THE KEEPER

THE KEEPER

TANA FRENCH

PENGUIN
VIKING

VIKING

UK | USA | Canada | Ireland | Australia
India | New Zealand | South Africa

Viking is part of the Penguin Random House group of companies
whose addresses can be found at global.penguinrandomhouse.com.

Penguin Random House UK,
One Embassy Gardens, 8 Viaduct Gardens, London SW11 7BW

penguin.co.uk

First published by Viking 2026

004

Copyright © Tana French, 2026
The moral right of the author has been asserted

Penguin Random House values and supports copyright.
Copyright fuels creativity, encourages diverse voices, promotes freedom
of expression and supports a vibrant culture. Thank you for purchasing
an authorized edition of this book and for respecting intellectual property
laws by not reproducing, scanning or distributing any part of it by any
means without permission. You are supporting authors and enabling
Penguin Random House to continue to publish books for everyone.
No part of this book may be used or reproduced in any manner for the
purpose of training artificial intelligence technologies or systems. In accordance
with Article 4(3) of the DSM Directive 2019/790, Penguin Random House
expressly reserves this work from the text and data mining exception

Set in 12.8/16pt Dante MT Std
Typeset by Six Red Marbles UK, Thetford, Norfolk
Printed and bound in Great Britain by Clays Ltd, Elcograf S.p.A.

The authorized representative in the EEA is Penguin Random House Ireland,
Morrison Chambers, 32 Nassau Street, Dublin D02 YH68

A CIP catalogue record for this book is available from the British Library

HARDBACK ISBN: 978–0–241–82376–7
TRADE PAPERBACK ISBN: 978–0–241–82377–4

Penguin Random House is committed to a sustainable future
for our business, our readers and our planet. This book is made from
Forest Stewardship Council® certified paper.

For Andrea, the editor every writer dreams of (of whom every writer dreams?).

If these books are anywhere close to what they should be, it's because of you.

I

Cal gets the first whiff of trouble when he's in Noreen's shop on a Saturday afternoon, buying eggs. The shop is in fact where Cal would expect to get wind of trouble, or of anything else underway in Ardnakelty townland, from pregnancy to potato blight. In spite of this, he more or less misses the hint altogether, because Noreen is coming at him with so much other stuff.

It's November. The townland lies still under rain, and has for weeks: what Cal's neighbor Mart Lavin calls a soft rain, one that doesn't fall but hangs in the air as a fine mizzle, coating you in a layer that only feels wet once you get indoors. The mountains, off on the horizon, are near-invisible, only a flick of outline here and there. Cal has battled it out with the rabbits for his last parsnips, and with the squirrels for the nuts from his handful of hazel trees. The tillage fields wait for ploughing under their green cover of clover and vetch; the cows still unhoused have left behind the tail-flicking irritability of summer and lie chewing the cud in slow, somnolent rhythms under a grey sky.

Cal has been in the West of Ireland long enough that he discounts this level of rain and walks to the shop. His house, an undistinguished 1930s cottage that he's gradually retrieved from dilapidation, is only a couple of miles from the village, and the road is in decent enough shape that he won't get himself too muddy. He leaves his door unlocked, a laxness that still gives him a spark of pleasure. Cal's previous neighbourhood, in Chicago, wasn't a bad one, but it had plenty of action, and some of that action would definitely have appreciated an unlocked door. Here, any form of action would have to be lost to end up at his place, and someone would notice it along the way and spread the word. If by some remote chance it does come calling, Cal's dog, Rip, can probably scare it off. Rip is a stubby little beagle cross, but he hasn't noticed that: he has both the bark and the self-esteem of a Rottweiler.

To the bafflement of his neighbours, who consider bitching about the weather to be a national duty, Cal likes this time of year. Autumn is when Ardnakelty comes into its own. Its summers and winters are half-assed by Cal's standards, but autumn is meant for nuance and there this place is expert, layering the air with the smells of earth and wet leaves, shading the land with every subtlety of green and gold, coding its weather hints in the slightest twist of breeze or shift of cloud. The last geese, straggling southward, send up their forlorn clamour. In the main street of the village, the colours of the little mismatched houses are muted; the air smells of turf smoke, and tentative piano notes weave through the rain from behind some lace curtain where a kid is practising. When Cal pushes the shop door open, the ding of the bell is blurred by the damp air.

The shop is small, warm, and bright, with bad country music playing cheerfully on a tinny little radio. Noreen is kneeling on the floor, bopping her rear end back and forth in time to the music and neatly whipping fake spiderwebs off her vegetable stand. 'There's yourself,' she says, through a mouthful of thumbtacks. 'These cobwebs are like they're made of glue, they stick on everything; I'll be here all day. Next year I'm not bothering my arse, I'm just putting that witch in the window and that's me done.'

'Can I give you a hand?' Cal asks. Cal is six foot four; Noreen is five foot one and not constructed for climbing. He comes in here expecting to fetch things off high shelves.

Noreen spits her tacks into a Ziploc bag. 'Go on, so; get down them pumpkins. Honest to God, I feel like I only put these up yesterday, and now here's me taking them down. It'll be the feckin' reindeers and Santys before I know it. My mammy always said that's how you know you're getting old: the years start flying in.'

'You haven't aged a day since I got here,' Cal says. He starts taking down miniature pumpkins from where they've been artfully tucked into the few square inches of free shelf space between soup mix, baby wipes, canned peaches, razor blades, envelopes, and everything else that keeps Ardnakelty running. 'If I didn't know you had all those great big kids, I'd swear you weren't a day over thirty.'

'G'way outa that. The wrinkles on me.'

'Thirty. Twenty-five, maybe.' Cal likes Noreen, even if some days she does make him feel like he should have had more coffee.

Noreen makes a *pfft* noise. 'I'm telling you, this week I feel like I'm a hundred. The kids threw a Halloween party, God help me. All the girls dressed up to the nines as sexy fairy murdered cheerleaders, you'd get more material in a bikini, and all the lads dressed up as themselves, lucky if they bothered their holes putting on a clean pair of trackie bottoms. And me running around like a blue-arsed fly, trying to make sure no one had a pocket fulla weed vapes or was riding anyone else down the back of the garden. I'm still recovering.' She shoots Cal a glance over her shoulder. 'Your Trey was invited. She didn't make it in the end, but she was asked.'

'Much obliged,' Cal says. 'She was sorry to miss it, but she had to take her little brother and sister trick-or-treating.' He has no problem stretching the truth in the name of harmony. Trey Reddy – who isn't technically his kid, but who counts as such for most practical purposes – has a less prickly relationship with Ardnakelty than she used to, but it's not friendly enough, and Trey isn't sociable enough, that anything short of a hostage situation would drag her to the Duggans' party.

'Speaking of invites,' Noreen says ominously, pointing her handful of spiderwebs at him. 'Where's mine?'

Cal is engaged to Noreen's sister, Lena, but not in the sense that either of them has any inclination to get married – they've both done that before, and feel once was plenty. The summer before last, Lena told Noreen they were engaged, for reasons that made good sense at the time, but what she hadn't taken into account was that once the reasons were gone, the engagement was still there. Neither of them was sure what to do about it. They couldn't call it off without people assuming they'd quarrelled, which would not only have complicated their lives but could potentially have made Noreen quit stocking Cal's favourite cheddar. In the end they decided to leave it be, in the faint hope that people would give up on it, but that's not how Ardnakelty rolls. The engagement has taken on a life of its own. People keep introducing themselves as Cal's new relations and asking where the wedding reception is going to be; Angela Maguire, who has a reputation for cakes, wants to know whether they prefer fruit cake or chocolate biscuit cake or a layer of each, taking into account that the young people like chocolate but it doesn't agree with Lena's aunt's digestion. Enough people hassled Lena about her ring that in the end Cal drove to Galway and bought her one, not a diamond but a tiny sapphire, since she likes blue. When he gave it to her she started laughing, and then he did too, but she wears the ring.

'We're still picking out the lettering,' he says. 'I got my heart set on the fancy curly stuff, but Lena's more of a straight-up-and-down kinda gal. Maybe you could talk to her, try and bring her around to my point of view.'

Noreen snorts. 'Jesus, Mary, and Joseph, I thought you'd more respect for me than that. Where would I be if I fell for that class of aul' rubbish, and me with four kids? Besides, you tried that one on me last winter.'

'Gotta get that lettering right,' Cal explains. 'Something this important, I wouldn't want to make the wrong choice.'

'You won't have any choices left if you don't set a date. Everywhere'll be booked out for years ahead. There's four townlands sharing Father Eamonn, and the poor man's still waiting on his knee replacement; he can't be standing up for two weddings in one day. And if you don't get the Breggan Court for the reception you'll be stuck with the Kilcarrow Arms up in town, and sure they gave half the county food poisoning at Georgia Healy's baba's christening. D'you want to spend your wedding night puking your guts up?'

'We were figuring on having the reception in Seán Óg's,' Cal says. 'All the toasted sandwiches people can eat.'

'You,' Noreen informs him, shaking a plastic vampire bat at him, 'you're lucky I don't believe a word outa your mouth, or I'd be taking a heart attack right here. You can't be having your reception in a dirty aul' pub, like some wee teenager that's after getting his girlfriend up the pole.'

'No one ever got food poisoning from a toastie,' Cal points out. 'Better safe than sorry.'

Noreen, throwing the bat into a big plastic box labelled HALLOWEEN, tuts at him. 'You didn't useta be this much of a messer. When you got here, you were well-behaved, so you were.'

'Lena's a bad influence,' Cal says.

'Put them pumpkins in that bin liner over there, they're going soggy already. All I'm saying is, you'd want to get a move on with the bookings. Once it gets to Christmas and New Year, there'll be people getting engaged right and left, and then where will you be?'

Cal is saved from answering this: the bell dings, the door flies open, and Tommy Moynihan strides into the shop like he's walking into a merger meeting. 'There's her ladyship,' he booms, rubbing his hands together. 'How's the form?'

Tommy is some kind of big shot in the meat-processing plant over towards Kilhone, which makes him Mr Big-Balls in this townland. This doesn't seem like much to get puffed up about, given that the townland would just about make a good-sized yard in backwoods North Carolina, where Cal comes from; Tommy, though, either hasn't noticed this or doesn't care as long as he's surrounded by the respect he deserves. He's got a farmer's solid bulk, a politician's frozen silver hair, a C-list cattle baron's ranch house, a Range Rover the size of a buffalo, and an annual family holiday to Mexico. Cal dislikes Tommy, although he acknowledges that this may be partly because Tommy's kid, Eugene, is a douche and Tommy's wife, Clodagh, looks at Trey like she's scanning for nits.

'Grand,' Noreen says, getting to her feet – Tommy, unlike Cal, warrants standing up – and dusting off the knees of her slacks. 'Up to my ears in mini Mars bars and Twix, lookit – I got them in for the trick-or-treating, the same amount as every year, but only half of them went. I heard people were getting theirs cheap off some fella that went round in a van.' She throws a rubber rat into the box with a vengeful snap. When she finds out names, which she will, Cal doesn't envy anyone who bought their candy on the down-low.

'I'll take a few of them off your hands,' Tommy says magnanimously. 'I'm a great man for the aul' Mars bars. You can keep your fancy artisan chocolates, isn't that right? Give me the good old-fashioned stuff.'

'Clodagh won't have Mars bars in the house,' Noreen informs him. 'She's going on the diet again, the one with the curly kale. I've that ordered in for her; tell her it'll be here on Thursday.'

'Ah, go on, give us a few packets there. What the missus doesn't know won't hurt her.' Tommy winks at Cal. 'Howdy, pardner.' Cal has been American for the entire three and a half years he's lived here, so the novelty should have worn off by now, but Tommy is apparently proud enough of spotting it that he needs to point it out every time they meet.

'Well, how de do,' Cal drawls, tipping his baseball cap. Noreen shoots him a behave-yourself glare behind Tommy's back. Cal gives her a mock-sheepish flinch and goes back to detaching skull-and-crossbones bunting from the shelves.

'Flying form,' Tommy says, rocking back and forth on his heels and surveying the shop. 'Flying form. We've Eugene down from Dublin for the weekend, so the missus says we need a bag of spuds and a rake of sausages. We can't be feeding a young lad on curly kale, amn't I right?'

Cal follows his nod to the window. Two people are standing outside, in the grey day that looks like twilight against the shop's brightness. Eugene – on the weedy edge of good-looking, wearing a long dark coat that's probably sophisticated business gear in Dublin but down here is just weird – is bent towards a tall blonde girl, talking fast. The girl has her head down and her hands tucked deep in her pockets. She's wearing a white puffy jacket and some kind of black leggings, but the leggings are erased by the dimness so that she looks like she's floating, about to drift away from him on the eddies of rain.

'Eugene's looking well,' Noreen says, peering out the window and rubbing away condensation. 'Who's that out there with him? God, I think my eyes are going on me, I'll be on the bifocals before I know it. Is that Rachel?'

'It is, o' course,' Tommy says. 'You couldn't keep them two apart. Young love, isn't it great?' This explains why Eugene is waiting outside, getting his pretty coat wet: he's too careful of his dignity to risk Noreen puncturing it in front of his girlfriend. Eugene has some hotshot job in finance, Cal isn't sure what and doesn't care as long as he doesn't have to hear about it, which means he avoids Noreen's when Clodagh Moynihan is in there.

'There you go,' Noreen tells Cal, pouncing on the fresh

opportunity. 'D'you see them two out there? They'll be getting engaged any day now. Won't they?' she shoots at Tommy.

'Ah, now,' Tommy says, tapping the side of his nose and smiling. 'I'm saying nothing.'

'Ah, they will. I knew as soon as Clodagh said she was back on the diet: she has to look her best for the engagement do. And I'll tell you one thing, mister' – this is to Cal – 'they won't be waiting any year and a half to set their date. They'll have the Breggan Court nailed down before the ring's properly on her finger. And that'll be one less date for you and Lena.'

'Oh-ho-ho,' Tommy says, clapping his hands together. 'Who's got cold feet?'

'Just leaving room for the young 'uns to get down the aisle,' Cal says. He drops the bunting into the storage box and goes to find his eggs. Noreen has earned the right to give him a hard time; Tommy hasn't, seeing as they've probably spent a grand total of less than ten minutes in conversation. Tommy, although he makes sure to grace the lower orders with his notice, represents a different echelon of local society from the guys Cal hangs out with. He dresses the same way, work pants and fleeces and puffer vests, but on him the getup looks like a costume, probably because it's always clean.

'Fair play. They're in a lot more of a rush than us aul' fellas, amn't I right?' Tommy guffaws and mimes elbowing Cal in the ribs, even though Cal is halfway across the shop. Noreen titters obligingly. Cal keeps inspecting eggs.

'I'd say it's Lena that's dragging her heels,' Tommy says, still grinning at Cal. 'Hah? She's been in that house a long time; she mightn't fancy leaving it to move down to your wee place, no harm to it.'

'You figure she oughta move?' Cal enquires politely.

'A change is as good as a rest,' Tommy says, like that means something. 'Will I have a word with her for you? Give her a nudge?'

Cal would pay good money to watch Tommy try to have a word with Lena. 'More haste, less speed,' he points out, since apparently this is what they're doing. Tommy laughs like he said something hilarious.

'There you go,' Noreen says, ringing up Tommy's sausages and adding them to the impressive heap of Mars bar packets on the counter. 'Keep those well hid from herself.'

'It'll be our little secret,' Tommy says. 'Don't be giving me away, now.' Noreen titters again, and Tommy pays and strides himself out.

'There's a bitta luck,' Noreen says with satisfaction, once the door's closed behind him. 'I thought I'd be stuck with them Mars bars; no one wants any more sweets in the house, after Halloween. But Tommy can't pass up a chance to be the big man.' She rings up Cal's eggs. 'And he won't be feeding Eugene feckin' sausages and spuds for the Sunday dinner. Tommy and Clodagh go into town for the big shop, is what they do, so she can get all the fancy ingredients for her Ballymaloe recipes. Then they come in here to honour me with their little bits and bobs.'

She frowns out the window at Tommy, who's clapping Eugene on the shoulder and talking up a big hearty storm. 'D'you know something? The pair a them don't look great. Eugene and Rachel, like. The way she wasn't even looking at him.' Noreen's warmth is even bigger than her nosiness; she's genuinely concerned, not just scouting for gossip. 'I know Eugene's an awful dose, but Rachel's pure mad about him. They're together since she was sixteen, sure; she's never been without him. If he's after getting himself some Dublin one, it'll break her heart. Do they look all right to you?'

'Dunno,' Cal says. He's disinclined to give the Moynihans any more conversational space than he has to. 'I'm not acquainted with either one of 'em enough to tell. You know anything about making soufflés? Trey read about them in some schoolbook and wanted to know what they were, so I said I'd give it a shot.'

Noreen goes off into a barrage of soufflé-related tips and variations. The window has misted over again, turning Tommy and Eugene and Rachel into blurred shapes swaying like scarecrows.

Lena has somehow found herself spending her Saturday afternoon driving over the mountain in a car full of teenagers. Seeing as she doesn't have kids, she didn't choose her car with this scenario in mind, but Trey had a football match in Lisnacarragh and her mam picked up an extra shift at the supermarket in town, so now Lena's Skoda has five kids squashed into each other's laps, elbowing and sniping and snickering and having a whale of a time. Trey and Kate's team won the match – the other three are just along for the crack, there not being much else to do around here at the weekend – so they're all on a high. Lena has already threatened to make them walk home twice. The narrow mountain roads, switchbacking and dipping, make for dodgy driving at the best of times; in this weather, with the spruce groves rising out of grey haze and the fields below veiled by the fine rain, their danger presses in close. In general, Lena sees no reason why teenagers should behave themselves – most of them will do that for long enough – but she draws the line at them sending her car down the mountainside.

'Missus,' says the freckly boy in the back – Ross, Lena thinks – leaning forward between the seats. 'Here, missus.'

'She's Missus Dunne, ya thick,' Aidan tells him from up front.

'She is not. She's married to your man Whatshisname, the Yank that lives at O'Shea's old place. Ya fuckin' thick.' Somewhere along the way, Trey's mates have filed Lena under Noncombatant Adult, meaning they don't worry that she'll squeal on them to the real adults for minor infringements like cursing.

'She is not,' Trey says. 'Why would he be in O'Shea's and her in her place, if they were married?'

'Exactly,' Aidan says triumphantly.

'If I was married to you I'd live in Australia,' Kate tells him.

'You won't be.'

'Fuckin' right I won't.'

'Missus,' Ross says, not to be sidetracked. 'Should Ciara here go out with Aidan?'

'Shut up, ya fuckin' Teletubby,' Aidan says, twisting around to hit him. He ducks. Lena slaps Aidan's arm back into place.

'She should give him a lash, amn't I right? He's a fine-looking fella—'

'Jesus,' Ciara says, covering her face with her hands and trying to disappear into her corner. Trey and the rest are laughing.

'You'd take him out for a spin at least, wouldn't you? If you were our age, like?'

'I'd need more info,' Lena says. She likes watching Trey in the middle of this. Trey spent her entire childhood on the defensive against Ardnakelty, which by age-old tradition considers the Reddy family to be more trouble than they're worth, so she turned out on the solitary side; by the time she started discovering things like mates and messing, it was late enough that Lena wasn't confident she'd get the knack. She enjoys the evidence that she was wrong. 'Is this fella just a pretty face, or can he do anything useful? Talk ye outa hassle? Build a house? Bake cakes? Play the guitar?'

'Kate plays bass,' Ross says, and punches Trey in the arm. Trey and Kate both hit him back at once. Lena's eyebrows go up.

'Hear that?' Aidan tells the rest. 'She says I'm a pretty face.'

'She needs fuckin' glasses.'

'Your ma needs fuckin' glasses.'

'Your ma needs a time machine and a johnny.'

'Your ma needs deez nuts.'

A scuffle breaks out. Lena leaves them to it. She likes

teenagers, or this bunch of them anyhow: the wildness and messiness of them, the rocket-fuelled energy shooting in every direction. They fizz with the glorious knowledge that they're untameable, that no rules, no matter how ferociously ingrained and enforced, are strong enough to hold them. Lena, even while knowing that's untrue, finds a deep pleasure in it.

She takes the opportunity, while they're occupied, to have a proper look at Kate in the rear-view mirror. She's seen Trey's friends here and there, mostly at football matches, but none of them are from Ardnakelty, so they're not kids whom Lena's known since they were born and before. Trey likes her life compartmentalised; it's only recently that she's been willing to allow even this much overlap. Lena and Cal, aware that one slip-up could have their privileges revoked, are careful.

Kate is tall and long-legged, with wide, cheerful features, a dark ponytail, and a smattering of freckles. Lena knows nothing about her except that she plays defence alongside Trey and can hold her own amid this shower, which seems like a decent start. She wonders what Cal will make of this, whatever this is. She reckons she'll have to talk him down from running background checks.

The scuffle has escalated to the point where Aidan is kneeling up backwards in his seat and Ciara, thrown sideways across the rest, is squealing. 'Quit that,' Lena says, raising her voice to carry over the noise, 'or I'll drive through a pothole and give the lot of ye concussions.' Aidan gets in one final punch and sits down, and the back seat subsides to an undertone of snorts and snickers. Lena slows the car down further. They're out of the spruce groves and onto open mountainside, amid wide stretches of heather; one mistake could send her wheel into a bog.

'I'm useful,' Aidan tells her, returning to the original issue. 'I swapped out the light fixture in the sitting room for my mam yesterday. That's useful.'

'Does your dad know yet?' Kate asks.

'He was in there last night watching telly. I'd say he saw it.'

'Not the light fixture, you dope.'

'I'm gonna tell him.'

'He's gonna lose the head,' Ross says.

'That's why you oughta tell him now,' Kate says. 'Give him time to lose the head all he wants, and then get used to it.'

'Aidan's dad thinks he's going onto the farm,' Trey explains to Lena. 'Only he's gonna be an electrician.'

"Cause Ciara doesn't like the smell of cow shite,' Ross says. Ciara hits him.

'I'm gonna tell him,' Aidan says to Lena. 'Just waiting for a good time.'

'You're grand,' Lena says. 'I'm saying nothing. I don't even know your dad.' She understands his worry. Unless Aidan has brothers, coming out as an electrician is likely to be a much bigger deal than, say, coming out as bi, or as an atheist. Regardless of how old-fashioned his dad is, a bi atheist farmer can keep the land in the family. Nothing matters more than that.

Lena's phone rings. It's Cal. Mostly Cal goes to Trey's matches, but today he got press-ganged into helping the McHugh brothers cut back their hedges. With the ploughing only a few weeks away, farmers are using this time to trim and mend, getting their land in order for winter. Sonny McHugh got pinned to a wall by a heifer and has one arm in a sling, so the McHughs are a man down. 'Here,' Lena says, putting the phone on speaker and handing it to Aidan. 'You hold that. And the rest of ye, keep quiet.'

'How's she cuttin'?' Aidan enquires into the phone, in his biggest, deepest voice. The back seat dissolves into giggles.

'Hey,' Cal says. 'That your fancy man?'

'He's spoken for,' Lena says. 'I'll stick with you a while longer.'

'They win?'

'Yeah,' Trey says, disentangling herself from the rest to lean forward between the seats. In spite of being sixteen, Trey is unembarrassed by Cal's existence, possibly because he's no actual relation to her. 'Three–two.' Kate throws in a whoop of triumph. 'This horse of a one was after me the whole time, trying to take the legs out from under me. I dodged and she went on her arse. She was yelling for a card, but the ref told her to get fucked.'

'Well, congratulations,' Cal says. Lena can hear the broad grin in his voice. 'You get soaked?'

''M grand,' Trey says. All of them got soaked, more or less. The car smells powerfully of steaming clothes, muddy boots, and body spray.

'You gonna be here for dinner, we can celebrate? I was gonna try making a soufflé.'

'The fuck is a soufflé?' Ross demands, in an undertone.

'Eggs,' Kate tells him.

'Posh eggs,' Ciara says. Another argument, lower-pitched, starts up over whether eggs can be posh.

'Yeah,' Trey says, to the phone. Trey's living arrangements sound complicated, but in practice they work with the ease of makeshift things that have built themselves around everyone's convenience. During the week she lives with her mother and the little ones, in a cottage at the foot of the mountains; at weekends she mostly stays on Cal's pullout sofa, so they can do their woodwork, mending and making furniture for whoever wants it, and so Trey can get a bit of peace. 'Going out after, but. With the lads.'

'Then we better get the soufflé right first try,' Cal says. 'Lena? You joining us?'

'Why not,' Lena says. 'I never had a soufflé before.' Cal, unlike her, enjoys cooking, even though he only took it up out of a belief that Trey needed to eat something other than hamburgers and grilled cheese and whatever boiled-into-submission stuff her mother came up with. Now he tries fancy things all the time, and mostly they work out. Even more than the food, which is good, Lena loves the care and concentration Cal puts into it. She could watch him cook all day, and find calm in the steady movement of his hands and the low patchy sound of him humming along to Steve Earle or Emmylou Harris.

'Me neither,' Cal says. 'And we might not have one tonight. I've got bread and peanut butter, just in case.'

'I'd eat soufflé,' Aidan tells the phone.

'Anyone Trey invites is welcome to whatever dinner we end up having,' Cal says. 'You talk to her. Well done again, kid. Tell Kate good job from me.'

'See you later,' Lena says, taking her phone back.

'Can I come eat soufflé?' Aidan asks Trey. Aidan is a charmer and a messer, the type to ask adults to buy him drink and somehow bamboozle them into doing it. He hasn't tried it on Lena yet, but she's seen him considering it.

'Fuck off,' Trey says. 'Make your own. You said you were useful.'

'What's all this about me being useful?' Aidan demands, outraged. 'Why do I have to be useful? How about the rest of ye, how are ye—'

'I made your granny that display shelf for her ornaments, that's—'

'How about Kate, how's she—'

'I fuckin' *scored*, from *defence*—'

The argument gets into full swing. Lena turns the car down the mountain, gorse branches rattling along the sides.

On the sidewalk outside Noreen's, Cal wipes mizzle off his phone and puts it away. The days are shortening towards winter; it's not even four-thirty, but already the sky has started to darken. All down the street, lights have come on in windows. Mrs Geraghty with the red door has her grandkids over; some of them are climbing on the armchairs, while a couple more are trying to put a leftover witch hat on the dog.

Tommy and Eugene and Rachel have headed off up the road. Tommy's big laugh, taking up as much space as possible, echoes off the houses. Cal feels like he missed something.

The instinct is a leftover, like a phantom limb that still feels the occasional twitch. For twenty-five years Cal was a cop in Chicago, where a well-developed radar for hinkiness was an essential multitool that did everything from smoothing your day to saving your life. He took early retirement specifically because he wanted to get rid of the job and everything about it, which mostly worked, but that instinct is still there. The difference is that nowadays most of the things it twitches at aren't exactly high-stakes, and aren't his problem anyway. After all that time on the job, Cal has a deep and heartfelt appreciation for things that aren't his problem, but not all of him has caught up with that philosophy.

'Sunny Jim!' a voice calls. Cal's neighbour Mart is sticking his fluffy grey head out of the door of Seán Óg's pub, which is conveniently located next to Noreen's, in case people need some fortification after their shopping. Mart is waving Cal over. 'Get in here.'

'I gotta go make dinner,' Cal says. Mart takes the pub seriously, and he expects the same respect from other people. If Cal goes in there, he'll be lucky to get out before midnight.

'The dinner can wait; you won't starve, the size of you. Come see what we've got here.'

Mart disappears. Cal succumbs to curiosity and heads into the pub.

Seán Óg's is Saturday-afternoon full, mainly farmers who've

finished up their weekend business early and need a pint or two on the way home. The place currently has no link to anyone called Seán, being run by a guy named Barty who mostly appears to be having second thoughts. It's a good pub, which is a credit to Barty, since the nearest alternative is far enough away that he could run a shitty two-tap dive and still get the clientele. Instead he knows what everyone drinks and when they should stop drinking it, brings out the ashtrays after closing time, and recently replaced the patchy linoleum flooring with something that looks almost exactly like wood, although he hasn't got around to the peeling textured wallpaper. Cal suspects that Barty harbours dreams of running a nice pub, someplace with craft beer and maybe a menu, scheduled live music instead of the occasional impromptu sing-along, and no smell of cow shit. Seán's has many excellent qualities, and Cal is fond of it, but no one would call it nice.

'Good man yourself,' Mart says, shepherding Cal towards the alcove where he and his cronies hang out. 'Barty! Get the big fella a pint.'

'I'll get it,' Cal says. 'I'm only staying for one.' The round system is inviolable: if he lets Mart buy him a pint, he has to stay and buy Mart one in return, or be branded for life as a scabby round-dodger, which is up there with sheep-rustling on the scale of social unacceptability.

'Aren't we all, sure,' Mart says. 'I'm not here at all, myself; I'll be in later, after the dinner, but now I'm mending walls. Only I had to welcome this gazebo back home.'

There's a clump of guys in the alcove, around a table littered with pint glasses and what look like little plastic dolls. The rest of the guys are younger than Mart – he's well into his sixties, although he's the little wiry type that never ages, while the rest are closer to Cal's age, hanging around the edges of fifty. Ardnakelty is too small to allow for much stratification; if you want company, you hang out with anyone who doesn't drive you crazy, and probably some people who do. Bobby Feeney is settled in the middle of the banquette, glowing with achievement like a new mama.

Over the summer, Bobby sold a few acres of poor grazing land to Tommy Moynihan, disregarding Mart's warning that getting his hands on land would only further Tommy's notions of upperosity. Bobby and his mama used some of the money to go on a pilgrimage to Lourdes and a bus tour of the Gems of South-west France. Most of the guys have had vacations in Majorca or Lanzarote here and there, when they could find people to look after their farms, but gallivanting around France is in a different league. Senan Maguire is ignoring Bobby completely, to stop him getting above himself, and talking loudly to Francie Gannon, who's ignoring both of them and staring moodily into his pint. PJ Fallon has his lanky legs wound around the legs of his stool and is gazing at Bobby like he just got back from the moon.

'Well, hey,' Cal says, pulling up a stool. 'You made it back. How was France?'

Bobby isn't used to being the centre of attention, and he's pink with the excitement of it, right up to the top of his little round head – Bobby looks like a kid made him from balls of Play-Doh. 'Amazing,' he says. 'Lourdes was a bit – you know. I knew there'd be rosaries, like, I just wasn't expecting that many. But the mammy was delighted; she'll be the queen of the bingo club now. And the rest of France is only brilliant.'

'He et the lot of it,' Senan informs Cal. 'Look at the state of him.'

Bobby is in fact even rounder than usual. 'They've gorgeous food,' he tells Cal. 'I had oysters and all.'

'Fuck me blind,' Senan says, staring at Bobby in disbelief. 'You. Eating oysters. We're in the shite now, lads; there'll be no living with him. Didja eat them with a shovel?' Senan is a big guy, with a face like a ham and a lot of forceful opinions. He and Bobby have been best friends all their lives, a fact that mainly manifests itself in Senan giving Bobby shit.

'You use a fork to loosen them,' Bobby informs him. 'Then you just neck them. Straight outa the shell.'

'I've seen it all now,' Senan tells the alcove. 'This gobdaw, with the sheep shite not washed off him, telling me how to eat oysters.'

'I heard they're like snots,' Francie says.

'They are, a bit,' Bobby concedes. 'Not in a bad way, but.'

'If some fucker asked me to pay top whack for a big snot,' Francie says, 'I'd tell him to shove it up his hole.' Francie has nothing against Bobby personally, but he's happiest putting a damper on things.

'You're missing the point,' Mart tells him. 'The big snot isn't important. It coulda been anything: a roasted hedgehog, say, or that beet soup the Russians go mad for. The point is, he hadn't et one before, and now he has. The scientists are after discovering that that's the best thing you can do for your health: try something new. It grows back the brain cells, when they're dying of boredom from doing the same thing every day. This fella's probably after adding a year to his life, just with them big snots.'

'I wouldn't eat hedgehog either.'

'No one's making you. Don't come crying to me when you die young.'

'I'd eat an oyster,' PJ says, having given this some thought – PJ, aware that his thought processes aren't the fastest in town, likes to give them time before he commits himself. 'Just the one, like. In case I mightn't get another chance.'

'Sweet fuck,' Senan says to Bobby. 'See what you're after doing? You'll have this whole place living on oysters and fuckin' caviar. Barty'll haveta order in champagne.'

'You're only jealous 'cause you haven't had champagne since that horse piss at your wedding,' Bobby says, smugly and surprisingly. Most times, Bobby can't come up with much more than an outraged sputter in response to the other guys' ribbing. The prestige of the trip appears to have put fresh sass into him. 'I'da brought you home some of the real stuff, if I'da thought you'd know the difference.'

'Oooh,' Senan says to the group. 'Burn, isn't that what the young people say? I wonder will I survive.'

'That reminds me,' Bobby says to Cal, ignoring Senan. 'I brought you this.' He digs into a supermarket bag at his feet and pulls out another of the small plastic objects. It turns out to be a figurine of the Virgin Mary. On closer inspection Cal realises it's a bottle, filled with some kind of clear liquid. The cap, in a tasteful shade of blue, is Mary's crown.

'That's holy water inside it,' Bobby informs him. 'Taken straight from the spring at Lourdes, and then blessed by a priest.'

'One for everyone in the audience,' Mart says, patting his on the head.

'Well, many thanks,' Cal says. 'I appreciate that. Do I drink it?'

'Use it as a mixer,' Senan tells him. 'Goes great with gin.'

'You do not,' Bobby says, shocked. 'Well, you might take a sup if you had cancer or something, maybe. I wouldn't say it'd taste nice, after being in the bottle so long. But mostly you'd use it to bless things with. Yourself, like, or your house. I put a bitta mine on the car, with the way people drive around here, and I was going to do the sheep, only I haven't enough to go round.'

'You can eat these,' Francie tells Cal, 'if you fancy a taste.' He pushes a tin of candy across the table.

'They're mints,' Bobby explains. 'Made with Lourdes water. Not blessed, like, so I don't know how much good they'd do you, but they're lovely. The mammy had the both of us sucking them on the flight all the way home, so the plane'd stay up.'

The candies are little white lozenges, each with Mary stamped neatly on the front. 'I wouldn't risk it,' Mart advises Cal, 'and you a Protestant. I'd say they'd burn the mouth off you.'

Cal, while not particularly religious in any direction, is iffy on the propriety of eating Mary. 'I better play it safe,' he says. 'Thanks. Besides, I don't figure they'd go with Smithwick's.' Barty helps him out by appearing at this moment with his pint. 'Here's to France,' Cal says, raising his glass to Bobby.

'I heard the French ones'd all go topless on the beaches,' Francie says. 'Is that true?'

'I wasn't on any beaches,' Bobby says. He looks like a kid realising he missed out on a candy store.

'Ahhh,' Senan says. 'Would your mammy not let you?'

'It's November,' Cal points out. He feels an obligation to take the heat off Bobby every now and then, although Bobby seems less in need of this than usual. 'How many bathing beauties was he gonna find in this weather?'

'More than he would here, anyhow.'

'Nah,' Cal says. 'Other way around. Here, you get five minutes of sunshine and everyone's out toasting themselves, regardless of how cold it is. Over there, they can afford to save it for hot weather. They're not gonna risk getting frostbite on their delicate parts.'

'When did you see topless women sunning themselves around here? Laid out in rows on the footpath in front of Noreen's, is it?'

'You never seen 'em? You oughta get out more.' Cal is enjoying himself. When he left all his old buddies back in Chicago, he missed this, the shove and jostle of being part of a group of guys. It's only recently that he's felt himself to have either the skill or the right to join in this one. His first couple of years here, he mostly kept his mouth shut, tried to get some handle on the intricate codes and undercurrents ricocheting around the table, and stayed ready to deflect the tests that got aimed his way. Things have shifted since then. Cal will never be what these men are, generations deep in this land; but he's engaged to Lena, the two of them are more or less raising Trey, just about every house in the townland contains some of his woodwork, and he's been useful in various other, less straightforward ways. If he wants to get in a pointless argument with Senan, he's earned it.

'So you're telling us,' Francie says to Bobby, returning to the main point, 'you spent two weeks in fuckin' *France*, and the best thing you spotted for the wank bank was a loada aul' ones on the bus tour?'

'That's some talk in front of her,' Mart says reprovingly, tapping one of the Marys on the crown.

'I am not,' Bobby says. He's getting flustered – Bobby is easily flustered, which is an unfortunate trait to have around here. 'And the bus wasn't just aul' ones.'

'It wasn't topless French crackers, I can tell you that much.'

'There oughta be that bus tour,' Mart says, diverted by this intriguing prospect from the serious business of putting Bobby back in his place. 'I'd go on that. When your mind does get in too much of a whirl from admiring the architectural masterpieces, you can take a wee break and walk round a cathedral.'

'Hang on a fuckin' second,' Senan says, putting down his pint. 'Stall the ball. Look at the state of your man. What's the story here?'

They all look at Bobby. He has in fact gone even pinker, right to the tips of his ears. He tries to hide in his glass, but when he comes back up everyone is still looking at him.

'What're ye on about?' he demands, without conviction.

'Holy Mother a the Divine,' Mart says in awe. 'Wouldja look at that. This fella was riding the arse off some French one down the back of the bus. Get the Pope on the line, lads: 'tis a Lourdes miracle.'

'I was not riding her,' Bobby says, stung past discretion. 'And she's not French.'

The alcove erupts in roars and fist-pumps and applause – 'Get up, ya boy ya!' 'Go on, ya good thing!' Cal joins in wholeheartedly. Bobby has always longed for a woman in his life, but they're thin on the ground in Ardnakelty. Up until a couple of generations ago, leaving town was only for the strongest-minded girls, or the wildest, or the ones with vocations; then things changed, and the girls, mostly unfettered by the farm legacies that hold sons in place, started heading off for somewhere that offers a wider range of options. Senan is the only one here who's married. The rest of the guys grew up eyeing their friends' sisters, slow-dancing at discos and taking for granted they'd all end up paired off with broods of kids running around their yards; instead one day they woke up and half the girls were gone, leaving the men to get old trudging the fields alone and coming home to silent houses. Bobby, humble about his own attributes, had more or less given up hope, but the wistfulness stayed.

'Let's have a look at her,' Francie says, 'before we go congratulating him. Show us a photo.'

'I'm not showing her photo to the likes of you,' Bobby tells him, trying to recover a little of his newfound poise. He's crimson.

'Why not? If she exists at all.'

'I don't blame the man,' Mart says. 'You've a low mind. He doesn't want her going in that wank bank of yours.'

'Wouldja stop. I'd say she's got a head on her like a melted welly.'

'She does not,' Bobby says indignantly. 'She's lovely-looking.'

'Is she a bit, ya know?' Senan enquires.

'A bit what?'

'You know. Unfortunate.'

'She is not! She's a receptionist. In an office.'

'You'd want to be sure. Before you get done for taking advantage.'

'You've a girlfriend?' PJ asks, trying to get this straight. 'An actual one, like?'

'Inflatable,' Francie tells him. Bobby manages to ignore this loftily and take a sip of his pint.

'Hey, congratulations,' Cal says, since no one else is doing it. 'Where'd you meet her?'

'On the bus tour,' Bobby says, turning towards Cal with relief. 'Her mammy and daddy were meant to be going for their gold anniversary, only her daddy did his back in, so Róisín went instead.'

'Róisín,' Mart says, pointing a finger and narrowing his eyes like a TV detective. 'Now we know she's Irish, anyhow. Or American, maybe.'

'She's Irish. What would I be saying to an American one?'

'Well, that's handy,' Cal says. 'She from near here?'

Bobby casts a wary look at the other guys. 'Near enough,' he says cautiously. 'Not local, like. But not Dublin or anything.' His face is slowly fading back towards its normal colour.

'Even better,' Cal says. 'You gonna see her again?'

'I'd say she gave him a fake number,' Senan says.

'I'm not bringing her next nor near any of ye,' Bobby says with dignity. 'She deserves better. I'm going down to see her next weekend.'

'Fair play to you,' Francie says, abandoning the ribbing and holding out his pint for Bobby to clink. Everything Francie says comes out sounding gloomy, but he means it: Francie missed out on his true love, so he understands the importance of these matters, even if he also understands the importance of giving people shit. 'May ye never give each other a minute's grief.'

'We won't,' Bobby assures him. 'Róisín wouldn't be into that carry-on. She's pure peaceful. 'Tis from being a receptionist; she has to deal with so many mentallers, nothing rattles her.'

'There you go,' Senan says to Francie. 'Go on and sell Big Tommy that field he's been sniffing at, and off you go on a bus tour and come back with a woman. If this fella can do it, anyone can.' Francie was engaged once, decades ago. It didn't work out – Francie was looking after his mother, who took longer than expected to die – but it's generally accepted as evidence that Francie, unlike, say, Mart or PJ, has romantic potential.

'I wouldn't sell Tommy Moynihan the steam off my piss,' Francie says. 'I don't trust that fucker.'

The weight of his voice shifts the key in the alcove. There's a second of silence. PJ, who is uncomfortable with unpleasantness, pokes at something imaginary in his glass.

'He paid me,' Bobby says, a little defensively. 'I made sure I'd the money in the bank before I booked the trip.'

'Maybe he did. But that fella's up to something. He won't be using me for it.'

'What would he be up to?' Senan demands.

'What does he want land for? He's sniffing around Rory Dunne's back field, as well, and the Kellys sold him the three-acre last month. And when Fat Pat McHugh died, Tommy had the Forge Field bought before the man was in the ground. Tommy's a fuckin' suit, him and his father before him. What does he want with farmland?'

'He fancies himself as your man outa *Dallas*, is all,' Senan says. 'He always did. The little fucker usedta wear a cowboy hat into school, when we were kids, till a few of the lads caught him and stuffed it down his kacks.'

'Then he'd be buying one big ranch for himself,' Francie says, 'not bits here and there that don't even connect up. He's a cute hoor, that fella. He's up to something.'

'Maybe he just wants land,' PJ says simply. 'Tommy never had land. I'd say he feels it, like.'

That gets a slight pause of acknowledgement. Tommy's status, though high, is undermined right at the foundations by his lack of land. Tommy is the richest guy around by a mile, and the best connected; Tommy has a conservatory and a water feature, and if you want your planning permission to go through, or your speeding ticket squared, Tommy is the guy who knows the guy who can get it done. Ardnakelty is pragmatic about giving him the show of respect that he requires in exchange, but the ass-kissing is underlaid by a fine sediment of something else. What Tommy has is lightweight, ephemeral. Banks can go bust, bribes can be outbid, compliant politicians can be voted out. A man who owns land can have and hold.

'It'd be like him,' Bobby says. 'He could never let anyone have anything he didn't. He made me sell him my Donkey Kong game that my uncle sent me from Canada, d'you remember?'

Mart is absorbed in carefully stacking the Mary bottles one on top of another, moving each one by its blue cap, like a chess piece. 'Don't you be slagging Tommy Moynihan, now,' he says, arching an eyebrow at Bobby. 'Saint Tommy brought jobs to this place. You're not allowed say a word against the man, don'tchaknow.'

'He can stick his jobs up his arse,' Francie says.

'Tommy's a cute hoor, all right,' Mart says. 'I wouldn't say he's got ambitions towards farming; that lad's too good to get his hands dirty. Was he talking to you at all, Sunny Jim?' He glances up at Cal.

'Nope,' Cal says. 'Not about my land, anyway.'

'How about yourself?' Mart asks PJ. PJ's farm borders Cal's few acres, on the other side from Mart.

'Ah, God, no,' PJ says, startled. 'Sure, myself and Tommy

wouldn't have much to say to each other. He'd nod to me in the street, only.'

'And I've heard nothing from His Lordship either,' Mart says. He considers his tower of Marys, decides the fourth one will lead to disaster, and changes his approach, arranging them in orderly single file. 'He's being awful choosy about location, did ye notice? All the bits he's chasing are over on the Kilhone side. If I hadta guess, I'd say 'tis something to do with that factory.'

For the last few months, there have been rumours of a factory being planned on the far edge of the townland. No one is sure what it's going to make – Cal has heard pharmaceuticals, industrial cleaning products, medical supplies, and something improbable to do with AI – but general opinion, with a few chronic dissenters, is in favour of it. A factory will bring jobs and money, maybe some road improvements, and possibly even decent broadband.

'That fucker knows something we don't,' Senan says.

'I'd say he knows they'll be bringing in workers,' Mart says. He places his pint in front of the lead Mary, so that they're all lining up for their turn. 'Specialised skills, they might need, that they can't get local. Tommy'll pull a few strings and get that land re-zoned to residential, no bother to him. Then he'll slap together a buncha town houses outa cardboard and gaffer tape, and sell them for a hundred-odd grand each.'

'And you playing straight into his hands,' Senan says to Bobby. 'Fuckin' typical.'

'I don't care,' Bobby says defiantly. 'I got Róisín outa the deal, and she's worth every bitta that land – sure, 'twas all rocks and weeds anyhow. Why shouldn't Tommy get something as well?'

''Cause he's a shitehawk,' Francie says. 'He'll get nothing outa me.'

'Go on and cut off your nose to spite your face, so. I'm happy.'

'I'm cutting off nothing. I didn't want a floozy anyhow.'

Bobby draws himself up to his full height, such as it is. 'Róisín's not a floozy,' he says. 'You apologise.'

Francie looks at him like he just grew an extra head.

'Fuck me sideways,' Senan says, rearing back on his stool to stare at Bobby. 'Look who found a pair of balls for himself, over in France. Did they sell those at the shrine as well?'

'That'll be the oysters,' Mart says. 'I heard they do mad stuff for the aul' manhood. D'you have to tuck it in your sock now?'

'You apologise to Róisín,' Bobby repeats. His chins are out.

'She's not fuckin' *here*,' Francie says.

'Here you go,' Mart says, pushing one of the Marys across the table. 'She can stand in.'

'I'm not apologising to a fuckin' bottle.'

'You are,' Bobby says. 'Or we can take this outside.'

Senan bursts out laughing. 'I'll have you as well,' Bobby tells him belligerently, pointing across the table.

'The blood's up now,' Mart says, watching with immense enjoyment. 'That's the hormones activating. Once he gets his leg over, there'll be no holding him.'

'I got this covered,' Cal tells Francie. On the off chance that Bobby manages to get his fist-fight on, a little pudgeball like him is going to be no match for Francie. While Francie wouldn't do him any physical damage, Cal feels that Bobby deserves to hang on to his newfound sass for a while longer. 'I'm from the South; we do apologies better'n anyone. Repeat after me—'

'I will in me hole.'

'"Dear Miz Róisín,"' Cal says. He has no idea whether this will work. A couple of years ago, Francie would undoubtedly have told him to fuck off back to the South and take his apology with him. Bobby folds his arms and waits pointedly.

'Fuck's sake,' Francie says. He looks around the table for support, but public opinion is on Bobby's side here; not that anyone cares about Róisín's honour, but everyone wants to see Francie apologise to a holy water bottle.

'Quit your whingeing and get on with it,' Mart says. To Cal: 'Wasn't it worth having the dinner late for this?'

Francie shakes his head in disbelief and raises his eyes to the ceiling, but he says, 'Dear Missus Róisín.'

'"I never intended to insult a lady,"' Cal says. '"Please accept my heartfelt apologies for my indelicate language."'

'I never intended to insult a lady. Please accept my apologies for my indelicate fuckin' language. Will that do you?'

'That's better,' Bobby says, mollified and settling back on the banquette. 'Watch your mouth, but.'

'That was poetry,' Mart says, raising his glass to Cal. 'No wonder Theresa Reddy's turning out so civilised.'

'Here,' Senan says, reaching for his Mary bottle. 'Give me that yoke. Mine's going up there.' He squints and aims the bottle towards the fishing net that hangs from the ceiling, tastefully scattered with glass balls and a wide variety of less probable objects that people have added over the years.

'You have some respect,' Bobby orders him. 'That's the Holy Virgin.' Bobby's new status appears to be going to his head. PJ, unsettled by this version, is edging away from him on the banquette.

'I'm not messing,' Senan says. 'I can't think of anywhere that needs a bitta sanctifying more than this fuckin' madhouse.' He tosses the bottle with a neat overhand snap right into the fishing net, where it lands between a stuffed Pikachu and a tube of sheep wormer.

2

When it comes to most things around here, Lena's standing policy is to avoid prying. This goes double when it comes to Trey. Trey defaults to silence anyway; when nudged, she clams up like a prisoner of war. Lena, who considers this the sensible response to Ardnakelty, doesn't nudge her. Once she's dropped off Trey's crowd, she drives all the way back to Cal's place without mentioning Kate's name.

'I like your mates,' she says instead.

'Aidan's a chancer,' Trey tells her. 'He was gonna ask you to get us a few cans for tonight, only I told him to get ta fuck.'

'Ha,' Lena says. 'Knew it.'

'How?'

Lena gives her a dry glance. 'Ah, God, no, I wouldn't have a clue about that kinda carry-on. Me and your mam never touched a drop till we were legal.'

Trey grins.

'You know not to get stupid drunk,' Lena says, pulling up outside Cal's gate.

Trey rolls her eyes, like she does every time. 'I don't get drunk.'

'Good. If you do, ring me or Cal, we'll come get you.' Lena doesn't ask where they'll be. The places have been handed down through the generations: a tumbledown Famine cottage low on the mountainside, the disused byre at the unwatched edge of Mossie O'Halloran's farm, the abandoned house down by the river. One or two of the kids who'll be drinking there tonight were probably conceived there.

'Thanksforthelift,' Trey says, all in one word, as she gets out of the car. Cal, who believes in manners, has been civilising Trey bit by bit, seeing as no one else was doing it. It's sticking, to some extent, although Lena suspects that Trey is mainly humouring Cal rather than coming to grips with the underlying principles.

'No problem,' Lena says. 'Tell Cal I'll get the dogs and be over in time for dinner.' Trey nods and heads for the cottage. Trey spent most of her life halfway up the mountains and she still walks like a mountain kid, a long, spring-kneed stride, buffered against tricky terrain. Lena can tell by the swing of her shoulders that she's happy. She finds herself smiling as she pulls away.

Lena's plans are held up by the fact that when she gets home, there's a baby-blue Mini Cooper in her drive and Rachel Holohan is sitting on her doorstep with some kind of case beside her. Lena doesn't get many visitors, and she has no idea what Rachel would want with her. Whatever it is, it doesn't look good. Rachel is normally all bounce and sparkle – Lena can't remember whether she's actually training as a Montessori teacher, or whether she just seems like she should be – but today she's huddled up like a wet bird, so deep in her thoughts and her furry hood that she didn't even notice the car pulling in. Lena hopes to God she's not running away from home and looking for a place to stay.

'Rachel,' Lena says, a few steps away.

Rachel leaps. 'Ohmygod,' she says, pressing her chest. 'You frightened the shite outa me. Jesus, sorry, I shouldn't say that, sure you live here, what was I expecting?'

'You're grand,' Lena says. She likes Rachel. To look at, Rachel has all the trimmings of someone Lena would find uninteresting: her hair is dyed platinum blonde with the bottom half in big smooth ringlets, she's an inch thick in fake tan and make-up, she has eyelashes like draught excluders, and she lives in yoga pants whose hems rise and fall with the temperature. She looks like she popped out of Instagram by mistake and someone should put her back in before she gets smudged. Since Rachel is from Ardnakelty, however, Lena has been seeing her around all her life, and she knows Rachel to be a gangling Labrador pup of a girl, cheerful, scatterbrained, inexhaustibly chatty, and good-humoured about her own gaffes. Lena favours people who don't match their exteriors. They give her something to wonder about.

'D'you know what,' Rachel says, struck by a thought, 'I think it's the weather. Honest to God, it's like a horror film, isn't it?' She waves her hand at the darkening fields, huddled under the rain. 'I'm sitting here expecting Freddy Croaker to jump out at me.'

'Freddy Krueger?' Lena suggests.

'That fella,' Rachel agrees. She stands up, dusts off her arse, and picks up the case, which turns out to be a cat carrier. 'Would you, if you've got time only, would you have a look at Pugsy? It's his face, my dad said maybe he got in a fight but sure Pugsy wouldn't fight a fly, he's fixed, lazy great lump, only the vet's closed.'

'Right,' Lena says. This makes a bit more sense of things. Back when she was a teenager, Lena had her heart set on being a vet, so she spent her school holidays volunteering at the vet's up in Kilcarrow town. That was thirty years ago, and mostly all she did was clean up dog piss and put flea drops on cats, but it takes longer than thirty years to shake off a reputation in Ardnakelty. People still bring animals to her, when the vet is closed or too expensive. 'Come on in and I'll have a look.'

Lena's dogs, Daisy and Nellie, come charging up to investigate – they're beagles, so their main priority is food, but a cat is interesting enough for them to put that on hold. While Lena shoos them out of the kitchen, Rachel pushes back her hood and looks around the room with frank curiosity. Lena is aware that her kitchen wouldn't be what Rachel's used to. Rachel's daddy owns the big home-goods shop up in Kilcarrow, making him the richest man in the townland, bar Tommy Moynihan. According to Noreen, Claire Holohan feels a duty to keep her house like a showroom, with new furnishings every year or two and a deep clean every Saturday, so as not to bring the family business into disrepute. Lena's kitchen is clean but messy, with battered furniture and stacks of books in odd places, a room that's been shaped to her convenience and liking by long, steady wear.

'Now,' Lena says, coming back from shutting the door on the dogs, who know cats are off-limits but who are still wounded by the injustice. 'Let's see this fella.'

Rachel plumps down on the floor in a tangle of long legs, unzips the carrier, and pulls out a fat ginger cat who has clearly decided this whole situation is beneath his notice. 'There,' she says, dumping him in her lap. 'Don't worry, he won't go for you, he's got no more fight than a, I don't know, a spud, and anyway he's got no teeth left.'

Lena sits down opposite her and offers the cat a finger, which he ignores. He's got a few scratches above one eyebrow, but they're shallow, the fine lines of blood already dry. This is nothing that couldn't have waited till Monday.

'He's been scratching himself,' she says, 'is all. Something's itching him. It could be ringworm, see how he's a bit baldy round the scratches? Or—' She tilts the cat's head to look inside his ear, which he bears with magnificent disdain. 'It could be mites, but the ear looks clean enough to me. You'd have to have the vet take a look. Till then, just give his claws a clip so he can't do too much damage, and wash your hands after you pet him.'

'Ah, that's great,' Rachel says, on a sigh of relief. 'Thanks a million. My dad says I'm a total sap about that cat, but I've had him since I was only little, d'you know the way? I'd be pure devastated if it turned out there was something wrong and I let him suffer.'

'No problem,' Lena says. She's aware that Rachel is bullshitting her. 'I did nothing.' She knuckles the cat's cheek and gets up to wash her hands. When she turns from the sink, Rachel is still sitting on the floor, pulling at a ringlet and letting it bounce back into place. The cat, done with this nonsense, has curled up in her lap and closed his eyes.

Lena knows she should offer her a cup of tea. Instead she dries her hands on the tea towel and waits. Whatever Rachel has come for, Lena isn't going to help her out.

Rachel blows out a breath and straightens her back. 'I'm gonna ask something awful nosy,' she says. 'You can tell me to feck off and mind my own business, I won't be offended or anything, honest to God. Just I'd love to know. Not outa nosiness.'

Lena looks at her. Under all the make-up and the chatter, she's taut and wan, like she's been hit by a shock and worn herself dazed trying to fight it. She's been crying.

'Ask away,' Lena says. 'I mightn't answer, but you're welcome to ask.'

'Right, so,' Rachel says. She presses her hands down on the cat, which opens one baleful eye and then shuts it again. 'D'you know back when you were married? Not the beardy fella, 'cause you're only going out, sure; Sean Dunne. That's right, isn't it?'

'It is,' Lena agrees. Sean has been dead more than six years, long enough that she can hear his name almost without pain. 'What about it?'

'OK, you know the way he didn't want you hanging around with people? I mean, obvi you didn't mind too much, 'cause you coulda just done it anyway, it's not like olden times when you hadta do everything your husband said or the priest would give out, or you coulda left him. But wasn't it terrible lonely, like? Did you not miss having girls' nights out, and calling round to people for the chats, and all that? And even now, like, 'cause it's still not the same for you as it is for my mammy and the rest of them, sure it's not. Is it awful tough? Or is it all worthwhile because you had your fella?'

Her upturned face is honest and worried. Lena bites down a flare of fury. Sean, dead and buried, is still in Ardnakelty's hands, being mauled and branded as they please; and, regardless of how many barriers she puts up, so is she.

'I don't know where you got that,' she says, careful to keep her voice even, 'but you've got it wrong. Sean never in his life told me who to hang around with. That's my own choice and always has been.'

'Ah, *shite*,' Rachel says, turning pink and slumping disconsolately over the cat. 'Now I'm after saying something stupid. Or it was my mammy that said it to start with, she said it was just like Sean to want you all to himself, just the two of ye, and the rest of the world could feck off – I think she usedta fancy him back in school, d'you know that? Only he never even looked at her, it sounds like, and sure she's happy as Larry with my dad, so that's grand. But it's not my mammy's fault, I was the one that went and said it to you. I'm an awful feckin' eejit sometimes.'

Lena isn't so sure. Claire, in school, was a skinny, vague little thing who spent half her time staring out the window and said 'What?' whenever anyone talked to her, but apparently she wasn't as oblivious as she seemed. Lena is starting to wonder how much of Rachel's chatter is an act, too, and what it covers.

'You're all right,' she says. 'Just, only two people ever know what goes on in a marriage. Anyone else who says they've a clue is pulling it straight outa their arse. Remember that.'

Slowly, with no drama, tears start to leak down Rachel's face. 'Sorry,' she says. She wipes them away with the back of a hand, smearing a swipe of mascara across her cheek, and looks at her hand ruefully. 'Now I'm feckin' crying again,' she tells Lena. 'I'd say I'm due my period, d'you reckon?'

It sounds like Rachel is having some kind of trouble with Eugene Moynihan, which isn't surprising, what with Eugene being a tosser. By now Noreen would have the kettle boiling, Rachel on the sofa, an arm around her, and a stream of comfort and interrogation pouring out at ninety miles an hour. But Lena has spent her entire adult life walling out Ardnakelty and its tangles, and now one of those tangles is sniffling on her kitchen floor. Allowing gaps in her boundary walls for Trey is one thing; allowing them for a near-stranger too dim or too desperate to heed the keep-out signs is another.

'I wouldn't know,' she says.

'I shouldn'ta bothered you,' Rachel says. 'Sorry. Just, you were the only one I could think of to ask. Everyone else around here, sure they wouldn't have a notion what I was on about. And then they'd go asking me questions, and then it'd be all round the townland before I even got home, and it'd all be even worse. I thought you might . . .'

The tears are coming down faster. Rachel fishes a bedraggled tissue out of her jacket pocket and dabs under her eyes, tilting her head back. 'I just don't want people upset,' she says. 'And I don't want them hating me. I'm a great big fat sap, I know I am, I oughta be all "Fuck the haters, it's a them problem", but I'm not made like that. Only it's Eugene, he doesn't like me arguing with him, and he's a load smarter than I am and it all makes sense when he says it, you know? And he was so patient explaining everything and I do appreciate it, honest to God I do, he only wants what's best for the two of us. Just . . .' She catches a huge sniffly breath that's on the edge of a sob. Her face, eyes closed tight, is clenched into a mask of wretchedness. 'I can't think,' she says. 'My head's melted trying. I wish I wasn't such a feckin' thick.'

'Listen,' Lena says. 'I haven't a clue what the story is here, and it sounds like I wouldn't be much good to you even if I did. But I'll tell you one thing I know for definite. Whatever you do, you'll piss people off along the way, whether that's Eugene or someone else, but the world won't end. If that's what you're asking.'

Rachel catches another long shaky breath. 'Yeah,' she says. 'I s'pose you're right, sure.' She gives her face one more dab and stuffs the cat back into his carrier, where he turns his back haughtily on the pair of them. 'The state of me, bawling my eyes out on you. I'm only morto with embarrassment here. I'm awful sorry. I won't bother you again.' She gets up off the floor, clumsily, trying to pick up the cat carrier at the same time.

'You're grand,' Lena says. 'Don't let people wreck your head. It'll sort itself in the long run.'

'Ah, yeah. Course. Thanks for, you know, having the look at Pugsy. I'll do that, with his claws. Thanks. Sorry again.' She pulls up her hood and is out the door and heading for her car at a half-run, stooped low over the cat carrier.

Lena watches the sweep of the Mini's lights, down the drive and out onto the road, before she shuts the door. It sounds like Eugene has decided that any wife of his is required to have posher friends than whoever Rachel hangs around with. Rachel, ditzy or not, understands what Ardnakelty will make of that.

Lena told Rachel the truth: she's cut off from this townland by her own desire, but that desire had nothing to do with Sean and came long before him. As far back as she can remember, she was planning a one-way ticket out, to vet training and then to Canada or New Zealand or anywhere far away that would have her. The plan changed shape when Sean came along.

Lena knew from the start he would never leave his land. She swapped her one-way ticket for him and hasn't regretted it, but it meant she had to set her distances inside herself rather than outside. She touches Ardnakelty at as few points as possible. She won't have the townland doing to her what it does, snuffling through the juicy innards of her life and her marriage and her mind.

She knows her distance makes people think she's cold, or strange, or uppity, and has no problem with those. She didn't know, and doesn't like, that it lets people think she's a poor pitiable victim.

Once she's ignored that for long enough, the sting will fade. She should have guessed at it, anyhow. This townland doesn't like being baulked. If it isn't fed what it wants, it'll make its own fodder.

It'll eat Rachel alive. Rachel is softer than Lena ever was; she's not made to hold out against a siege. Against her own instincts, Lena thinks about ringing Claire, but she doesn't have Claire's number and is on none of the WhatsApp groups for sports clubs and school classes and the Tidy Towns. Noreen would have the number, but getting it from her would set off a tornado of questions and surmises, and Rachel doesn't need that.

Rachel will find her own way, the same as Lena did. Lena lets the dogs back into the kitchen and gives them their dinner. She got Nellie and Daisy after they were dumped half-starved on a roadside; watching them, sturdy and glossy and secure, still gives her the same warmth she takes from the new ease in Trey's walk.

While they eat, she leans back against the counter and thinks about Sean. For the first year after he died, she would do anything not to think of him; she worked herself to exhaustion every day and walked herself to exhaustion into the night, to keep her mind from reaching for him. These days she sets out time to think of him, deliberately and regularly, so that the man she knew won't be lost.

Claire had Sean right, or close to it. He wanted very few things, but he wanted those with an intensity that seemed incapable of being sated. Even when he and Lena lay down together, he could never get her close enough. Sometimes she wondered if the flaw was in her, not in him; if she had bent her mind so hard to withholding parts of herself, she couldn't stop. But Sean was like that about other things. The farm was family land, owned free and clear for generations, but he never felt it was his enough. Lena came to think he would never be easy unless he cut himself open, put her and the farm inside, and sewed himself back up tight.

Lena wanted him just as deeply, but differently. She has a knack for contentment that he never had. She was happy with him. To her surprise, she's happy again, without him.

The window is dark; the warm kitchen light catches in the haze of raindrops on the pane. Cal and Trey will be wondering where Lena is. 'Come on,' she says to the dogs, and they follow her out to the car, snorting at the cold outside air.

'Another one bites the dust,' Mart says, on the way home. He's giving Cal a ride – Cal took a while to get accustomed to Ardnakelty's attitude towards driving home from the pub, but they sanded the cop reflex off him in the end. Mart's car smells of sheep dip and his dog, Kojak, and has no shock absorbers to speak of, but so far it's got him home. 'There'll be wedding bells before next Christmas. Can you picture Bobby in a tux? He'll look like the fuckin' Penguin.'

'Jeez, man,' Cal says. 'You're as bad as Noreen. They just met.'

'Bobby's smitten,' Mart says, taking one hand off the wheel to light the rollie in his mouth. 'You saw the state of him: smitten ta fuck.'

'She might not be,' Cal points out.

'Doesn't matter. Bobby's a nice fella, but he's not what you'd call a sex symbol, God love him. If this Róisín one is courting him, 'tis one of two things: either they're made for each other in heaven, or else she's in the humour to settle down and she reckons wee Bobby's the best she'll get. Either way, they'll be headed down the aisle by the time I can get my suit dry-cleaned. Racing yourself and Lena to the altar.'

'Love is in the air,' Cal says. 'You'll be next.'

He's only ribbing Mart, who considers women to be interesting in the abstract but not a field in which he has any urge to get personally involved, like space travel or raising ostriches. Mart snorts smoke out of his nose. 'I will not. Who'd want the likes of me? Now that J.Lo's gone back with your man.'

'Don't underrate yourself,' Cal says. 'You've got conversation. A lot of women value that.'

'I never underrated myself in my life, bucko. I'm looking at it from the other perspective, is what I'm doing. Think it over: d'you know who'd want me? Some widow woman that's got time on her hands and needs a new project to keep her occupied. I'd make a first-rate project, so I would. The efficient type could roll up her sleeves and get stuck right in here. The wardrobe alone could keep her going for years.' Mart bounces the car over a pothole, for emphasis.

'You could fix up her wardrobe, instead,' Cal points out. 'She might need some good hats.' From the neck down Mart's wardrobe is the standard farmer ensemble, mainly pilled fleeces and well-aged work pants, but he also owns Ardnakelty's most varied collection of headgear. Today, in deference to the weather, he's wearing a shiny yellow sou'wester.

'I'm not sharing my hats with no one,' Mart says. 'A woman would disrupt my lifestyle. I can't be doing with that.' He rolls down his window to let the smoke escape, out of consideration for Cal. Cool damp air sweeps in. 'Wee Bobby hasn't a clue what he's after getting himself into. There's the logistics of getting back and forth to wherever she is, and the social minefield when he introduces her to this place, and there's the joys of living with two women in the same house – and that's before you even start in on the emotional territory, and the question of when he's allowed out to the pub. There's a reason why all the old love songs are sad ones, Sunny Jim: because love's a head-wrecking little bollocks.'

'Me and Lena are doing fine,' Cal points out. 'No one's head's wrecked.'

'Ye are,' Mart concedes. 'The two of ye are getting along swimmingly. I'd say "so far", only that'd be impolite. But the difference is, ye've both got a bitta experience under your belts, so ye can spot the pitfalls. Bobby's got no more experience than a baba – apart from the aul' internet porn, and that's grand in its own way, but I wouldn't say it prepares you for marrying a receptionist from Tipperary.'

'How do you know she's from Tipperary?' Cal asks.

Mart lets out a wheeze of laughter. 'I don't. I'll test it on Bobby tomorrow and see does he look caught out.'

He pulls up in front of Cal's gate. Cal's windows are lit; in the kitchen, Lena is at the cupboards, her thick ponytail falling down her back as she reaches for plates, while Trey's cropped brown head moves back and forth behind her. Their faces turn between the work and each other; they're talking. 'Off you go now and enjoy the aul' domestic bliss,' Mart says, 'and don't be wasting any sentiment on me. I'll admit there was a time when I usedta get the odd craving for a woman, back when the sap was rising, but that was in a different millennium, sure; I'm all recovered now. I wouldn't have one if she was handed to me on a plate.'

'Fair enough,' Cal says. 'Thanks for the ride.'

Mart is still looking out the window at Cal's house, the car idling and his hands loose on the wheel. The windshield wipers give a soft intermittent swish. 'What I wouldn't mind having,' he says, 'is a son, or two or three. Or daughters, sure. I'm not one a them sexists; that's for eejits that have no sense of practicality.'

'I'd pay to watch you change a diaper,' Cal says.

'I'd manage,' Mart says with dignity. 'Like I was telling Francie, I'm a great believer in the new experiences. But that's not my point. My point is, I've no plans to go dying in the foreseeable, but it'll haveta be done sooner or later. I've no quarrel with that. But what happens then, Sunny Jim?' He smiles across at Cal. In the faint light from the dashboard, his face is a mass of quick-moving creases. 'That's the million-dollar question, hah? What happens then?'

'Are we talking about the afterlife?' Cal asks. 'It's only six-thirty.' If he had thought Mart was that drunk, he might not have taken the ride.

Mart snorts. 'I am in me hole. I wouldn't discuss that kinda carry-on with a Protestant anyhow; sure, all ye have to offer is fire and brimstone, and there's no getting up a worthwhile conversation around that. If there's any such thing, I'll deal with it when I get there. No: I'm talking about the land.'

His face turns to look up the road, towards his farm. It's too dark to see anything but the strip of tarmac and the falling rain in the headlights, but Mart can see it anyway. 'That won't die when I do,' he says. 'If you wanta get philosophical about an afterlife, sunshine, there it is in front of you: that land. That was my daddo's afterlife, and then my father's, and now 'tis mine. Only what do I do with it? I've no childer to leave it to. The brothers are emigrated or dead, or both for all I know. I've cousins by the dozens, but half a them would sell the land to Tommy Moynihan or some other gombeen man for shitey town houses, and I've got no way of knowing for certain which half is which. What do I do, to stop a perfectly good afterlife from going to waste?'

Cal is silent. He doesn't come from farming stock; he has nothing to offer here.

Mart puts the car into gear, with a ferocious grinding noise. 'I shoulda found some young one that fancied a baba or two but couldn't be arsed putting up with fellas' nonsense,' he says, 'and come to an arrangement. 'Tis a bit late for that now, sure. I'll haveta interrogate the cousins. You can dust off the aul' detective skills and give me a hand.'

'I'm no match for any cousin of yours,' Cal says, and Mart laughs. Cal gets out and waves his thanks, and Mart lifts his hand in response as the car bumps off up the road, headlights glittering on the dripping hedges.

Cal's front room is bright after the dark road and smells of varnish from the back-room workshop, where he and Trey have been finishing up a shoe cupboard for Michelle Healy. The dogs, his and Lena's, come bouncing over to welcome him and check out where he's been. Normally Trey's dog, Rip's litter-mate Banjo, would be there too, but Trey has been leaving Banjo at her mama's place more often these days. Cal suspects she might not want to trail a dog behind her everywhere, like a little kid. He hasn't asked in case he's right.

Lena is kneeling by the fireplace, laying out kindling; in the kitchen half of the room, Trey, her hair still rucked up and damp from the shower, is setting the table. ''Bout time,' she says. ''M *starving*.'

'So let's get this show on the road,' Cal says. He dumps the eggs on the counter, along with a packet of mini Twix bars that Noreen threw in to get them out of her sight, hangs up his jacket, and bends to kiss Lena. Lena is tall and fair, with deep curves and deep blue eyes, and to Cal a room feels warmer with her in it. 'Congratulations,' he says, holding up a hand for Trey to high-five.

'Lisnacarragh were fuckin' raging,' Trey says with satisfaction, slapping his palm. 'They thought they were gonna flatten us like ten–nil, just 'cause they have your woman that the scout came to look at. She didn't even score.'

'She didn't reckon on Trey and Kate,' Lena says. Trey is small for a defender, at around five foot five, but she's wiry, fast, and used to taking advantage of being underestimated. 'The face on her, when you intercepted that high cross.' Over the past couple of years, Cal and Lena have both gone from being clueless about football to understanding the offside rule.

'They'll know better next time,' Cal says. 'We're gonna need ham and cheese for this, chopped up small. You do that, I'll do the eggs.' He's talking to Trey. Lena doesn't cook; it's one of the things she decided to leave in her old life, when her husband died. Cal has no problem with this. He likes cooking, and he likes the opportunity to differentiate their relationship from her marriage. He doesn't know much about her marriage, any more than she does about his, but he knows it was a powerful thing and not one she thought she'd ever be able to leave behind her.

'Lisnacarragh's used to having things their way,' Lena says. 'They'll be out for revenge. When's the rematch?'

'Coupla weeks,' Trey says, pulling ham and cheese out of the fridge. 'My boots're in tatters. When's Michelle Healy paying us?'

'Her cupboard's about ready,' Cal says. 'One more coat of varnish and we'll take it down to her. I'll lend you the money till then, if you need new ones sooner.' He knows better than to offer to buy Trey the boots outright. A couple of years back, even the suggestion of a loan would have gotten his head bitten off.

'Nah. I'll be grand till then. Get the cash outa Michelle before you give her the cupboard, but. She's a hoor for not paying her bills.'

'Damn,' Cal says, getting out bowls to separate the eggs. 'I'll have to get you one boot for Christmas and the other one for your birthday.'

'I know what I want for Christmas,' Trey tells him. 'Can you teach me to drive?'

'Sure,' Cal says. The thought of her driving on these roads gives him the heebie-jeebies, but he was a backcountry kid himself and he knows how it works: she'll drive whether he teaches her or not, so he'd rather she do it right. 'You need some kinda permit for that?'

Trey makes a *pfft* noise. 'Prob'ly.'

'OK,' Cal says, resigning himself to figuring out the admin side of this, which both Trey and her mama would ignore until some form of shit hit the fan. 'Next year maybe you can drive yourself to school, instead of riding that damn bike.' Trey adores her bike, a sleek navy Diamondback that she bought with her woodworking earnings, but from Cal's perspective her biking these roads is at least as bad as her driving them, and a lot wetter.

'Mightn't be in school next year,' Trey says.

'Kid,' Cal says. 'You gotta finish school.' They've had this conversation before, never to anyone's satisfaction.

'How come?'

'Gives you options.'

'Don't want options. I'm gonna be a woodworker. I don't need my Leaving Cert for that.'

'I know that. And if you decide you want to try out something else, a few years down the line, you oughta have that choice.'

Trey twists one corner of her mouth and goes back to chopping ham, but Cal can tell the conversation isn't over. He keeps separating eggs, and waits.

'When we were up in town, last weekend,' Trey says. 'I was talking to Sam Murray.'

Sam is a woodworker in a big way, too big to feel any competition from Cal and Trey's back-room operation. He's thrown them jobs a few times, when he was overloaded or when someone needed something smaller and more fiddly than he wanted to bother with. Cal likes him – Sam is young and cheerful, with enough energy to furnish Dublin Castle if the chance came his way – but he's startled by the thought of Trey deliberately getting into a conversation with the guy. Trey mostly doesn't talk to people unless she has a concrete objective, or no choice.

'Huh,' he says. 'How's Sam doing?'

'You were gone to the shops,' Trey says, a little defensively. 'I saw him coming outa the pub.'

'Fair enough,' Cal says. 'What'd he have to say?'

Trey pulls more ham out of the packet, although it looks to Cal like she's done plenty already. 'I asked him if he'd take me on. As an apprentice. He said yeah, no problem. He's approved, like, to have apprentices. He could register me, so I'd get my qualification at the end.'

She's still got her head down over the ham, just giving Cal the odd quick sideways glance, but he can feel her alert and waiting for his response. Lena has turned from the fireplace to watch them, but she's staying quiet.

'Well,' Cal says. 'That's great to hear. That fretwork must've impressed him.' He catches the relief loosening Trey's face. He doesn't know whether to be proud that she had the chops to talk to Sam, or worry that she left him out because she thought he wouldn't approve. 'Sam's the real deal; you'll learn stuff from him that you won't get from me and YouTube videos. Did he say when he had in mind?'

'Any time, he said. Just let him know.'

'Well, even better,' Cal says. He rummages through a drawer for the whisk. The kid doesn't need to be hanging out in some workshop, among big hairy guys talking big hairy talk and sending her to buy new bubbles for the spirit level. Let her goof off with her buddies a while longer, bitch about homework, catch up on being a kid; once she moves on from that, there'll be no moving back. 'You can take all the time you need. Finish school, get your licence so you can drive yourself into Kilcarrow every day, get back to him then.'

He's ready for the argument, but Trey just shoves the chopping board towards him. 'That much?'

'Yeah,' Cal says. 'Sure. And the same amount of cheese.' He's not reassured. Trey doesn't give up that easily; he's never known her to give up at all, unless she decides she actually wants to. He waits, but Trey is neatly pulling the cheddar packet open, not looking at him. Lena strikes a match and sets it to the firelighter, and Cal gets started on the egg whites.

The soufflé works out. Trey finishes hers in a hurry and checks her phone, which has been demanding attention from her coat pocket. 'Gotta go,' she says.

'You can't bike if you're gonna drink,' Cal says. 'You want a ride?'

'Nah. Ross's brother's giving us a lift. Thanks.'

'He going drinking with you?'

'Nah. He's *twenty*. He's only driving us 'cause Ross said he'd do his share of cleaning the cattle sheds.'

'If he's drinking, you don't take a ride back with him. You call me and I'll come get you.'

Trey rolls her eyes, throws on her coat, gives Rip's jowls a quick rub, and heads out the door. Cal manages not to ask where she'll be. He would love to tell her to bring her buddies over here, he'll stay out of their way; but even if Trey would go for it, which she wouldn't, he has no desire to be the guy who invites random teenagers over to do teenage things at his place. He and Ardnakelty know each other well enough that no one gets weird about Trey hanging out here, but her friends aren't from Ardnakelty.

'She'll be grand,' Lena says, getting up to clear the table. 'She's got sense.'

'She better,' Cal says. He blows out a long breath. 'I didn't see that coming.'

'Sam Murray?'

'Yeah. I knew she wanted an apprenticeship, but I didn't think she'd go out looking. Not yet, at least.'

'I thought she might,' Lena says. Cal looks up at the touch of remoteness in her voice, like she's thinking something she's not going to share, but Lena has her back to him, rinsing plates. 'I expected further away than Kilcarrow, but.'

Cal has had the same thought. Sam would at least keep Trey here. Cal can't tell whether he's right or wrong to want that; whether the kid needs to be in his keeping for a little bit longer, or whether he just doesn't want her to go.

He doesn't ask if Lena is in favour of letting Trey quit school, in case she says yes. Lena cares plenty about Trey, but she does it differently from Cal. She's never shared his ferocious urge to protect the kid. Cal and Lena are harmonious; their only minor clashes have come out of that discrepancy, and Cal doesn't feel like having one tonight. He gets up and finds two glasses and the bottle of bourbon.

'You know Kate, that's on the team with Trey,' Lena says. 'What's she like?'

Cal glances over quickly. He didn't have Kate down as the type to give people grief, but you never know. Lena, though, has lost that tint of reserve. Instead she looks mischievous.

'She seems like a good kid,' he says, 'from what I can tell. I don't want to talk to any of 'em too much, in case I'm wearing the wrong shirt or breathing funny or something.' Cal's own daughter, Alyssa, is grown now, but when she was Trey's age, he could be a near-fatal embarrassment just by accidentally glancing in the wrong person's direction. 'How come?'

'I think Trey might be going out with her. Or thinking about it, anyhow.'

Cal stops with the bourbon bottle in mid-air. 'What? How do you know?'

'I don't know for definite. Just the talk in the car. One of the lads sounded like he was slagging them.'

'Holy shitballs,' Cal says. He can't think of anything to do except stand there. Lena is grinning. 'I mean . . . Shit. I didn't see that coming. She's just a kid.'

'She's sixteen,' Lena says. 'Did you have a girlfriend by then?'

'Yeah. I guess. But Trey, she's . . .' Cal leaves the bottle on the counter and takes a walk around the room, to get his head straight. 'No. It's not the same thing. The kid, what with everything, she's young for her age. Too young for that.'

'Looks like her and Kate mightn't agree with you,' Lena points out. Her face is still amused.

'I bet they don't. That's my point. The fact that she doesn't even realise she's too young, that shows she's way too young.' Cal knows he sounds like he's babbling, but he's not kidding. When Trey first showed up in his back yard, more than three years ago, she was half feral and the world's enemy; she knew plenty about dodging trouble and making it through hard times, but almost nothing about being a person among people. Cal has been teaching her those skills as best he can, and the kid is a fast learner when she feels like it, but neither one of them is magic. She's come a long way, but not far enough to go around having relationships like some kind of grown-up.

Lena is laughing. 'Cool the jets,' she says. 'I'd say they're only at the stage of being awkward around each other. It could take them months to get any further, if they ever do.'

'Damn,' Cal says, rubbing a hand down his face. 'I need that drink.' He goes back to the counter and starts pouring the bourbon, with ginger ale for Lena, on the rocks for himself tonight. 'How old's Kate?'

Lena settles herself on the sofa. 'Trey's age, give or take, if they're on the same team. I like the cut of her as well. She has a laugh, and she takes no shite.'

'She treat people right?'

'She does, yeah. From what I've seen, anyhow.'

Cal brings the drinks over. 'You know anything about her family?'

'You could have them over for dinner,' Lena suggests helpfully. 'Suss them out, ask about Kate's prospects, get their fingerprints. Trey'd never talk to you again, but sure you haveta make sacrifices in this life.'

'Seriously,' Cal says. 'You know anything?'

Lena turns to put her feet up on his lap. 'She's a Carroll, from Knockfarraney. If it's the ones I'm thinking of, her dad's Mattie Carroll, he's a cattle man – not in a big way, like, but he does well enough – and her mam's Lucy-Anne. I was in school with the both of them. Lucy-Anne was good crack, and Mattie had more sense than a teenage boy oughta. See?' She lifts an eyebrow at Cal, over the rim of her glass. 'Lovely and respectable.'

'Well,' Cal says. He takes a big swig of his bourbon. 'That's good.' He almost wishes Lena hadn't told him, not tonight, coming right on top of the apprenticeship thing. It feels like he only just got a good firm handle on what Trey needs from him and how to provide it, and now out of the blue she's come up with a brand-new set of needs. Presumably someone should talk to her about healthy relationships and whatever the hell, specially since she didn't grow up with any kind of example, what with her father being worth even less when he was around than when he wasn't. Cal would bet his life her mama hasn't covered this territory; Sheila Reddy does her best according to her lights, but her best doesn't get into much emotional depth. Cal himself has no idea of how to even start. His ex-wife, Donna, did all that stuff for Alyssa, or at least he assumes she did, since Alyssa turned out pretty great. But he can't dump this on Lena. Trey doesn't look to Lena for counsel. Mostly she doesn't look to anyone, but when she does, it's to him. Cal doesn't know how to have this talk with any kid, but he sure as hell doesn't know how to have it with a girl, let alone a girl who apparently likes girls. He wants someone to sit him down and explain in small words how he got himself into this.

'At least she's not gonna come home pregnant,' he says. 'We're not gonna need to, I don't know, fix her up with contraception or . . . Jesus.'

'Did you reckon she was gay?' Lena asks.

'I never thought about it before. I didn't think I *needed* to think about it any time soon.' Cal leans his head back against the cushions and takes a breath. 'Is she gonna get any flak?'

Lena sips her drink and considers that. 'Not around here. People think she's odd anyhow, this won't make any difference; and they don't go looking for reasons to go after the Reddys, not any more. She might get a bitta hassle from a few people in school, maybe. But she's got mates now, and so has Kate. Between them all, they'll beat the shite outa anyone that needs it. She'll be grand. She's tough.'

'I know she is,' Cal says. He doesn't know how to say that that's the problem, not the solution. The kid was tough for too long; she deserves the chance to be soft.

'Wait and see,' Lena says gently. 'It could turn out great.'

'Yeah,' Cal says. 'It could.' Apparently love is in the air, just like he said to Mart. It's out of season. That kind of stirring belongs in spring, with the birds flirting and the buds unfurling. This restlessness in the dark evenings, under the rain, has a different feel. He finishes his drink and puts the glass on the coffee table, so he can rub Lena's feet.

By unspoken agreement, Lena doesn't sleep over when Cal has Trey; it would feel unseemly, the two of them sharing a bed with her right outside their door. That night, after Lena goes home, Cal stays up. Mostly, when Trey goes out, he lies awake in bed with his light off till he hears her come in, so she won't feel like he's hovering. Tonight he makes up the sofa bed and then sits at the kitchen table, reading in the small warm circle of light from the hanging lamp. The type blurs; he needs reading glasses. Rip, sprawled in his corner, runs and huffs in his sleep, chasing the rooks he never can catch.

It's past one in the morning, the fire has burned low and the room is cold, when he hears Trey's key turn quietly in the lock.

'What's up?' she says, when she sees him there.

'Nothing,' Cal says. 'Couldn't sleep. You have a good night?'

'Yeah,' Trey says. She's red-nosed from the cold. She breathes on her hands.

'You look freezing,' Cal says, getting up. 'Here.' He puts a mugful of milk in the microwave and gets out the cocoa powder. Trey drops down beside Rip and digs her hands into his fur, to warm them.

Cal watches her, as the microwave hums and she murmurs to Rip. She's probably had a drink or two, but she's not drunk or anywhere near it. She never is; the kid has spent too much of her life on the defensive to be comfortable with the idea of letting her defences down. She looks at ease, like the night was a good one. He wants to ask if Kate was there, but he knows better than that.

'Aidan's gonna ask Ciara to go out with him,' Trey tells him.

'Well, about time,' Cal says. The microwave dings; he stirs

cocoa powder into the hot milk. 'Whenever I take you guys anyplace, they're making goo-goo eyes at each other the whole way.'

'He was waiting till she decided,' Trey explains. 'She was worried it'd be too complicated or something, I dunno. With all of us being mates.'

'Hold on,' Cal says. 'Back up the truck. So Ciara already knows he's gonna ask her out? And he already knows she's gonna say yes?'

Trey gives him a look like he shouldn't be allowed around people. 'Yeah. He said it to Ross and Ross said it to Kate and Kate said it to Ciara, and then the other way round, till they decided.'

'So they're already going out. If they've agreed to go out, they're going out.'

'Nah. He didn't *ask* her yet. They reckon next week.'

'Damn,' Cal says. 'This an Irish thing? Or a Gen Z thing? Or just your buddies?'

'What? How'd you ask girls out? Send a message by dinosaur?'

'Watch it,' Cal says, mock-offended, pointing the spoon at her. Trey is grinning. 'I went up to the girl and said, "Hey, Susie, you're looking mighty fine today, you wanna go to the movies Saturday?" And then I held my breath till I found out if Susie was gonna say yes or if the whole school was gonna be laughing at my sorry ass.'

'She say yes?'

'Sure she did. We dated for a whole three weeks, till her daddy found out. The point is, we didn't have the whole thing *negotiated* in advance by ambassadors. What's gonna happen if any of you want to get married, someday? International summits?'

'You're just old,' Trey tells him, getting up and coming over for the hot chocolate.

'Maybe,' Cal says. 'But I managed to ask Miss Lena out without asking Mart to ask Miss Noreen to ask her for me.'

The idea catches Trey in mid-sip, and hot chocolate goes down her nose. Cal watches her cough and laugh at the same time. 'I guess I oughta be relieved you guys can ask someone out without making a TikTok,' he says.

Trey wipes her mouth with the back of her hand and pulls herself up to sit on the counter. After a moment she says, 'How come you don't want me apprenticing with Sam?'

Cal puts the milk back in the fridge. When it comes down to it, he has no say in what the kid does. He's not her daddy, or anything else that matters. She showed up a few years back, looking for his help because her big brother was missing, and now somehow here they are. If she wants to quit school tomorrow, he can't do a damn thing about it. So far, neither one of them has brought that up.

'I do,' he says. 'Sam's a good guy, he does good work, and you've gotta move on from here sometime. Just not yet.'

'I'll still do our stuff,' Trey says. 'Even if I'm apprenticing.'

There's something in her voice, almost like reassurance, that makes Cal close his eyes against it for a moment. 'Well, wait and see how much time you've got,' he says. 'Sam might keep you pretty busy. It'll be fine, either way.'

Trey nods, twisting around to get the packet of Twix bars out of the cupboard. Cal can't tell whether she's convinced or not.

'Just finish school,' he says.

'That's another year and a half.'

'Kid,' Cal says. 'That's not a long time.'

'Year and a fuckin' *half*.'

'Sam'll wait.'

'He mightn't. He'll take on someone else.'

'Then somebody else'll take you. You do good work.'

'School's stupid,' Trey says. 'Wanta be doing something real.'

'Well, I get that,' Cal says. 'I felt the same way. And now I wish I'd got more out of it while I had the chance.'

'I'm not you,' Trey points out.

'I know that. I'd just like you to have more'n I do.'

'What's wrong with what you've got?'

Cal looks at her, sitting there chewing one of Noreen's Twixes, with her jeans dirty and gorse in her hair from whatever her and her buddies were doing, perched on the countertop the two of them made themselves out of a half-burnt oak that they salvaged after a fire on the mountain. 'Nothing,' he says. 'Not a thing in the world.'

Trey gives him a look that means *Well then*. He doesn't know how to tell her that that's his point. He can't explain that she's spurring time along, whipping it faster than there's any need for. Cal is old enough to know, not only that he can't afford that, but that no one can.

Shhh, he wants to tell her. *Just stay still a minute.* When Trey first started spending time at his place, she could stay still for hours on end, watching the rooks in his oak tree squabble and make mischief like a bunch of middle-schoolers, or waiting for one of the rabbits in the back field to line itself up in her rifle sights. Now it seems like she never stops moving. Even sitting right there on the counter, swinging her feet, she's going too fast.

'I'll finish this year, anyhow,' she says, like she's offering a compromise. 'Now I've started.'

'Well, that's good,' Cal says. 'We'll figure out the rest along the way. Now get some sleep.'

He lays a hand on her head for a second, on his way to his room. For a moment he thinks she's about to say something, but then she just waves at him with her Twix bar. Cal lies in bed with his eyes open for a long time, listening to her washing out her mug and brushing her teeth and murmuring to Rip, till the line of light under his bedroom door blinks out.

3

The phone drags Cal out of sleep. The room is middle-of-the-night dark. His mind shoots to Alyssa and he grabs for the phone, but the screen says MART.

'Hey,' he says. 'What's up?'

'Rise and shine, Sunny Jim,' Mart says. 'I hate to interrupt your beauty sleep, but we've got a bit of a situation. There's a girl after going missing.'

'Who?' Cal sits up fast, before he remembers Trey is on his sofa bed. Not all of his mind is awake yet. He switches on his reading light and shields his eyes.

'Rachel Holohan. Never came home tonight. She's not answering her phone, none of her pals know anything, and her mammy and daddy are climbing the walls. They're asking for people to go out and have a look for her. She left her car, so she can'ta gone far if she's on her own, but there's an awful lotta ground to cover all the same.'

Cal doesn't ask whether they've called the police. The Garda station up in Kilcarrow is open for a few hours a few times a week; the nearest twenty-four/seven place, in Castlerea or Roscommon or wherever, isn't going to send a search team out here in the middle of the night because a grown woman neglected to phone home.

'Rachel,' he says. He remembers that afternoon, the blonde girl drifting on the fine sweeps of rain, her face turned towards nothing; the nagging twitch, off in a corner of his mind, that said he was missing something. 'She goes out with Eugene Moynihan. He know anything?'

Mart snorts. 'He says not, but he'd say that regardless. Eugene hasta take good care of himself, sure; he's awful precious. I'm meeting PJ at my gate in ten minutes. I'll see you there.'

It's twenty to four. Cal dresses fast and warmly, and takes the flashlight out of his night table. He's planning to leave Trey a note in case she wakes before he gets back, but when he opens his door she's sitting up in bed, rumpled and blinking in the stripe of light from his room.

'What's the story?' she asks.

'Rachel Holohan's missing. Me and some of the other guys are gonna go look for her. Make sure your phone's charged up, I'll check in.'

'I'll come.'

Cal almost says no. The night, with one girl already wrapped away somewhere inside its implacable vastness, feels unsafe; and this could turn out to be no job for a kid. But he doesn't like the idea of Trey here alone. He doesn't actually think there's a crazed spree killer roaming the back roads looking for young girls to snatch up, but he doesn't feel like taking anything for granted. 'OK,' he says, turning the light on. 'Put on plenty of layers, and stick right by me.'

Trey starts pulling on her clothes over her pyjamas, while Cal laces up his boots and finds the spare flashlight in a kitchen drawer. 'Where'd you guys go tonight?' he asks.

'Mossie O'Halloran's old byre. In case it started raining again.'

'How'd you get home?'

Trey sits on the floor to put on her runners. 'Ross's brother. He wasn't drinking.'

'You see anyone out there? Car, pedestrian, anyone?'

'Passed a coupla the McHugh lads driving home from the

pub, on our way back. And some car lights on the Knockfarraney road while we were at Mossie's, but too far away to see who. No one else.'

'OK,' Cal says. 'If you think of anything, let me know.' He zips up his jacket and tosses Trey her wool beanie. In his corner, Rip has lifted his head to watch, unsettled by the urgency in the air.

'You want me to text the others, see if they saw anything?'

'Nah,' Cal says. This could be, probably is, a dumb kid having a blow-up with her boyfriend and storming off; the last thing the situation needs is every teenager in three townlands awake at this hour and firing up the Snapchat rumour machine to warp drive. 'Maybe tomorrow, if she hasn't shown up by then. Let's go.'

The night is cold, a thick cold that clogs the air. The rain has stopped, but there's still a patchy layer of cloud blocking the sky, with only a smear of dull white where the moon rides high. Cal points his flashlight at the road and they head for Mart's place. Here and there among the fields, windows are lit: Ardnakelty is awake and on edge.

'Rachel's decent,' Trey says. 'Don't know what she's doing with that prick Eugene.'

Cal has never formed any impression of Rachel Holohan – he's aware that such a person exists, but he couldn't pick her out of a line-up, as long as the rest of the line-up had blonde hair and fake lashes. If Trey speaks well of someone from this townland, though, it means something.

'Well,' he says, 'maybe her and that prick Eugene had a fight, and she's run off to give him a scare. And she'll be home before morning, when she gets too cold.'

Trey ups the pace and says nothing. Cal can feel her nerves humming. When her big brother went missing, people told her he had run off, too. It didn't end quickly or well.

The flashlight picks out Mart and PJ, waiting at Mart's gate, long-shadowed and mismatched. PJ is wearing so many layers that he has a fat guy's body balanced precariously on his long skinny legs; Mart is origamied around his crook and has the sou'wester jammed well down over his ears.

'And you brought your assistant,' he says, dropping his smoke in a puddle. 'Good on you; the more pairs of eyes, the better. Tommy Moynihan's coordinating the search, giving us the benefit of all them leadership skills. I told him we'd take this stretch, from the main road down to the river. We're not searching every corner of every field – no point in spending hours on that in the dark, when we can do it quicker and better in the morning. We're just looking to see has the young one got hit by a car and left at the roadside, or gone for a walk and collapsed in a faint, or maybe got herself tangled up in a tree.'

His eyes pass over Trey and meet Cal's. Cal gets the message: the kid could end up seeing something she shouldn't. He's already aware of that, and not happy about it. 'Makes sense,' he says, giving Mart a blank look back.

PJ is shifting from foot to foot, glancing around like he might spot Rachel at the foot of a wall. ''Tis fierce cold,' he says worriedly. 'I brought the hot water bottle with me, in case we'd find her and she might need warming up quick.' He opens his jacket to reveal one of the reasons for his bulk: his belly is bulging with something tucked inside his fleece.

'Good thinking,' Cal says.

'Myself and PJ'll head up this way,' Mart says, pointing his crook towards the main road, 'and the two of ye can work your way down to the river. If ye find anything, or if ye find nothing, give me a bell and I'll update His Nibs.' He touches a finger to his hat and stumps off up the road, with PJ loping beside him.

'How the fuck would she get stuck in a tree?' Trey demands. Tension is making her prickly. 'She's not a fuckin' cat.'

Cal aims never to lie to Trey. 'He means she could've hanged herself,' he says. 'He didn't want to say that in front of you.' Trey makes an irritated *pfft* noise and goes silent.

They have about two miles of road to cover, curving between drystone walls and fields and the occasional farmhouse. They head back the way they came, sweeping the flashlight beams down the verges, over long grass and tangles of dead wildflowers. The dark is windless and silent; small things scuttle away at their approach, and watch from hiding as they pass. The air smells, more powerfully and intricately than by day, of ripe earth, sodden leaves, and manure. Far off, spread out across the fields, other small lights swing and zigzag. A long call comes to them faintly, too distant to hear the name, if they didn't already know what it is.

Cal left the living-room light on, but his place doesn't look welcoming; it has a defensive air, fists raised to repel invaders. He has to make himself lift the flashlight beam to sweep the big oak tree where his rooks roost – the branches are probably too high for climbing, but he doesn't like the thought of it looming behind them swollen with the unknown. The rooks stir on their perches and bitch him out for waking them. Apart from them, the oak, bared for winter, is empty.

Cal can still feel the tension off Trey, in the sharp flicks of her flashlight beam and the hard pace she sets. 'The Holohans live out the other side of the village,' he says. 'Right?'

'Yeah. That big white bungalow off the Lismore road, with a loada flower beds out front.'

'Well then,' Cal says. 'I don't see any reason why she'd've wound up all the way over here.'

After a minute Trey says, 'You reckon she's OK?'

She has to know that Cal has no more information than she does. It catches him by the heart, that she still has enough little kid left in her to look to him for impossible reassurances. 'I don't know enough about her to make any solid guesses, kid,' he says gently. 'All I can tell you is, most people who go missing come home.'

Trey says nothing. A rustle of grass and a long sigh send them whipping their flashlight beams over the wall, into a field. A clump of cows, still unhoused by someone aiming to scrape a bad year's feed over the long winter, gaze back at them with mild, reproachful surprise. Trey lets out a hiss of breath between her teeth.

'Most likely that's all we're gonna find,' Cal says. 'Creatures that just want us to leave them in peace.'

Trey, turning back to the road, doesn't answer. For a second her flashlight catches on a pair of eyes, low to the ground and flaring luminous white, before whatever it is whisks away.

The years of living on her own have sharpened Lena's alertness. When Sean was there with her, the world stopped at the walls of their farm; anything beyond that could go disregarded. When he died she got the farm off her hands as fast as she could, keeping only two acres in case she wanted a garden or a horse someday, but instead of contracting, the boundaries of her awareness disintegrated altogether. Now her senses catch the smell of Sunday roast blown from Ciaran Maloney's house, or the scurry of sheep half a mile away roused by a passing fox, or the shadow of a cloud moving over the mountain. Probably this is her mind's response to being a woman alone in the middle of nowhere, but it brings her pleasure rather than fear. She's always loved this place, through all the people tangling up her feelings about it; anything that brings more of its details to her notice is welcome.

What wakes her is nothing she can put her finger on. The house is quiet. If anything or anyone were nearby, the dogs would have warned her, but no movement comes from the kitchen. Only the air feels wrong, charged up with a fine electric hum too high to hear.

Lena gets out of bed and goes to the window, shivering a little as the cold strikes her. Outside, the immense stretch of darkness is spattered with bright windows. Between them, smaller points of light bob like will-o'-the-wisps.

It's past four o'clock, but Lena knows Noreen will be awake. Sure enough, she answers on the second ring.

'Helena! Is Cal after finding something?'

'I'm not at Cal's. What's going on?'

Noreen lets out a gust of breath. 'God, for a moment there I thought . . . 'Tis Rachel Holohan. She's after going missing. You know Rachel, Claire's one, the blondie—'

'I know her.'

'I'm awful worried, Helena. I was saying to Cal just this afternoon, I saw her there with Eugene and they didn't look great, d'you know the way? Rachel's pure mad about that fella, but he's a sleeveen little fecker, if the boss's daughter was giving him the glad eye up in Dublin he'd give Rachel the aul' heave-ho like a shot. And she'd be only devastated. She's better off without him, but sure they don't think that way at that age, everything's the end of the world—'

Lena says, 'When did anyone see her last?'

'Now I heard this from Claire, and she's up to ninety, why wouldn't she be, so I mightn't have it right, but anyhow. Eugene's down for the weekend – honouring us with his presence, aren't we the lucky ones.' Noreen isn't normally bitchy; worry is sharpening her. 'So Rachel spent the day with him. She left him around half-four and he says she was grand then, and she musta gone home sometime after 'cause her car's there, but Claire and Fintan were over in Athlone doing a bitta shopping and they et there and didn't get home till half-eight, so they missed her. They thought she was meeting up with Eugene again in the evening, so they weren't worried that she wasn't there when they got home, they just thought he'd come and got her—'

Lena moves out to the kitchen, leaving the lights off. The dogs stir and raise their heads, and pad sleepily over to her for pats. She rubs behind each of their ears in turn, and they lean heavily against her legs, pleased at the unexpected company.

'Only then last thing at night Eugene rang the house, he said he was trying to get on to Rachel to say good night but she wasn't answering. He never saw her in the evening. She was never meant to go back out with him at all. No one's seen her. I wasn't even here, we brought the kids into town to the pictures, I'm driving myself mad thinking if I'da only been here I mighta looked out and seen her – Claire and Fintan are going mental, all the men are out looking—'

Lena says, 'I saw her.'

'What? You did? When?'

'She came here. Around half-five, maybe, or a bit before. Her cat had scratches; she brought him over for me to have a look.'

'Helena! How was she? What kinda form was she in, like?'

Far off in the darkness outside the kitchen window, more lights waver along invisible trails. 'She seemed grand,' Lena says. If Rachel is off somewhere trying to make a decision in peace, or just having a good cry for herself, the last thing she needs is to come back to a townland that knows all her business; specially since it sounded like that business wouldn't make her popular around here. 'A bit worried, maybe, but I reckoned that was just the cat.'

'You'll have to tell Claire. Go on, ring her now and ring me back after.'

'You ring her,' Lena says. She doesn't want to talk to Claire. 'It's years since I saw her; I'd be intruding.'

'I could, I suppose. Just, the state she's in, I wouldn't wish it on my worst enemy . . .' Noreen's voice cracks. 'God, Lena, some days I almost wish I'd never had kids, d'you know that? It's too much, honest to God it is. It's more than any woman could take. When something like this could happen any day, outa nowhere, one minute everything's grand and the next . . .' She sniffs and catches a shaky breath. 'God, wouldja listen to me, making a big aul' drama outa nothing. Rachel can't have gone far, without the car; she'll be home by morning and I'll feel like a right eejit. Come here, I'd better go ring Claire. I'll let you know if I hear anything.'

Lena puts her shoes on and finds her torch. If Rachel came here once, she might have come back. Daisy, whose tolerance for society is limited, has gone back to bed, but Nellie is delighted at the genius idea of a late-night outing. Lena keeps her close to heel.

The old stone byre where Sean's ancestors kept their cattle is empty, just a scatter of hay left from years ago, when Sean and Lena used it to store feed. The shed is full of the clutter that belongs there, and nothing else. No one is huddled against the house's walls.

Lena finds herself walking quietly, on her own land, and deliberately makes herself step more firmly. Under the sweep of the torch beam, the grass lies wide and bare. Nellie has the beagle passion for spotting everything and sharing it all, but the only time she alerts is to a mouse-sized skitter among the grass. An owl swoops low over Lena's head, warning her off his hunting ground, but apart from him there's no one, and no sign that anyone's been and gone.

She goes back inside and makes herself tea. Noreen and every woman in the townland will be doing the same, while their phones hop out of their pockets with the woodpecker drilling of notifications, information and speculation and emotion zipping through the air like insects. Lena stands at the kitchen counter, warming her hands on the mug and watching the lights move outside the window.

The road splits, the main fork heading for the village, a narrower lane winding off towards the river. Flashlight beams crisscross the village road: Tommy Moynihan and his leadership skills have things covered. Cal and Trey head for the river.

The cold has worked its way through Cal's boots; he can't feel his toes. 'How you doing, kid?' he asks.

'Grand.' Trey flicks her light over a patch of mud churned by sheep tracks. The only human ones among them are from man-sized wellies.

'You freezing?'

'Nah.'

Cal can smell water up ahead, a clear cold note cutting through the rich autumn tangle of scents. His flashlight catches the thick strip of woods that borders the river. 'You got a little more left in the tank? No point monkeying all around those banks in the dark, but we might go down as far as the water, see what we see.'

'Yeah. No problem.'

She looks sleepy, but not exhausted. Trey is mountain-kid hardy; no amount of exercise is enough to tire her out. 'OK,' Cal says. 'Tomorrow you can sleep till noon.'

'Was gonna anyway.'

'Till two,' Cal says. He hopes either one of them can sleep, after tonight is done.

The river has good perch fishing; sometimes Cal and Trey catch dinner there, or don't, depending on the river's mood. It's narrow enough that a kid could throw a stone across it, but fast and rocky; you need to know its tricks. The approach is thick with growth left to its own devices and accumulating in layers: fallen leaves ankle-deep over a thick bed of other years' leavings, brambles and underbrush hip-high, and far above that the spread of trees, alder and birch and willow, their trunks coated in moss. Even on a summer day it's a dim place, flickering with sunbeams and midges. On a night like this the bank is a new kind of dark, closer and unsettlingly personal, with the ceaseless, restless rush of the river somewhere up ahead.

'Stay behind me,' Cal says. 'Right behind me.'

There's a path to the water, but it's nearly invisible even in daylight, and they lose it after only a few steps. They pick their way through the snarl of undergrowth, swearing every now and then when they snag on brambles or stumble into a sudden dip. The flashlights find nothing but branches in every direction, crisscrossing till their patterns lose any meaning and start to feel like hallucinations. The sound of the water keeps them on track; without it they'd be wandering in circles, lost just yards from the road.

'Listen,' Trey says, stopping.

Sounds come from upriver, getting louder against the noise of the water. Something big is crashing through the undergrowth.

'Hey!' Cal shouts.

A man's voice calls something back – Francie Gannon, could be, from the deep note – and a beam blinks between the trees. Cal swings his in answer.

'How long till it gets bright?' Trey asks.

'Couple of hours. We're not gonna stay out all that time. We'll take a look at the riverbank and go home. I'll head back out once it's light.' Come daytime, if the search isn't over, it'll be a different thing. Tommy Moynihan's pull will get the whole machine up and running with no delays: lines of Guards in high-vis jackets poking long poles into undergrowth, dogs hurrying their handlers along a scent, radios crackling, journalists arranging their eyebrows and their voices into their favourite sombre curves. Cal has been here long enough to feel the extra dash of urgency that prospect brings to the situation. This is Ardnakelty business, and Ardnakelty has a strong preference for dealing with that itself, without any contribution from outsiders. A couple of years back, Cal would have slept through this night like a baby and heard the story the next day when he went into Noreen's for his shopping, or when Mart felt like a gossip break. The shift still has the power to startle him: it seems almost unthinkably strange that he should be here, his flashlight one point in the constellation that spans the townland, searching this low cold landscape for a girl he doesn't know.

The river, coming into view between the slants of tree trunks, is running high and fast. In the flashlight beams it's a cold white, slashed with black. Trees lean low enough that the current drags at their branches. The flashlights catch nothing worth checking out, which is what Cal expected. With the river in this mood, anything that went in there would be swept straight down to the Shannon and out to sea.

He's turning away, ready to say something about heading home, when he hears the shout from upriver again. It has a different note this time.

'Come on,' Cal says.

They wade through the undergrowth like they're wading through bog, in a ludicrous broken waddle that never makes it to a run. Trey, built for this terrain, starts to overtake Cal, but he waves her back behind him. The shout rises again and he yells, 'We're coming!'

Above the bend in the river, a white shape hangs in the water, ragged black streaks radiating where it splinters the current. On the side of the bank, a light bobs wildly, and something dark is scrabbling. It's a man, clambering awkwardly down the steep bank, flashlight between his teeth.

'Wait!' Cal shouts, and the light stops moving. Cal pulls his phone out of his pocket and passes it and his flashlight to Trey.

'Point one so I can see where I'm going,' he says, 'and one at whatever that is in the water. If we both fall in, you call Mart for help. Don't come in after us. Got it?'

'Yeah,' Trey says. She shoves his phone in her pocket and aims the flashlights. Cal starts down the bank, steadying himself on branches and dodging the ones that grab at his face. The earth is boggy with rain, which helps him dig in for footholds under the layers of slippery leaves. He just hopes the whole damn bank doesn't slide into the water.

The man is Francie, braced precariously at the river's edge, hanging on to a bush and panting. 'It's her,' he says.

She's face down in the water, hair streaming wide, one hand outstretched towards them and wavering like a signal. Her jacket has snagged on some hidden thing that juts out from the bank at the bend, a root or a branch. Without it she would be gone, halfway to the Shannon on this sinuous, unstoppable movement. Close up, the noise of the river is chaotic, a relentless roar crammed with mutters and trills.

'OK,' Cal says. She's far enough from the bank that one of them will have to step in. He's heavier and stronger than Francie. He hooks one arm around a leaning willow and reaches to grab Francie's wrist with the other hand. 'I got you.'

Francie is knee-deep at the first step. He rocks when the current hits his legs, but Cal's grip holds and he finds his balance. He leans out, his shadow rippling and breaking on the water, to catch Rachel's hand. Twice the water moves her and he misses. His wrist is taut and shaking with the effort and the cold. Cal knows they don't have long before the water numbs his legs to uselessness. Trey, on the bank above them, stays silent and trains the lights on the white shape.

Francie shakes himself and leans out again. This time his fingers hook around Rachel's wrist. Slowly he backs towards the bank, tugging her with him, her body careening wildly between his pull and the current's.

When Francie's footing is solid, Cal lets go of him and grabs Rachel's arm. Her jacket is thick and slippery, and at first the snag holds her fast, but finally they rip her free and tow her in. Waterlogged, she's impossibly heavy and unwieldy, stubbornly resisting them.

'Flat bit here,' Trey says, indicating with one of the flashlights. She's moved closer, down the bank. Cal wants her not to be there, not to see them manhandling Rachel through these ludicrous, humiliating sprawls. He wants to cover her eyes.

They drag Rachel to the flat stretch of bank and lie her on her back. Cal tilts her chin, sweeps her mouth with his finger, and feels at her neck for a pulse. There's nothing. Her throat is as cold as the water. Her eyes, half open, stare up at the sky.

Cal pulls her jacket open and starts compressions, blocking her face from Trey with his body. Rachel smells of river water and the unimagined things hidden deep beneath it. A rush of thick froth bubbles out of her mouth and he feels ribs snap under his palms. It's been a million years since he did this and he knows he could be doing it wrong, but there's no one here to do better.

He stops, heaving for breath, and presses his fingers into her throat again. Francie, on one knee beside him, dripping, says nothing. Trey's torch beam flattens his face to a featureless white mask, dark holes for eyes.

There's no pulse. Cal lifts his head and shouts up to the treetops, with the full power of his voice behind it, 'Here!'

After a moment he hears, wordless over the jumble of the river, men's voices taking up the call and passing it on, growing farther and fainter across the trees and the fields. He bends back to the compressions.

Francie says, close to him so Trey won't hear, 'She's gone, man.'

'I know,' Cal says through his teeth, between compressions. He doesn't look up when he hears voices coming closer, underbrush breaking. Francie shouts back, and Trey sweeps one of the flashlights as a guide.

'Her father,' Cal says. 'Keep him back.' Francie nods and scrambles up the bank. Cal keeps going till a hand grips his shoulder and Senan's voice says, 'Take the child home.'

In this weather there's no sunrise. The black sky pales slowly through gradations of grey, and the fields match it, blurred under a thin shifting mist. The lights ranging the roads have gone out, but the ones in house windows are still on, weak against the growing day. The landscape feels unreal, ready to vanish at any instant. Cal's body, trudging home down the muddy road, feels the same way: something that's had all the solidity leached out of it, leaving it at the mercy of any wind that might come blowing.

'She's dead,' Trey says. 'Right?'

'Yeah,' Cal says. It strikes him that he doesn't even know how old Rachel was, maybe twenty or twenty-one. That seems like something he should have known, like maybe then he could have done better CPR and brought her back.

'You worked like mad on her all the same.'

Cal can't tell whether she's asking why, or looking for reassurance that they did their best, or offering that comfort to him. He doesn't want that. His feelings aren't Trey's job. 'Yep,' he says. 'I went all out. It wasn't gonna make any difference, she'd been gone a while, but you gotta try.'

Trey nods and goes silent. Their feet crunch on the muddy road; Cal's shoes, sodden with river water, squelch at every step. Over the walls, in the fields, the winter-sparse grass is weighed down with dew.

When they shoot rabbits for dinner, Trey takes the deaths in her stride; what she can't handle is anything wounded and suffering. 'From all I hear,' Cal says, 'drowning's about the most peaceful death there is. No pain or anything.'

Trey nods, but she doesn't come out of her silence. Cal asks, 'You know Rachel?'

'Nah. Seen her around, just. She was dacent to me, even back when everyone else was shite. Bought Alanna an ice lolly one time, when we were down the shop.'

'Well,' Cal says. That doesn't sound like a lot, but Trey's bar is low when it comes to the village. 'She sounds like a good kid, all right.'

Trey says, 'You reckon Eugene kilt her?'

The thought has occurred to Cal, but he discarded it. 'Nah,' he says. 'Eugene's a jagoff.' He doubts Trey knows what a jagoff is, but he doesn't have it in him to rummage for a better word. 'He talks big, but he couldn't kill anyone. By pushing a button, yeah, sure, but not like that.'

Trey considers that and acknowledges it with a tilt of her head. 'Someone else coulda,' she says.

Most kids would have gone straight to accident or suicide, but Trey has known people to die by violence before. Cal feels like, no matter how hard he works, he can never get her assumptions to go back where they should be.

'The Guards'll look into that,' he says. 'But mostly, when someone dies young, no one killed them. Mostly they had an accident, or things got to be too much for them and they couldn't think of another way out.'

'That's stupid,' Trey says flatly.

Cal doesn't have the wherewithal to get into mental health and empathy tonight. All he wants to know is that Trey's not going to go stirring up the townland with hints about murder, and that she's going to be able to get some sleep. Everything else can wait till after that. 'Maybe,' he says. 'I'm just telling you, that's what mostly turns out to have happened. If you've got other ideas, don't go around saying them. To anyone. You got that?'

Trey rolls her eyes. 'Wasn't gonna.' Cal believes her. Not saying things is one of Trey's main skills.

The kid seems like she'll sleep just fine. He can't be certain – she has an iron-clad aversion to showing any kind of upset – but her walk, hands in her coat pockets, head tilted back to scan for the outline of the mountains amid the cloud, looks OK. Trey likes to know she's done everything she could. They did that tonight; it didn't work out.

They round the bend and Cal's place comes into view, rising grey out of the grey mist around it. The light in the window is pale and watery. For a fatigue-tangled second Cal expects to find the house the way it was the day he first got here, weeds crowding the doorstep waist-high, streaked paint on bubbling wallpaper, broken furniture tumbled in corners and saints askew on the walls. Then the waking rooks start shuffling their feathers and asking hoarse questions, and Rip catches the signal and sends out a barrage of welcoming barks. Trey, at Cal's elbow, yawns hugely and shudders all over like a dog coming out of water.

'Come on,' Cal says, picking up the pace. 'Let's go get warm.'

4

The next days are strange. Cal is waiting for half the townland to find excuses to stop by: deaths are prime conversation material, and the people who found the body are going to be the juiciest cuts off the joint. Besides, Ardnakelty expects the benefit of his professional expertise, whether he has any that's relevant or not; he's ready to field questions about what the Guards are likely to be doing and thinking. But no one shows up. A nice Guard with a countrywoman's broad, good-tempered face comes to take Cal's and Trey's statements, and goes away again. There's no funeral, and no plans for one; Rachel's body is in Galway or somewhere, being examined and tested and autopsied. Out in the fields, men trudge back and forth and whistle to their dogs – livestock and land take death for granted and move on, leaving no room for pauses – but the townland lies under a new layer of silence, heavier than the cloud and the fitful rain.

Trey answers the Guard's questions readily and doesn't bring up the subject again. Cal leaves her plenty of open spaces, while they put the last coat of varnish on Michelle Healy's shoe cupboard, but the only things she drops into them are ordinary comments about school and her buddies – Aidan and Ciara have apparently managed to establish that they're going out, and are now trying to organise their first date, a process that sounds like it could take months and a trained negotiator. Once or twice the silences have a finely balanced quality, like Trey is on the edge of saying something, but nothing comes out. If the kid is still having thoughts about murder, she's keeping them to herself.

Cal wonders, at first, whether the lack of talk about Rachel is due to the likelihood of suicide. She could have gone into the river by accident, except he can't see what she would have been doing out there in the first place; by day the river is all wholesome pleasures, fishing and pretty scenery, but he can think of only one thing it would have had to offer her by night. People might be keeping their mouths shut to spare her family's feelings, till the official verdict comes in.

When he goes down to Noreen's for his shopping, though, the shop is full of women who stop in mid-sentence when they see him; some of them turn away to hide red eyes. He grabs a few necessities and pays as fast as he can. People are talking, they're just not talking to him.

Although it probably shouldn't, it comes as a chilly surprise to find there are still doors that shut in his face. That was fine and dandy back when he saw Ardnakelty as a wayside inn, somewhere pretty to rest and recover while he figured out the next thing. But he's here now. There is no next thing; instead there's Trey, and Lena, and Rip, and the nursing chair Con McHugh wants to give his missus for Christmas.

Something about this death means that Ardnakelty is subtly changed by its shadow. Cal, who knows how this place can run wild on rumours, hopes it hasn't gone down the same line of thought as Trey and decided that Rachel Holohan was murdered. Suicide is bad enough, and hard enough to get past, but it happens, especially in the dark dregs of the year: old guys up the mountain whose shotguns won't stop whispering to them, lost boys taking ropes out to the trees they used to climb. Murder is different. Even a hint of it shakes a place to the bone, setting in motion things that can't be predicted or controlled. Suicide requires nothing but grief, which is hard enough; murder makes demands.

He doesn't ask Lena what she thinks. She's staying silent too: she told him Rachel came to her place that evening, something about a hurt cat, but she offered no commentary beyond that and hasn't mentioned Rachel since. Cal knows her well enough to know when there's no point in asking questions.

Truth be told, Cal doesn't think all that much about Rachel herself. The cold creature he pulled from the river, or the crack of her ribs under his palm, hits him in the gut now and again, but he didn't know her and has no sense of the life she lost. The ones who won't leave his mind are her parents, although he doesn't know them either, beyond the occasional scrap of small talk in Noreen's. There were times, when Alyssa was younger, when he feared for her. The thought of that fear solidifying, changing from a corrosive shadow to the rest of someone's life, makes him get up from wherever he is and go find stuff to do.

He's been staying away not only from Noreen's but from Seán Óg's, picturing a sombre silence where he'll count as an intruder. When he finally gets fed up and heads down to the pub, though, he finds it precisely its usual week-night self. It's maybe two-thirds full, guys in for a couple of pints and a chat after their dinner, rather than a serious session. One corner has brought out the cards and has a ferocious game of Fifty-Five in progress; three guys at the bar are having their usual argument about the merits of various sheep breeds, which has been going on at least since Cal moved here, without anyone altering his position an inch; in the alcove, Mart and his posse are enjoying Senan being outraged about something. Cal was planning on just buying his own pint, in case he's not welcome to stick around. Instead, he gets a round in and joins them.

'Thank fuck,' Senan says. 'You're the only one that'd know what I'm on about; this shower are living in nineteen fuckin' eighty, they're looking at me like I'm speaking Swahili. Your young one has a smartphone, hasn't she?'

'Yeah,' Cal says, passing out the glasses. Apparently he was right to buy a round. He's not an intruder after all, at least not here and not today.

'Has she got the Snapchat?'

'Yeah. Is that bad?' Raising a teenager has got even more fun since Alyssa was coming up. Donna would probably say it just feels that way because Cal is doing more of the hard part this time, but he disagrees. When Alyssa was sixteen, neither he nor Donna had to figure out what the hell a Snap streak was and whether it could do her any harm.

'Has she got an AI on it?'

'Don't think so,' Cal says. 'She doesn't use Snapchat much, from what I know. It has AI?'

'They give you one. Like a fuckin' pet parrot or something. My young fella comes in to me—'

'Which one?' PJ asks. PJ likes to have things clear in his mind.

'Finbarr. The one that's thirteen, or fourteen, or whatever he is now. He sits his smelly self on the sofa next to me, and he tells me he'll have his AI rate my rizz. The fuck is a rizz?'

'Sounds dirty,' Francie says.

'That's what I thought. I tell him I'm not letting that yoke anywhere near my rizz, and the little bollocks rolls his eyes at me. Then he tells me to give him my best chat-up line.'

'Pay attention, now,' Mart tells Bobby. 'You can try these out on the lovely Róisín, if you run short of conversation.'

'We don't,' Bobby says smugly. 'We could talk for hours, so we could, and never get bored once.' Francie mimes retching.

'What'd you give Finbarr?' Cal asks Senan. He's kind of taken aback by the level of normality going on. He wonders if this is Ardnakelty's way of announcing, obliquely, that it's decided Rachel fell in the river by accident.

'I'm not giving that little gobshite my good lines,' Senan says. 'They're too powerful to be put into inexperienced hands. He'd have half of second year pulling each other's hair out over him by Christmas. So I tell him to ask the AI yoke, "Are you a terrorist?" And it says – hang on.' He pokes at his phone. 'It says, "I'm sorry if there was any confusion, but I am not a terrorist. I'm just here to chat and help you out with anything you need. Is there something else you'd like to talk about?"'

'Your Finbarr's on a list now,' Mart tells him.

'Everyone's getting their knickers in a twist about this yoke taking over the world,' Senan says, 'and it's so thick it can't even tell when it's pulled. So I have the young fella type in, "Because you've hijacked my heart." And that fuckin' yoke says, listen to this, "Haha, that's a classic pickup line! I'd give it a solid seven out of ten for effort. It's always fun to use cheesy pickup lines to break the ice." The cheeky little—' Words fail Senan: he stares around the alcove, holding up the phone at them like an exhibit. 'I got patronised by something that doesn't even fuckin' *exist*. Your man Zuckerberg or someone pulled it straight outa his hole, and now it's giving me shite.'

'That's your pickup line?' Cal says. 'How the hell are you married?'

'He's got a hundred acres,' Francie reminds him.

'And a ten-inch mickey,' Senan says. 'And at least my missus never divorced me.'

'Yet,' Cal points out. 'She know you've been hitting on AIs?'

'Angela'll be only delighted,' Francie says. 'She's no need to worry about him doing the dirt on her; even the fuckin' internet won't have him.'

'Ah, now,' PJ says consolingly. 'Seven outa ten isn't bad.'

'Don't you go patronising me as well,' Senan tells him. 'Let's see you do better, go on. Give us your best shot and see do I ride you.'

'I haven't got a chat-up line,' PJ says, startled. He's blushing at the thought. 'I never needed one yet.'

'Course you've got chat-up lines. Everyone has chat-up lines. When we were young fellas going to the disco, what did you do to get the shift? Did you just stand next to a one and hope she'd plant the lips on you?'

'Well, God almighty, lads,' Mart says, putting down his glass. His eyes have gone over Cal's shoulder. 'Wouldja look what just sauntered in.'

Cal turns to look. The door is swinging closed behind Tommy and Eugene Moynihan, Eugene brushing rain from his coat sleeves, Tommy pulling off gloves. The swirl of cold air they've brought with them skims into the alcove.

'That's some fuckin' brass neck,' Senan says, low.

The card game has paused mid-hand. Tommy nods to the pub, with a fine balance of his usual geniality and a gravity to fit the circumstances. Only a few heads nod back.

'A pint of Guinness and a bottle of Heineken there, Barty, when you're ready,' Tommy says. After a moment Barty puts down his glass-cloth and starts pulling the pint.

Tommy finds a table and arranges himself at his leisure on the banquette, and Eugene copies him. Eugene favours his mama more than his daddy: he's middle height and narrow all over, with dark hair and a face that's good-looking as long as you get it at the right angle and don't have high expectations in the way of chins. He's the kind of smug little prick who Cal reckons spent much of his schooldays getting his head flushed down the john, although apparently not regularly enough to do much good. Today his subpar chin has a defiant set that doesn't suit him.

No one says a word. Bobby's mouth is open and round; PJ

looks as shocked as if Tommy just unzipped his pants and pissed on the floor. Mart's face and Senan's are grim.

'Ah,' Tommy says, smiling over at the card-players, 'the aul' Fifty-Five. Who's winning there?'

Red Geraghty mutters something.

'You took a tenner off me at that, last time I was in,' Tommy says, waving a finger at Red. 'Deal us in there, go on. Give me a chance at revenge.'

The card-players glance at each other. One of them starts to say something, but a small sharp movement from another guy cuts him off.

Cal is starting to understand why no one's been talking to him. Whatever's going on here is the kind of complicated that could take years to explain.

'I'll go easy on ye,' Tommy says, grinning. 'I'll leave ye the shirts on your backs.'

Out of nowhere, Francie leans back on the banquette and starts to sing.

'In Dublin city, where I did dwell
A butcher boy I loved right well
He courted me my life away
But now with me he will not stay . . .'

Francie has a good voice, the right fit for the slow melancholy song, deep and rich enough to take up all the space in the pub. Seán Óg's has plenty of musical nights, when the scrawny old guys in the opposite corner bring out the fiddle and the tin whistle, or someone has a guitar, and everyone takes their turn at singing. This isn't that.

'There is an alehouse in this town
Where my love goes and sits him down
He takes another on his knee
And he tells to her what he won't tell me . . .'

Tommy Moynihan is smiling slightly, nodding along like he's

appreciating the entertainment. Eugene is glancing sideways at him and trying to do the same, but his smile comes out as a tooth-grinding smirk.

Senan starts to hum along with Francie. Mart takes it up, and then Bobby and PJ and someone outside the alcove. After a minute, Cal joins in. Mart's eyes move to him, briefly, and then back to Tommy.

'He went upstairs and the door he broke
He found her hanging from a rope
He took his knife and he cut her down
And in her pocket these words he found . . .'

The hum has spread throughout the pub, a low drone rising beneath Francie's voice. Not everyone is joining in: some guys stare down into their pints or fiddle with their phones. Eugene's smirk has tightened into something closer to a snarl.

'Oh dig my grave both wide and deep
Put a marble stone at my head and feet
And in the middle a turtle dove
So the whole world knows that I died for love.'

The deep hum holds and fades, and the pub is silent. Everyone watches Tommy and Eugene.

Eugene makes it about twenty seconds before he cracks. His face is red with outrage. He struggles to get up, shoves the table away, and storms out of the pub. He tries to slam the door behind him, but it's slow-close and won't slam.

Tommy looks around the room, taking his time. His jowls are weighted down with disappointment in every one of them.

'Eugene's not in great form,' he says. 'Sure, who am I telling; ye all know the trouble the poor young fella's had. I thought a pint and a bit of company would do him the world of good, but it looks like we'll have to come back when everyone's feeling a bit more like themselves.'

He takes out his wallet and puts a twenty on the table. 'Please accept my apologies,' he says, with sad dignity, to Barty. 'If I'da known it'd cause you this kind of disturbance, I'da gone elsewhere today.'

He stands up, straightens his coat, and casts a last look of profound reproach around the room. Then he follows Eugene out. The door creeps shut behind him.

Red slaps down a card on the table. 'How many of your ewes needed a hand with the lambing this year?' one of the guys at the bar demands of his buddy. 'If you had Suffolks—' Barty, left with an unclaimed pint, leans against the bar in resignation and takes a long swig of it himself.

'Right,' Senan says to PJ. 'We're getting you a coupla chat-up lines whether you want them or not. Here' – to Bobby – 'what line did you use on Róisín? If it worked for you, it'll work for anyone.'

'I asked her did she know how long till the bus stopped next,' Bobby says. 'My mammy's bowels were at her something fierce. 'Twas the rich food.'

'Christ almighty,' Senan says, from the heart.

'There's hope for you yet,' Francie tells PJ.

PJ looks back and forth between them all, trying to puzzle out what he's expected to do with this information. 'Back when I was single,' Cal tells him, 'I mostly just went in with "Hey, how's your day been going?"'

PJ looks like he suspects Cal of yanking his chain. 'That's not going to do the job for this fella,' Senan informs Cal. 'She'll say, "Grand" or "Shite" or whatever, and he'll just stand there. The man needs a line.'

'OK,' Cal says. 'Then what you've gotta do is find one that works with your strengths and your weaknesses. Like, if you don't figure you can pull off being all flirty—'

'He can't,' Francie assures him.

'Then you use that. Like, "Hey, I'd love to talk to you, but

I'm no good at picking people up. How 'bout you try to pick me up instead?"'

'Not bad,' Mart says judiciously, nodding to Cal. 'I'd say that'd get you a shift off the AI. Probably not a feel, but.'

PJ thinks that over. 'But what if she doesn't?' he asks. 'Chat me up, like.'

'Merciful Jaysus,' Senan says, raising his eyes to heaven.

'She mightn't,' PJ says.

'She might not,' Cal says. 'But she might laugh, and then you've got a foot in the door.'

'She might not,' PJ points out, clearly feeling himself on firm ground with this line of argument.

'The bitta uncertainty is what gives the flavour,' Mart explains. ''Tis like betting on a horse. You'd get no crack outa it if you already knew you'd picked the winner.'

'What're you shiteing on about?' Francie demands. 'I'd be only delighted if I knew I'd picked a winner. The same with women. If I was after suspense, I'd go to the fuckin' pictures. I'm after the ride.'

'When was the last time you did either one?'

The argument gets into its stride. Cal looks around the pub. Red has won the hand and is raising his fists in triumph; the guys at the bar have moved on to swayback in Scottish Blackfaces. Barty is halfway down Tommy's abandoned pint.

Ardnakelty, unlike Trey, has this firmly down as a suicide. Cal isn't as relieved as he would have expected to be. Apparently suicide, or this one at least, makes demands of its own.

The good-tempered Guard comes to Lena's place, too. Someone told her about Rachel's visit, which makes Lena the last person who saw Rachel alive, or anyhow the last one who'll admit to it. The Guard's name is Breege, and Lena likes her; she manages to give the death its weight, without either pretending she's personally devastated or implying that she can make it all better. Lena explains how people sometimes bring her their animals, and tells her about Rachel's cat's ringworm, and Breege nods and writes it down. Lena says nothing about Eugene, or Sean, or haters, or the rest of it. Whatever drama was going on there, it wasn't hers and she's not touching it. If anyone wants Breege to know the story, they can tell her themselves.

They won't. Even Rachel's parents, if they know it, might or might not share it. Ardnakelty has no time for Guards. The townland will run its own investigation, spreading unseen below the official inquiry like ancient trailways underlie the brash modern roads; it'll reach its own conclusions, and deal out its own justice.

Whatever those conclusions are, they won't meet Lena's standards. They'll be based almost entirely on whether and where it suits this place to assign blame. The decision will be made gradually, collectively, via multiple intertwined algorithms complex enough to blow a computer to smithereens. Rachel herself will barely even factor into the equation.

Lena finds herself thinking about Rachel, the little she knew of her, the same way she thinks about Sean: deliberately, to protect against that erosion. She feels no guilt – the townland would gleefully heap that on her, if they knew the details of Rachel's visit, but Lena rejects it. Guilt would be arrogance. It would mean believing that she could have stooped like the Virgin Mary from a pedestal and, smiling in her infinite compassion, lifted Rachel out of her despair and set her back on her feet, all fixed. Lena no longer believes that any man or woman can be another's salvation.

Noreen, who rings Lena every day, doesn't notice that Lena is close to silent on the subject of Rachel. She's ringing to talk, anyhow, not to listen. Noreen's place in the village comes at a price of its own, like everything around here. As the universal provider, she fires out supplies, information, advice, and sympathy with the speed and force of a tennis-ball machine, but the dynamic doesn't allow for her to have needs in return. No one expects Noreen to cry on their shoulder or spill her worries on them. She stores all that up and gets it out of her system on Lena, who can be relied on to have few opinions and not to pass anything on.

'She didn't leave a note,' Noreen says, a few days in. 'That's what they were looking for, didja know that? All around the old footbridge – that's where they think she went in, off the bridge, something about the currents, or anyhow that's what they told Claire – but they never found one. Is that not odd, like? Would you not expect her to leave a note?'

Lena has got back from work late. She works part-time at a stable out the other side of Boyle; officially she just does the books, but sometimes she hangs on to give a hand with the horses or take one out on a trail ride, and this week she's been doing one or both every day, regardless of the weather. She was making herself a sandwich when Noreen rang. She puts the phone on speaker, leaves it on the counter, and goes back to slicing bread.

'I wouldn't have a clue,' she says. 'I'd say some people do and some don't.'

'I know. You're right, sure. I just wish she had; to keep things clear, d'you know? I know that's not right, saying the poor child shoulda done things different, and her in that state, but still.' Noreen speeds up when she's frazzled. It makes Lena turn calmer, which speeds Noreen up even more. 'Come here to me, Helena. When are they going to send her home?'

'They'll do it as soon as they can,' Lena says. Rain ticks fitfully against the window. She's lit the woodstove, but the kitchen, after just a few hours with no one but the dogs to fill it, still feels chilly and damp. She changes her plan, throws the cheese back in the fridge, and gets out sausages instead. The house needs the smell of something warm and rich.

'They wouldn't give Fintan a date,' Noreen says. 'They told him they were running tests. What's that mean? What kinda tests?'

'How would I know?'

'What does Cal say?'

'I haven't asked him.'

'Well, ask him, so. He'd know how they work. The, what's that I'm looking for, the protocols, or whatever they call them, procedures?' Noreen cracks a bite off something crunchy, maybe a carrot stick. When Noreen is nervy, she eats.

'I'd say that's all different in America,' Lena says. 'From what Cal's told me, anyhow.'

'It might be, all right. Sure, they're mental over there; their police have guns and all. Who knows what they'd be at.' For a moment Noreen sounds daunted, but then she rallies. 'Get Cal to talk to the Guards, so. Tell them they need to get a move on.'

'Why would they listen to him?' Lena enquires. She focuses her mind on arranging the sausages in the pan. She has plenty of practice keeping her calm with Noreen, but her stock of it is low right now.

'He's a feckin' detective! They've that thin blue line yoke, sure, they haveta listen to each other, how else d'you think Paudie Nagle still has his licence, and him driving like a maniac, only for his brother—'

'Right,' Lena says, before the torrent can drown her. 'I'll pass it on.'

'They oughta send her home,' Noreen says. She catches a sudden hard breath, like she's reaching the last of her control. 'Honest to God, Helena, they oughta do that. 'Tis feckin' barbaric, leaving Claire and Fintan waiting like this. Claire hasn't slept since; if she doesn't get Rachel home soon, we'll be burying the two a them together.'

Lena says nothing. The sausages spit in the pan. A gust of wind slams rain against the window, and then drops away.

'And it's not only the family,' Noreen says. ''Tis grand for you, sure, you wouldn't notice the difference, but everyone's getting themselves into a terrible state. If we could have the wake and the funeral and all, that'd be the end of it; everyone could leave it then. But with it hanging over us, people can't stop talking, and then they wind each other up worse. That aul' gobdaw Tom Pat Malone, didja hear what he's saying?'

'Haven't seen him,' Lena says. Tom Pat enjoys a reputation as a great character, but she considers him a predictable little chancer.

'He's saying he heard the banshee, the night before Rachel went. Didja ever hear the like? That fecker's deaf as a post, he wouldn't hear the banshee if 'twas sat on his own bed – if it even existed, like. He's only saying it for notice, but he went and said it to a buncha kids, and now Freya Kelly won't go to bed in case she hears the banshee. And Doireann feckin' Cunniffe was in here yesterday banging on about having a premonition. I nearly told her to stick her premonition up her arse, I'd my mouth open on it before I caught myself. I can't be saying that kinda thing to customers, I'll be outa business.'

'You shoulda clattered her,' Lena says. 'And then asked her why she didn't have a premonition and dodge.'

'Doireann Cunniffe's not the point. Everyone knows what she's like. The point is, if they leave it much longer sending Rachel home, people'll start saying worse. They're hinting already, some of them. Nothing you could put your finger on, you know the way. Hints, only.'

Noreen leaves a gap so Lena can ask what kind of hints. When she doesn't, Noreen changes her tack. 'Didja call round to Claire?' she demands.

'I've been working,' Lena says. Sometimes she annoys herself. All it takes is a good dose of Noreen, and she turns into a kid making excuses.

'But you didn't call round to Clodagh Moynihan, sure you didn't?'

'Jesus,' Lena says. 'Have I ever?'

'Some people are. Outa sympathy for their loss, like, 'cause Rachel was practically engaged to Eugene.' Noreen cracks off another bite with a vicious snap. 'Loss, me hole. None of the Moynihans ever gave a shite about anyone but themselves. There's some awful lickarses around here, d'you know that?'

'Well,' Lena says, 'you couldn't pay me to go near Clodagh, if that helps.'

'Call round to Claire, but. Do it tomorrow, if you're not in work.'

'Why would I call round to her?'

'Feck's sake, Helena! The poor woman's after losing a child.'

'When Sean died,' Lena says, 'the last thing I wanted was randos turning up on my doorstep.'

'I know, yeah. I feckin' know. Miss Independent, that's what you've always been. Wouldn't answer the door, wouldn't pick up the phone, no one saw hide nor hair of you for months, I was so worried I couldn't sleep at night— Claire's not like that.'

'I haven't a clue what Claire's like,' Lena says. She stabs a sausage hard enough that it splits. 'That's my point. Why would she wanta be stuck making chitchat with someone she hasn't talked to in thirty years?'

'Jesus, Mary, and Joseph, why d'you always have to make everything difficult? Call round to show her you're on her side.'

'No one told me there were sides,' Lena says.

Noreen makes an explosive noise of sheer exasperation. 'Someday I'll murder you, d'you know that? I'll feckin' brain you with a biscuit tin, and your Cal can haul me off to jail where I'll get a bitta feckin' peace for once. O' course there's sides. How would there not be sides?'

'Then there's sides,' Lena says. 'I'm not on one.'

'Right,' Noreen snaps. 'That's grand. Away you go and leave the rest of us to do the dirty work, like always. I don't know why I even bothered asking.'

'I'm not leaving you to do anything,' Lena says. She doesn't pick up the phone, in case she ends up throwing it. She just stands there with a fork in her hand, talking to her countertop like a lunatic. 'Call in to whoever you want, or don't. I'm not making you do it.'

'You are, yeah. Claire needs people round her. There's not enough women in this place that we can afford to have one that doesn't do her bit.'

'My bit,' Lena says. 'And what would that be, now?'

''Tis one thing when it's just the Tidy Towns, or the tea after mass, everyone knows what you're like, but now here's every woman in this place taking turns bringing Claire lasagnas and walking the dogs for her, and you can't even—'

'I bring Trey and her mates to the football. I even make them fecking sandwiches. That's my *bit*. The rest's nothing to do with me.'

'And that's another thing,' Noreen snaps. 'You're making that child as bad as yourself. She wouldn't be caught dead going around with Ardnakelty kids, oh God no. Tell us, go on: when you bring her mates to the football, where are they from?'

Lena says, 'Trey can go around with whoever the fuck she likes.' The dogs look up at the note in her voice.

'She can, yeah. And when she grows up without a single friend in this townland, will you be proud of yourself then?'

'Who says she needs friends around here? Who says she'll even be here, in a coupla years' time?'

'D'you know what?' Noreen's voice is rising. 'That's only a

brilliant idea. The pair of ye oughta feck right off, to Dublin or London or somewhere no one'll ever expect anything from ye, God forbid. Leave this place to people that actually appreciate it.'

'D'you know what that sounds like?' Lena says. 'That sounds like paradise.' She's used to fighting with Noreen, having done it all her life, but this feels different; it bites deeper.

'Great. That's a plan, so. Off you go, and don't be wrecking my fecking head any more.'

'You're the one that bloody rang me,' Lena says, but Noreen has already hung up.

'Get fucked,' Lena says to the phone, loud enough that the dogs come over to help. Nellie has brought her favourite toy, a well-chewed old runner, which she drops at Lena's feet to make things better.

'Good girls,' Lena says, looking down at their worried faces and calming her voice. 'Noreen can go and shite, amn't I right?'

The dogs, reassured by her tone, wag and press against her, agreeing from the heart with whatever she thinks. The sausages have burned on one side. Lena blows on them till they're cool; then she sits down on the kitchen floor and shares them out between Nellie and Daisy. She's lost her appetite.

When Cal took early retirement, he expected it to be lazier than this. That was the one thing that gave him doubts: he's not the kind of guy who's at ease sitting on his ass doing nothing, and he figured all that leisure would itch at him pretty fast. He put off the problem by buying a fixer-upper house, and he had some vague ideas about travelling around Europe once that ran out of work for him to do, but it turned out he'd just forgotten how country life works. If his house or his land doesn't come up with something that needs doing, his neighbours will. No farmer is going to let an able-bodied man go to waste. Cal has learned, among other things, how to drive a tractor, how to fill a clamp for silage, and how to shear a sheep, although Mart claims that if Cal did his whole herd, the first one would be ready for shearing again by the time he got done with the last.

This afternoon he's chopping firewood. Everyone for miles around has a lavish supply of this, gleaned after the fire that swept the mountains the summer before last – Cal had his doubts about the legality of this, but no one showed up to object, so he rolled with it. A few old oaks came down here and there, and Cal and Trey saved what they could for furniture and those countertops, but most of the casualties were spruce. Cal considers spruce to be no good for anything except firewood, and not much good for that, but it's been seasoning long enough that at least it shouldn't coat his chimney in creosote and start a fire of its own. He and Mart worked out a deal: Mart, who has more shed space, stores Cal's wood till he needs it, and Cal, who has better joints, chops for both of them.

The weather is right: not raining, although it's considering it, and not too chilly, only the first hint of frost to tell Cal he's getting this job done just in time. He hasn't lost the boyhood knack; the axe-blows ring clear and satisfying, and the wood splits cleanly into fireplace-sized pieces, spreading the tang of spruce through the air. On an upturned bucket, Mart's boombox is playing Linda Ronstadt to help things along. When Cal has worked up a sweat, he pulls off his fleece and wipes his face on it. He takes a minute to let the air cool him, and to look out across the fields to the mountains. The dark smudges of spruce groves are fewer and farther between than they used to be, but heather and gorse have run riot over the ragged black scars the fire left behind. The mountains, with millennia of experience in regeneration, let the ash settle and went to work without missing a beat. After just one summer's worth of growth, no one would guess anything ever happened.

Mart, who's trundling alternate wheelbarrow-loads of split wood to his back door and to Cal's red Pajero, wolf-whistles at him. 'Wouldja look at them muscles,' he says admiringly. 'D'you remember the state of you, when you first got here? A belly on you like Santy, you had, and I could tell by your face you were riddled with the cholesterol. That's what the food in America does to a man. Over here you wouldn't even be allowed sell it as food, most of it; you'd have to label it "industrial by-product, not for human consumption". And now look at you. Giving Jean-Claude Van Damme a run for his money.'

'I still got a belly,' Cal says, slapping it.

'That's only a bitta curve, sure. Curves are in, boyo; d'you not keep up with your fashion magazines? You're a credit to this place. We oughta put you on the tourist websites, as an advertisement. Before and after Ardnakelty.'

'You're just buttering me up so I'll keep going,' Cal says.

Mart grins. 'You're doing a great job there, Jean-Claude. Keep at it. Although,' he adds, struck by an inspiration, 'who I did oughta get down here to help me is wee Bobby. I need a way to get that fella talking when he's working too hard to be on his guard.'

'He's still keeping quiet about Róisín, huh?' Cal says, picking up the axe again.

'The little fecker's turned cunning,' Mart says, outraged. ''Tis true what they say, that love changes a man. Bobby Feeney never had a cunning bone in his body, and now will I tell you what he done?'

'Uh-oh,' Cal says.

Mart puts the wheelbarrow down and settles himself on a stack of old tyres to do the story justice. A lifetime of farming has tattered Mart's joints; he sits down when he can, which isn't often. He pulls off his hat, which today is a bright blue beanie with a pom-pom on top, and fans himself with it.

'Sunday afternoon,' he says, 'I'm in the kitchen minding my own business, making myself a cuppa tay, and what do I see out the window only Bobby's bockety aul' Passat heading up to the main road. Bobby's got no reason to be out and about on a Sunday afternoon. So didn't I hop in the car and follow him – at a safe distance, like. Sure, I'd nothing better to do.'

Cal lifts an eyebrow at him, between blows: farmers never have nothing better to do.

'I'm as entitled to a break as any man,' Mart says with dignity. 'Ask the union fellas up in Dublin: they'd have your arse in court before you could spit, for denying me my break. Anyhow I wasn't planning on following him the whole way. I've no interest in being a spectator to whatever that lad calls courting. All I wanted was to see where Señorita Róisín is from, the way I can ask around and find out who her people are and whether she's a dacent match for our Bobby.'

'Awww,' Cal says. 'Stalking him for his own good.'

'That's exactly what I was doing. But did the little fecker appreciate it?'

Cal doesn't have the breath to answer, but the question is rhetorical anyway. 'That fella,' Mart says, with mounting injury, 'that shneaky specimen, drove the pair of us up and down every side road in the county for the guts of an hour. In the end I lost him. There's me driving in circles like a feckin' eejit, trying to work out how to get home, when I get a text. I pull out my phone' – he mimes it – 'and who is it only the man himself. And the text says, not a word of a lie, the text says, "Fuck off home and don't be annoying me, Róisín doesn't need the life frightened outa her by your ugly mug."'

Cal, tossing split wood into an old feed sack, is grinning. 'Good for Bobby,' he says.

'Good for Bobby, me arse. I'm only looking out for him. He oughta be thanking me.'

'Maybe he doesn't need looking after,' Cal points out. 'If he's smart enough to be one step ahead of you.'

Mart doesn't bother answering that, beyond a snort. 'What I'm only dying to know,' he says thoughtfully, pulling his tobacco pouch out of his pocket, 'is whether he's invited her for a night out to meet the aliens.'

'Mart,' Cal says, lowering the axe. 'You can't tell Róisín about the aliens.'

Bobby has been convinced, ever since he was a teenager, that the mountains are some kind of pit stop on an interplanetary back road. He has decades' worth of notebook entries – he wants to show them to Cal, but the ribbing he gets in the pub leaves him too shy – where he's recorded lights moving on the mountainside, weird shapes in the sky, flattened patches of heather. Sometimes, when his mammy is feeling well enough to be left alone, he spends the night up on the mountain with his phone camera and a pair of night-vision goggles. Bobby has never been lucky enough to see a real live alien, but he holds out hope.

'I'll tell the woman sweet shag-all,' Mart says, affronted. 'Unless she turns out to be a right geebag that'd make his life a misery, and he's too blinded by the hormone explosion to notice. Then I might haveta drop a hint or two, in his own best interests.'

'Come on, man,' Cal says. 'The guy's happier'n I've ever seen him.'

'I'm saying nothing. I'm wondering, is all.' Mart examines the amount of tobacco in his rollie paper and sprinkles in a little extra. Apparently this conversation has more substance to it than Cal recognised; it's going to take a while. He goes back to his wood-splitting. On the boombox, Linda is singing 'Heart Like a Wheel', rich and sweet enough to make heartbreak sound like something to wish for.

'Every relationship,' Mart informs Cal, 'has its crossroadses. Not just the romances; alla them. Them moments where either ye'll go your separate ways, or ye'll come out in better shape than ever. I don't know about you, bucko, but if I was Róisín the Receptionist, I'd see the little green men as a bit of a crossroads.'

'Maybe she's into aliens too,' Cal points out. 'They can hold hands in his hide, or whatever he's got up there.'

Mart licks his rollie paper and considers that. 'Maybe,' he acknowledges. 'It'd be a great excuse for a bit of a cuddle while they wait. I'd say the odds are against it, but.'

'It'll be fine,' Cal says. 'If she really likes him, one weird hobby isn't gonna be a dealbreaker.'

'Maybe not,' Mart says. 'But I won't be easy in my mind till I know herself and Bobby have made it past that. The thing about the crossroadses, boyo, is that they're fierce unpredictable. Take yourself and myself: if you think about it, Sunny Jim, we've had our own crossroadses along the way. Haven't we?'

'That's one way to put it,' Cal says.

'There's been times when our relationship coulda easily gone tits-up. But here we are, getting on like a house on fire.' Mart smiles sweetly at Cal, tilting his head to the lighter. 'Who woulda thought, hah?'

'I just keep you around for the rides home from the pub,' Cal says. 'You quit offering, then we'll have a crossroads.'

Mart has a giggle at that. Mart likes it when Cal gives him shit; he sees it as a sign that he's getting Cal into the swing of the local customs. 'Or,' he says, 'take the Moynihans. They're having a bit of a crossroads these days – not among themselves, now. With this place.'

The touch of extra weight on his voice is so delicate that it's practically imperceptible, but Cal is familiar with Mart's ways. Like everyone else around here, Mart is constitutionally incapable of going at anything directly – Cal puts it down, vaguely, to centuries of British rule, the concealment reflex that's beaten into the colonised. It took him months to figure out that anyone who refused a cup of tea probably wanted one, but he's got better at reading the code. Apparently they've reached a point where Ardnakelty – or at least Mart's personal corner of it – wants him to know something, or wants something from him, or both.

'Yeah,' he says. 'I got that.'

Mart cocks his head at him. 'I thought you mighta done, all right. Part of it, anyhow. Tell us, Sunny Jim: what'd you get?'

Cal says, 'Folks think Rachel Holohan killed herself 'cause Eugene was cheating on her.'

'Near enough,' Mart says. 'There's some debate about the details – there's people that think he was cheating, and people that think he was giving her the aul' heave-ho, and people that think he was treating her bad, and people that think 'twas a bit of all three. But that's the gist of it. That's why Tommy has Eugene taking leave from work to stay down here, sure: so everyone'll get the message that he's pure devastated about losing the love of his life, he's got no bitta fluff pulling him up to Dublin, he's a poor injured innocent and nothing else. I'm not convinced Tommy's made the right call there, myself, but that's what he's at.'

'If I wanted people feeling sympathetic,' Cal says, 'I'd get Eugene as far away as I could. Kid's short on charm.' He keeps chopping. This conversation needs spaces in which he can evaluate things, before he opens his mouth.

Mart snorts appreciatively at that. He smokes and watches Rip bowing and wriggling, trying to convince Mart's black-and-white sheepdog, Kojak, to come play. Kojak, flopped in the grass, ignores him. They've always been good buddies, but Kojak is getting old, and Rip doesn't understand.

'Father Eamonn gave a rousing aul' homily on Sunday,' Mart

says, 'about personal responsibility. I wasn't there myself, but that's what I'm told. According to His Holiness Father Eamonn, now, everyone's got personal responsibility for their own actions and their own sins. We're not to be putting any of it on anyone else. It doesn't matter what anyone done on a person along the way; God won't be factoring that in when he does the accounting.' He squints up at the mountain, gauging the rags of mist that hang around its crest line. 'There's an interesting moral question there, Sunny Jim. If a fella does his woman wrong, just for example, and she goes in the river, whose slate does the sin go on? What would the Protestants have to say about that?'

'I'm not much of a Protestant,' Cal says. 'And suicide's not much of a sin in my book. It's just a sad thing.'

Mart cocks an eyebrow at him. 'That's very diplomatic of you altogether,' he says. 'After our wee singsong in the pub, the other night, I thought you'd more opinions than that. Or were you only humming along to keep the rest of us company?'

His eyes, half hidden among their cheery creases, are bright and sharp on Cal's.

'I've got opinions about the Moynihans,' Cal says. 'I don't like 'em.'

While this is true, it's not important. The fact is, Cal was sitting right there with the guys, giving Senan shit about his pickup lines and expecting someone to buy the next round, when Tommy and Eugene walked in. He didn't have the right to opt out as soon as things got complicated.

Mart nods, acknowledging the validity of the point. 'You're in good company,' he says. 'Plenty of people don't; myself included. But the thing is, Sunny Jim, there's people that do. Not *like* them, now, but there's people that'd lick Tommy Moynihan's boots clean and thank him for the honour. Tommy's brought jobs to this place, bucko. Jobs.'

His eyes flick sideways to Cal, to make sure Cal knows to be adequately awestruck. 'I'm not impressed, myself,' he adds. 'If Tommy sorted out them nitrate derogations, say, or if he got rid of my paperwork for me, I might chance the odd lick of the boots now and again; but the opportunity to work my arse off in a meat-processing plant for shitey wages to buy that fella first-class flights to Cancun doesn't set my heart aflutter. For some people, but, them jobs put him within a spit of the Sacred Heart. The McHugh boys, now: there's eight of them, and only enough land for four to farm. The other four got jobs off Tommy. They won't hear a word against the man, or his family.'

'Makes sense,' Cal says.

'It does not. Tommy's not doing them a favour; he's making money offa their backs. They're fuckin' peasants, is what they are, tugging their forelocks to the squire and missing the bigger picture altogether. You'd expect better of farming men.'

Mart blows out a long, scornful plume of smoke. 'They're stuck in the past,' he says, 'is what it is. You don't know what 'twas like around here, bucko, when myself and Tommy were young lads. There was nothing. If you weren't in line to inherit land, you had nothing: no way to earn a living, and no woman'd look at you. You packed up your bits and bobs and off you went to England or America or Australia. Plenty never came home. I've two brothers out there somewhere, Sunny Jim, or then again maybe I don't. Maybe they died of the drink in mouldy bedsits years ago, and no one knew to tell me.'

Cal nods and keeps chopping. He understands that this story isn't just Mart's; it's community property, a thing carried in common by every family scattered across these fields. From her bucket, Linda mourns for all the lost loves.

'The McHughs and the rest of themens that lick up to Tommy,' Mart says, 'they haven't kept up with the times. They haven't got it into their heads that things are after changing. Nowadays there's more jobs than you can ate. The businesses do be crying out for workers. When the young people emigrate nowadays, 'tisn't 'cause they can't find a job; 'tis 'cause they have a job, and they still can't get a house to live in. But themens still fall on their knees and give thanks when they hear the word *jobs*.'

Rip is still bugging Kojak, bouncing in circles around him. 'Rip,' Cal calls over. 'Sit, boy.' Rip gives him an affronted look, but he sits, as slowly as he can get away with. Kojak gets up, shakes himself, and stalks over to Mart.

'And now,' Mart says, 'we've got Father Eamonn shoving his oar in. Tommy's fierce generous at the collection plate, and he was awful loud about following Father Eamonn's orders when it came to them votes on the gay marriage and the abortion. So I wouldn't say Father Eamonn's basing his opinion on purely theological grounds.'

'Uh-oh,' Cal says. 'You allowed to shit-talk a priest? Or are you gonna have to bring that up in confession?'

'I would if I went, but I don't so I won't. And I never liked the fat fucker anyhow. But there's people that listen to him. And meanwhile, there's people like myself and Senan and Francie, that's not big fans of Tommy and the amount of say he has around this place.' He glances over at Cal. 'That's something we'd keep to ourselves, but, as a general rule.'

'I heard you guys bitching about Tommy before this,' Cal says.

'Amongst ourselves, you did. In the privacy of our own corner, in like-minded company. No one'd cross the man to his face.'

This startles Cal. He's never known Mart to be intimidated by any man, or any woman, except possibly Noreen. 'Or what?' he asks.

'Or else,' Mart says. He rubs Kojak's head. 'Let's say you wanted planning permission or a bitta re-zoning, so your son could build himself a house on your land, maybe: you could kiss that goodbye. Or let's say you were a farmer: you'd have inspectors calling out to you three or four times a month, and they'd find something every time – maybe there'd be a blocked gutter, or a wee crack in your concrete, or a species of weed they didn't like the look of, and next thing you knew, you'd be up to your ears in penalties. There's plenty of people in high places that owe Tommy a favour or two. D'you know Eoin Duggan? Dessie's cousin?'

'Stocky redheaded guy with a big chin?' Cal says. He's liking Tommy less and less. He's also not crazy about the implication that this is, all of a sudden, information he needs.

'That's the boyo. When Tommy got the lovely new Range Rover, a coupla year back, didn't the poor lad discover it wouldn't fit in his usual space outside the church, for mass. So he wanted the space Eoin always used; 'tis wider, d'you see. Only Eoin needed the width for his mammy to get in and out, so he told Tommy to get fucked.'

Mart draws on his rollie, watching Cal to make sure he's getting all the nuances here. 'After that day,' he says, 'Eoin couldn't get behind the wheel without being pulled over. If he left Seán Óg's, he was breathalysed. If he headed into town, his treads were too worn, or his headlight was aligned wrong, or he was outa his lane. Inside two months, Eoin had enough points on his licence that he was off the road. And the first time he got a lift to mass, what do you think he found parked in his space?'

'Nice to know I was right about the guy,' Cal says, reaching for the next log. In fact, it's not nice, and he wasn't right. The bitching he heard along the way was all small-scale stuff: Tommy Moynihan's conservatory is a poncy eyesore, Tommy Moynihan got the bin lorry's route changed because it was waking him up too early, Tommy Moynihan expects Noreen to save him the good bacon even if other people come in first, Tommy

Moynihan got his brother-in-law the council contract to resurface the road. All of it confirmed Cal's opinion that Tommy was a prick. He got no hint, ever, that the guy was this kind of dangerous, or this kind of thorough.

Cal has encountered Ardnakelty power structures before, but not this one. What he's seen in action has been the power of backcountry men, men who would never in a million years call in the official authorities to fix a problem, even if it would do any good; who do it themselves instead, neatly and ruthlessly, maintaining the rule of a law constructed from unspoken codes and understandings that run generations deep. What Mart's talking about is something that exists on a different level: the power of rich men on golfing terms with the authorities, far-seeing men who analyse situations in terms of profit and formulate long-term plans, and who never do anything themselves.

In three and a half years here, Cal never spotted this feature of the landscape. Every time he thinks he finally counts as settled in Ardnakelty, the place comes up with something that makes him feel like a big dumb greenhorn all over again.

'People don't cross Tommy Moynihan,' Mart says. 'What happened in the pub the other night: Tommy wouldn't be used to that kinda treatment at all, at all.' He smiles a small, grim smile down at Kojak, remembering. 'But a girl's dead, Sunny Jim. That changes things. There's going to be crossroadses popping up everywhere you look, the next while. You won't be able to go out your door without tripping over one.' He turns his smile to Cal. 'D'you remember them days when you were just a blow-in, bucko, and no one gave a shite what you thought? We've come a long way.'

The pile of logs has shrunk to a scattering, and Cal's muscles are burning. He puts down the axe and rolls his shoulders, tilting his head back to look up at the sky. The cloud has taken on a purplish tinge that he knows; rain is on the way. 'What is it you want?' he asks.

Mart cocks his head enquiringly. 'Did I ask you for anything?'

'Not yet,' Cal says. 'But when you tell me stuff, mostly you want something.'

He expects a grin of acknowledgement, but he doesn't get it. 'I'm clarifying the situation, is all,' Mart says, 'while I've the opportunity. Just in case.'

He drops his rollie butt and grinds it out with his boot. 'I've a feeling,' he says. 'D'you know how some people'd get the aches in their bones when the weather's turning bad? Like that, only different. And whatever else about you, Sunny Jim, you're a useful lad to have on side in a crisis.'

Cal says, 'What kind of crisis?'

'I've a feeling,' Mart says. He jams his blue beanie down over his ears, so the pom-pom sticks up straight on top of his head, and stands up, wincing as his hip jabs him. 'Just a feeling.'

He nods at the split wood. 'That oughta do us for a while. Fair play to you, Jean-Claude: we'll be lovely and warm for the winter. When the frost comes in, yourself and the missus and the young one can snuggle up in front of that and toast marshmallows.'

He hefts the feed sack into the wheelbarrow, dumps the boombox on top, and trundles off towards his house, with Kojak loping at his heel and Linda still singing her heart out. The rain is starting.

5

The crossroads shows up two days later, when Cal is on his roof, replacing a handful of broken slates before the winter winds hit. Cal had never owned an old house before this, and one of the things he didn't expect is that it needs constant tending, like a living creature. He figured he'd get it back into shape and that would be that, but something always requires his care: the tiles on the front step wear loose, or the paint on the window frames peels, or grasses take root in the chimney pot. Mostly this doesn't come to Cal as a bad thing, although he knows that would be different if he was busier or less handy. He likes the thought of the house moving and changing through the seasons the same way the land does, responding to his attentions and flourishing under his hands. Right now, though, amid the general atmosphere of unease, that feels like a bunch of sentimental bullshit. He just checked the slates last autumn, and all of these were fine then. There's a damp patch on the workshop wall that makes him think the gutter is failing; the bathroom sink isn't draining right, and he hates screwing around with plumbing, especially plumbing that some clown half-assed in the eighties. He doesn't feel like he's keeping the house happy and thriving, he feels like the whole thing is just plain falling to pieces, on purpose, faster than he can patch it.

He hears the crossroads coming before he sees it; there's no point in having the most expensive car in Ardnakelty unless you can make everyone else listen to its bellowing. He looks up to watch the black Range Rover charging too fast along the twisting road, between the stone walls and the half-clipped hedgerows. He reckons Eugene is driving. The car is being handled deftly, but with a young man's assumption that it's everyone else's job to get out of his way.

Cal takes for granted that the Moynihans are aiming for the main road and town, seeing as there's no one around here worth their attention. It's only when the Range Rover passes PJ's place and starts slowing down that he realises where it's headed. By the time Eugene has manoeuvred through Cal's gate, and parked a standoffish distance from his low-class Pajero, Cal is down the ladder and waiting in front of his house.

Tommy is in the passenger seat, and he's first out of the car, settling his beige farmer jacket on his shoulders and striding across the yard with a hand lifted to Cal. Rip, bubbling over with energy after a morning of being bored at the foot of the ladder, is bouncing and wiggling at the prospect of visitors. 'Sit,' Cal says.

Eugene follows Tommy at a snappy pace, picking up his feet like a city boy. Eugene doesn't have exactly the demeanour Cal would expect from someone in his circumstances. The kid looks like he's grieving hard, all right – he's lost weight, and there are purple bags under his eyes – but what he mainly looks is tense and irked, like he considers the entire situation utterly unacceptable. He has the air of a man about to file an elaborate grievance with HR.

'Howdy there, chief,' Tommy says, coming to a stop a few yards from Cal. Tommy is taller than most men around here, but Cal has a couple of inches on him; Tommy tends to stay well back, so he won't have to look up. 'How's the form?'

'Hangin' in there,' Cal says, wiping his hands on his work pants. 'Lord willing and the creek don't rise.' Noreen isn't here to glare at him; if he wants to give Tommy the full boy-howdy treatment, he can. This time he's not just yanking Tommy's crank. Whatever Tommy wants, Cal isn't inclined to give it to him, and he's always found big-dumb-redneck to come in handy against people who enjoy looking down on other people. He doesn't like thinking in these terms, of adversaries and strategies, but here they all are.

'You've got this place looking great,' Tommy says approvingly, inspecting Cal's cottage. 'I hope you know we all appreciate what you've done here – amn't I right, Eugene?' Eugene gives a tight nod and says something that has the appropriate words in it. 'This place was an eyesore, so it was,' Tommy tells Cal. 'I'd be ashamed to pass by it. And then you came along and rescued it for us.'

'Glad to be of use,' Cal says.

'I'd say it keeps you on your toes,' Tommy says. He holds out a hand to Rip, but Rip is too well-behaved to cosy up to anyone without Cal's permission, which he's not about to get. 'If you're not too busy, could you give us a few minutes of your time?'

'Well,' Cal drawls, scratching the back of his neck and squinting up at his roof, 'I reckon I might could take a break. All's I was doing is patching up a coupla loose slates, and I don't guess they'll fall off in the next half-hour.'

'I'd say you'll have to take a break anyhow,' Tommy advises him, examining the layer of cloud with a critical eye. 'It's going to lash any minute. All this rain must be a bit of a shock to you, hah?'

'We got rain in America,' Cal says. 'Sometimes we even get a lot of it.'

'Everything's bigger over there,' Tommy says, like he's coming up with something clever, 'even the rain. Ours does the job, though. Could we step inside, before it has us drownded?'

A few days ago Cal might have brought them inside, just out of manners, but now he doesn't feel like letting this goombah call the shots. 'Aw, shucks,' he says, tipping back his baseball cap. 'Y'all went and picked a bad day for that. The house ain't fit for company.'

'Ah, now,' Tommy says, smiling, 'you're selling your missus short there. I'd say Lena keeps the place fit for a king.'

'Well,' Cal says blandly, smiling right back, 'mostly Miz Dunne does her housework, and I do mine. And sometimes, I gotta confess, my mama would slap the sugar out of me if she could see the results.'

Tommy laughs, and Eugene gives a brief snigger. Cal feels that Tommy needs to do a better job of training Eugene, if he wants the kid to follow in his footsteps. Eugene has a genuine talent for hitting the wrong note.

'We're not fussy,' Tommy assures him. 'If 'tis good enough for you, man, 'tis good enough for us.'

'I wouldn't feel right about it,' Cal says, shaking his head regretfully. 'Inviting two fine men like y'all to sit down in a place that ain't up to any of our standards. I'll always take the opportunity to shoot the breeze with good neighbours, but today we'll have to do it in God's living room instead of mine.' He waves a hand in the general direction of the scenery. Behind Tommy and Eugene, the rooks are starting to swoop over to investigate the Range Rover.

Tommy isn't going to push it any harder, when he won't win. 'That's a lovely way of putting it,' he says approvingly, scanning the fields. 'Sometimes it takes an outside eye to make us see what we've got, isn't that right?' That part is to Eugene, who deigns to nod, although he's displeased and not hiding it well. Cal smiles at him. 'I wouldn't want to mislead you, but,' Tommy adds. 'We're not just here for the company, fine though it is. This is a professional call, you might say.'

The Moynihans' house is about the only one in Ardnakelty that doesn't have any of Cal and Trey's work in it. Cal hasn't missed the message: in Tommy's eyes, he's not important enough, or maybe not permanent enough, to be worth patronising. He finds it interesting that this has suddenly changed.

'Gee,' he says, 'I'm honoured, but I'm plumb up to my ears with Christmas orders. I can give you the number for a guy up in town who does good work, though.'

After a second of bafflement, Tommy throws back his head and laughs heartily. 'Ah, God, no,' he says. 'We've got a bitta miscommunication going on here. Your furniture's great stuff, I've seen it here and there and I'm well impressed, but we're sorted for all that – at the moment, anyhow; sure, I'll call back over as soon as we need anything. No, I'm talking about another kind of professional call.'

'That so,' Cal says.

'It is,' Tommy says, rearranging his posture to indicate serious conversation and shifting his tone to a sombre one. Eugene, looking off past Cal's head, doesn't bother to follow his lead. 'I don't know how much you'll have heard, now. But you know what happened to poor Rachel Holohan. You were there when she was found, sure.'

'I was there,' Cal says. 'That was a terrible thing.'

'Oh, it was, all right. Tragic. The poor girl.' Tommy shakes his head and leaves a moment of silence. Eugene blinks fast.

'And you might know,' Tommy says, snapping out of it, 'herself and Eugene here were as good as engaged.'

'I do seem to recall Noreen mentioning something along those lines,' Cal says.

'That's right, o' course: you were there when she was making guesses about the engagement do.' Tommy smiles sadly. 'Noreen's always been sharp as a tack. She wasn't far off there, was she, Eugene?'

This is apparently Eugene's cue. 'I was going to ask Rachel that weekend,' he says. Eugene doesn't talk like his daddy.

Tommy has the full Ardnakelty accent, rich as farm dirt; Eugene has scrubbed all that away till he could be from anywhere in this country, as long as anywhere had a decent selection of concept restaurants and craft beer. His voice is tight; he doesn't like trotting out this story for Cal's inspection. 'I had the ring and everything.'

Cal looks mildly puzzled and waits.

'He had it all planned to ask her on that old footbridge over the river,' Tommy says, letting his voice go deep with melancholy. 'He was only waiting for a break in the weather, the way he wouldn't haveta drag her out there in the rain. The Lovers' Bridge, people usedta call that, back in the day. The two of them had associations with it, isn't that right, Eugene?'

'Yeah,' Eugene says. His mouth has pinched tighter.

'Huh,' Cal says. He would have expected Eugene to pull some staged baloney with rose petals in a fancy country house. 'That's right about where they think she went in, ain't it?'

Eugene's head flicks away. 'The exact location hasn't been confirmed,' Tommy says smoothly. 'I'd say we're better off staying away from speculation, amn't I right? There's enough of that going around.'

'You might have a point there,' Cal says. His attention is on Eugene's reaction. The kid isn't just irked at the indignities of this situation. It comes across that way because that's his accustomed mode, but once you get a closer look, Eugene is furious.

'The thing about a loss like this,' Tommy says, taking back the conversation, 'is that everyone goes looking for some reason behind it. You can't fault them for that, sure. A senseless tragedy's too much for any man to handle. 'Tis only human nature to try and understand it.'

Cal can see why Tommy wanted to take this indoors. This is the kind of speech that would work best from a leather armchair, in an atmosphere of dignified gravity and pipe smoke, or else around a kitchen table with a pot of tea and an air of neighbourly collaboration. Cal's front yard isn't giving Tommy a lot to work with, but he's doing his best.

'But people round here are that desperate for answers,' he continues, 'they're lashing out. There's accusations flying left and right; mad stuff altogether. People are so off balance, they wouldn't know what they're saying, half the time. You mightn't credit this, but I'm told there's people saying Rachel was, we'll put it nicely' – he cuts his eyes significantly at Eugene, who's gritting his teeth hard enough that Cal waits for the crack – 'that she was seeing someone else, the last while, and she was afraid Eugene would find out. Now I know that's a dirty lie, and Eugene knows it too, but you can't stop people talking.'

Tommy shakes his head, sorrowing over the townland's weak-mindedness, and keeps a sideways eye on Cal. Cal shakes his own head obligingly. 'Some people just get born with a ten-gallon mouth,' he says. More rooks have congregated on the Range Rover. He holds out hope that they'll shit on it, but the rooks have never yet done anything he wants them to, and he doesn't expect them to start now.

'And then,' Tommy says, his voice swelling with emotion, 'then we've got Eugene here. If any man needs answers, 'tis him. But Eugene's not throwing around any accusations. He's just wearing himself half to death, trying to think of a reason why this coulda happened – ah, now, there's no shame in that, son.' He puts a hand on Eugene's shoulder. Eugene twitches. 'You were mad about Rachel; you deserve a reason why she's gone, and your whole future with her.'

Eugene is focusing intently on somewhere in Cal's back field. Cal doesn't like the kid, but he feels a touch of sympathy for him today.

'My young lad's heartbroken, Mr Hooper,' Tommy says. 'He's putting on a brave face, but I'll be honest with you: myself and the missus, we're worried about our boy. We'll do whatever it takes to help him.'

'Huh,' Cal says. 'I'm sure sorry to hear that.' He's getting clearer on what Tommy is here for. 'You know who you oughta talk to, is the priest – Father Eamonn, ain't that right? I heard that, way back when the Maguires lost a baby, Father Eamonn did a fine job of explaining how God's always got a good reason.' Senan still spits on the ground when he hears Father Eamonn's name.

'Oh, we are, we are o' course,' Tommy says, dipping his head piously. His swoop of silver hair doesn't budge. 'But I'm a practical man. If there's reasons here on earth that could give Eugene some peace of mind, I think he deserves to have them. You're a father yourself, isn't that right? If a child of yours was left like this, you'd do anything in the world to help.'

Tommy, like the rest of Ardnakelty, has this filed as a suicide. Cal says, 'You want someone to find out why Rachel did it.'

'I do. And the missus was saying it feels like a miracle, that we've got a man with your skills right here in the townland.' Tommy gives Cal the gracious nod of one important man to another. 'If there's any man that can help us, it's you.'

'I'm not a PI,' Cal says.

'Oh, I know that, o' course,' Tommy assures him, hands going up to repel the very thought. 'We wouldn't want anyone like that. We couldn't have some stranger going around the place poking his nose in – specially not at a time like this, with everyone up to ninety. But someone like yourself, now. A man that's well-known and well-liked. You could have a few conversations here and there without upsetting anyone's feelings.'

'Not my style,' Cal says.

'I'm not talking about giving your neighbours the third degree, man,' Tommy says, all reasonableness, with a quirk of an eyebrow that says Cal is being dramatic. 'Nothing that'd get you in anyone's bad books. I'm talking about having the chats, is all. Hearing what there is to hear. Setting rumours to rest, before they do too much harm. You'd be doing the whole place a favour, not just my poor lad. And around here, we don't forget people who've done us a good turn.'

'Maybe I should've made myself clearer,' Cal says. 'I'm not your PI.'

Just for a fraction of a second, he sees the flare of savagery in Tommy's eyes. Then it's gone, and Tommy is sighing regretfully, nodding his head. 'Well,' he says, 'that's a shame. I thought I'd chance my arm, but I can't blame you for sticking to the carpentry. I'm sure you want a bitta peace and quiet, after all the years of dealing with thugs and reprobates. The aul' peace and quiet's a great thing, if you can get it.'

'I do my best,' Cal says. Rip is twitching to go for the rooks. Cal puts a hand on his head to settle him.

'And I'll tell you what I'll do,' Tommy says, 'just to show there's no hard feelings. If you ever feel like going legit with the carpentry business, paying the taxes and doing the VAT and all that, I've a friend in the Revenue who can sort you out like that.' He snaps his fingers, smiling straight into Cal's eyes.

'Well, if that ain't mighty obliging of you,' Cal says, smiling right back at him. He hears the threat loud and clear.

'Although you mightn't be allowed to go legit,' Tommy says, struck by the thought. 'What with you being a Yank. But don't you worry: when my fella sets his mind to something, he finds a way.'

'I'll be sure and keep that in mind,' Cal says.

'Do, man. Don't forget it. Neighbours oughta look out for each other, isn't that right?'

'Reckon so,' Cal says. He almost wishes he could keep Tommy talking a little longer. Two of the rooks have taken a liking to the Range Rover's windshield wiper and are working together to detach it, bracing their feet on the hood so they can put their backs into tugging.

'Thanks for the chat,' Tommy says. 'If you change your mind, let me know any time. Any time at all.'

Eugene is already throwing Cal a jerky nod and whisking around to head back to the car. Tommy gives Cal one more smile before he follows.

Cal squats down by Rip and rubs his neck, watching, while Eugene shoos the rooks away with furious flaps of his arms and the two of them get in the car, and while Eugene reverses out the gate in one sweep without checking if anyone's coming. Then he climbs up his ladder, ignoring Rip's gusty sigh, and gets back to work on his slates. Rip could use a good long walk, but Cal wants to think, and he thinks best when he's getting something done.

The fact that Tommy wants reasons implies that he hasn't found them at home. Eugene wasn't dumping Rachel, or cheating on her, or whatever else the townland has come up with. It could be a ruse – Tommy could have been aiming to produce the exact impression he did produce – but Cal doesn't think so. The flash of rage when he found himself baulked was real.

Eugene could be keeping things from his daddy, of course. Some struggle is going on there. Eugene didn't want to be here, but Daddy is the boss man, and Eugene doesn't like that one bit.

That feeling is jabbing Cal again, the insistent prickle of something hinky in the air. He wonders why Tommy cares so much about Rachel's reasons, and why he isn't taking the opportunity to frame this as an accident: mix-up over the romantic rendezvous, Eugene thought they'd cancelled and Rachel didn't, one slip on the rain-wet bridge with its too-low walls, no blame for anyone and a great big helping of sympathy with all the fixings for everyone involved. He wonders if Tommy shares

Trey's suspicion that this was neither suicide nor accident, and if he does, why.

Cal understands what he's just done. Even without what Mart said, he would have turned Tommy down – he's not going to run around hassling grieving people just to soothe Eugene's delicate feelings, let alone for whatever reason Tommy is keeping to himself. But a few days ago, he would have turned him down differently. Up until today, Tommy had him pegged as a clueless Yank who was humming along in the pub because he thought it was one of those quaint Irish singsongs. That's gone for good. Whatever's going on, Cal is inside it now.

He's OK with that. Cal doesn't like guys like Tommy, who carefully collect power and use it to force their will down other people's throats. He worked with enough of them, back on the job, to develop an allergy. If the rest of Ardnakelty is dealing with one of those guys, Cal might as well deal with him too.

Tommy was talking out of his ass about the rain. The layer of cloud hangs sulky and apathetic, like it could stay put forever without doing anything to justify its existence. Out in his top field, Mart is moving sheep, guiding Kojak with sharp calls and neat flicks of his crook. He spots Cal on the roof and waves, and Cal lifts a hand back. He needs to talk to Mart.

The rooks, deprived of their windshield wiper, are sneaking up on Rip, who's too busy sprawling in a martyred attitude at the foot of the ladder to notice. Cal pulls off another broken slate and tosses it at them, and they scatter, yelling rude words, while Rip leaps up to chase after them.

It's Trey, of all people, who brings the next piece of news. By five o'clock it's dark enough that Cal has finished up with his roof, under a thickening sky, and gone inside to thaw his fingers. Lena has come over for dinner; she's setting the table and telling Cal the latest story about her boss, whose people skills don't match her horse skills and who may be about to go viral after losing the head with some woman who went into a stall to make a TikTok with the cute horsie. Lena tells a story well, and Cal appreciates it; he needed the laugh. He's found himself not in the mood for cooking, but he's dug a chicken casserole out of the freezer and stuck it in the oven, so at least the place smells good.

Trey bangs in with Banjo, both of them damp, and Banjo looking muddy and guilty. 'He went in the ditch after a rabbit,' Trey says, dropping her bike helmet and kicking her schoolbag into a corner. 'And Mr Moore gave us fuckin' weekend homework. Entire essay on *Yeats*.'

'You're not into Yeats?' Cal asks. He's at the fireplace, arranging kindling and firelighters.

Trey, digging an old dish towel out of the cupboard under the sink, rolls her eyes.

'I never was either,' Lena says, laying out plates. 'The man sounds like an awful dose.'

'Up his own hole,' Trey says. She sits down on the floor to get the mud off Banjo's legs before he can spread it everywhere. The other three dogs have come stampeding over to greet them and check out what scents they've brought in, so Trey is half-submerged in a wriggling mass.

'Hey,' Cal says, turning to snap his fingers at the dogs. 'You can say hello once he's clean. Bed.' He points to the corner by the fireplace.

'Get back here,' Trey says, grabbing Banjo as he makes to follow the others. 'What's *that*?'

She's pointing her chin at the Virgin Mary bottle, which is on the mantelpiece. Cal originally stuck it in a drawer, but he figures Bobby might stop by for romantic advice at some point – Bobby considers Cal to be an authority on these matters, seeing as he's managed to get together with two different women and only one of them has dumped him so far – and his feelings would be hurt if the bottle was nowhere to be seen.

'Bobby brought it back for me from France,' Cal says. 'Got holy water in it.'

Trey rolls her eyes again, more elaborately this time. 'Hey,' Cal says, balancing one of his split logs on top of the kindling pile. 'The guy was being nice.'

'Bobby's a fuckin' dope,' Trey says. She appears to be in the mood to bite someone, possibly due to Yeats.

'Maybe, but he's a dope who did a kind thing. Don't knock that.' Trey lets out an extravagantly irritated sigh and concentrates on Banjo, who wants to play tug-of-war with the dish towel.

'God, that takes me back,' Lena says, pausing with a handful of forks to look at the bottle. 'My granny had one a them. She used to put some on us before exams.'

'You can put some on your Yeats essay,' Cal tells Trey.

'Mightn't even do it,' Trey says.

'You gotta do your homework. Do it right after dinner, then you can forget about it.'

'Nah. Gotta head.'

'You going out with the guys?' Cal asks.

'Nah. Home.' Trey wards Banjo's paws off her jeans. 'I'll do the essay tomorrow. C'n I come round before lunch?'

It's Friday. It's been more than two years since Trey spent a Friday night at her mama's place. 'Sure,' Cal says. 'Any time.'

He can't find anything else to say. Just a month or two ago, he about had to roust Trey out of his place when he felt she'd been there long enough. He wonders if she's dodging another conversation about staying in school, or if her buddies have been giving her shit for sleeping at his place. Either of those is possible, but he can't escape the feeling that he's making up fancy hidden reasons where none are needed, looking for something that would be fixable. The kid is sixteen; she has friends her own age, a social life, just like he wanted for her. She doesn't want to spend her weekends hanging around with some old guy. At some point he should find a careful way to let her know that, if she's got better things to do than help him build Con McHugh's wife's nursing chair, she doesn't have to.

'Here,' Lena says. She sits down on the floor beside Banjo, so she can distract him while Trey cleans him up. Banjo, delighted with all the attention, rolls over to let her at his belly.

Trey, rubbing at Banjo's back leg, says, 'They're sending Rachel Holohan home.'

Cal and Lena both stop what they're doing.

'The medical examiner said suicide,' Trey says. She hasn't looked up. 'She drank antifreeze.'

'Where'd you hear this?' Cal asks.

'Ross's cousin's a Guard. He said it to Ross's da, 'cause Ross's da was freaking out that there was some mad serial killer around, and Ross's sisters weren't allowed go anywhere so *they* were freaking out. And Ross heard.'

'Jesus,' Lena says. 'Look who's getting the news fresh off the tree these days. You'll be giving Noreen a run for her money.'

Trey makes a face. Her relationship with Noreen has improved a lot since the days when she routinely stole stuff from the shop, but both of them still hold a certain level of grudge.

'You sure Ross got it right?' Cal says. 'Something like this, I'd've thought Noreen would've heard about it.'

'She probably did,' Lena says. 'She's not speaking to me 'cause I didn't call round to Claire Holohan, and 'cause this one here hangs out with foreigners from the wilds of Knockfarraney. Or something.'

'None a her business who I hang out with,' Trey says.

'That's what I told her,' Lena says. 'Noreen has trouble with the idea that anything in this world isn't her business.'

Trey makes a *pfft* noise that dismisses Noreen and her opinions. 'Ross got it right,' she tells Cal. 'He's sharp.'

'Well,' Cal says. 'That explains some stuff.'

'What stuff?'

'Something Tommy Moynihan said. He was over here this afternoon, him and Eugene.'

Lena raises her head from Banjo.

'Tommy sounded pretty sure Rachel did it herself,' Cal says. 'I was wondering why he didn't pitch it as an accident, so no one could blame Eugene. He must've heard the news already.' Going by Mart, Tommy has at least a couple of Guards in his pocket.

Lena is watching him. She says, 'What did Tommy want here?'

'Tommy wanted me to go poking around and figure out why Rachel did what she did,' Cal says. 'And whether she was stepping out on Eugene.'

'What did you say?'

'I told him to shove it where the sun don't shine,' Cal says. Trey looks up, startled and grinning. 'Not in those exact words, but he got the idea.'

'Ah, cool,' Trey says. 'And you keep telling me to be mannerly.'

'I was mannerly. I just don't like the Moynihans much.'

'Lotsa people don't,' Trey says. 'I heard Tommy and Eugene got drummed outa Seán's, the other night.'

'Well,' Cal says. Lena has gone back to Banjo; he goes back to the fire. 'Not exactly. We sang 'em a song, is all. Maybe they just didn't enjoy our singing.' He's not looking at Lena, but he feels her head turn sharply again.

'You were there?' Trey says.

'Yep,' Cal says. He holds a long match to a firelighter and watches it catch.

'What'd they do?'

'Left.'

Lena says, 'Was Mart Lavin there?'

Lena has never liked Mart, or trusted him. Cal isn't entirely clear on whether he likes Mart himself – the things he knows make that question a complicated one – and by most definitions of the term, he doesn't trust Mart as far as he could throw him; he relies on him, when he has no choice, but that's not the same thing. Somewhere along the way, though, that's stopped being the part that matters. 'Yep,' he says.

'Didja tell him about Tommy calling round?'

'Not yet,' Cal says. 'He's been out on his land all afternoon.'

'Don't say it to him,' Lena says.

Cal is taken by surprise. Regardless of Lena's views on Mart, her position has always been that Cal's choices are his problem; when he wants her opinion on them, getting it out of her is like pulling teeth. Cal has always believed that if he started living his life in some way she couldn't accept, she would simply walk away from him, sooner than ask him to change it.

'He must've seen Tommy's car,' he points out. 'You could see that thing from space.'

'Then he already knows, and you've no need to tell him.'

'Well,' Cal says, 'he might be interested in the details.'

'Mart Lavin's interests aren't your problem,' Lena says. 'Whatever he's at, you don't need to get involved in it.'

Trey has gone silent, but she's watching. Trey doesn't like it when Cal and Lena disagree, no matter how tamely. Cal doesn't know how far her parents' fights went, before her daddy took off for good and all, but he knows they got a lot worse than a child should have seen.

'I'm not getting involved in anything,' he says. 'There's nothing to get involved in. I'm just keeping Mart up to speed.'

'Because he's planning on trouble. Let them make their own trouble without you.'

'This isn't some big deal,' Cal says. The fire has taken hold;

he focuses on carefully balancing another piece of wood on top with the tongs. He wants Lena to leave it.

'Not yet, maybe,' Lena says. 'Give it time. I had Noreen telling me there's sides, the other day, and trying to make me pick one.'

'I don't mind being on the guys' side,' Cal says. 'Better'n being on Tommy's.'

'What's the difference? Mart's the same as Tommy: both of them aiming to run this place and everyone in it.'

'Well,' Cal says, 'I like Mart a whole lot better'n I like Tommy.'

'That's not the point,' Lena says. Her hand on Banjo has stopped moving; she's turned towards Cal. 'Why would you be on any side? When those lads ran Tommy outa the pub, it wasn't because of Rachel Holohan. It's because of stuff that happened before you ever heard of this place. Tommy wouldn't sort their planning permission unless they donated to his pet councillor, or his daddy did something on their daddies back in the sixties. Nothing to do with you.'

Banjo, neglected, butts at Lena's thigh to get her attention back. 'No,' Trey says in an undertone, shoving his nose away.

'I was sitting right there,' Cal says. 'What was I supposed to do?'

'You coulda done nothing. Sat there, drunk your pint, and let them sing their hearts out.'

'Those are my neighbours,' Cal says. He keeps his voice mild, for Trey. 'I hang out with them. We help each other out. I'm not some tourist that just stopped here for a few pints.'

'You're not, no. That doesn't mean you haveta do whatever Mart Lavin wants. First it's only singing a song, now you're off to feed him info about Tommy, then there'll be something else— You've no idea what you'll end up doing, down the line.'

'Gonna walk the dogs,' Trey says abruptly, standing up.

'Before it rains.' Back when Cal was married, if he and Donna argued, Alyssa would look for ways to distract them with something pretty, or make them laugh. Trey just leaves.

'They'll get muddy again,' Cal says.

Trey shrugs, zipping her jacket.

'Dinner's gonna be ready.'

'We'll be back before then.'

Cal almost orders the kid to sit her ass down, but he's not sure whether it would work, or what he would do next either way. Trey snaps her fingers for the dogs – Daisy ignores the whole thing and Banjo rolls his eyes to indicate he's too exhausted to move, but Rip and Nellie bounce up – and heads out without another look at him or Lena.

'Jesus,' Cal says, when the door slams behind them. 'We could've saved that for later.'

Lena lifts her eyebrows. 'Why would we?'

'Because. The kid doesn't like when we fight.'

'That wasn't fighting. That was disagreeing.'

'You think she knows the difference?'

'Then she needs to learn,' Lena says. She gets up, brushing dog hair off her jeans. 'The odd disagreement isn't the end of the world. Do you want her reckoning she's been dumped, the first time herself and Kate don't see eye to eye?'

'I just want her not stressed out,' Cal says. 'That's all.' He's not sure how he's ended up arguing about arguing, when he didn't even want to have the argument in the first place. 'And we don't even know that she's going out with Kate.'

'She already knows couples don't always agree,' Lena points out. 'What with her mam and dad. If we hide it, she'll only be worrying about what goes on when she's not around. And how's she supposed to learn to sort things, if she never sees us do it?'

'What did she learn tonight? She walked out. She didn't see anything that'd do her any good.'

'And when she walks back in, we'll still be here, no harm done. She'll see that.'

'She better walk back in soon,' Cal says. 'Or she's gonna be eating cold casserole.' He feels like he should have just kept his mouth shut, about everything.

Lena goes to the cupboard and takes down tumblers. Cal, watching her, feels the annoyance drain out of him. He loves watching Lena do things; he loves the contained grace that comes not from any thought of being seen, but from strength and competence. Right now of all times, he doesn't want to be at odds with her. What he wants is to go over to her, wrap his arms around her, and pull her close. He doesn't expect her to shoulder his mood and smooth it out for him, but just her physical self always improves things.

'Listen,' he says. 'Things around here should settle down now, with Rachel coming home. Even if Mart's thinking about trouble, it could all blow over.'

'Noreen said the same,' Lena says, 'more or less. Once Rachel's buried, everyone can move on.' She sets out the glasses on the table. 'Mostly I wouldn't call Noreen naïve, but I might haveta make an exception.'

Cal dims the overhead light, to bring out the flicker of the fire. He wants the room to feel cosy, homey. Instead it takes on a contracted, huddled air, like some attack has brought down the electricity and left them cut off, with nothing to do but endure till the next thing happens.

'Hey,' he says. 'I'm not gonna let Mart get me into anything I don't want to be in.'

'You're a grown man,' Lena says. 'I shouldn'ta tried to tell you what to do. You can get involved in whatever you want, as long as you don't expect me to get involved as well.'

'I know better than that,' Cal says.

Lena doesn't smile. She says, 'I don't like this for Trey.'

'Probably you're right, and no harm done.'

'I don't mean us arguing. She'll be grand.'

'Then what?'

'You heard her,' Lena says, 'the other night. She wants that apprenticeship in town. And there's Kate.'

Cal isn't sure where this is going. 'I thought you were fine with Kate,' he says. 'And with Sam.'

'I am. They're not the problem.' Lena goes to the sink to fill the water jug. 'With how much she hates this place, I always thought she'd be outa here the day she left school. If she gets herself an apprenticeship and a girlfriend, she might end up staying.'

Among the few things Cal knows about Lena's husband is that he was the reason she turned down a place in vet school in Edinburgh. 'Do you wish you'd left?' he asks.

Lena glances at him, over her shoulder. 'No,' she says. 'Not saying it's been all sunshine and roses, now, but if I could go back, I wouldn't do any different.'

'Well then,' Cal says. 'The kid might end up feeling the same way.'

Lena watches the water filling the jug. Cal thinks she's not going to answer, but after a minute she says, 'There's you saying you won't let Mart Lavin rope you into anything. But you never sat down and decided it was a great idea to run the Moynihans outa the pub, or that you'd only love to be part of whatever gang wars Mart's got planned. You just got sucked into it, before you even had a notion what was going on.'

Cal finds it hard to argue with this. Ardnakelty always has had this knack. It sneaks up around you so expertly that by the time you realise it's there, you're already neck-deep in its operations.

'Maybe,' he says. 'But if I'd had time to think it over, I'd've done the same thing.'

'That's your call,' Lena says. 'But it's not going to stop there.

And Trey's watching you do it. What she's seeing is that if she stays here, that'll be her. Getting sucked into things. Or else spending all her time fighting not to be.'

Cal hasn't put much thought into what Trey's future in Ardnakelty might look like, at least not in those terms. He's been kept amply occupied by smoothing down her relationship with the place to the point where no one gets hurt, and trying to make sure she has the grades and the woodworking skills and the basic level of civilisation to build herself a future at all, not to mention clothes that fit and something approaching a nutritious diet. He wasn't aware that analysing the large-scale psychological implications was on his to-do list.

'Well,' he says, 'we can't load her onto a bus and throw her out of town. Even if we wanted to.'

'If she stays,' Lena says, 'it'll be 'cause of us. Not only, but partly.'

'That kid's not gonna stay anywhere she doesn't want to just 'cause of you and me,' Cal says. Even a little while back, he might have thought differently, but it looks like he would have been wrong.

'If you hadn't come here, Trey'd be outa this county by now. Gone.'

'And that definitely would've been bad,' Cal says. 'Out there all alone with no education, no qualifications, no family, no nothing.' The thought is a comfort. He may not be what Trey needs any more, but he's been some use along the way.

'Maybe,' Lena says. She pours water into the glasses and sets the jug on the table. Behind them, the cold seeps through the window to slide along their backs.

Cal hates the thought of Trey in this mood walking out into the dark, and the thought of each of them sitting alone while this tight, hunkered-down evening closes around them. 'Seeing as we've got the house to ourselves tonight,' he says, 'you want to stay over?'

For a minute he thinks Lena's going to say no, she feels so distant. Then she draws a long breath and turns to him. 'Yeah,' she says. She's not smiling, but she reaches out a hand and takes his. 'Good idea.'

The oven timer rings. 'I'll go get Trey,' Lena says. She gives Cal's hand a squeeze and lets it go. She shrugs on her jacket, tucking her ponytail inside the collar, and goes out the door.

Cal turns off the oven, leaving the casserole inside to keep warm. Then he sits down at the set table, listening to the restless crackle and snap of the fire, and waits for someone to come home.

It's dark as midnight, a sullen, dripping dark that feels like it's prepared to stay unbroken till spring. Lena knows this road like she knows her own house, but she switches on her phone torch anyway, so she won't step in a puddle. She's annoyed with herself, Cal, and Mart Lavin, in more or less equal proportions. She wishes she lived somewhere like Australia or Canada, where she might run into the kind of wildlife that could be looking for hassle. She's in the mood for a fight.

Trey hasn't gone far: Lena finds her sitting on PJ's wall while the dogs explore the verges, out of sight in the darkness but still audible as they rustle and snuffle. 'Hiya,' Lena says. 'The dinner's ready.'

'Yeah,' Trey says, without moving. 'I was gonna come back now anyhow.'

'You coulda just stayed put,' Lena says. 'It's not like myself and Cal were about to go at each other's throat. We'd it all sorted out by the time you got to the gate.'

Trey shrugs, a short hard shrug that means *Nothing to do with me*. Lena props her arse against the wall beside Trey and plays her phone torch idly over the empty field across from them. The grass is thin and patchy; Skippy Gannon left his cattle unhoused too long, trying to save on silage after rain scuppered the harvest. The place has a neglected look.

Trey says, 'Didja ever know anyone that kilt themselves with antifreeze?'

'There was a fella over the other side of the mountains, a long time back,' Lena says. 'Before you were born, probably. He drank antifreeze.'

'What's it do to you?'

'I've only seen dogs,' Lena says. 'It tastes sweet, so they'll drink it if they find it. First they act like they're drunk. After a couple of hours they have seizures, or they go unconscious. If you don't treat them quick, they die in a day or two; faster if they drank a load of it.'

Trey says, 'Now everyone's gonna say Rachel kilt herself for definite.'

'Most people say that already.'

'Yeah,' Trey says. 'You reckon she did?'

'I've no opinion,' Lena says. 'I didn't know her well enough for that.'

'People are saying she done it 'cause that tosser Eugene broke up with her. That'd be fuckin' thick.'

She's giving Lena a look like a question. 'If you want my opinion on that part,' Lena says, 'for whatever it's worth, I don't believe people die over a break-up. If the rest of their life was in bad shape as well, then maybe. Or if their head wasn't working right, one way or another. The break-up might be the last straw, but it's not the reason.'

'I wouldn't,' Trey says flatly. 'Fuck that.'

'I'm delighted to hear it,' Lena says. 'Neither would I.'

Trey glances sideways at her. 'You're not gonna break up with Cal, but.'

'I wasn't planning on it,' Lena says. She caught the sudden sharp note in Trey's voice. Trey has grown up trained to be constantly on the alert for land mines, mantraps, fault lines. 'I wouldn't say Cal is, either. We make each other happy, and we're old enough to value that. We don't always agree on everything, but we're old enough to value that, too. Are you going out with anyone?'

She feels Trey retreat inside herself, weighing up her answer. 'Nah,' she says, in the end. 'Thinking about it.'

'Pick someone you like,' Lena advises her. 'Not just someone you fancy. Someone you'd want for a friend.'

Trey nods, one definite jerk, accepting this as solid. She slides off the wall and starts towards Cal's. Lena falls in beside her and watches her face in the phone's faint light bouncing back off the road. It's intent, rather than dreamy. She's going into this with the same focus she brings to other things that matter.

'Rachel didn't seem like her life was messed up,' Trey says, after a minute. She's kicking a rock along the road. 'Or like her head wasn't right.'

'Maybe not,' Lena says. 'You'd never know what's going on in people's lives, or in their minds.'

Trey scoops the rock back to the centre of the road with a deft flick of her foot. 'Everyone's got antifreeze.'

'Most people would, all right. For the car, or for the sprayers when there's frost. Your mam probably has. Make sure Banjo can't get at it, or the little ones.'

Trey says, 'I don't reckon Rachel done it herself.'

'Fair enough,' Lena says equably. She doesn't agree, but she wants to hear this.

'I never did. But with what you said about the antifreeze: no fuckin' way. Why would she go for something that takes days? And where they could treat it, if they found her?'

Lena knows well that not every suicide takes the quickest

or surest route. Rachel might not have known about the delay, might have just wanted a fail-safe to go with the river, might have reached for whatever she found handy. She might have been hoping, with some part of her, that she'd be found in time.

She says, 'What d'you reckon happened?'

'Before I heard about the antifreeze, I thought either she went to dump Eugene and he lost the head, or else some fucker tried to do something to her. Donie McGrath, maybe. She fought back, and he shoved her in the river.' Donie McGrath is the local scumbag. Lena is with Trey on this much: that sounds right up Donie's alley. 'But it wasn't. If Eugene lost the head, he'da just hit her; he wouldn't go fucking about with antifreeze. And how would Donie give it to her?'

'No girl in her right mind'd take a drink off Donie,' Lena agrees.

'Then I thought it coulda been someone else like Donie, only that hides it better. Someone that seems all right, so she'd take a drink off him. Why would he poison her, but? He'd roofie her, just.'

'That'd be simpler, all right,' Lena says. She doesn't like the amount of thought Trey has put into this. She was happier back when the whole of Ardnakelty could have gone up in smoke and Trey wouldn't have bothered to look up from her sandpaper, as long as Cal was OK.

'Unless,' Trey says, 'he wasn't like Donie. He didn't wanta do stuff to her. He wanted to kill her.'

She's keeping her voice low, like someone might be crouched behind a wall to listen. Lena watches Cal's windows, up ahead. 'Only thing is,' she says, 'why would anyone want Rachel dead?'

Trey pauses to dig her rock out of a pothole with her toe. 'I reckon she knew something,' she says, 'or she found out something, and she was gonna say it. And someone around here wanted to shut her up, so they gave her antifreeze and fucked her in the river once she was too drunk to fight back or swim out. Coulda been Eugene – Cal says he hasn't got the nads, but it doesn't take a lotta nads to put antifreeze in a drink. Or it coulda been someone else.'

She gets the rock free and sends it off up the road again, bouncing in the phone's beam. 'Only no one's ever gonna say that,' she says, ''cause then there'd be all kindsa hassle. Everyone'll just say she kilt herself. End of story.'

Lena goes still inside. This is, at least in part, her doing.

'I doubt it,' she says, once she's got her thoughts together. 'Rachel didn't seem like the type to rock the boat. She was a great one for keeping the peace, same as most people round here. If she found out something dodgy, she'da just kept her mouth shut.'

'Like you said,' Trey says. Her voice has a flat note; Lena can't tell whether it's defeat, or bitterness, or something else entirely. 'You never know.'

They walk on in silence. Lena wants to say something, but she's too afraid she'll make a balls of it. She remembers Trey, just a couple of years back, burning to defy this place any way she could find.

They stop at Cal's gate, waiting for the dogs to catch up. 'Tell me something,' Lena says. 'Are you planning on poking around, looking to find out what happened?'

Trey whistles a long up-flicking note for the dogs. 'Nah,' she says. 'She wasn't my mate or anything. No point, anyhow. Even if I found out, nothing I could do about it.'

Lena believes her. 'Right,' she says. She should be relieved. Cal would be.

The dogs come running; Lena hears the rush and patter of their paws on the road, long before they materialise out of the darkness. Trey gives her rock one last hard kick up the road towards Mart's place, and turns in at the gate.

The sun has been up for hours, but it still feels like dawn, a heavy gray dawn that the land can't shake off. The birds are silent. The long grass and weeds sag with dew or rain; when Lena turns off the road onto the narrow river path, they wet her jeans to the knees.

The bridge is a single low arch, so old that the stones seem to have smudged into one another with wear. It's just wide enough for a car, but for the last few decades cars have used the new bridge below the village. This one is no longer marked on maps; only locals wanting a shortcut, or looking for a romantic walk, cross here. The land is taking it back: bare trees lean out over it on either bank, creepers hang thick on its sides, and the weeds grow high around each base. In a few years, unless the council forgets about it altogether, it'll probably be labelled unsafe, then cordoned off, then demolished.

By then it'll be haunted. Rachel will be another dot on the luminescent map of ghosts stretched across the countryside, between the old woman waving down cars on a Kilhone back road and the half-faced shotgun accident on Crannagh Hill. She'll have been transmuted from a real girl, with gangly legs and fake lashes and a spoilt cat, into a myth to scare kids who never knew her. *My brother says a girl jumped off there 'cause her boyfriend dumped her, and if you go on it at night she'll appear and drag you over with her. My mam says that's a loada shite, there was never any girl. My cousin saw the ghost. Dare you to cross the bridge at midnight, dare you to touch it.*

Lena stands at its centre, looking downstream. The river runs high and rampant, a rich brown churned to white in streaks. On Lena, the bridge's wall comes to mid-thigh; Rachel was the same height as her, give or take. The stones are wet underfoot, and moss grows in their cracks. One bad slip would do it, or a stagger if antifreeze was wrecking your balance, or one shove; or you could just lean forward, and let gravity do the hard part for you.

That's still what Lena believes happened. But where she feels no responsibility for that, she feels the full weight of Trey standing at Cal's gate, her face half turned away to look down the dark road, saying *Nothing I could do about it*. In Trey's mind, you do this townland's bidding or you'll land in the river, and it'll all be covered up like it never happened.

Lena knew she thought that way. She was the one who taught Trey that lesson: spread the story that suits this place and bury what doesn't, or the price will be too high. She loved Trey's blazing, unbending rebellion, and she bent it to the townland's will. She doesn't consider that she could have done anything different in those specific circumstances, and somehow Trey has never held it against her, but she hasn't forgiven herself.

She told herself it wouldn't matter too much, in the long run, because it was only for a few years. The minute Trey was old enough, she would be out of here like a bullet out of a gun. Lena, of all people, should have remembered that people don't always leave the places they intend to leave.

If Trey is going to make a life here, she needs solid proof that she doesn't have to follow this place's orders and live by its rules, that it doesn't always get to choose what stays hidden and what comes to light. Whatever was behind Rachel Holohan's death, Trey needs it spread out and flown high over this townland for everyone to see, not twisted and knotted into whatever shape is most convenient. Lena owes her that.

6

When it comes to reconciling with Noreen, Lena knows her timing is lucky. Rachel is coming home: that means Noreen won't be wound to snapping point any more, and it also means she'll be in need of someone to talk to. All the same, Lena goes in armed. Noreen adores Nutella to the point where she won't have it in the shop, never mind the house, because she doesn't trust herself around it. Dessie gets her a jar on her birthday and one at Christmas, and the rest of the time she does without. Lena goes into town and buys the biggest jar of Nutella she can find.

When she dings the shop door open, Noreen tries to give her an icy glare, but she's not constructed for icy glares, either physically or constitutionally, and it comes out looking more like she's holding in a belch. 'Ah, Nore,' Lena says, penitently. 'Don't be looking at me like that. Here: I brought you an apology.' She holds up the jar.

Noreen purses up her mouth and sniffs. 'It'd take more than that,' she informs Lena, but Lena can tell she's wavering. Noreen enjoys a good fight, but she hates holding on to a grudge; it gets in the way of conversation.

'We were a pair of snappy cows, the other day,' Lena says. 'No way round it. Mammy woulda made the two of us say Hail Marys till we were ready to behave ourselves and make up.' She sees Noreen's mouth twitch. 'I'll do it if I have to. Is that what you want? Hail Mary full of grace—'

'Jesus, go 'way outa that,' Noreen says, clapping her hands over her ears. 'Triggered, isn't that what the kids say? I'd never admit it to Father Eamonn, but whenever I hear that, all I can see is the look on Mammy's face, and her standing over us glaring.'

'There's one for the therapist,' Lena says. She pulls herself up to sit on the counter and opens the jar.

'What therapist? Have you got a therapist?'

'God, no. What for?'

'I thought Cal mighta got you into it. You know what the Americans are like: mad for the therapy. Does Cal do it?'

Lena fishes a couple of spoons out of her jacket pocket and hands one to Noreen. 'Where would he even find a therapist, around here?'

'On Zoom, sure. Wee Freya Kelly wouldn't go to school, and Alice found her a Zoom therapist that's all the way down in Wexford, and now she does breathing and she's grand. Cal could have a therapist in Chicago or anywhere.'

'Not that I know of,' Lena says. 'But I suppose there's always secrets in a relationship.'

'I don't think Dessie has any secrets,' Noreen says. She takes a big spoonful of Nutella and leans her elbows on the counter to lick it pensively. Her perm helmet is ragged at the edges, and she looks like she might have lost a bit of weight; her face, normally plump and neat, has a touch of sag under the eyes and the chin. 'I know that sounds like wishful thinking, but d'you know something, Helena, I actually wish he did have. Some days I wouldn't even mind if they were bad ones, as long as they were ones I didn't see coming a mile off.'

'They wouldn't be bad ones,' Lena says, scooping out her own spoonful. 'Dessie's a good man.' She means it. Dessie Duggan wouldn't be her style, but she appreciates the affectionate stolidity with which he not only weathers but tempers the force of nature that's Noreen. Lena's private opinion is that without Dessie, Noreen would have reached a level of overdrive where someone, possibly Lena, would have knocked her on the head just to get some peace.

'Ah, he is, yeah. I'm not complaining. Just, we've our silver anniversary next year, didja realise that? Twenty-five years. I can't remember the last time he did anything I wasn't expecting.' Noreen sucks on her spoon and gazes into space, considering. 'I'd say you and Cal still get surprises about each other,' she says. 'Do you?'

'We do, yeah,' Lena says. 'I reckon that's one reason we're in no rush to move in together. This way the surprises get spread out; they'll last us longer.' In fact, Cal himself was a big enough surprise that she's still getting her head around it. Until he came along she took for granted, without regret, that she'd used up that part of herself with Sean.

'Are you going to actually get married? Ever, like?'

'Being honest,' Lena says, 'probably not. We're happy. I wouldn't wanta risk messing that up.'

'Fair enough, I s'pose,' Noreen says, after a moment, sounding only half convinced. 'I won't go buying meself a hat, so. I'd just . . . I'd love to see you settled, d'you know? After everything.'

She's looking up at Lena appealingly, hoping she won't take offence. Lena is touched. 'I'm settled,' she says. 'This is as settled as I get. And sure, it's not like being married would make any difference. I was good and married to Sean, and then one day he was gone.'

'True enough,' Noreen acknowledges, with a sigh. She reaches over to take another spoonful. 'Double-dipping,' she says. 'And me always telling the kids only a savage would do that. After the last coupla weeks, but, if this is the worst I'm doing, I'm only delighted with myself. I oughta be hoovering up the Valium.'

'Things'll get better,' Lena says. 'Like you said. Now that they're letting Rachel come home.'

Noreen closes her eyes against that for a second. 'She's going to the funeral home up in town on Monday. They're not having a viewing, I'd say 'cause it's been so long that— D'you know what, Helena, I can't even think about it, I'll be in tears right here—' Noreen tips her head back, so she won't run her mascara, and takes a couple of deep breaths till she has herself under control again. 'Anyhow,' she says. 'The funeral's on Wednesday, once the last of Fintan's sisters flies in. And God forgive me, if Father Eamonn says one feckin' word about the sin of suicide, I'll haveta be dug outa him. I know that's his job, sins and all that, but there's a time and a place.'

'It'll be grand,' Lena says. 'I'll sit on you till you get a hold of yourself.'

Noreen's eyes pop. 'Helena! Are you coming? To the funeral?'

'Ah, yeah. I can't let you get yourself arrested. Who'd run this place?'

'Jesus,' Noreen says. She's staring at Lena, spoon suspended in midair, like she's wondering whether to book her a doctor appointment. 'Actually, like?'

'Look at that,' Lena says. 'People can still surprise you, even when you've known them all your life. Dessie could be next.'

'How come? I'm not giving out or anything, that's great, just I never expected—'

Lena shrugs. 'I thought about what you said, after. I reckon you've a bit of a point. Not a whole one, like, but a small bit.'

'I've always got a point,' Noreen informs her, recovering her poise. 'You oughta listen to me more. Are you going to call round to Claire?'

'Feck's sake,' Lena says. 'Don't rush me, girl; one step at a time. How's she doing?'

Noreen sighs and reaches for the jar again. 'Like you'd expect. The older ones are home, so at least she has them around her.'

'Have they any idea why Rachel mighta done it?' Lena asks. It takes an effort, like poking her finger through a membrane and hearing the tiny decisive pop.

'They haven't a clue. Not a notion. Claire says her course was going grand, she got on great with the family, she never seemed depressed or anxious or any of that, everything was grand. Isn't that terrible? Some of the girls think it'd be even worse if she knew the reason, 'cause probably it'd be something small that Rachel woulda got over if she'd only given herself the chance. But I think it'd be worse not knowing. You'd never stop wondering, like. If it was something where you coulda helped, if only she'da said it . . .' Noreen's mouth trembles. She takes a bite of her Nutella to manage it.

'What do you reckon yourself?' Lena asks. 'If anyone has an idea, it'd be you. Even if it's not solid enough that you'd say it to Claire.'

Noreen gives her a faintly puzzled look. 'I reckon there was something up between herself and Eugene. Most people do, sure.'

'What kinda thing? Did she say something to someone?'

'Not that I heard. Just, I saw them together that afternoon, and they didn't look great. And she didn't have any other reason, or not that anyone knows about. So . . .'

'Would she have found herself another fella, maybe?'

Noreen's puzzled look sharpens into wariness. 'Where'd you hear that?'

'I didn't,' Lena says. 'I wouldn't blame her, is all.'

Noreen has straightened up from the counter, chins out. 'Why would it matter? The poor girl's dead; what's it to anyone, either way? And since when did you give a shite about who's riding who around here?'

'I'm not just asking outa nosiness,' Lena says. 'It's 'cause of Trey.'

That knocks Noreen off track. Her eyes widen. 'Are you worried about her?'

Lena shrugs. 'She keeps asking about it, is all. Why Rachel did it, why anyone would. I reckon she just wants to understand, but I don't like her thinking about it all the time, d'you know the way? I don't like it being on her mind. She seems grand, but so did Rachel, didn't she?'

The catch in her own voice takes her by surprise. She shrugs again and concentrates on scraping her spoonful level on the edge of the jar.

Noreen gives a sudden, shaky puff of laughter. 'Ah, no, sorry,' she says, flapping a hand, when Lena looks up raising her eyebrows. 'You've every right to be worrying; God, aren't we all. Just, there was you, back when Sean was alive: "I'm not having kids, feck that, too much hassle, too much worry . . ." And now here's you in the same boat as the rest of us, worrying yourself mental over a child.'

'At least I dodged changing nappies,' Lena points out. Her reasons for staying childless weren't the ones she gave Noreen. She wasn't going to let any child of hers be ruled and shaped by Ardnakelty, but neither was she going to raise one behind her barricades; those were her choice, not one she had the right to make for anyone else. And yet, even though Noreen's wrong, she's somehow managed to be right. Here Lena is, exactly where she said she'd never be, battling this townland over a child.

'I'd take a mountain of nappies over this,' Noreen says. 'I would. With the nappies, and them not sleeping, and getting sick in your hair, at least you know where you are.'

'I would as well, to be honest,' Lena says. 'I'm well used to cleaning up shite, with the animals. I'm not used to this.'

'I always thought you'd do great with kids,' Noreen says. 'All of mine adore you, you know that, don't you? Honest to God, it's a great comfort to me, knowing if there's something they don't wanta tell me, they could go to you.'

'You mightn't like what I say to them,' Lena warns her. 'I'm a bad influence, remember?'

'Ah, stop that. I wouldn't mind what you say. Just so's they have someone they can talk to.' Noreen takes the jar back off Lena and stirs it absently. 'There's a few people saying Rachel mighta been playing offside,' she says. 'That's why I wanted to know where you heard it.'

'What people?'

'Ah, eejits, just. Michelle Healy, people like that. Gossipy aul' bitches, throwing muck at someone who's not here to defend herself.'

Lena asks, 'What does Mrs Duggan say about it?'

Mrs Duggan is Noreen's mother-in-law. Back when Lena and Noreen were kids, she ran the shop, along with its associated information network; now she spends her days immense and motionless in an armchair at Noreen's sitting-room window, trawling the street with pale, flat, expressionless eyes, but she still finds ways to get hold of what she wants. Mrs Duggan is even better at intelligence-gathering than Noreen, her tastes run darker, and unlike Noreen, she never parts with any of her hoard for free.

'She's said nothing. Sure, Dymphna wouldn't know much about the young people's goings-on, only what she hears from me and the kids. But I'll tell you this' – Noreen points her spoon at Lena – 'when Rachel was alive, I never got one sniff of her doing any such thing. Not a sniff. And I woulda known – sure, the dogs in the street woulda known; Rachel couldn't hold her water, God rest her, if you asked her for the time she'd give you her life story. I'd bet any amount of money that poor girl never in her life looked at any fella but Eugene Moynihan. Isn't that a terrible thing?'

'It is, yeah,' Lena says. She finds herself short of breath; it takes her a second to understand why. Here she is, involved. She's only put one toe into the river, but she can feel the surging voracity of the current sucking at her.

'If I hear anything about why she done it,' Noreen says, 'I'll let you know. To settle the child's mind.'

'Thanks,' Lena says. 'That'd be a big relief.'

Noreen has gone back to drawing swirls in the Nutella with her spoon, not looking at Lena. 'D'you actually wanta feck off to Dublin or somewhere?' she asks. 'Or were you only saying that 'cause I annoyed you?'

'Ah, I was just being a narky cow,' Lena says. 'Like I told you, I'm settled. I'm grand.'

'That's what I thought. Just, the kids'd miss you terrible, and I would as well, and you never know, do you? With people. You can't ever be sure.' Noreen is welling up again. 'Look at Rachel, just the day before she was in here buying hair spray and giving out 'cause the damp was wrecking her curls, and now . . .' She gives a huge, gulping sniff, puts a hand over her mouth, and starts to cry.

After a second, Lena scoots along the counter and wraps an arm around her shoulders. Noreen drops her head onto Lena's chest, disregarding her make-up altogether, and sobs like she's been saving it up for weeks. Lena sits there, holding her, and is taken aback by how natural it feels. The last time she hugged a woman was twenty years ago, when their mam was alive.

The bell dings and Mouth McHugh charges in, mud-splattered and halfway into a rant about the weather. He takes one look at the pair of them, stops in his tracks, horrified, and backs out. Lena and Noreen explode laughing. They clutch each other, rocking and laughing and gasping for breath till it sounds like sobbing all over again.

Mart, of course, spotted Tommy's car at Cal's place, just like Cal told Lena he had. He shows up around lunchtime, squelching across the field to Cal, who is taking advantage of a break in the rain to cover his vegetable beds with a layer of manure and straw, against the coming winter. Today Ardnakelty is being beautiful in a way that has an eerie tinge: the air is cold and still, filled with a haze that leaches colour away so that the greens fade into greys towards the horizon, like the fields are slowly turning to stone.

'Morning,' Cal says, straightening up on his spade, when Mart gets close enough. He's alone; Kojak took one look at the muddy field and flopped down in the shelter of the wall, to wait for Mart to finish his business.

'D'you know what that there mansion needs?' Mart says by way of greeting, pointing his crook at Cal's house. 'A name. You're here almost four years now, man, and here's everyone still calling this the O'Shea place, like you don't exist. Give it a name, and get a good big plaque for your gatepost. That'll put manners on them.'

'Half the house names around here, I got no idea how to even say them,' Cal points out, 'let alone what they mean. If I try naming this place, I'm gonna end up calling it Horse's Ass Hill or something.'

Mart hoots with laughter at that. 'Horse's Arse oughta be Tonecapall, if I'm remembering my Irish right. That's got a lovely ring to it. Go on, do it. I'll pay for the plaque.'

'I get enough shit in Seán's as it is,' Cal says.

'The lads'd enjoy themselves,' Mart concedes, 'but they'd come round in the end. You've earned naming rights; you have the place in great shape altogether.' He squints over at it. 'How's the aul' roof getting on?'

'Ready for winter,' Cal says. He goes back to his bucket of manure, courtesy of Skippy Gannon's cattle. He knows where Mart is heading, but he feels like making Mart do a little more of the work.

'Ah, that's great,' Mart says, smiling at him. 'I thought maybe Tommy Moynihan interrupted you before you had it done.'

'Nope,' Cal says. 'His timing was good.'

'Was he looking for a sideboard? I'da thought Clodagh's taste would lean more towards marble, with a bitta chrome on the side.'

'Tommy was looking for a personal PI,' Cal says. 'He wanted me to ask around, try and find some reasons why Rachel Holohan went in the river.'

Mart's eyebrows shoot up. 'Was he now,' he says. 'And what didja say to him?'

'Told him he'd got the wrong guy,' Cal says.

That sends Mart off into a fit of giggles. 'God almighty, I'da given a lot to see that,' he says, wiping his eyes. 'The great Tommy Moynihan, being told to stick it up his hole by some Yank that's only here a wet weekend. How'd he take it?'

'He wasn't happy,' Cal says. 'But hey, neither was I.'

Mart gives him a long look and a nod. The giggles have fallen away. 'Well,' he says. 'There you go, Sunny Jim. That's one crossroads behind you, anyhow. How does it feel?'

Cal has finished spreading the manure. He wipes his spade clean on the grass and moves on to the straw, which is also courtesy of Skippy. Straw is in short supply this year, after the summer's rain, but Skippy wouldn't take money. Cal is going to make him a display shelf for his father's old World War II models.

Mart watches him work. 'Rachel drank antifreeze,' he says. 'Didja know that?'

'I heard,' Cal says. 'I'd like to know why Tommy's so set on finding out her reasons. He said it was 'cause Eugene's upset, but I don't see that guy shelling out hard cash just to settle Eugene's feelings.'

Mart ruminates over that for a while. 'D'you know what age Tommy is?' he says suddenly, miffed. 'He's not a kick off sixty. You wouldn't credit it, wouldja? You don't see that fucker hobbling around on any aul' crook, and there's hardly a wrinkle on him.'

'A soft life'll do that,' Cal says. 'If you'da got yourself an office job, you'd look like George Clooney right now.'

'"A fine figure of a man,"' Mart says. 'That's what people say about Tommy. D'you hear anyone saying that about me?'

His eyes, squinting off at the mountains, are absent; he's talking to let his mind work. 'They say it behind your back,' Cal says. 'You oughta hear Noreen. I think she likes you.'

Mart grins automatically. 'I'll tell you what I think,' he says. 'We've the local elections coming up next spring. I think Tommy's setting up young Eugene to go into the aul' politics, God help us all. It runs in the family, sure: Tommy's dad, the Boss Moynihan, he was a county councillor, and he woulda been a TD, only for he had a heart attack and hadta take things easy. We all thought Tommy was headed the same way, in his young days – every time a pothole got fixed, there was Tommy at the door with a leaflet about how 'twas all his daddy's doing – but he changed his mind, in the heel of the hunt. I'd say once he got his hands on Clodagh's daddy's money, the entrepreneurial spirit took over.'

He watches a lone blackbird hop amid the sparse grass, searching for food. 'And now, Sunny Jim,' he says, 'now Eugene's got big and bold enough for the torch to be passed, only here he is in this place's bad books. Tommy can't afford to wait for that to blow over. If Rachel had reasons that weren't Eugene's fault, Tommy'll want to wave them under our noses. On the other hand, if Rachel had any reason that might come out at the wrong moment and look bad against Eugene, he needs to know.'

Mart nudges a scattering of straw into better alignment with the toe of his boot. 'I'd say he's wondering was Rachel up the duff,' he says. 'That'd scupper Eugene good and proper, if it got out. Breaking it off with a young one, or even doing the dirt on her, that's one thing; that could happen to a bishop. But getting her up the pole and then leaving her high and dry: that wouldn't go down well at all, at all, even with the forelock-tuggers. Or,' he adds, struck by an idea, 'he might wanta know did Eugene give her a disease of the unmentionables.'

'Jeez, Mart,' Cal says.

'Tommy'll be hoping 'twas the other way round, o' course,' Mart says, disregarding that. 'That Rachel was the one playing offside on Eugene, and her conscience got to her. That'd clear the decks, all right. The Moynihans wouldn't be getting run outa Seán's then. And it'd be great for Eugene's prospects. People'd have to give the poor betrayed cratur the vote.'

It has a strange feel, listening to Mart turn over the possibilities for inspection, the same way Cal would have listened to his partner bounce around a case back on the job. It layers in with the strange feel of the landscape, and the strange, dislocated feel of this last week or two. 'You don't even know he's running,' Cal points out. 'You pulled that outa your ass.'

'I'm exploring the possibilities, is all, Sunny Jim,' Mart says. 'Just exploring. Staying one step ahead.'

'Eugene always acts like he's too good for this one-horse place,' Cal says. 'You think he's gonna give up his cushy job in Dublin to hang around here listening to people bitch about potholes?'

'Eugene'll run for what he's told to run for, bucko. Tommy's the law in that house.' Mart smiles at Cal. 'And, sure, what's there to complain about? A good salary and a big expense account and a fat pension, and everyone around here treating you like you're Tom Cruise and Richard Branson rolled into one, and all you've to do for it is throw a few shapes now and again about the drink-driving laws or the EU regulations. 'Tis a great gig altogether. Sure, I'd do it myself, only I couldn't stick listening to all them Dublin accents. Eugene'll be on the pig's back.'

'That's if he gets in,' Cal says. 'You gonna vote for him?'

'I will in me hole. I'd enough of that lot with the Boss. If you think Tommy's a nasty piece of work, bucko, you shoulda seen his daddy.'

'I've seen enough Moynihans to last me a while,' Cal says. 'Thanks anyway.'

'You're safe enough. The man's dead thirty year or more; the second heart attack did the job.'

Mart is looking out over the landscape again, eyes narrowed, like there's something there to see besides empty pastures. The fields have the utter stillness of animals that could be sleeping or watching.

'There was a woman in it, back when I was a wee lad,' he says, 'and the Boss Moynihan was forcing her. Everyone knew it, and no one did a thing. Not even her husband. No one woulda approved of them making a fuss, d'you see, after all the Boss did for this place; 'twoulda been ungrateful. Uppity, like. "I own this town," that's what the Boss usedta say. And he did, bucko.'

'Well,' Cal says. 'Ain't this place just full of surprises.'

He had it brought home to him a long time ago that Ardnakelty has plenty of dark things buried under the sweet soft greens, but this one hits different. Cal knows why. When that story began, he was thousands of miles away and probably still in diapers, but now he's part of it. He got woven in, not when he told Tommy Moynihan to take a hike, but at some unremarked moment along the way when that decision became inevitable. He's starting to understand what Mart meant about crossroadses.

'I wonder if he'd get away with that now,' Mart says. The blackbird, alarmed by something, has taken off; his eyes track its curves across the grass, till it vanishes into the treeline. 'On the one hand, Sunny Jim, hashtag metoo; but on the other hand, it takes more than a few years and a hashtag to change a place. In this country we're fierce proud of how modern we are; we'd bulldoze every bitta history in the place for data centres, if it'd get us a pat on the head off the big corporations. But some of the old ways don't bulldoze easy.'

'Looks like Tommy thinks things have changed,' Cal points out. 'If he's worried that something about Rachel could get in Eugene's way.'

'Ah, well,' Mart says, 'the aul' elections are a tricky thing to manage, Sunny Jim, from Tommy's perspective. You can boss a man into promising you his vote, but once he gets into the polling station, he's his own man again. Sure, isn't that the beauty of democracy? If this place takes against Eugene, they mightn't say it, but they'll do it.'

He leans over, with an effort, to gather a handful of straw and scatter it on a patch that Cal missed. 'If there's interesting information floating about,' he says meditatively, 'I wouldn't mind having a look at it myself.'

'What for?'

'I won't know till I see it, sure. Isn't that my point? One step ahead, boyo: that's my favourite place to be.'

'If you go poking around,' Cal says, straightening up, 'Tommy's gonna find out. Then he'll go poking around to figure out why you're poking around, and you'll chase each other in circles all over the townland. And everyone'll just end up worse upset than they already are.'

Mart cocks his head and gazes at Cal like he just did

something unprecedented and refreshing. 'Do you know, Sunny Jim,' he says, 'I think that's the first piece of advice you ever gave me. Amn't I right?'

'I told you how to fix that faucet,' Cal says.

'Arrah, that doesn't count; you got it off YouTube. This was advice.' He smiles at Cal. 'That's what the crossroadses do: they change things. Didn't I tell you?'

'All the times you've given me advice,' Cal says, 'I figure it's my turn.'

'Fair enough,' Mart concedes. 'There's a difference, but. I'd always think my advice through, before I go handing it out willy-nilly. Would you say you've done the same?'

'Sure feels like it to me,' Cal says. He goes back to his straw. He's having to spread it thinner than he'd like, but he can't ask Skippy for more. Mart would give him some, but Cal doesn't like owing Mart.

Mart whacks his crook sharply on the vegetable bed, to get Cal's attention. 'Listen to me there, bucko. What you're missing is that Tommy won't just go away if the likes of yourself and myself ignore him. If he's trying to put you on the payroll, that means he can't afford to wait around hoping the answers fall into his lap. He's going to keep looking. If he doesn't get the ones he wants, or if he gets ones he doesn't want, that's when he'll turn interesting. I don't mind that myself, once it doesn't get outa hand, but we both know you don't like things interesting.'

Cal looks at Mart, and Mart looks back at him. 'This time you want something,' Cal says.

'I'm no different from Tommy,' Mart says, 'or from yourself. I'd only love a few answers. If I'm not to go looking for them, then maybe someone that's better fitted for the job should do it.'

'Huh,' Cal says. 'Seems like everyone around here's looking to get themselves a personal PI.'

Mart gives him an odd look, from under his hat brim. 'I'm

not talking about any PI, Sunny Jim,' he says gently. 'I'm only saying: Tommy's up to something, and a bitta clarity here could prevent a loada hassle. All round, like.'

Cal says, 'You reckon I should be expecting hassle from Tommy?' This has been at the back of his mind.

Mart smiles at him, his wrinkles deepening till Cal can't see his eyes. 'Ah, God, no. In the ordinary run of things, you'd get some nonsense offa him, all right. But these days Tommy's got too much on his plate to waste time annoying some fella just for having the nerve to say no.' He taps Cal's boot with the point of his crook. 'If I'm wrong, but, you know to tell me. Isn't that right?'

'I can handle Tommy,' Cal says. 'I just like being prepared.'

'You handled him yesterday, no problem to you,' Mart agrees. 'But here we are having this conversation all the same. And you're right to have it.' He fluffs up the straw that his crook flattened. ''Tisn't about handling anyone, Jean-Claude, or not yet. 'Tis all about communication. You communicate with me, and I'll communicate with you, and we'll all be good and prepared if things get interesting.'

He nods to Cal and trudges off, his crook sticking in the muddy ground. Kojak lifts his head and starts laboriously picking himself up. The hazy air slowly fades them both to grey, statues moving deeper into the stone fields.

The closest Lena willingly comes to cooking is making blackberry jam, which she does at the end of every summer, with berries from the brambles that grow rampant along the verges. She started off doing it because to her tastes the shop-bought jams were all sugar and no flavour, but she found a satisfaction stronger than she expected in the process: gathering this place's overlooked wild bits and pieces, with no permission needed from anyone, to make something she loves. She wonders if this is how the old wise women got their start, showing appreciation for their home places and sidestepping the regime via jam.

She takes a dozen jars out of her kitchen cupboard, packs them into a cardboard box, and loads them into the boot of her car, with some old cushions to keep the box from sliding about. She hopes to God Almighty she won't need all twelve, but she might as well be prepared for the worst. The dogs, excluded, give her heart-rending looks from the front window as she drives off.

As well as being better than the shop-bought stuff, Lena's jam has practical uses. Dropping round with a spare jar of jam is unassailably innocent – odd, coming out of the blue, but then everyone knows Lena is odd. And it comes with built-in boundaries: generous enough that she'll be invited in for a cup of tea and a chat, but minor enough that, even within the complex Ardnakelty barter system, no one will feel an obligation to repay the favour.

She starts off with Michelle Healy. Michelle is minding her toddler grandson and she mainly wants to talk about her daughter Georgia, who is apparently considering ditching the child's father and getting together with some fella who walks like a duck, and what should Michelle do about it? Michelle is the kind of relentless oversharer who makes words fall out of other people's mouths in response; even Lena, practised at saying nothing, barely manages to keep herself to something vague about not pressuring kids in case they push back. At least Michelle is frazzled enough, what with preventing the toddler from launching himself off furniture, that she doesn't register Lena moving the conversation from Georgia's love life towards Rachel Holohan's. Michelle heard that Rachel had a bit on the side, all right, but no one said who it was; and anyway Michelle only heard it from Julie Quinn and sure Julie'd believe anything, that's the problem with this place, if Georgia goes off with that duck-footed fecker everyone'll think she was riding him all along and he's the baby's dada and what should Michelle do about that?

Julie Quinn, surrounding herself with a jungle of houseplants since the last of her kids emigrated, would be happy to talk all day about anything Lena fancied. She heard from Laura Barry that there were rumours going around about Rachel, but she feels bad for listening, because her Niamh was pals with Rachel, and Niamh says there's no way. Niamh can't get time off work to fly home for the funeral; she's all the way over in Birmingham, on her own, grieving her friend. The thought makes Julie's eyes well up. Lena holds her hand, with its bitten nails. Julie gives her a potted begonia on her way out.

Laura Barry, who was the boss bitch in school and never liked Lena, is the only one to give her funny looks, but the jam forces her to provide twenty minutes of stilted chitchat, including the information – delivered with wide doll-eyes and a little pursed mouth, like Lena is committing a social gaffe by bringing up the subject – that Yvonne McCabe did mention Rachel had been spreading her wings a bit, but Laura doesn't think it's really fair to speculate, and did Lena want another cup of tea or . . . ?

Yvonne McCabe, still in her work clothes, is genuinely delighted to see Lena. She rousts a squad of noisy teenagers out of her kitchen, opens the jam on the spot, whips out scones to go with it, laments what this will do to her diet, and wants to hear everything Lena's been at since they last talked. It takes Lena forever to pick her way out of that and onto Rachel. Yvonne heard from Doireann Cunniffe that Rachel might have been messing about a bit, but sure why wouldn't she, if she was going to spend the rest of her life stuck to that gobshite? Yvonne reckons he can't even do the business without admiring himself in the mirror the whole time and patting himself on the back at the end. Lena laughs before she knows she's going to.

Doireann Cunniffe is easy. She spills the whole story

practically without assistance, which is lucky, because Lena is very close to being done with this. Doireann is also the only person who has no doubt that the rumour is true, because she heard it direct from Clodagh Moynihan, who heard it direct from Rachel herself. She pulls her cardigan closer around her shoulders – the house is overheated, but Doireann is always cold – sniffs up the drop at the end of her nose, leans in close enough that Lena can smell her hair spray, and talks a mile a minute in a breathy undertone. Clodagh would never have said a word, only she's off her head with worry about her Eugene, with people putting it about he was stepping out on Rachel, and isn't there a terrible lot of uncharitable types around here who love to think the worst? and at least Rachel had the decency to feel guilty and come clean to Clodagh, although she wouldn't say who the fella was but sure Doireann supposes you can't blame her, and Clodagh's that kind-hearted she never breathed a word to Eugene, just told Rachel it had to end, and isn't it a lesson to all of us that you never know what someone might be hiding, no matter how innocent they look. By the time Lena can disentangle herself from the spreading morass of unrelated gossip – Georgia Healy's been seen out and about with a new fella, and Doireann always had a hunch there was something about that baba, and Doireann's hunches are never wrong, it gives her the shivers sometimes – she's right on the verge of faking some medical emergency, if she had the brainpower left.

She drives home with all the car windows open, so the wet earth-smelling wind can blow her clean. Her mind is flooded with voices and names and crockery patterns. It's been thirty years since she talked to any of these women beyond cordial chitchat in Noreen's shop. She's raw, like every one of them stuck to her and ripped bits off when she pulled away. She never wants to see blackberry fucking jam again.

Within twenty-four hours all those women will have talked

to each other, and to everyone else. *Come here, you'll never guess who called round to me . . .* They'll comb through the conversations and spot the overlaps. Then they'll dig out possible explanations to pick over, and choose the ones that suit their own desires: Lena is a ghoul, and a filthy-minded one at that; Lena is feeling guilty because Rachel went to her and she did nothing to help; That Time of Life is sending Lena off her rocker; she's obsessed with Rachel because Rachel was Sean Dunne's secret love child. There isn't a single thing she can do about any of it, only sit still and let them tattoo her all over with their favourite patterns.

She got what she was after, anyway, or at least some of it. There's not a chance in hell that Rachel told Clodagh Moynihan she was cheating, and only a fool like Doireann Cunniffe would believe that – Clodagh picked her mouthpiece well. Tommy never needed Cal to find out whether Rachel was running around on Eugene; he knows fine well she wasn't. Probably he wants to find out what was in her mind, but meanwhile he wants that rumour spread; either to make Eugene into the poor innocent victim, or to keep people looking at that instead of at something else, or both.

Lena still reckons Rachel did this to herself, but she has a growing certainty that the Moynihans had some hand in it, more than she first thought. Something means they can't afford to let this death be; they need to get it in their grip and bend it, full force, to the shape they want.

She's well aware of what this means. She needs to back off, fast and far, and let the Moynihans and Mart Lavin's lot fight it out to have their way with all that's left of Rachel Holohan. Every bit of good sense she has, as well as thirty years of hard training, is tugging her to do it.

She's not going to. Underneath the rawness, a small part of her is sparking with triumph: she's getting somewhere. She pictures the look on Trey, the dawning change as she realises this place's rules don't have to rule her.

Lena's phone buzzes – Cal, probably, wondering if she'll be over for dinner. Lena ignores it. The only thing she wants less than jam is people; even Cal.

She realises that she's not going to tell him any of this. He'd bring it straight to Mart Lavin, to be knitted into whatever cunning piece of intricate manipulation Mart currently has under way.

One of the reasons Lena first wanted Cal was because nothing about him came from Ardnakelty. Every man she'd ever known had grown up twisted by the unceasing pulls of this place or one exactly like it. She knew Cal must have his own slants and twists built in, like everyone else, but she welcomed those because they had not one thing to do with this place. He came to her clean of it. Now here he is, waist-deep in its tangles.

Lena is doing this for Trey, not for Mart Lavin's use or anyone else's. She speeds up, to strengthen the wind coming into the car. She's nowhere near the river, but her head is bursting with its sound, the roar and the jabber.

7

Trey bikes over to Cal's on Saturday, just like she promised she would. She scribbles down something or other about Yeats, and they make a start on Con McHugh's wife's nursing chair – the baby is due at the beginning of January, so the chair needs to be ready for Christmas. They've never made one before, so they've been reading up and sketching for a while, working out their design based on the rocking chair Cal made for Lena a few years back. They're starting with the seat: tracing the pattern onto a thick slab of cherrywood chosen for its pretty grain, carefully cutting around it with the jigsaw, scooping out its hollow with curved draw knives. Its shape feels good in the hands. Curls of wood shavings fall to the dusty floor, and in the corner the radio plays quietly, some woman with a sweet undemanding voice singing about nothing much.

Trey is quiet. She looks tired; there are purple smudges under her eyes. Cal, expert at reading her various silences, can't tell what's under this one, whether she was just up late or whether she's drudging through the afternoon till she can take off into her real life. *Go on*, he wants to tell her. *You go run with your buddies, do dumb stuff you shouldn't, laugh your asses off. It's OK; I'll take care of this.* He knows he can't do that. Trey needs the money; her mama has nothing spare to give her. Cal would give her an allowance in a heartbeat, but she wouldn't take it.

He talks into her silences, about what to make for dinner and what poetry he liked back in English class and whether they should think about buying a bandsaw. If he keeps his mouth shut too long, he starts getting edgy: about Trey and school, Trey and Kate, about what she'll do for money if Mart was wrong and Tommy Moynihan sics his Revenue friend on their woodworking. Cal has never been much of a worrier, not over things that aren't right in front of his face. He wonders if this is what a midlife crisis looks like.

The kid sticks around to make chicken parmigiana and green beans, and to eat them, but as soon as they've washed the dishes she slings her schoolbag on her back and heads for her mama's place. Cal takes Rip for his evening walk, among the squelching leaves and the whiffs of turf smoke, and then doesn't know what to do with himself. Nothing on Netflix looks good. He thinks of calling Lena, but he doesn't want to mess with their routine two nights running; it feels like a surrender, an admission that things are shifting and there's nothing he can do but let them all be dragged along. The house is cold, a sullen cold that pushes up through the floor faster than the heating can drive it out. In the end he goes to bed early.

He's restless enough that he's half awake when, sometime after one in the morning, his phone beeps. It's Trey.

Can you come over

Cal sits up and looks at the phone. Trey has never called him in her life – according to her, only old people use phones for making phone calls – but this has every indicator of something that requires an actual conversation. He calls her.

It takes her a few rings to pick up. 'Yeah,' she says, warily, like she's doing something weird and suspect. 'So can you come over?'

'What for? Everyone OK?'

That gets a beat of silence. ''Cause,' Trey says eventually. 'We got Donie McGrath here.'

In the background Cal hears an excited murmur of other voices, tightly kept down. 'Where? Who's we?'

'My house,' Trey says. 'I *told* you.'

'Kid,' Cal says. 'What the hell?'

Trey blows out air impatiently. 'Can you just come? We're out the back of the house. In those trees up against the mountain. Can you not let my mam see you?'

'OK,' Cal says. He can't think of any way this makes sense, and definitely not a single way it could be good. Donie McGrath is the town lowlife; he has the temperament and the vocation for serious scuzzbaggery but not the brains, so he spends his time hanging around the fringes of anything squirrelly he can find, doing the real guys' grunt work and making his mama's house shake with gangster rap. There's no good reason why Donie and Trey should intersect. 'I'm on my way. Just hang tight and don't do anything dumb. We clear?'

'Yeah,' Trey says. 'Can you bring a torch? Mine got broke.'

'Sure,' Cal says. He's already pulling his pants on. 'See you there.'

He sticks to running lights and low speed till he's passed Mart's place. Then he turns on his high beams and floors it.

Sheila Reddy and her kids live in an old grey cottage a few miles away, tucked in under the mountain. Cal pulls over a couple of bends before the gate and leaves his car on the shoulder. The cloud has thinned just enough that the moon is a white haze, and he can see to make his way up the road towards the Reddy place, every window dark at this hour. He climbs over the wall and skirts the edges of the yard, keeping his flashlight off but ready, dodging Sheila's flower beds and heading for the grove behind the house. In among the trees is a light, faint but steady.

'You were ages,' a voice says in an undertone, from the shadow of a big oak. Cal has his feet braced and the flashlight raised before he realises it's Trey.

'What's going on?' he says.

'Over this way,' Trey says, and heads into the trees. Cal follows her, his feet sinking into layers of soggy leaves. The dark is thicker in here. He turns on his flashlight, cupping it with his hand to let out only a trickle of light so he won't trip over fallen branches.

They do in fact have Donie McGrath, very thoroughly. He's face down on the ground, with Aidan sitting on his back, Kate sitting on his thighs, Ciara sitting on his ankles, and Ross standing at his head with a phone flashlight pointed at him and a thick branch at the ready. Even in the dark and under three teenagers, Donie is recognisable. He's a fat little no-neck fuck – flabby couch-potato fat, not farmer fat – wearing the kind of tracksuit that Cal associates with multiple low-level felonies.

'Can he breathe?' Cal asks.

'Who gives a shite?' Trey says.

'Gonna be a lot more paperwork if he can't,' Cal says. Trey tilts her head, acknowledging this.

As they get closer, Donie comes to life and tries to wriggle himself free. 'Gonna kill ye all,' he informs the kids.

That gets snorts of laughter out of them. 'Not if we kill you first,' Aidan points out.

'He's gonna stink us to death,' Kate says. 'You should shower more often, d'you know that?'

'Bitch,' Donie says. 'Gonna kill you.'

'Well, look at that,' Cal says. 'He can breathe.' He goes around to Donie's head and squats down, outside spitting range. It's been a few years since the two of them last met, but Donie didn't enjoy the experience, and Cal is pretty sure he remembers it vividly.

'Well hey there, Donie,' he says. Donie has grown out his hair into a mullet that ought to be illegal, but he still has the stringy little bangs, held in place by so much gel that the night's events haven't budged them. 'I like the new hairdo.'

'Fucking prick,' Donie says, predictably.

'Language,' Cal says. 'There's young 'uns present.'

'Get them *off* me.'

'What's your rush?' Cal says. 'It's a beautiful night; it's not even raining. You just enjoy the fresh air awhile. Are his hands free?'

'Course not,' Trey says, affronted. 'We brought that garden wire stuff my mam has for the roses.'

'Great,' Cal says. He straightens up. 'Can you four keep an eye on him while Trey brings me up to speed?'

'No problemo,' Aidan says cheerfully. He bounces on Donie's spine. Donie lets out a whoof like a deflating air mattress.

Cal jerks his head at Trey to follow him, and heads deeper into the trees. Once they're far enough away for privacy, he stops.

'Kid,' he says. 'I'm gonna ask you again: what the hell?'

'Little shitebag's been hanging around our house at night,' Trey says. 'For weeks. Threw stones at our windows, poured pig shite all down the front door. Smashed up my mam's flower beds. Left a fox with the head taken off it on our step. Don't know where he got a fox; that little scut couldn't catch a fuckin' slug. Prob'ly roadkill.'

'Why didn't you tell me?'

'Didn't need to. 'M not a kid. I knew I could sort it myself. Or with the lads, anyhow.' Trey flicks her head backwards at her buddies. Cal swings the flashlight over to check on the situation. Aidan, still sitting firmly on Donie's back, waves. Ross is tickling Donie's nose with a long twig.

'We looked around during the day,' Trey says, 'till we found a buncha cigarette butts and a coupla empty cans over there, in the trees. So we knew that was where he was watching from. Then we just hid out here at nights waiting, and when he showed up tonight, we jumped him. We didn't know it was Donie, so we were thinking it'd be a fight, but it was like fighting a fuckin' marshmallow. Me and Kate coulda taken him on our own, no need for the rest.'

'For Chrissakes,' Cal says. He looks at her, standing there with her hair messy and a scratch down her cheek from wrestling around in undergrowth with that asshole, and feels a rush of warmth so strong it almost overwhelms him. No wonder the kid has been tired, no wonder she's been leaving Banjo to look after her family, and no wonder she wanted to spend most of her nights here. He has an urge to grab her and give her a bear hug, or a noogie, or something. 'You goddamn dumbass. He could've had a knife.'

'He did,' Trey says promptly. 'It was in his pocket, but. We figured it would be. Why would he be waving it about, all on his own out here?' She fishes a sizeable flick knife out of her jacket to show Cal.

'Jesus,' Cal says. 'Gimme that.' He takes the knife away.

'I woulda borrowed your gun,' Trey says helpfully, 'only I figured you'd say no.'

'No shit,' Cal says. The weight of the knife in his pocket makes him feel weak at the knees. 'You're still a dumbass.'

'We got him,' Trey points out, unfazed.

'Yeah you did,' Cal says. He finds himself suddenly and ferociously proud of her, which is probably the wrong response. 'And then you didn't know what to do with him.'

'We didn't think about that part,' Trey acknowledges. 'Aidan wanted to beat the shite outa him and dump him back on his mammy's doorstep, and Ross wanted to pull his kacks off and shove him in the river, but I said no. I wanta know what he was at, giving us hassle. He wouldn't tell us.'

'Well,' Cal says, 'with Donie, you just gotta know how to talk to him. I've had a productive conversation with him before, I can probably do it again.'

'I know, yeah. That's why I texted you.'

At least Cal still has a use in her life, even if it's only working over some Z-list mope. He can do that. He glances over at Donie, who has started squirming again – not with any real intent, just from the instinct to make things difficult. 'You do anything lately to piss Donie off?' he asks. 'You or any of your family?'

'Nah. Haven't even seen him.'

'You sure? Maybe he saw Maeve down in Noreen's and said something inappropriate, and she told him to fuck himself, something like that. Would you know?' Maeve is thirteen, but that wouldn't bother Donie.

Trey shrugs. 'People tell Donie to get fucked all the time. He'd just laugh at her.'

'True,' Cal says. 'How about anyone else? Your mama have beef with a neighbour, anything like that?' Donie is for hire. Donie also has the attention span of a fruit fly, except where money is concerned. If he's been hanging around here for weeks, Cal is betting there was cash involved.

'Not that she said. Maeve had a fight with her mates coupla weeks back, but she always does, and anyway it's sorted now.'

'Nah,' Cal says. 'OK, let's go find out. I like a challenge.'

Donie has got bored of wriggling and is lying still again, staring glassy-eyed at nothing. 'He's a frisky one,' Aidan says proudly, giving him a clap on the shoulder. 'I might keep him for a pet.'

'You'd never get him housetrained,' Ciara says.

'Just auction him off,' Kate says. 'My uncle's pigs went for two euros twenty the kilo. What d'you reckon he weighs?'

'Too much,' Ross says. 'The little fucker rolled on me, when we were taking him down; fuckin' flattened me. He needs to go on a diet.'

It's not bravado; they're genuinely having a blast. They're not one little bit worried about Donie, regardless of his flick knife and his general unsavouriness. On the one hand, they all have a bad case of teenage immortality; on the other, Cal agrees with them that, while Donie would have shanked any of them during the struggle without batting an eyelid, he's unlikely to have the follow-through for revenge plots. Cal plans to eliminate any possibility that they're all wrong.

'Have him stuffed and stick him on the wall,' he says. 'Who's got that garden wire?'

'Me,' Ciara says, waving it.

'Do his ankles,' Cal tells Trey. 'I like things nice and thorough.'

'Fuck *sake*,' Donie says.

'Hey,' Aidan tells him reproachfully. 'You heard the man: language. I don't want to get corrupted.'

'Except by Ciara,' Ross says. Ciara gives him the finger.

Cal aims his flashlight at Donie's ankles, Ciara scoots out of the way, and Trey squats down and starts tying them. Donie tries to kick out. Ciara gives him a smack on the leg, like a mama smacking a kid's hand away from a hot pan, and he settles down.

'Good,' Cal says, when Trey's done. The kid is thorough; someone is going to have a long night with a pair of wire cutters. 'Now you all head over there a ways. Me and Donie need some privacy. I'll text you when you can come back.'

'Aah,' Aidan says, miffed. 'We're the ones that caught him.'

'I know that. Do you butcher your own cattle, since you're the ones that raised them? Or do you leave that to the professionals?'

'You gonna butcher him?' Ross asks. 'Can we watch?'

'I haven't decided yet,' Cal says. Donie is lying still, a sullen lump ignoring the whole situation, like a toddler refusing to get dressed. 'Depends how bad he pisses me off.'

'Come on,' Kate says, getting up and dusting Donie residue off her jeans. 'Let the man get to work.' She pulls Aidan up after her and gives Cal a quick nod of approval. Cal, what with everything else on his mind, hadn't realised he was being evaluated. Apparently he's passed, at least so far.

He watches Trey and her buddies head off into the trees, shoving and snickering and hissing at each other to keep it down. Once their light gets far enough, he turns his attention to Donie. Donie, all trussed up, looks like a great big grub.

'Donie,' Cal says. 'My man. Long time no see. How'd your finger heal up?'

Donie tries to spit at Cal, but he doesn't have the angle. Cal takes a walk around him and points the flashlight at his hands, which are tied behind his back. Trey and her buddies didn't skimp on the garden wire; a crisscrossing snarl of it reaches halfway up Donie's forearms. One of his middle fingers is bent at an unnatural angle, halfway down, and has a lumpy look.

'You shoulda taken that to a doctor,' Cal says. 'What do you do when you want to give someone the finger? Use the other hand?'

'Untie me, man,' Donie says. 'They done it too tight. It's killing me.'

'And I've got a pain in my ass, son,' Cal says. 'We'll just have to suffer. What are you doing here?'

'Went for a walk,' Donie says.

'Son,' Cal says, still leisurely scanning Donie up and down with the flashlight, 'you and me go back, you know what I'm saying? And I gotta tell you, Donie, as a friend, I'm concerned about you. You're going downhill. I knew you were a scumbag, but I never thought you were the type of scumbag that goes around peeping on little girls changing into their nighties.'

'I don't peep on anyone.'

'Sure you do. Which one was it? The thirteen-year-old, or the seven-year-old?'

'Fuck off. I'm not into that.'

'Huh,' Cal says. He wanders over to Donie's head end and shines the flashlight in his face. He's gauging how scared of him Donie is. Donie is a pretty basic system, operated via a couple of simple dials: who can give him most, and who can scare him most. Cal has no intention of giving him anything. After their last encounter, Donie ought to have a useful level of fear going on here, but then again, Donie doesn't have much power of retention. If something isn't hurting him in the moment, he has trouble establishing any emotional connection to the fact that it might. 'Then what are you doing here?'

Donie, squinting into the flashlight beam, grins. 'Told you. I was out for a walk.'

'That's right,' Cal says. 'You did mention that.' He moves over to Donie's side and gets a good grip on the wire between his wrists. 'I like to think I'm a memorable guy, son. I'm vain that way. So it hurts my feelings, Donie, it pisses me *right off* when you forget one of the most important things about me, which is that I *don't like mopes being fucking predictable.*'

He yanks his handful of wire upwards, not hard enough to dislocate Donie's shoulders, but close. Donie opens his mouth to yell, and Cal gets a foot on his neck and shoves his face into the wet leaves. After a few moments he steps away and lets Donie flop back onto the ground. Donie blows and heaves and spits dirt.

'That refresh your memory?' Cal asks.

'You ripped my fuckin' *arms* out.'

'Nah,' Cal says. 'That was just a reminder.'

'What'd you do that for?'

Cal squats down by his head. Donie's pasty face is squished up against the ground, and he smells powerfully of stale sweat and cigarette smoke. 'If I have to work you over to make you talk, Donie, I'll do it good. And once you're done talking, I'll take you into town and dump you on the Guards' doorstep, and I'll tell them I caught you peeping on little girls and you came at me with a knife. And I'll have five witnesses, plus the knife, to back me up. You see that ending well for you, son?'

'Fuckin' sliced my *arms* open,' Donie says, flexing his wrists experimentally and grimacing.

'Last chance before I get bored,' Cal says. 'You here off your own bat, or did someone pay you?'

Donie grins up at him. He has to be scared by now, but Donie's emotions don't soak through all the layers; his eyes are still flat, like nothing much is happening. 'You wanta make me a better offer?'

'Nope. Who was it?'

'Nah, man. I don't wanta piss him off.'

'Probably not,' Cal agrees, 'but you don't want to piss me off either, and I'm here and he's not. Talk to me, or I'm gonna do it right this time.' He takes hold of Donie's wrist wire again and braces his feet.

'I'm fuckin' *talking*!' Donie yells.

Cal stops. 'Keep it down,' he says. The lights in the house are still off.

'It was Big Tommy Moynihan. Not himself; he sent his young fella. Little fuckin' ladyboy, thinks he's great. Holding his coat in like he didn't want it touching me.'

'I don't blame him, son,' Cal says. 'You look like you got diseases they haven't even named yet. What'd Eugene say?'

'Said his dad wanted Sheila Reddy scared. Nothing hands-on, he said, to start with anyhow. Just a bitta hassle.'

'He say why?'

'Nah, man. Not my problem. Maybe she pissed him off. Moynihans are all pricks.'

'When was this?'

'Last month sometime, I dunno.'

'You talk to them since?'

'The ladyboy rang me coupla weeks back. I gave him the update. He said keep going, I said that'll cost you, he posted me the cash – fuckin' pussy wouldn't send it off his phone, too scared he'd get in *trouble*.' Donie snickers. 'So I got back on the job. Take this shit off me, man.'

'You need a better career plan, son,' Cal says. He's thinking. Donie isn't going to be a problem any more, but Tommy is a whole different question. 'This one isn't working out for you. What are you now, headed for thirty? You planning on spending the rest of your life smearing shit on doors and getting beat up by kids?'

Donie shrugs, and winces when his shoulders don't like that. 'I do what I want, man.'

'Follow your dream,' Cal says. 'Just do it somewhere else. You come back here, I'm gonna beat the living daylights outa you, and then I'm gonna get what's left of you put on the sex offenders register. Same thing if you give any of those kids any shit. We clear?'

Donie works a piece of underbrush out of his teeth with his tongue and spits. 'Yeah. Whatever.'

'Good call,' Cal says. He doubts Donie could even identify any of the kids, apart from Trey, and Donie knows better than to go after Trey.

'Listen, man,' Donie says. He tries to squirm around to make eye contact. 'You say nothing to Moynihan, and I'll say nothing. Hah?'

'You're done talking,' Cal says. He moves back from Donie and texts Trey. *Get everybody back here.*

'I need a smoke,' Donie says.

'I don't smoke.'

'They're in my pocket.'

'I don't touch you unless I have to,' Cal says. His phone beeps: thumbs-up emoji. He glances up and sees pale flickers of light zigzagging among the trees. Trey and her buddies take shape out of the dark, quick as deer, in a rush of small rustles and the crunch of leaves. Cal catches Trey's eye and gives her a nod.

'What'd he say?' Aidan demands.

'Didja beat him up?' Ross wants to know.

'He looks OK,' Ciara says, disappointed, inspecting Donie's face. Donie grins and blows her a kiss.

'Same as he was,' Kate agrees. 'Ugly as fuck.'

'Aah,' Ross says. 'Then why'd we haveta leave?'

'Shut up,' Trey says, to all of them. 'Listen to him.' She jerks her head at Cal.

They shut up. Their faces turn obediently towards Cal.

'Me and this guy are done here,' Cal says. 'He won't be back. Ain't that right, Donie?'

'Fuck you,' Donie says sullenly.

'That means yeah,' Cal tells them. 'I'm gonna take all of you home, then I'm gonna take him back where he belongs.'

'What was he at?' Kate wants to know.

Cal looks at her. She has a straight stance and steady eyes. She looks like the only one, apart from Trey, who has some inkling that this might be more than an awesome way to pass a few nights; whose mind sees the outlines of a bigger picture.

'I'm not gonna tell you right now,' he says. Ross and Aidan make indignant noises, but he keeps talking to Kate. 'You've earned it, but I'm not clear on the details of what's going on here yet. Till I am, I'm gonna keep my mouth shut, make sure I don't screw anything up. I'll get you up to speed as soon as I can.'

'We done all the dirty work,' Aidan says, outraged. 'That fucker *farted* on me.'

'Quit whingeing,' Trey says. 'He'll tell you when he can.'

Cal is still looking at Kate. She gives him that steady gaze for another second; then she nods. 'Right,' she says. 'What do you want done with him?' She flicks her head at Donie.

'We'll stick him in my trunk,' Cal says. 'Let's go.'

Cal is pretty sure that untying Donie's ankles won't do them any good – Donie isn't the cooperative type, he'll slump on the ground and refuse to move – so they haul him to the car like a trussed animal, Cal and Aidan hoisting him by the armpits, the rest taking turns to wrangle his legs. Donie finds the whole thing entertaining. Once he tries to lick Aidan's face, and sniggers when Aidan yells and almost drops him.

They load him into the trunk, which is conveniently screened off from the rest of the car, for dog reasons. Donie accepts this without much reaction, like it's a regular part of his routine. Trey jumps into the passenger seat, and the rest of the kids pile into the back somehow. 'Mister,' Aidan says, leaning forward between the seats, as Cal pulls out onto the road. 'You gonna say this to our parents?'

In the corner of Cal's eye, Trey's face turns towards him. By rights he should have a long sit-down with every set of parents involved. But if Tommy Moynihan has the Reddys in his sights, Cal needs Trey and her buddies to keep talking to him.

'Nope,' he says. 'You're old enough that your parents are your problem. You want to tell them about this, it's your call.'

'No fuckin' way,' Aidan says.

'Toldja,' Trey says triumphantly to Aidan.

Donie starts kicking something, without much heat, just to create a nuisance. 'Simmer down back there!' Kate yells. 'This fella's trying to drive!' When Donie kicks harder, she starts to sing at the top of her lungs.

The five of them sing 'She Looks So Perfect' all the way down the twisting dark roads, over the sound of the engine and the smooth rush of air against the windows. The headlight beams stretch out far in front of them, seizing hedges and stone walls into vivid life for a moment before releasing them back into the night. Aidan has Ciara on his lap, with his arms around her, and they're all swaying back and forth to the song. Cal didn't think Trey was even acquainted with that kind of music, but she knows all the words.

Cal drops off various kids at discreet distances from whatever houses they're supposed to be at, and they vanish expertly into the dark, waving cheerfully. Then he and Trey head back towards Ardnakelty.

Donie has quit making a ruckus, but he still gives the occasional token kick. 'He's alive, anyhow,' Trey says, nodding backwards at the trunk.

'Yeah, well,' Cal says. 'You can't have everything.'

Trey grins. 'What'd he say?' she asks.

'He says Eugene Moynihan hired him.'

'The fuck?' Trey sits up straight. 'Why?'

'Keep it down. 'Cause Tommy wanted your mama scared.'

'Why the *fuck* would that arsehole—'

'Donie doesn't know.'

'*Says* he doesn't.'

'He doesn't. Would you tell Donie anything, if you were Eugene?'

'He hasta have *some*—'

'Not now,' Cal says. 'We'll talk about it later.'

Trey shuts her mouth. For a minute she glances over her shoulder at Donie, like she's considering taking another shot at him, but in the end she settles back in her seat and watches the road disappear under the Pajero's tyres. The simmering quality of her silence and the set of her jaw both say she's thinking up things to do to the Moynihans. Cal is going to have to defuse that, but first he needs to deliver Donie back where he belongs. He's looking forward to that part.

His mind is on the Moynihans, too. If Mart is right – and when it comes to this place, Mart is mostly right – Tommy Moynihan's main focus right now is Eugene's political career, and Cal can't see any way that would be furthered by hassling a bunch of kids and a woman who stacks supermarket shelves. On the other hand, he can't see Tommy putting time and energy into side quests, what with everything else on his plate. This makes no sense.

The Moynihans haven't quite worked up the balls to put in a remote-controlled gate, but of course their place has a fancy motion-activated security system, which blasts floodlights in Cal's face as soon as he turns in between the tall concrete gateposts. He pulls right up to the front door. 'You stay in the car,' he says. 'Keep your head down.'

Trey doesn't bother answering that, just hops out and slams the door. On second thought, Cal sees no point in dying on this hill. Donie knows Trey. Regardless of whether Tommy sees her face, he's going to hear what she did.

'Wave to the cameras,' he tells Trey, as he gets out of the car. He grins and waves like a maniac.

Trey snorts with laughter and does the same. 'C'n I moon them?'

'No,' Cal says, going around to the back of the car.

'Why not?'

''Cause I don't want to see that. Evening, Donie.'

'What the *fuck*,' Donie says, outraged, when he's struggled into a sitting position and taken a look around. 'We were gonna keep Moynihan outa it, man.'

'You were,' Cal says. 'Me, I don't give a shit whether you get paid or not. Let's go.'

Donie expresses his sense of betrayal by deciding his limbs don't work. Cal and Trey have to manoeuvre him out of the car chunk by chunk, while he stares sulkily up at the lid of the trunk, and haul him to the doorstep by his armpits. He slumps and lets his feet drag; Tommy is going to have to get someone to rake his pretty gravel smooth.

Tommy, alerted by his app or his butler or whatever, is waiting for them in the doorway, wearing pyjamas and a plush maroon bathrobe that looks like someone just steam-cleaned it. Cal considers sticking with tonight's direct approach and just punching Tommy in the face, but he knows better. Tommy is no Donie.

They dump Donie on the doorstep. Tommy takes a step back and raises his eyebrows, looking for an explanation.

'Evening, Mr Moynihan,' Cal drawls. 'I'm right sorry to disturb your beauty sleep, but me and Trey here, we found something of yours at her mama's place. So we brought it back to you.'

Tommy inclines his head to stare at Donie. 'My God, man,' he says. 'Is that Mrs McGrath's young lad? What's after happening to him?'

'He's safe and sound,' Cal says. 'Or close enough. No need for a reward; just being neighbourly. Like you said to me, the other day: neighbours gotta look out for each other.'

He nods to Tommy and gets back in the car. Trey slams her door good and hard, for emphasis.

'So,' Cal says, starting the car, 'where'm I taking you?'

'Yours,' Trey says. She's craning her neck to watch, in the rear-view mirror, as Donie tries to wriggle himself up to standing, and Tommy ignores him to gaze after them. 'Can I?'

'Sure,' Cal says. This is the first moment he's had to let the relief sink in. He almost reaches over to mess up her hair, or something. 'Course you can. Text your mama.'

Trey rolls her eyes, but she pulls out her phone. 'How come you didn't ask that fucker why he sicced Donie on us?'

''Cause he wouldn't tell me, and I can't make him. I was a cop too long to ask questions when I won't get an answer. Sets the wrong tone.'

Trey nods, acknowledging that. 'Hang on,' she says suddenly, as they round the bend towards the village. 'Pull over.'

'You OK?'

'Yeah. Turn your lights off.'

'What for?' Cal says, but he pulls over on the shoulder and switches off the lights.

'Back in a minute,' Trey says. She slides out of the car and is over the wall like a fox.

Cal leans across to her door, but she's already invisible, just a rustle in the field, and he can't call after her; any sound travels for miles out here. 'Shit,' he says, to no one.

He sits there, hoping no one happens to pass by, and listening. In spring and summer, the nights around here are alive with creatures mating, hunting, fighting, raising their babies. With autumn, things turn silent, as birds leave and animals draw deeper into the warmth of hidden shelters; only a few creatures are out and about tonight. Their sparse scattering of noises seem sudden and loud as warnings.

After what feels like an hour but is actually only sixteen minutes, Cal hears that rustle again, and a shadow drops over the wall. 'Let's go,' Trey says, hopping into her seat. 'Keep the lights off.'

Cal moves off as quietly as the Pajero can manage. 'What'd you do? They see you?'

'Nah,' Trey says, with scorn. 'I wasn't gonna go into Moynihans', with them stupid floodlights. I just kept low and went up to the corner of the wall. Tommy wouldn't bring that little scut inside his house, all mucky and everything; I knew he'd talk to him outside.'

'You hear anything?'

'Yeah. Tommy wants us out.'

'Who? Out like what?'

'Like out. Outa our house. Donie said – he was just sitting there on the step like a fuckin' kid; Tommy musta done his wrists with wire cutters, and Donie was poking at his ankles like he was waiting for his mammy to come do it for him. Donie was bitching about wanting money, and Tommy was like, "I don't owe you anything. I was paying you to get them out. They're still fuckin' there. And now they know it was you, and you've been warned off, I'll have to start from scratch. I oughta be getting a refund off you." Then he slammed the door and Donie started banging on it with the wire cutters, so I done a legger in case Tommy called the Guards.'

'Tommy's not gonna call the Guards,' Cal says, before he realises: Tommy isn't your standard country boy who considers the police to be useless at best and a royal pain in the ass at worst. Tommy has plenty of uses for the Guards, and regardless of how dirty his hands are, he can call them in all he wants.

Trey says, in a voice that's set for warfare, 'We're not leaving that fuckin' house.'

'Damn right you're not,' Cal says. His anger at Tommy is rising, too, but it can wait; he needs to think. This still doesn't make sense. There was a time when running the Reddys out of town would probably have won a few votes, but that time is over, and anyone with Tommy's connections would know that. This has to be personal. 'You guys piss Tommy off? Or Eugene? Or Clodagh?'

'Never even see 'em. Don't wanta.'

Cal is thinking about the ugly story Mart told him, about Tommy's daddy and the woman. He wonders what Sheila would say, if she was asked whether she's had any problems with Tommy. It's not a question Cal could ask her, but Sheila and Lena go way back. Then he wonders what Rachel would say.

'You reckon they want the house?' Trey asks. 'For Eugene to live in, or something?'

The Reddys' place is a chunky little cottage, about the same vintage as Cal's, that they rent from some kind of cousin-in-law of Lena's – Cal still doesn't have all the relationships straight around here, but he doesn't spend too much time on it, since the simplest thing is to just assume everyone is related half a dozen ways. The cottage has three bedrooms, a faint year-round smell of damp, and cracks in unsettling places. Even if Mart is right and Eugene is planning on moving back to the boonies to run for office, Cal can't imagine that Tommy would want the place for him.

'Nah,' he says. 'It wouldn't be up to their standards. No conservatory.'

'Then what the fuck?'

'I dunno, kid,' Cal says. 'We'll find out.' Mart would laugh his ass off: apparently Cal is turning out to be someone's PI after all. 'Meanwhile, you tell your mama to make sure the house is in good shape. Food in the fridge, clean clothes on everyone, no dirty dishes lying around.'

'We already *do* that. How come?'

''Cause,' Cal says. 'Now that Tommy can't use Donie any more, he's gonna go looking for another way to scare you guys out. I reckon there's a decent chance he'll try siccing Child Protective Services on you, or whatever it's called around here.'

'*Fuck* him,' Trey says, clear and hard. 'He better not.'

'You just stay one step ahead,' Cal says, 'and it'll be fine.' He's nowhere near as relaxed about this as he's trying to sound. 'You guys been going to school lately?'

'Yeah. Mostly.'

'Good. Then he can't use the truant officer. Any of you been stealing from Noreen?' Trey used to shoplift from Noreen on a semi-regular basis, partly out of need, partly as a fuck-you. A while back Cal explained to Trey that this left him obligated to pay her debts, and that was the end of that.

'Not me,' Trey says promptly. 'Swear to God. And not Alanna. Don't think Maeve and Liam do, but I dunno.'

'Tell them if they do, they need to quit. All of you need to be squeaky-clean, the next while, till we figure out what's going on here.' Cal peers out the windscreen, trying to spot his turn. He's taking the long way home, skirting around the village, where a car at this hour is unusual enough that Noreen or someone wakeful might take a look out their window. 'How much do the little kids know about what's been going down?'

'They heard him throwing rocks at the windows, but I told them it was my mates messing. Maeve saw the flower beds. The shite on the door, and the fox, I found those, so I got rid of them before anyone saw.'

Cal swallows down, for now, the thought of Trey cleaning up Donie's messes. 'How about your mama?'

'She knows most of it. Not about me and the lads hiding out for Donie, like. But she saw the stuff he did.'

Cal doesn't fool himself that he has the measure of Sheila Reddy, or anywhere near it. Sheila had a tough life, married to Trey's daddy; it turned her into a tough woman, one who thinks along strange concealed lines.

'Did she have any guesses about who was doing it?' he asks. 'Or why?'

Trey shrugs. 'Nah. I left Banjo with them,' she adds, a little defensively. 'When I went out.'

'I know,' Cal says. As a guard dog, Banjo is about as useful as a cheese sandwich, but he makes a good alarm system. The thought of the kid trying to balance living her life with protecting her family makes him wish he had dislocated Donie's shoulders while he had the chance. 'You did good. But, kid: leave it, for now. Don't do anything.'

'Like what?'

'Don't give me "like what",' Cal says, craning his neck for the next turn, which should be hidden among the hedges somewhere, unless he's lost. 'Like anything. About Tommy, or Eugene, or Donie. Not till we get a better idea what's going on here. I know you want to start cracking heads, and I don't blame you. But with a guy like Tommy, you don't get mad, you get smart.'

'So I'll find out what's going on,' Trey says. 'Like I just did.'

'Well,' Cal says. He needs to be careful. If he forbids her to do something she's going to do anyway, all that will change is that she'll keep it to herself. 'You can keep your ears open, talk to people, see what you pick up. But you gotta be subtle. Nothing that anyone would notice.'

'Turn's there,' Trey says helpfully, pointing.

'Kid.'

'OK,' Trey says, after a second. 'For now.'

'I got your word on that?'

'Yeah.'

Trey takes her word seriously. 'Good,' Cal says, swinging into the turn. 'If we need to do something, we'll do it, don't worry. Just not yet.'

Trey nods. 'Thanks,' she says gruffly, to her window. 'For coming over, and everything. Sorry for getting you outa bed.'

'It's fine,' Cal says. 'I'm glad you did. Only thing I wish is that you'd called me in earlier. I'm right here, I might as well come in handy.'

'Yeah. I know.'

'I mean it,' Cal says. 'You wanna do something nice for me, in exchange for tonight? Next time, call me in *before* you've got some mope tied up with garden wire.'

Trey rolls her eyes. Cal can't tell whether she'll do it, but he hopes she's at least accepted the option. 'And, kid,' he says. 'The part about the Moynihans, and that stuff you heard. I'd rather you kept that to yourself, for now. We don't need it spreading all around town. You don't need to lie to your buddies; just let 'em think we dumped Donie at home.'

He knows he might be asking too much. Her buddies are the centre of the universe; keeping things from them is against nature. Trey nods promptly, though. 'Ross'd talk,' she says. 'Aidan wouldn't, but he'd tell Ciara, and she would.' She glances over at him. 'Kate won't.'

Her face in the dashboard's glow, shadowed in strange places, looks older and mysterious. 'OK,' Cal says. 'You gonna tell her?'

'I reckon. Yeah.' She watches to see if he's going to cut up rough.

'All right,' Cal says. 'You know her; your call. Just keep in mind, kid: Tommy's a scuzzball, and we haven't figured out what he's playing at. The less Kate knows, the safer she is.'

'She won't care,' Trey assures him.

'Oh well then,' Cal says. He manages not to point out that Kate's mama and daddy might care a lot. Being responsible for Trey is about all he can handle right now; Kate's mama and daddy are going to have to look out for themselves. 'The rest of 'em gonna tell people about Donie?'

'They might,' Trey says, after a second. She looks younger again and anxious, watching him to see if she screwed up. 'Prob'ly. I can tell them not to, but . . .'

'But the story's too good to waste,' Cal says. 'Don't worry about it. Donie doing Donie-type crap isn't gonna raise anyone's suspicions. You guys'll probably get a medal for taking him down.'

Trey grins, reassured. 'C'n I have the knife?' she asks.

'No,' Cal says. They're coming up towards Mart's place; he dims his lights and slows down to a crawl. 'And if you make one single sound before ten in the morning, I'm gonna whup your ass.'

Trey, unintimidated, grins again and settles back in her seat to start texting somebody. As Cal turns in at his gate, he hears her humming 'She Looks So Perfect' to herself.

8

Lena waits till early Monday afternoon, when Sheila will have finished her shift at the supermarket but the kids won't be back from school yet, to call over. It's still new to her, knowing Sheila's schedule well enough to predict when she'll be home. Back when they were teenagers, Lena and Sheila were close enough that they're in all each other's wild memories. Their men took them in different directions, and for a long time neither of them wanted the other, or anyone. Things have been changing. When Sheila's house burned down and her husband ran off for good, the summer before last, she came down off the mountain, got herself a job, and started unfurling out of years of heavy silence into someone Lena recognises. She's the only person in Ardnakelty whom Lena counts as, give or take, a friend.

It's drizzling, but Lena's wax jacket is solid and Sheila lives only a mile and a half away, so she walks. Lena considers driving around here to be a pure waste, not of petrol but of Ardnakelty. Her feelings about the people have never managed to touch her deep joy in the place itself, both intimately familiar and inexhaustible: no matter how well she knows it, there's always a new pattern of lichen spotting a stone wall, or a strange swirl of clouds over the fields, or a different shading to the scent of the air. It was one of the things that kept her alive, after Sean died. She walked the roads for hours, trying to walk her mind empty, and along the way she lost the option of feeling that the world had stopped. Lena is unsure whether this is symmetry or irony:

Sean kept her in this place with him, and then the place kept her here without him.

When she has to step onto the verge to let a car pass, mud squelches under her runners; over the walls, the fields are waterlogged and the grass is sparse. The winter is going to be a hard one: this spring it rained enough to delay all the planting, and the last few months it's rained enough that the harvest was whatever scraps the farmers could grab during brief dry spells. Above the fields, the mountain, unaffected, flaunts its full autumn richness, yellow gorse and dark spruces and a hundred shades of gold and brown.

Sheila is home. Her kitchen is small, darkened by the loom of the mountain behind it, but she's made it a good place to be. Her house on the mountainside was clean but scraped bare and drab, like she had enough in her to meet the minimum but nothing more. Here the walls are painted a bright turquoise and hung with small watercolours and kids' drawings, the worn floor tiles are waxed to a shine, and there are straggly plants in pots on the windowsill.

The red checked tablecloth is laid out with a teapot and mug, an open box of éclairs, and one half-eaten on a plate. 'When I was a kid,' Lena says, 'that's what I swore I'd do, once I grew up. Cake for lunch, and stay up all night. You're living the dream.'

'I am,' Sheila agrees. She finds Lena a plate and a mug. 'One day last week I had pick-and-mix sweets for my lunch. Nothing else, just sitting here stuffing my face with bonbons and jelly babies. I'll be fat as a fool.'

'You won't,' Lena says. She says it as fact rather than reassurance. Sheila is tall, long-limbed, and bony, the type that never puts on weight. She's nothing like Trey, who is far enough from striking to be near-invisible when she wants to be. Sheila's face is all hard, sweeping curves, and her rough auburn hair is pulled back in a ponytail that shows them starkly. Sheila used to be beautiful; even now that she's too weather-worn for beauty, Lena likes looking at her.

'I always thought I'd like to be fat,' Sheila says. 'It'd be great after a hard day: you could sit there on the sofa and have plenty of yourself to get hold of. All that lovely soft stuff, all your own.'

Lena is grinning, and Sheila grins back at her. 'You watch,' she says. 'I'll be bursting outa these jeans in no time.'

She pours the tea. Lena settles back in her chair and warms her hands, cold from the walk, on the mug. 'Cal said Donie McGrath was giving you hassle,' she says.

Sheila nods. 'He won't be back,' she says. 'They caught him Saturday night, Trey and her pals. I was watching them, out the window.' She puts an éclair on Lena's plate. 'Was that Cal with them?'

'It was,' Lena says. 'But it was Trey and her mates that did the spade work; Cal just helped them tidy up. They had Donie all trussed up and ready for market before he even got here.'

Sheila smiles a little. 'I like her pals,' she says. 'She doesn't bring them around much, but I like what I see. They take no shite.'

'The young people nowadays are better about that,' Lena says. 'D'you remember Sister Breda? Hitting us with the ruler for talking, screaming at us that we oughta be disgusted with ourselves if we wrote off the lines, and it never even crossed our minds to say anything. If anyone tried that on Trey, she'd tell them to get fucked and walk out.'

'She would,' Sheila agrees. 'I'd like to see it.'

The éclair is good: fresh from a bakery, not packaged stuff. Lena asks, 'Did Trey say why Donie was hassling you?'

Sheila shrugs. 'Donie likes upsetting people,' she says. 'And here's me with a buncha kids, and no man in the house to give him a hiding. I'm not easy upsetted, but he wasn't to know that.'

Lena says, 'Tommy Moynihan hired him to do it. He wants you outa this place.'

Sheila puts her mug down on the table and stares at her.

Lena asks, 'Was Tommy at you?'

Sheila's eyes meet hers with complete understanding. Both of them have spent enough years alone to know how many men believe that a woman without a man is fair game: the ones who lean too close in the shop and grin knowingly, stare at the wrong parts and press against you in ways that can't be proved and make sly comments about you being lonely; the ones who offer you a lift home and slide a hand up your thigh; the ones who show up on your doorstep, late at night after a few drinks, some sheepish, some cocky, some frightening, all of them taking for granted they have a right to come in.

'Not Tommy,' Sheila says. 'He never even gave me one look that was outa line. Did he with you?'

'No,' Lena says. 'The worst he ever did was patronise the fuck outa me. But I thought I'd ask.' She knows that, whatever she's had to deal with from men, Sheila has had worse. The widow of a respectable farmer is in a different category from a woman who's been used and abandoned up the mountain by one of the good-for-nothing Reddys.

'He's not that kind,' Sheila says. 'He likes having people under his thumb, but he likes doing it here.' She touches her forehead. 'He wouldn't do it with his own body.'

'That'd be beneath him,' Lena agrees. She told Cal she'd ask, but she's unsurprised. Cal doesn't have the measure of Tommy yet. He hired Donie rather than do his own dirty work; the distance is part of the power. 'Has he anything against you? Or does Clodagh?'

'Clodagh wouldn't talk to the likes of me,' Sheila says. 'I turned down a job off Tommy last month. He didn't seem bothered, but you'd never know with that fella.'

'A job? At the plant, like?'

Sheila shakes her head. 'Tommy said a pal of his needed a

shift manager for his shop over in Athlone, and he'd put a word in for me. 'Cause of my situation – that's what he called it, my *situation*.' The corner of her mouth lifts with amusement.

'God, he's some tulip,' Lena says. 'Is that why you turned it down?'

'I don't want favours off Tommy Moynihan,' Sheila says. 'And anyway it woulda meant moving to Athlone.' Lena's eyebrows go up. 'Tommy said that like it was a great thing: a fresh start, he said. Like he thought I'd get down on my knees and kiss his hand.'

Lena says, 'He really wants you outa this place.'

'I know, yeah. I haven't a notion why he'd give a shite.' Sheila, lifting another éclair from the box, seems undisturbed. 'I'm going nowhere. I only just got back down here, sure.' She flashes Lena a quick, almost shy smile. 'I've friends at work now, didja know that? I went for lunch with them, the other day. And myself and Yvonne McCabe, d'you remember her? We take turns getting the kids from school.'

Lena says, 'Cal reckons Tommy's trying to get Eugene onto the county council. He thought maybe you knew something about Eugene that could scupper his chances, so Tommy wants you gone before you talk.'

Sheila looks up from the éclair. She says, 'Did Cal send you to ask me?'

'No,' Lena says. 'Or yes and no, more like. He wants to find out why Tommy's out to get you, 'cause he's worried about Trey. It isn't just him, but. I'd love to know as well.'

'Trey's grand,' Sheila says. 'We're staying put.'

'I figured that, yeah,' Lena says. 'But she wants to know what's going on around here, and I don't see why she shouldn't.'

Sheila thinks this over. 'What good would it do her?' she asks.

'She's talking like she wants to stay here,' Lena says. 'To live, like; after school. I'd rather she didn't do it the way either of us did.'

They look at each other, across the small cheery table and the sweet smell of tea, seeing in each other's face the wild girl and everything that brought her to here. The rain murmurs, soft and ceaseless, against the windowpanes.

Sheila nods, accepting that. 'I know nothing about Eugene,' she says. 'How would I?'

'That's what I figured,' Lena says. 'Cal's feeling protective, is all. When he gets like that, he goes after every answer he can come up with. Like clay-pigeon shooting: he fires them all out there and sees how many he can take down.' Sheila smiles. Her smile still has an out-of-practice look to it, like she's doing something risky.

'I figured that one would get shot down,' Lena says. 'What I wondered about was Rachel Holohan. Something was on her mind, to make her do what she did. I wondered if you had an idea what it was, maybe, and Tommy wasn't happy about that.'

Sheila shrugs. She puts a hand to the side of the teapot, checking the temperature. 'I'd say Rachel just had more weight on her than she could hold,' she says. 'The Moynihans are awful heavy. Once you got in under them, you'd never get out. You wouldn't be able to breathe, even.'

'They'd be a lifestyle choice, all right,' Lena agrees. 'I wouldn't fancy it myself.'

'That's one reason I wanted Johnny,' Sheila says. 'Everyone thought 'twas only 'cause he was a fine thing, but I wasn't that thick. I wanted Johnny 'cause there was nothing to him, only the laughs and the rides. He was light. I felt like, if I wanted to, I could always get out from under him.' She gives Lena a sudden grin. 'Not like that.'

'I wasn't thinking any such thing,' Lena says, mock-primly. 'You've a filthy mind.'

Sheila grins again, but her mind's not on it. 'Your Sean was different,' she says. 'He'd weight to him.'

'He did, yeah,' Lena says. 'I knew if I took up with him, I wouldn't get out. I wanted him enough that I was all right with that.' This is as close as she's come, ever, to talking about Sean with anyone. It feels dangerous. Part of her is pulling to get up and leave.

'I oughta have wanted that,' Sheila says. 'But I didn't. So I went with Johnny.' She gets up to turn the kettle back on, taking the teapot with her. 'I wasn't reckoning on the kids. I was on the pill and all, but Emer came anyway. There's no man in the world that can hold you down like a child.'

She dumps the tea bags in the bin and reaches into a cupboard for fresh ones. 'Rachel came here,' she says.

Lena looks up, startled. 'When?'

'The night she died. Six, maybe. On my doorstep, mascara all down her face, saying please could she ask me something.'

'Did you talk to her?'

Sheila nods. 'The little ones were in watching the telly, so I brought her in here and made her tea. I was curious why she thought of me. I never said two words to the girl in my life.'

When she thinks about it, Lena feels like she shouldn't have been surprised. If Rachel wanted to ask a woman whether her man was worth losing her friends, Sheila would be the obvious place to go.

'She wanted to know about Johnny,' Sheila says. 'Me and Johnny. She knew plenty already. She knew how, when he done the legger to London, he done it with money he talked outa Fiona Kelly, saying he was in love with her.' The corner of her mouth lifts wryly. 'The poor young one didn't mean to say that; it slipped out. She was awful worried then, in case I didn't know. I knew everything Johnny did.'

Lena nods. Johnny was never any match for Sheila. If he thought he was, it was because Sheila let him.

'She wanted to know what I done about it,' Sheila says. 'Did

I say anything to him, all the times he was talking people outa their money, or selling them stuff he'd robbed offa someone else. How did I try and stop him. Did I threaten to leave him. Did I ever warn people what he was at.'

This isn't what Lena was expecting. She finishes off her tea, to make room for the reheat, and starts rearranging her thoughts.

The kettle boils, and Sheila pours a dash of water into the teapot. 'I told her,' she says, 'themens around here can look after themselves. I done it for long enough; they can do the same. I done nothing about Johnny till I needed to. I watched him, is all. I kept my eye on him. And when I needed to, I put a stop to his gallop.'

She swirls the water and dumps it out in the sink. 'I don't reckon she believed me,' she says. 'She was sitting there, big eyes on her, "Ah yeah I know, people can be total bastards and they were treating you like shite, prob'ly it served them right, but like, what did you say to him?" She thought I was just sore at people for cutting me off when I married Johnny, and when it came down to it, I wouldn't stand by and watch while he fucked them over. She had it arse-backwards. I'm not sore at anyone, but I wouldn't lift a finger for any of them. That girl was softer than I am.'

'I thought the same thing,' Lena says. 'Were we ever that soft, back in the day, and we just don't remember?'

'If I'da been soft,' Sheila says, 'I'd be dead. And if you'da been soft, you'da lost your mind a long time back. We liked playing at it, is all, while we had the choice. That Rachel one was soft as butter straight through.'

She fills the teapot and brings it back to the table. 'That girl was like a child,' she says. '"But what didja *do*, what didja *do*?" Like a child that thinks it's all a storybook, and they wanta know what the hero done next to sort it all out and get the happy ending. A grown woman knows sometimes there's nothing to be done, so you do nothing.'

'She called round to me as well,' Lena says. 'Just before she came here. Asking was it 'cause of Sean that I've no mates around here, and did I mind or was it worth it. I thought Eugene wanted her to ditch her pals and get posh ones instead.'

'Clodagh done that,' Sheila says. 'When she started going out with Tommy, remember? She was always a snobby bitch, but she started acting like she'd never seen the rest of us before in her life.'

'Noreen says she's after joining a bridge club in Boyle,' Lena says. 'For golfers' wives only, don'tchaknow. They take turns making the canapés.'

That makes both of them snort with laughter. 'Jesus,' Sheila says. 'I'd do myself in as well, if I had Clodagh Moynihan dragging me into that.'

'From what you say, but,' Lena says, 'that's not what was worrying Rachel. I had it wrong. Eugene was up to something that'd fuck people over.'

Sheila nods, pouring the fresh tea. 'Eugene and Tommy,' she says. ' "He's always done what his dad says, he doesn't know how to say no to him . . ." That's what she said. And a loada talk about Eugene being a good person.'

'Did she say what they were at?'

'She wanted to tell me,' Sheila says. 'I wouldn't hear it. This is the first time in my life, since I left school, that I've had a bitta peace. I wasn't giving it up for some young one I never even talked to before.' She picks icing delicately off her éclair with the tip of her fork. 'It wouldn'ta made any difference anyhow. Like I said, she was soft as butter. I couldn't change that. Whatever she wanted off me, I didn't have it.'

Lena is hearing Noreen's voice: *Sure, the dogs in the street woulda known; Rachel couldn't hold her water, God rest her.* And

Trey's, clean and sharp as a blade coming down across the homey check tablecloth. *I reckon she knew something, or she found out something, and she was gonna say it. And someone around here wanted to shut her up, so they gave her antifreeze and fucked her in the river.*

Maybe Cal is right and Eugene wouldn't have the guts, Lena has no idea. What she knows is that Tommy doesn't let anything stand in his way, and that Eugene, raised from birth to believe that his right to whatever he wants springs from being a Moynihan, would never have the guts to say no to Tommy.

She says, 'D'you reckon she was in bad enough shape that she'd kill herself?'

'I reckon she had enough weight on her that she couldn't keep going,' Sheila says. 'With the Moynihans and their messing.'

Lena says, 'She coulda broken up with Eugene.'

Sheila gives a dismissive flick of her chin. 'She couldn't do without him, she said. Any woman can do without any man, but she didn't wanta know that. There's women that think it mustn't be real love if they can live without it. But she said even if she could, Tommy wouldn't let her walk away, not with whatever it was she knew. "He'd do something to me, tell people shite about me or have me thrown outa my course or something, he'd run me outa town..."'

'That'd be his style, all right,' Lena agrees.

'She couldn't get out from under,' Sheila says, 'so she went into the river.' She sucks the icing off her fork and glances across at Lena. 'Did you never wanta?'

'Not like that,' Lena says. It's true. When she wanted to walk into the river, it was never because she felt weighed down. It was the opposite: in the wake of Sean's death she felt hollowed, scraped fine as gauze, the whole merciless world roaring right through her like she was made of nothing.

'I did,' Sheila says matter-of-factly. 'Plenty of times. Only there were the kids. They weighed me down too much for that, even.'

'Did you say it to anyone?' Lena asks. 'That Rachel came here?'

Sheila shakes her head. 'Like I told you,' she says. 'Themens can look after themselves.'

It occurs to Lena that next time Noreen gives her shite for not doing her bit, she can point to Sheila as an example of how it could be worse. She says, 'So why does Tommy want you gone?'

Sheila shrugs, uninterested.

'Cal's worried,' Lena says. 'He thinks Tommy'll come after you some other way. Child Services, maybe.'

Sheila lifts her head and looks Lena full in the face. Her eyes are ice-blue and beautiful. 'You tell Cal,' she says, 'if Tommy tries anything like that, I'll tell the world that Rachel came here crying 'cause Eugene usedta beat the living shite outa her. Let's see him get onto the council after that.'

Lena has no doubt that she'll do it, and do it well. A couple of years back, or even a couple of weeks, that would have accomplished nothing except getting Sheila shunned for slandering the great Moynihans, but things are different now. Things are finely balanced, and shifting in ways she can't predict.

'I'll say it to Cal,' she says. 'I don't know whether it'll ease his mind or not, but I'll give it a go.'

'Would you back me?' Sheila asks.

The words reach Lena strangely, like a forgotten language out of a vanished life. She can't remember the last time anyone asked her to back them on anything; everyone knows better.

'I would, actually,' she says. She would love to ask Noreen whether this qualifies as doing her bit.

Sheila grins at her the way she used to grin before Johnny or Sean or any of it, back when they were sixteen and about to climb in the jacks window of the disco in town. 'I thought that, all right,' she says, and she gives Lena the last éclair.

When Cal moved here, it took him a while to get back into the swing of only making the trip into town every couple of weeks, to stock up on a while's worth of needs. He had got used to Chicago, where just about anything he forgot would be less than ten minutes away. Once he got reminded, though, this routine settled on him with the familiarity of childhood, when town was a monthly event that involved good pants and a spit-comb. He likes the advance thought it requires, the way it obliges you to see life in broad stretches rather than in urgent, unpredictable snippets.

He went to town just last week, but he could use another can of varnish, and Noreen doesn't stock the ice cream Trey likes. While he's there, he might as well drop in to the station and shoot the shit with Garda Dennis O'Malley for a while. Cal has always got along well with Garda Dennis, but it's occurred to him that his relationship with the local Guards might not stay the same now he's pissed off Tommy Moynihan. If he wants to shoot the shit with Garda Dennis, he should probably do it fast.

What Sheila told Lena gave him a certain amount of reassurance – at least Tommy doesn't appear to have anything personal against the Reddys. But the other things she threw into the mix have added enough complications that Cal could use a little police-level clarity on some facts.

He buys the varnish first, as an indicator that Garda Dennis is just a collegial afterthought. With the can swinging from his hand, he heads for the Garda station.

He gets lucky and finds it open. The station is a tiny, boxy building, painted white and blue and set down neatly amid a row of boxy little painted houses, like something out of a kid's toy set. The street is empty, all the houses huddled against the rain, which sweeps in sheets against the station's front wall and flows down the yard in a layer deep enough to soak Cal's pants cuffs.

Garda Dennis is at the front desk, and he's spilled something on his keyboard. He's dabbing it carefully with a paper towel and saying minor cuss words at it in a reproachful undertone. He matches the station: in his spotless uniform, with his rosy cheeks, he's round and neat as a figurine. He looks like he spends his work hours getting himself into humorous predicaments involving rascally stray mutts.

'Afternoon,' Cal says, wiping his feet on the mat. 'I catch you at a bad time?'

Tommy hasn't got to Garda Dennis yet: his face lights up when he sees Cal. Being a Chicago PD detective would horrify Garda Dennis, who is a man in the right place and happily aware of it, but hanging out with someone who used to be one is apparently the next best thing to meeting Clint Eastwood. 'Ah, God, no,' he assures Cal. ''Tis great to see you. I'm after making a mess of this yoke, lookit; I had the cuppa tea and the biscuit in the same hand, and it all went wrong.'

'Been there, done that,' Cal says ruefully, pushing back his jacket hood. 'A few months back I got a text when I was making stew, figured I could answer it and stir the stew at the same time. I've got a brand-new phone now.'

'I'll leave this to dry for a bit,' Garda Dennis says, eyeing the keyboard doubtfully, 'and then we'll see.' He pushes it away and wipes his fingers on the paper towel. 'What can I do for you?'

'Not a thing,' Cal says, 'except pass the time if you're not too busy.' He puts down his can of varnish on the floor and rubs rain off his face. 'My fiancée, she asked me to pick up her shoes that were getting re-soled, since I'm in town. But they're gonna be another half-hour, so I figured I'd drop in, get outa the rain and say hi.'

Garda Dennis's eyes widen. 'You've a fiancée?'

'Yep,' Cal says, a little sheepishly. 'Me and Lena Dunne, we've been together a while now, we figured we might as well make it official.'

'Ah, God, congratulations,' Garda Dennis says, his face splitting into a huge grin. He gets up and leans across the counter to give Cal a heartfelt, slightly sticky handshake. 'Being married is great; I know some fellas complain about it, but I'm not joking you, 'tis the best thing I ever did. You won't know yourself.'

'Thanks,' Cal says, grinning back. 'I'm a lucky man.'

'Lena Dunne,' Garda Dennis says. 'She'd be a local woman, am I right? Her sister's Noreen Duggan that runs the shop in Ardnakelty?' Garda Dennis takes pride in knowing the people on his beat, wide though it is; he needs to redeem himself for having overlooked Cal's engagement.

'That's right,' Cal says. 'Ardnakelty born and bred.'

'Born and bred and buttered,' Garda Dennis says comfortably, settling back into his chair. 'Fair play to you. There's fellas that go mad for the foreign ones – and I'm not saying they're wrong, we've a loada Brazilians here in town and every one of them's a fuckin' stunner. But for settling down with, like, you can't beat an Irish girl. Them Brazilians'd be a bit much for every day. You'd be moithered the whole time, just looking at them; you'd never get a word out. You can have the crack with an Irish girl.'

'Well,' Cal says, with a grimace. 'Mostly I do. Right now, I gotta say, not so much.'

'Wedding jitters, hah?' Garda Dennis asks sympathetically. 'The weddings is hard on the women; all the mammies and aunties and sisters sticking their oar in, 'twould wreck anyone's head. She'll be grand once 'tis all done and dusted. Take her somewhere nice for the honeymoon. Somewhere with a bitta sun, to make up for all this.' He waves at the door and the rain.

'It's not that,' Cal says, ducking his head and rubbing the back of his neck, uneasy. 'The wedding, we haven't even set a date yet. It's . . . You heard about Rachel Holohan, right? The girl that drank antifreeze, jumped in the river?'

'Ah, God, that was a terrible thing,' Garda Dennis says. His round face creases with upset. ''Tis always worse when 'tis a young one; specially a lovely-looking young one like that. I'd say I'm not supposed to think that any more, it'd be sexist, but all the same.'

'It's shaken up Ardnakelty pretty bad,' Cal says. 'And Lena, she's shaken up worse'n most.'

'Did she know the young one well?'

'Sort of,' Cal says. 'Rachel dropped in to Lena, just a few hours before she went into the river; around five-thirty that evening. Lena's working herself up thinking maybe Rachel had already drunk the antifreeze, and if she'd got her to a doctor, everything would've been fine.' A thought strikes him. 'You might know, is that true? Or can I tell her the antifreeze came later, she's worrying over nothing?'

Garda Dennis puckers up his face and rubs his nose with the effort of trying to remember. 'God,' he says. 'Your man did say what time she took it, the medical examiner, but I can't . . . Come here to me, I've the report right in the back.' He starts extracting himself from his chair, which is a snug fit. 'You just hang on there a sec, and we'll see what we can do.'

The posters on the station walls haven't changed since Cal first came in here, more than three years ago; a little yellower and more tattered now, they're still begging people to wear their seatbelts, follow these ten farm safety tips, and quit running diesel across the border. Cal reads over them and listens to the rain and to Garda Dennis, in the back room, peacefully discussing with himself where that report might have gone. Garda Dennis isn't a dumbass, he's not dishing the dirt on the investigation over pints in his local; but in his mind, if nowhere else, Cal is still a police officer, and there's nothing wrong with sharing information with him.

Cal doesn't like himself very much right now, using Lena as a pry tool, but he couldn't think of any other way to get the info, short of claiming to be unhealthily obsessed with a girl he barely knew, which would have been more moral but definitely not smarter. He especially doesn't like the realisation, which only came to him as he said the words, that they're partly true. Lena is different, since Rachel died. She's always had a remoteness somewhere in her, but now it's spread, like colour spreading slowly through water. Even with her head on his chest, she feels miles away. In some way he doesn't understand, Rachel's death has done something to her.

'Here we go,' Garda Dennis says, reappearing from the back room with a file held up victoriously in both hands. 'We'll see now can we settle your missus's mind.'

'I'm much obliged to you,' Cal says. 'I appreciate this more'n I can say.'

'Ah, you're grand,' Garda Dennis says, waving that off, a little embarrassed. 'We can't have this spoiling the run-up to your wedding. Ye'll need all your wits about you just for the guest list, sure.'

He settles back down behind the counter and starts going through the file, licking his thumb to turn each page. The file looks too thin to hold something that's shadowed a whole townland. The rain hammering the roof makes the building feel even smaller, a tiny bubble of calm.

'Now,' Garda Dennis says, planting one stubby finger firmly on the paper. 'I knew 'twas in here somewhere. Here we go: "The ethylene glycol" – that's the antifreeze, amn't I right? – "the ethylene glycol was ingested less than an hour before death." And she died at' – he runs his finger down the page – 'between eight and midnight – I'd say your man had an awful time working that out, 'cause of her being in the water, but that's what he said. So that'd mean . . .'

His lips move while he does the math. 'Seven o'clock,' he says. 'That's the earliest she coulda drunk it. What time did she leave your missus's house?'

'Like quarter of six,' Cal says.

'No way had she taken it by then, so,' Garda Dennis says triumphantly. 'And there's nothing your missus coulda done.'

'Well, that's good news,' Cal says, taking a deep breath of relief. 'That's gonna be a big weight off Lena's mind. And off mine. You know how it is: you see your woman worrying, you'll go a long way to fix it.'

Garda Dennis nods hard enough that his cheeks bounce. 'That's love, sure,' he says. 'Last week there, my missus thought she heard a rat up in our attic. I knew fine well there was nothing there – the dog woulda been going mental – but she couldn't sleep; she does be petrified of the rats. So up I climbed. In with the dust and the spiders. I sat in that attic the rest of the night, with the torch in one hand and the poker in the other, watching for a rat that was never even there.'

He's gone a becoming pink. 'I might be an awful eejit,' he confesses. 'The lads all say she's got me by the bollocks. But you shoulda seen how delighted she was, when I came down in the morning and said there wasn't a scratch all night. 'Twas worth it.'

'That's love,' Cal agrees. 'Nothing dumb about that; I'd've done the same. And I guess there's nothing weird about Lena worrying, what with her being the last person to see Rachel.'

He leaves a pause there, in case Garda Dennis wants to correct him on that, but Garda Dennis is still nodding understandingly. 'She's racking her brain,' Cal explains, 'in case Rachel said something that could've tipped her off. She says Rachel mostly just talked about her cat, it had got scratched up, but Lena's afraid she missed something.'

'She wouldn'ta done it 'cause her cat wasn't well,' Garda Dennis reassures him. 'The poor girl was a bit flighty-like, from what I hear, but she wasn't straight-up mental.'

'I didn't know her myself,' Cal says, 'but that matches what I heard.' He wonders who told the Guards that Rachel was flighty-like. 'You guys ever find out why she did it?'

Garda Dennis shakes his head. 'Not a clue. None of the mental health, everything grand at home, everything grand at college, everything grand in the love life. She went out with Tommy Moynihan's young lad,' he adds, impressively, like he's saying *She went out with JFK Jr's kid*.

Right about here is where Cal would love to amble off down a tangent about the Moynihans and their doings, but he knows better. When Tommy comes calling to warn the Guards against Cal, he doesn't need to hear that Cal has been in digging for dirt on his family. 'I knew that part, yeah,' he says. 'They seemed like a pretty happy couple to me.'

'Ah, God, yeah. Young Eugene had the ring bought and all. A few people thought they mighta been having some hassle, one way or another, but that's only gossip; all her friends said no, the two of them were happy out. Earlier this year they had a bitta trouble over where they'd live once they were married – he works in the finance up in Dublin, d'you see, and she was a home bird, she had all her friends and family round here, didn't wanta leave the place. But that was all sorted. They'd been looking at buying a bitta land round your way, for to build a house. I'd say Eugene was going to work remote,' Garda Dennis adds knowledgeably.

That fits with Mart's guess about Eugene running for the council; he can't do that from the big city. Cal has always got the impression that Ardnakelty doesn't meet Eugene's high standards. He wonders how Eugene felt about his daddy and his girlfriend teaming up to keep him there.

'Eugene seems pretty cut up about it,' he says.

'In tatters,' Garda Dennis says, with a mixture of solemnity and relish. 'That's what he is: in tatters.' He rubs his bald spot, trying to come up with something that'll help. 'Maybe she just imagined he was going off her,' he suggests. 'And she got herself in a state over that.' He looks hopefully at Cal.

'Well, that's a thought,' Cal says, with an impressed lift of the eyebrows that makes Garda Dennis sit up a little straighter. 'Anything like that on her social media, or her texts? She call Eugene a coupla dozen times that evening?'

'Not a thing,' Garda Dennis says promptly, proud of knowing this one right off the bat. 'He rang her a few times, but she didn't answer. And there was a buncha texts from her pals – about someone's twenty-first the next weekend, like, and who was going to wear what dress, so's they wouldn't match. But she never tried to get in touch with anyone.'

'Well,' Cal says, troubled again. 'Maybe, maybe not. Lena, she went to bed early that night, and she thinks maybe she might've heard a knock at the door, sometime in her sleep. I figure she was dreaming, but she's got it in her head that was Rachel coming back again, looking for help. Did you guys pull the location history off her phone, maybe I can reassure Lena she never came back that way?'

'Oh, God, I wouldn't say so,' Garda Dennis says, startled. He gives it a shot anyway, paging methodically through the file, but he comes up shaking his head. 'Sure, round here we haven't got the resources you'd be used to in Chicago,' he explains, a little abashed. 'We wouldn't go around getting location histories unless 'twas on a suspect, say, who's done something a bit serious, or on a missing person. We couldn't do it for something like this.'

Cal doesn't disillusion him on the resources of Chicago PD. 'You gotta prioritise,' he agrees.

'But if you'll take a bitta advice off a married man . . .' Garda Dennis leans forward conspiratorially across the counter, his round blue eyes earnest. 'If I was you, I'd tell your missus we have that location history and Rachel was miles away all night long. Sure, what harm? That's my number one tip for marriage: if you can make the other half happy, and no harm done to anyone, don't miss the chance.'

'Sounds like good advice,' Cal says, grinning at him. 'I'll take it, and hope she does the same.' He stoops to pick up his can of varnish. 'I won't keep you from the job any longer. Those shoes oughta be ready by now. Thanks again for taking the time.'

'Ah, not at all,' Garda Dennis says, from the heart. 'Sure, you'da done the same for me back when you were on the job, amn't I right?'

Cal feels a small, sharp pinch of sadness. He doesn't miss his old job even a little bit, but there's a warmth in having this one place where his past self still exists in Garda Dennis's mind, a ghost with a badge and a caseload and a mouth full of cop slang in cop rhythms. Soon, as soon as Tommy Moynihan can fit it into his busy schedule, that'll be gone.

'That's right,' he says. 'Any time.'

'Don't have the reception in the Kilcarrow Arms,' Garda Dennis advises him, picking up his keyboard and paper towel again as Cal turns to go. 'I was at one there this summer, and God almighty, I was never that sick in my life. I thought I was turning inside out. Get the Breggan Court.'

The nearest café is a depressed little side-street joint with a lot of worn Formica and a strong smell of fried eggs. Cal shelters there, in spite of the fact that their coffee tastes like its main ingredient is burnt hair. By now he understands the weather around here well enough to know that the rain is what Mart would call 'down for the day' and there's no point in trying to wait it out, but he wants to think, while Garda Dennis's info is still fresh in his mind. This place is, for obvious reasons, always empty; he's not going to run into anyone else up from Ardnakelty and wanting company.

He gets out the notebook where he keeps shopping lists and woodwork measurements, and finds a clean page.

> *4 p.m.: Outside store with Tommy and Eugene*
> *4:30 p.m.: Leaves Eugene*
> *5:30 p.m.–5:45 p.m.: At Lena's*
> *+/– 6 p.m.–6:30 p.m.: At Sheila's – last known sighting*
> *Between 6:30 p.m. and 8:30 p.m.: Goes home, leaves car*
> *? evening: Possible plan to meet Eugene – family thinks yes,*
>   *Eugene says no*
> *8:30 p.m.: Family gets home, house is empty*
> *Between 7 p.m. and 11 p.m.: Antifreeze*
> *Between 8 p.m. and 12 a.m.: Time of death*

At six-thirty, Rachel was upset and worried, but not on the edge as far as anyone could see. Within a few hours, she was drinking antifreeze. Something, or someone, happened in those hours.

He finds himself wondering whether anyone checked the Holohans' supply of antifreeze to see if any was missing or not, and whether anyone went looking for a discarded container. He also wonders where Rachel was, all that blank stretch of time between Sheila's house and the river. He wishes the Guards had pulled her location history, and ideally location histories for all the Moynihans and that little shitbag Donie McGrath, but he doesn't blame them for not doing it. Cal has seen Irish detectives in action on a murder case, and found no fault with their work, but this wasn't a murder; this was just an undistinguished small-town tragedy, a part of the inexorable snowfall of girls and boys who every day slip through the world's fingers and melt away. If it occurred to anyone that it might be something heavier or darker than that, Tommy Moynihan would have ground out that thought under his heel like a cigarette butt.

The Guards did what they were supposed to do. Then they withdrew, leaving the townland under its rain and its silence, to deal in its own ways with anything that remained.

The waitress puts down Cal's scone and shuffles away without making conversation. The scone tastes like lukewarm Play-Doh. Cal takes two bites to keep the waitress's spirits up, and leaves the rest be.

Maybe sweet-natured Garda Dennis is right, and the whole thing was a big tragic mix-up. Rachel's family thinks she and Eugene had planned to meet up that night; Eugene says they hadn't. But if Rachel was waiting alone at the meeting place and thought Eugene was ghosting her because of whatever the hell was going on, she would have at least tried getting in touch with him before she reached for the antifreeze and the river.

Cal is less certain about Eugene than he was. Eugene may be a wimp, but wimps are the ones who lash out most frantically when they're backed into a corner, like for example if they and their daddy are up to something squirrelly and their girlfriend is getting cold feet. And Eugene may not be the boy genius he thinks he is, but he's smart enough that if he had done something bad to Rachel, he'd have made sure to leave a bunch of missed calls on her phone. Cal would love to know where Eugene was from seven o'clock that night, or at least where he says he was. Even if he'd wanted to bring up the subject with Garda Dennis, there would have been no point; no cop around here is going to ask Tommy Moynihan's young lad for anything that resembles an alibi.

Cal tells himself he's not acting like this is a murder; he's just acting like there's something hinky here, which there is. He flips to a fresh page.

Tommy:

1. Reddys
2. Rachel
3. Eugene council?
4. Land

Tommy has been trying to run the Reddys out of town; he's trying to find out something or other to do with Rachel's death; if Mart is right, he's trying to launch Eugene into local government. And way back before Rachel died, Francie was warning darkly that Tommy was up to something – something to do with buying land, although no one ever settled on a solid suggestion as to what that might be. Cal can't see how those four lines of business might connect up. It's possible that they're unrelated, of course, but that would make Tommy one hell of a multitasker. The guy is canny enough and experienced enough to prioritise when the pressure is on. If he's still running all four of those lines, at a time like this, Cal is ready to bet they're all four knotted together.

Going by what Rachel told Sheila, Tommy and Eugene are up to something that would harm people around Ardnakelty – possibly something illegal, but not necessarily, given that Rachel didn't mention going to the Guards. The amount of resources Tommy is willing to pump into it suggests that it's something big.

Cal doesn't like any of this. He has no clear line of sight on anything, and he can't see to an ending in any direction. He didn't like this feeling back on the job – any case could turn bad, but these were the ones that had a tendency to turn bad in ways he never saw coming. He sure as hell doesn't like it popping up in his own life.

The rain is thickening, coating the windows till the street outside is invisible. The waitress has vanished; the weary clatter of half-hearted washing-up filters out from the back room.

Cal is aware that his urge to fix stuff isn't always a good thing, but what he's doing here isn't coming out of his own urges, misguided or not. On a personal level, he feels no drive to do anything but let Rachel Holohan rest in peace. This demand comes from outside him; from Sheila Reddy making it clear that the Moynihans are, somehow, a threat to this place.

Skippy Gannon gave Cal straw for his vegetable beds; Angela Maguire is planning his wedding cake. Senan brought Cal for a few pints with Lena's three wary brothers, all of whom used to play Gaelic football with Senan, making his character reference the most powerful one Cal could have. PJ helped him clear the brambles that were reaching out to choke his back field, and while they were at it he raised his clear tenor shyly over the snapping of the shears and taught Cal the words to a bunch of folk songs, so now Cal can sing along when the pub turns musical. Bobby brought him a bottle of holy water. Cal's feelings about Ardnakelty are complicated, with plenty of tangles and reservations, but his feelings are beside the point; they're nothing but fuss and fluff, beside the solid fact that he lives here. Regardless of Lena's objections, he can't switch that on and off at his convenience. When he has something the townland needs, he has an obligation to provide it.

What he has to offer is a little woodworking skill, and the muscle-power to pack a silage clamp or mend a drystone wall, and the fact that he used to be a detective. He understands now why Mart gave him a funny look when he said something about everyone wanting a PI. Tommy looked at Cal and saw a PI for hire, but Mart just saw a guy who lives here.

The coffee has gone cold. Cal reads over his timeline once more and puts the notebook away. He figures, seeing as he's already gone and pissed off Tommy Moynihan, he might as well find a moment to have a chat with Eugene.

9

When it comes to matters of local protocol, Cal tends to triangulate Noreen's opinion, Mart's opinion, and Lena's if she has one, which she mostly doesn't. This lets him avoid both the risk of missing some exclusively masculine angle and the risk of becoming the fall guy in an elaborate set-up if Mart feels things are getting boring around here.

Lena has no opinion on whether Cal should go to Rachel Holohan's funeral, but Mart and Noreen are both adamant that he needs to be there. Noreen, with a fresh little worry-line running across her forehead, assures Cal it doesn't matter that he barely knows the family – "Tisn't about that, there'll be plenty there that's the same as yourself, it's just so they know we're all there for them. Sure when our mammy died I remember Valerie Nagle showed up, d'you know Val? With the hair? Ah, you do – I hadn't spoken to her since we fell out when we were sixteen, but it meant the world to me, we're back friends now . . .' Mart's take is different. 'Strength in numbers,' he explains. 'You sit with us in the hotel after, Sunny Jim, and do what we do, and 'twill all be grand.'

'I've been to funerals here before,' Cal points out. 'I'm not gonna disgrace you.'

'Not this one you haven't,' Mart says, and he stumps off, crook-backed over a wheelbarrow heaped with some substance that smells like it should be bubbling.

Mart is right: it's not like the other funerals Cal has been to.

Those were people like Dumbo Gannon, who had a heart attack on his sofa, and Senan's father-in-law, who was just plain old. The grief had the same tornado ferocity that Cal remembers from his mother's death, but like his, it was something within nature, something that would eventually wear itself a resting place. The grief in this cold church has no place anywhere and never will. It's a ravenous creature out of folktales, hunting forever with no rest or respite.

Kilcarrow church is modern and ugly, an incoherent combination of concrete, red carpet, and pine. People are weeping, but the acoustics muffle their sobs to a jagged pulse under Father Eamonn's surround-sound intonations. The stained-glass windows are dulled by the darkness outside.

It's a big church, but it's crowded – Cal can't tell whether this is support, rubbernecking, duty, or a little of all three. Just about everyone he knows is there, including a couple of guys who only come down from the mountain a few times a year, and plenty of people he doesn't. He's at the back, wearing his good clothes – he doesn't own a suit, his life here not offering many occasions that require one, but he does have a pair of navy pants and a blue shirt, and shoes he can polish. To his surprise, Lena, who hasn't been to church since her own mother's funeral, is beside him. She gave no explanation, and he hasn't asked. She's wearing a trim blue dress and the kind of shoes he didn't know she owned, and her hair is pulled into a smooth bun. He finds both of them slightly unsettling, like they've strayed into some alternative universe where they lead very different lives.

To his even greater surprise, Trey is on his other side, with clean jeans and brushed hair. 'What?' she said, at the look on his face when she walked in his door that morning.

'Nothing,' Cal said. 'I didn't expect you to come along today, is all.'

Trey, rubbing dog hair off her jacket, shrugged. 'Rachel was sound.'

'You've got school.'

'I'd be the only one there. Everyone's going.'

'Kid,' Cal said. He knows Trey well enough to spot when she has an agenda. 'We talked about this. We're not gonna do anything yet.'

''M not *doing* anything. Everyone's always saying I oughta be more *sociable* with this place, and now when I—'

'When did I ever say that?'

'Noreen does.'

'Since when do you listen to Noreen?'

'Rachel was sound,' Trey said. 'And fuck the Moynihans,' neither of which Cal could argue with.

It takes him a while to notice that something is screwy about the seating arrangements in the church. Rachel's family is up front, on the right-hand side. Right-hand side is for family, Cal knows that much, but he would have expected the Moynihans to be over there too, seeing as Eugene and Rachel were practically engaged. Instead, they're taking up the front left pew. Neither family looks at the other, even once.

The coffin is white, heaped all around with flowers. Girls who look like Rachel go up the aisle two by two, carrying things to lay on top of it, things she loved too dearly to leave behind. In this strange setting they pick their way like nervous deer, ready to leap at any startle. Most of them are crying.

Father Eamonn says smooth nice things about Rachel, and smooth compassionate things to her loved ones. Then he takes a minute, bending his head to build suspense. Father Eamonn has a cascade of jowls and he talks funny, letting his voice rise and die away in an arc that's presumably meant to sound spiritual but that to Cal's ears just sounds phony.

'Tragedy,' he says, lifting his head, 'can bring a community together, or it can tear it apart. Each and every one of us in this church today has a duty to make sure it does not tear us apart.'

He pauses impressively. Trey is picking something off the pew in front with her fingernail. Cal nudges her and shakes his head.

'We will feel the temptation,' Father Eamonn says, gripping the pulpit to lean closer to the mike, 'to assign blame. This is a temptation to sin. Judge not, lest ye be judged, says Our Lord Jesus Christ in the Sermon on the Mount. If we have the audacity to take judgement into our own hands, we are defying Our Lord's word, and we are inviting his harshest judgement on ourselves. Let us pray today that we will all have the strength to resist that temptation.'

Something moves through the church, a scattered rustle almost too low to hear, a mutter that goes on too long.

Outside the church, the line to shake hands with Rachel's family is near-silent. People have their heads down against an ill-tempered wind that drives fine rain in their faces whichever way they turn. Lena pulls her jacket hood up.

'I can't remember the last time I saw the sun,' Noreen says, next to her. 'Honest to God, I can't. I'm watching reality shows, what's that one where they make eejits of themselves in Ibiza, just so's I won't forget what it looks like.'

Step by step, the line shuffles forward. Rachel's brother and sisters, home from their faraway places, look dazed by the brutal impossibility of the day. Claire and Fintan look near to dead themselves. Their faces have fallen in around their bones, and Claire's eyes are swollen as if she's been beaten. One of her sisters is trying to keep an umbrella over her, but her too-big black dress is clinging with rain.

'I'm sorry for your trouble,' Lena says. 'Rachel was lovely, all her life.'

Claire holds on to her hand. 'She went to you,' she says. Her voice is hoarse and stilted, like words have come unmoored from their meanings. 'That night. Did she say anything to you?'

'She was there about the cat,' Lena says. 'Those scratches he had. I told her it was nothing to worry about.' The lie comes harder than she expected. 'She took great care of that cat.'

'She was mental about him,' Fintan says. He clears his throat, and then does it again. 'Pure mental.' Lena remembers him back in school, the time he ate the copper sulphate on a dare and the substitute teacher freaked out, and Fintan pretended to collapse and the teacher ran out of the room and never came back, and everyone was twisted laughing. He had no idea this was lying in wait for him. None of them had any way of knowing. Trey and her mates have melted off to sit on the churchyard wall, unbothered by the rain, inscrutably watching the strange adult rituals.

'I'm glad she went to your place,' Claire says. She hasn't let go of Lena's hand. Hers is fever-hot. 'You were always kind. I'd like if the last face she saw was kind.'

Lena can't remember if she was ever kind to Claire, or if she was ever kind at all. 'You only hadta look around that church,' she says, 'to see how much she was loved.'

Claire and Fintan nod, pressing their lips tight against more tears. Over to the other side of the church door, at a discreet distance, is another line. People are queueing up to tell Eugene Moynihan they're sorry for his trouble. Now and then they glance up against the rain, checking who's joined them and who's watching.

The afters are in the Kilcarrow Arms, an old red-brick mansion that sometime in the 1950s turned into a haphazard combination of hotel, restaurant, bar, and function room. Even when it's not giving people food poisoning, the Kilcarrow Arms doesn't have much to recommend it, being shabby in a non-quaint way and staffed by people who look like they're making plans to lose a fake nail in your drink. It coasts on the fact of being the only place in town with a room that can hold a couple of hundred people. Cal isn't sure how long this shindig is meant to last, but if he has to, he can sneak Lena and Trey out to get a burger somewhere.

'There you are,' Mart says, appearing at his shoulder and steering him towards an awkward-shaped nook that's apparently standing in for the pub alcove: Bobby, Senan, and Francie are squashed around a table that holds a surprising number of pints. Mart has also dressed up for the occasion, meaning he's not wearing wellies and his pants aren't held up by baling twine. 'Senan's after getting in a rake of pints, the way we won't have to fight our way to the bar for a while. You can get the next round.'

Cal looks around for Lena and Trey, who have somehow disappeared. The crowd has segregated itself neatly by gender, age, occupation, and other factors that Cal can't decipher; he catches Lena's fair head amid a group of women he didn't even know she knew. Trey has materialised among a bunch of teenagers at a corner table discreetly tucked away from adult sightlines. Cal can tell, from Aidan's rapt expression as he nods along to whatever Ross is saying, that under the table he's pouring something extra into his glass. He catches Trey's eye and gives her a warning look; she gives him back a blank one. He ups the warning level. She ups the bafflement.

'Don't be fussing over the child,' Mart says, planting Cal on a stool. 'She's grand; if you don't have her fit to be let out in public by now, you never will.'

'Get that into you,' Bobby says, shoving a pint across the table to Cal.

'Don't bother,' Francie says. He's eyeing his glass at arm's length, like he just found a bug in it. 'The head on that is a fuckin' disgrace.'

Cal takes a swig of his pint. 'I'm not a Guinness man,' he says, 'but even I can tell that's shit.'

'To match the day that's in it,' Senan says. He's in a dark mood. Today has got to him, and Senan is used to being able to hit back at things that get to him. 'And the weather, and that fuckin' priest. Drink your pint and quit your whingeing. You've still got your young one, haven't you? What else do you want?'

'Not a thing,' Cal says, and means it. He downs some more of his shitty Guinness.

'They'd a great turnout, anyway,' Bobby says, trying to find a positive. 'Everyone's here, only the lads that couldn't leave the farming.'

'And look what we've got to make up for the farmers,' Mart says, digging a bony elbow into Cal's ribs and pointing with his chin. 'I was right about Sir Tommy's grand plan. I'm right that often, boyo, sometimes I amaze myself.'

The Moynihans have taken over a big table across the room from the Holohans', but they've given pride of place in the centre of the banquette to a scrawny little guy with an out-of-date check suit, a beat-up fedora, and the colourless, lipless, lashless face of someone Jimmy Cagney would fist-fight. Tommy and Eugene are sitting one on each side of him, like favourite courtiers, nodding wisely at everything that comes out of his mouth. 'Who's that guy?' Cal asks.

'Fuck me,' Senan says. 'Innocence is a beautiful thing. Don't tell him; today's been bad enough already.'

'Where have you been these last few years, Sunny Jim?' Mart demands. 'D'you live under a rock? That's Dickie O'Shea.' And when Cal still looks blank: 'Our TD, man. Our congressman, is that what you'd call it? The fella that goes up to Dublin and gives the city politicians an earful about treating us better. Not that they pay him a blind bitta notice, but it gets him in the papers and he has a rare aul' time.'

'And a rare aul' load of wee brown envelopes,' Francie says.

'That fella's the biggest landlord in the West,' Mart says. 'Apartments, he owns, and pubs, and hotels. All on a TD's salary.'

'If I was the biggest landlord in the West,' Cal says, 'I'd have a better suit than that one.' He doesn't want to get into politics, not on a day when everyone is already on edge.

'Jesus, man,' Mart says, 'you'd never make it in politics. Dickie's had that suit since the first time he put his name on the ballot; he wouldn't trade it for pure silk satin Armani. That fella might have enough in the bank to buy and sell the lot of us, but as long as he's wearing that yoke, Dickie's a man of the people, don'tchaknow. No notions about Dickie. Just like yourself and myself. There's an awful lotta fools around here, Sunny Jim.'

'I voted for Dickie,' Bobby says, offended.

'Course you did,' Senan says. 'That's the man's point.'

'What you do,' Mart tells Bobby with magnificent disdain, 'doesn't even count as voting. You just tick whatever box your daddy did. That's not voting. That's taking a stroll down to the polling station and back.'

'It is so. He got in, didn't he?'

'The Holohans know Dickie Whatshisname?' Cal says. They didn't strike him as the type to hang out with politicians.

Senan snorts. 'They don't have to know him. They couldn'ta kept him away with a cattle prod.'

'We're meant to be honoured,' Francie explains. 'That an important man like that would take time outa his day to pay his respects to one of ours. And then we'll all vote for him.'

'If that shitehawk shows his face at my funeral,' Mart says, 'I'm relying on the four of ye to get him by the shiny suit and throw him out, arse over tip. But that's not the point. The point is, I told ye, and I was right: Tommy wants Eugene in politics. D'you know how round your way, Sunny Jim, the politicians'd always be on the telly endorsing each other? That's what that is right there. Dickie O'Shea sitting down for chats over a pint that Eugene bought him: that's an endorsement.'

That could explain why Eugene is still hanging around Ardnakelty: Tommy has him cosying up to Dickie O'Shea, while Rachel's death means there's something in it for Dickie. 'Whole lot cheaper than TV time,' Cal says.

'While we're on the subject,' Mart says, to Cal. He dabs a bit of beer foam tidily off his lip. 'We had a wee chat there not too long ago, yourself and myself, about the great Tommy Moynihan and the joys of communication.'

'I remember that,' Cal says. Senan and Bobby and Francie are all watching him. 'Communication and clarity, both.'

'That's the one,' Mart agrees, smiling at Cal. 'That was a great aul' chat. I was wondering if you'd found any bits and pieces of clarity to communicate, on your travels.'

Cal has been considering whether to tell Mart the various stuff he's picked up, but it's too nebulous; it'll just get people all worked up and raring to go, without any direction to go in, and that never ends well. 'No clarity so far,' he says. 'But I'm working on it.'

'Are you?' Francie asks.

'Yeah,' Cal says.

Senan says, 'I heard Donie McGrath got caught shiteing about at the Reddy place.'

Cal translates this, which a couple of years back would have sounded like a non sequitur, without effort. Senan wants to know whether Donie's bullshit had anything to do with Tommy, but he also wants to know whether Cal is only taking an interest because Trey was under threat.

'Donie's a detail,' he says. 'I'm gonna want a lot more clarity than that little asswipe can give me.'

Senan nods, knocks back the last of his pint, and swaps the

empty glass for a full one: his questions have been answered to his satisfaction. 'There ye go,' Mart says to the table, like Cal has proved a point he was arguing. 'Here's to clarity, and the sooner the better.'

Cal drinks to that. He finds he's slightly surprised at himself, like he just navigated a complicated conversation in a language he didn't realise he spoke well enough to pull it off.

'Ah, Jesus,' Francie says, his face puckering with disgust. 'Would ye look at that fuckin' lickarse.'

Dickie O'Shea, being a busy man, is leaving. Eugene has walked him to the door, so he won't get lonely, and is shaking his hand like they're posing for a photo op.

'Christ on a fuckin' bike,' Senan says. 'If that little scut knocks on my door asking for a vote, I'll give him such an almighty kick up the hole, he'll land in the fuckin' Atlantic.'

'There's an upside, mind you,' Mart says. 'There always is. I'm only dying to see Eugene Moynihan in a polyester check suit.'

The minute Lena steps inside the hotel bar, Yvonne McCabe grabs her arm and whisks her over to a table that's apparently become the base for middle-aged Ardnakelty women who are on the easy-going side – the high-maintenance table, led by Laura Barry, is across the room, sipping gin and slimline tonic – and who aren't close enough to Claire Holohan to gather around her. This is exactly where Lena wants to be, but she still feels the urge to run for the hills.

'Look who I found,' Yvonne says triumphantly, presenting Lena to the group. Lena knows all of them – Philomena Doherty, Julie Quinn, Melanie O'Halloran – or she did once upon a time, back in school. Since then they've got used to not knowing Lena any more, beyond brief pleasant small talk in Noreen's. The last time she sat down for a drink with this lot, the drinks were mostly illegal.

'Here,' Yvonne says, pushing a glass into Lena's hand. Back in the day, Yvonne was the one all the boys fancied: a little thing with a ton of blond hair, a figure that hit you straight in the eye, and the kind of matter-of-fact cheerfulness that made everything feel less daunting. Nowadays her hair is cut short and spiked up, and her figure has relaxed into a series of lavish bulges; the cheerfulness hasn't changed, but it would take more than that to make Lena feel undaunted here. 'Vodka and Coke, the real stuff, fuck the diet shite on a day like this. I got a spare while the going was good. If you want anything else, you'll have to catch a lounge boy, and good luck with that.'

'This is great,' Lena says, sliding onto the banquette. 'Thanks.' Sooner or later someone is going to bring up her factfinding excursion with the jam, but not yet. It'll take a while and a couple of drinks before Rachel is mentioned. The funeral was more than anyone could take; they need to catch their breath before they head back into that territory.

It'll come. When Yvonne grabbed Lena's arm, probably she was genuinely glad of the chance to bring Lena back into the fold – the two of them always got on – but that was incidental. Ardnakelty wants to find out why Lena Dunne, after all these years, has been taking an interest in local affairs.

Lena is grand with that; she has her answers ready. What she wants to find out is whether anyone around here knows what Eugene was doing that had Rachel worried.

These women won't tell her. All of them were born wearing the prime directive like a birthmark: say nothing. Talk plenty, keep the chat flowing, but when it comes to anything that has weight, saying it would only lead to trouble. Everyone here will say nothing expertly, but Lena is still fluent in her mother tongue, even if she refuses to speak it. She'll know, by whether they warn her off, if there's something they're keeping unsaid.

'Jesus,' Philomena Doherty says, inspecting Lena up and

down. Phil is still short and square, she still drinks pints, and she still looks like she's brandishing a camogie stick even when she's not. 'Why do you look ten fuckin' years younger than I do?'

'It's 'cause she's got no kids,' Yvonne explains. 'I usedta be all fresh-faced as well, no eyebags or anything, up until I had the kids. Remember that?'

'You can have one of mine,' Phil tells Lena. 'Have Jack. I'd a pound of mince in for the dinner last night, and the little shite came in from training, fried it up, and et the lot. Between slices of batch bread. He's a fuckin' savage.'

'At least he fried it,' Julie Quinn says. Julie has big brown eyes that always look worried; back in school, she was the one constantly anxious about getting in trouble, whether she'd done anything or not. 'That's a step in the right direction. Niall woulda put it in the microwave. He did that with sausages once, and all the skin peeled off.'

'Step in the right direction, me arse. He didn't bother his hole salting it or anything, and when I got in he came to me complaining that it tasted like shite. I nearly took the head off him.'

The conversation swings into horror stories about things people's kids have done. Lena could offer stories about Trey that would stop the other women in their tracks, but she has no intention of doing it. She knows fine well that she'll have to part with some currency here, if she wants anything useful, but Trey isn't currency.

Noreen is eyeing Lena across the room, the way she'd eye a dog that probably shouldn't be off the leash. Lena gives her an angelic smile and a finger-wave. She's safe: Noreen can't rush over to supervise her, because she's stuck dancing attendance on her mother-in-law. Between her weight and her arthritis and her sciatica, Mrs Duggan hardly ever leaves the house; Lena can't imagine how Noreen and Dessie got her into the car, let alone into the church and up the hotel steps. But when Mrs Duggan wants something, people get it for her, and nothing would have convinced her to miss out on today. She's throned in the middle of a banquette, draped in yards of purple velvet, a little purple hat clamped to her twist of black-dyed hair, with Noreen and Dessie firmly staked down on either side of her.

'I could smell it from out on the landing, I'm not joking you,' Melanie says. Everyone has started laughing, pressing their hands over their mouths to hide it, Julie hissing at Mel to stop. 'When I pulled it out from under his bed, it was *green*. I thought it was going to reach out and grab me. I told him, next time I'm taking him up to Dublin Zoo and leaving him there. Where he belongs.' Lena finds she's laughing too. Somewhere along the way, she forgot that she likes these women.

'I'd say you can smell Sophie's room from here,' Yvonne says. 'The *perfume*, my God. Some influencer had it, on TikTok, and now they're all drowning themselves in it. Didja ever leave an apple in your schoolbag till it went squashy, and then spray the bag with air freshener to stop your mammy finding out? That's what she smells like.'

Everyone is laughing too hard, rocking in their seats with the effort of keeping it down. Lena has heard women bitch about their kids plenty of times, but this has a different edge, sharper and more urgent. These women are brandishing the stories the way they'd hang amulets and scrawl symbols, masking their children's preciousness from whatever malevolent thing weaves through the air scanning for prey. This is protection.

'Sure, the girls'd melt your head just as bad as the lads,' Phil says. 'Louise came in to me this morning, right, waving some top in my face, and she said she couldn't wear it 'cause her arms look funny. She was annoyed with *me*. Like her arms are my fault, or it's my job to fix them. There's nothing wrong with her arms, and if there was, what the fuck am I meant to do about them? Shove her back up there and start over?'

Yvonne splutters on a mouthful of her drink. The laughter has reached a suppressed intensity that sounds painful.

'D'you know what,' Phil says to Lena, whacking Yvonne on the back, 'just take the lot of them.'

'Ah, don't be saying that,' Julie protests, dabbing under her eyes where her mascara is running. 'You'll miss them once they're gone.'

There's a splinter of silence. The laughter is wiped away like it never happened. No one turns to look at Claire Holohan.

The room swirls like water, groups eddying together and apart, people carried from one to the next on the current. The mood has the same ceaseless ebb and flow: surges of weeping, talk, laughter, silence, all sweep across the room, dissipate, and re-form into something else. Everyone looks stiff and weird in their good clothes, and the whole afternoon has the queasy, rudderless sway of a nightmare. Cal feels like he's been here forever, but the flat grey outside the windows hasn't changed.

'Now,' Francie says, arriving back at the table and putting down his precarious handful of pints.

'About fuckin' time,' Senan says, reaching for a glass. 'Were you waiting for the horse to piss?' He's snapped out of his dark mood and turned loud. He's nowhere near drunk – Senan is big enough, and practised enough, to hold a lot of booze without showing it – but his eyes skid too unpredictably and he puts his glass down too hard. He looks like he might welcome an argument.

'I've had plenty,' Cal says. 'I gotta drive home.'

'Don't we all, sure,' Mart says. 'No Guard's going to pull anyone over on a day like this. Sure, that's the sergeant over there, lookit, at Tommy's table. With the pint in his hand.'

'Sandwiches,' says a teenage waitress who's clearly been dragged in for the day by her mama. She shoves a tray of wilted triangles at them.

'What kind?' Bobby wants to know.

The waitress examines them. 'Egg?' she says doubtfully. 'And those ones are ham.'

'Don't be tempting us,' Mart tells her, slapping away Bobby's reaching hand. 'We're all on a diet here. So we'll fit into our bikinis for Christmas in Tenerife.' He pats his scrawny middle. 'I'm going great guns, but some of these fellas, naming no names' – he wiggles his eyebrows extravagantly at Bobby and Senan – 'they'd go through those gourmet yokeymajigs for a shortcut, and then where would we be on the beach? Man-boobs galore. 'Twouldn't be a pretty sight.'

The waitress is trying to figure out whether he's yanking her chain, and whether or not he wants sandwiches. 'Wouldja have any lettuce?' Senan asks her. 'I'd murder a lettuce.'

'Don't be making demands, you; this lady's got enough to be doing. D'you know who'd only love a few egg sandwiches, but,' Mart tells her, struck by the thought. 'See that table over there? The big fella with the grey hair, he'd sell his mammy for the sniff of an egg sandwich. Give him our share, go on.'

The waitress looks doubtfully back and forth between their table and Tommy's. All the guys give her encouraging nods, and in the end she drifts off, still glancing back dubiously over her shoulder.

'Now,' Mart says happily. 'That lot won't be able to say no. Tommy'd ate slurry, sooner than look snobby in front of the populace.'

'He's a braver man than me if he eats them sandwiches,' Senan says.

'I do love a good game of Russian roulette,' Mart says. 'When 'tisn't my own guts on the line.'

'I'm starving,' Bobby says dolefully. At a long table at the end of the room, a scrawny kid with an unconvincing moustache is ladling soup from a tureen into bowls, for a line of the kind of old women who can't be killed by anything short of a lightning strike. Bobby eyes him wistfully. 'I'd eat the hind leg off the Lamb of God.'

'We'll bring you for chips after,' Francie says. 'You big baby.'

'Here,' Senan says to Cal. 'Is your young one going into the politics as well, is she?'

'Huh?' Cal says. 'She's gonna be a woodworker.'

'That's what I thought. What's the story there, so?'

Cal follows the angle of Senan's chin to Trey, who has paused by the Moynihans' table on her way somewhere and is having what looks like a chirpy chat with Tommy Moynihan.

'What the hell,' Cal says.

'Exactly,' Senan says.

Cal resists the impulse to get up out of his seat and remove Trey from her conversation by the back of her hoodie. 'Huh,' he says. 'Maybe Tommy wants a chair fixed.'

'I thought you told that fella to do his own dirty work,' Mart says.

'Yep,' Cal says. Nobody looks anything like puzzled. Evidently the guys know all about Tommy's attempt at hiring himself a PI. 'From what I know about Tommy, he might need telling more'n once.'

'Your young one doesn't look like she's telling him to fix anything himself,' Senan says. Trey says a few more cheery words to Tommy, gives him a nod, and heads for the door to the bathrooms, dodging the sandwich waitress. The amiable look falls off Tommy's face the second she turns away. He watches her the way a man with a flyswatter watches a fly, right up until the waitress catches his attention and he slaps on a big cheesy smile like he expects her to ask for a selfie.

'I gotta take a leak,' Cal says, standing up.

'I would if I was you, Sunny Jim,' Mart advises him. 'Take your time; get the job done right.'

Cal makes his way through the crowd as fast as he can, dodging anyone who's going to want a chat. He knows damn well that he should postpone this conversation till he has guaranteed privacy and a cool head, but he doesn't give a shit. This room is filled up with grief and fear, lapping at every parent's chin till they're gasping for breath, they're craning to keep above water. People are whipping their heads back and forth to check on great big teenagers like they're watching toddlers. And Trey picked now to get into it with Tommy Moynihan. Here Cal was getting all misty-eyed, thinking she was growing up; any eight-year-old without an actual concussion would know better than that.

He hangs around in the badly lit corridor outside the john like a pervert, being absorbed in his phone. The corridor smells of drains and has the kind of wallpaper that looks like someone's gramma put a curse on anyone who removes it. It's a couple of very long minutes, during which Cal gets increasingly pissed off, before Trey comes out drying her hands on her jeans.

''M not getting drunk,' she says, after one look at Cal's face. 'Aidan only has a little flask between all of us.'

'Come here,' Cal says, heading for the far end of the corridor, so he can quit looking like a creep.

Trey follows him. 'What?'

'What'd Tommy Moynihan want?'

Trey gives him an impossibly blank look. 'Huh?'

'Kid. I'm not in the mood.'

'He didn't want anything,' Trey says, after a second. 'I was the one that went over to him.'

'Well, even better,' Cal says. 'What for?'

'Asked him does he fancy a new dining-room table. Told him we're booked up till summer, but we can fit him in then if he wants.'

'Right,' Cal says. 'What'd he say?'

'He said nah, he's grand, he'll come find me if he needs me. I said no problem, any time, I'll be right here.'

With her hair neat, she looks less like a wild mountain creature and more like an actual member of society. She understands exactly what Tommy Moynihan meant, and she made sure he understood exactly what she meant, too. For better or worse, she's learning to speak Ardnakelty's language.

'Tommy's dangerous,' Cal says. 'Get that in your head right now.'

'I *know* that.'

'No you don't. You say it, but you don't act like it. You think he's just some old guy with stupid hair, he can't do anything to you. If Tommy wants to mess you up, he can mess you up bad.'

'I know all that. I'm not fuckin' thick.'

'So what the hell are you poking him for?'

Trey's chin is set hard. ''M not *poking* him. I didn't go in there saying hey, fuckface, who're you gonna hire to rub shite on our door now that we bet up Donie? All I done was say I'd make him furniture. 'Cause that's what I *do*.'

Cal knows that hot grey glare well. He supposes he should be grateful for small mercies – a few years ago she would have thrown rocks through Tommy's windows or some shit like that – but he's not. 'Right. So you're telling me you were trying to, what? Make nice with Tommy? Kiss and make up, after the other night? I look dumb to you?'

'I fuckin' live here,' Trey says. 'Tommy Moynihan better get used to it.'

Cal looks at her, standing there with her feet planted on the sticky carpet and her chin out, unblinking. She's staking her claim on her territory, starting to draw the fierce, clumsy lines that will gradually define the shape of her life. He wants to reach out and put his hand on her head, but he doesn't do it. He can't tell whether he'd be holding her steady or holding her down.

'I guess he had,' he says.

Trey watches him, seeing the anger fade. 'I knew he wasn't gonna say yes,' she tells him. 'I wasn't gonna get us stuck making a table for that prick.'

'Good,' Cal says. 'The only thing I feel like making him is a knuckle sandwich.'

Trey grins. 'Tomorrow me and Kate are gonna walk Banjo past Moynihans',' she says. ''M hoping he'll piss on that stupid fountain yoke. C'n I bring Rip as well?'

'Sure,' Cal says. 'He could use the exercise; he's getting chunky. Make sure you wave at the cameras.'

Trey waves with her middle fingers. 'No you don't,' Cal says. 'You be—'

'Yeah yeah yeah,' Trey says, 'be mannerly,' but she's still grinning as she heads off back to her buddies.

'So tell us,' Mel says, leaning forward too far across the table to Lena. 'This fella of yours. What's he like?' They're a few drinks in. Mel's lipstick has worn patchy, and her curls – as red as ever, but dyed now – are starting to break loose from their twist.

They've covered Julie's mammy's chemo, Yvonne's new boss, Mel's husband's refusal to get a decent cover for the slurry pit till she threatened to leave him, and the parent feud on Phil's camogie team. It's Lena's turn. 'I'm saving a fortune on furniture,' she says. Cal isn't currency, any more than Trey is.

'I'd say you feel like a young one,' Yvonne says dreamily, 'going out with him.' She's settled back on the banquette, swirling her straw in the glass parked comfortably on her stomach. 'Come here, that could be why you look younger, as well.'

'Why would she feel like a young one?' Phil says. 'He's no toy boy. What age is he?'

'The same as myself,' Lena says. 'A year older.' She's not used to being in a conversation this size, never mind being the focus of it. The speed and the overlap and the tangents, coming at her from all sides, are making her feel lightheaded.

'D'you mean 'cause she's getting the ride?' Mel asks Yvonne. Julie squeals and slaps Mel's arm; Mel whacks her hand away. ''Cause they haven't been together long enough to get bored with it, like the rest of us?'

'You've a filthy mind, d'you know that? No, what I mean is, he's foreign. Girls like us – our age, like – we never went out with foreign fellas.'

'We did,' Julie objects. 'My sister married an Australian.'

'Because she emigrated to *Australia*,' Phil says. 'Who was she supposed to marry? A fuckin' Somali?'

'I shifted a Spanish student one time,' Mel says reminiscently. 'At a disco in Athlone. He was a fuckin' woeful kisser, it was like shifting a Labrador' – 'Oh Jesus!' from Julie – 'but I was over the moon with myself all the same. I was the only one that had got off with anyone that wasn't some kinda cousin.'

'Exactly,' Yvonne says, waving her glass to focus everyone on her point. A bit slops out onto her hand, but she ignores it. 'In my entire life, right, I never got off with anyone that was from outside this *county*. 'Cause when we were that age, there was no one around only Irish fellas. You hadta emigrate to find anyone else. But the young ones nowadays, loads of them'd be going out with fellas from Brazil, or Nigeria, or Poland. Lena's like a young one.'

'That's me,' Lena says. 'Young at heart.'

'I'll tell you one thing,' Phil says. 'If you wanta marry a foreign fella, you're lucky you sold Sean's land first. The Dunnes went buck wild over that, amn't I right?'

'They had conniptions,' Lena says. She isn't drunk, but that same reckless looseness is filling her up. Sean's family might as well be her currency; let them come in useful at last. For a moment she wonders what it would have been like to be able to bitch about them to these women, back in the nightmare months after Sean died, instead of gnawing herself to the bone with silent fury. 'They'da been welcome to buy the land themselves, but they didn't want that. They thought I oughta let his nephews work it for the rest of my life, and then leave it to them in my will. One of Sean's brothers, right, I'm not saying which one, but listen to this: outa the goodness of his heart, he came up with a budget for me. An actual spreadsheet, like, for me to live by. How I could cut back here and do a bitta overtime there, and then I wouldn't need to charge them rent. He emailed it to me.'

Everyone's gobsmacked and laughing at the same time, and Lena finds herself laughing too. 'He'd a link in there to where I could get cheap toilet roll,' she says. 'In bulk, like, and store it in the shed.'

'The brass neck on him,' Mel says, jaw-dropped. 'Was that Kenny?'

'Not telling.'

'I bet it was. Didja tell him to stick his budget up his hole?'

'I couldn't be arsed. I just went ahead and sold the land. Never heard from him and his spreadsheet again.'

'If you think they had a conniption then,' Phil says, 'imagine what they'd say now, if you still owned that land, and you marrying a Yank. You could leave it to him.'

'They'd have aneurysms,' Lena says. 'The whole lotta them at once. It'd sound like fireworks going off.'

'The Dunnes are all awful high-strung,' Julie says. Mel elbows her and she claps a hand to her mouth, horrified. 'Ah, no, Jesus, I didn't mean Sean, I only meant—'

'You're grand,' Lena says. 'They are. I oughta know.' Everyone bursts out laughing again, and after a second even Julie joins in.

For the last few minutes, Lena has been feeling someone's

eyes on the back of her head. When she turns round, she meets Dymphna Duggan's concentrated stare across the room.

On either side of her, Noreen and Dessie are intent on conversations of their own, but Mrs Duggan is watching Lena. She lifts one hand and beckons.

'Oh Jesus,' Yvonne says, cringing. 'Does she want me or you?'

'Me,' Lena says. She puts down her glass and stands up.

'The Lord be with you,' Yvonne says behind her, as she heads off into the crowd.

It's a long time since Lena was in a room with this many people. What presses on her, more than the shoulder-bumps and the clatter of voices, is the smell: hundreds of perfumes and damp coats and cigarette-smoked jumpers, all clotted together along with the thick savoury reek of undefined soup. She breathes through her mouth and tries to remember the smell of her yard under rain.

Mrs Duggan has all her jewellery out for the occasion. She's draped with gold: curly brooches, rings, a thick crucifix. 'Lena Dunne,' she says, smiling up from her banquette. Her voice is flat and slow, as heavy as her body. 'You scrub up well.'

'Thanks,' Lena says. 'You're looking well yourself.'

'I'm in great form,' Mrs Duggan says. 'Great form altogether. 'Tis a while since I had a day out.' She lifts her sherry glass to Lena. 'I didn't think I'd see you here.'

'I was in school with Claire,' Lena says.

'You're feeling fierce sociable these days,' Mrs Duggan says. 'I hear you've been calling in here and calling in there, handing out the blackberry jam like there's no tomorra.'

Lena says nothing. Mrs Duggan sips sherry and watches her.

'If you're feeling sociable,' she says, 'don't be leaving me out, now. You brought me some a that jam before, d'you remember that?'

'I do, yeah,' Lena says.

'I thought you would, all right,' Mrs Duggan says, with a small private smile curling her thin mouth. 'I liked that. I et it on soda bread. You'll make me soda bread, won't you, Noreen?'

'I will, o' course,' Noreen says promptly, over her shoulder. Noreen has been managing to keep her conversation snapping along while also maintaining a wary eye on Mrs Duggan and Lena.

'Now,' Mrs Duggan says to Lena. 'Let you call round to me with another pot of that jam, and we'll be sociable together.'

'I'll see if I have any left,' Lena says.

'Ah, you do,' Mrs Duggan assures her. 'If you look hard enough, you'll find one. Call round to me then.' She dismisses Lena with a lift of her chin and turns her attention to scanning the room.

On her way back to the table Lena runs into Trey, dodging through the crowd with the agile expertise of someone accustomed to school corridors. 'There's some fuckin' eejits going around with sandwiches,' Trey says, by way of greeting. 'They look like they'd give you the shites.'

'Don't eat 'em,' Lena says.

'Wasn't going to,' Trey says. 'Look—' She jerks her chin at a girl meandering past with a half-empty tray and an air of distaste for the whole experience. 'Someone oughta trip her up,' she says. 'Flat on her fuckin' face.'

Lena shakes off the residue of Mrs Duggan and looks at Trey properly. 'Are you starving, is it?' she asks.

Trey shakes her head impatiently. ''S not that,' she says. 'Just, they oughta have more respect. I know your woman Rachel doesn't care, she's dead, but they oughta at least have dacent sandwiches.'

'They oughta,' Lena says. 'Yeah.' She wishes sharply that she could ward off danger from Trey the way Yvonne and the rest do with their kids, by bitching about her eating habits or her schoolwork or her fashion sense: small piseogs, to guard kids who come from solid homes where safety has always been the default. Trey, after the various things life has thrown her way, needs stronger stuff than that.

'Go home,' she says. 'I've things to do here still, but Cal can take you.'

'Nah,' Trey says, unfazed by the change of subject, and she heads back to her mates, nipping around people like they're defenders.

Seeing as he's there, Cal goes to the john. He could do with a minute or two of quiet.

He doesn't get it. Eugene Moynihan is at the sinks, with the water running, staring at himself in the mirror. He looks like he might have been there a while.

'For fuck's *sake*,' he says, when he sees Cal. 'Leave me *alone*.'

He sounds too weary even to be obstreperous. 'I'm not aiming to bother you,' Cal says gently. 'I'm sorry for your loss.'

'Whatever,' Eugene says. He looks down at his hands, which are loose in the sink like he forgot them there. 'If you've changed your mind, talk to my father, not me. I don't give a shit whether you do what he wants or not. In fact, I'd rather you didn't. OK?'

'I'm not planning to,' Cal says. It sounds like Tommy might not have shared the details of the Donie episode with Eugene, which is unexpected but convenient.

'Great,' Eugene says. 'Congratulations.'

Cal is expecting him to walk out, but Eugene just stands there. He's swaying very slightly forward and back. Some of it could be exhaustion, but Eugene has also had a little more booze than he probably should have. 'It's all gone to shit,' he says, mostly to himself.

Cal leans against the wall with his hands in his pockets and puts on his listener face, which is an approachable blank, ready to nod mildly at anything up to and including cannibalism. He had no intention of seeking out a conversation with Eugene today, of all days, but here they both are. He's interested in hearing what, besides the obvious, has gone to shit.

'I know, son,' he says. 'This is a bad day. But from all's I hear, you got better ones ahead.'

Eugene looks around sharply. 'What are you talking about?'

'Well,' Cal says, 'word is, come springtime you're set to be our new councillor, or whatever it's called. Did I get that wrong?'

'That,' Eugene says, and snorts. 'Yeah. Whatever.' He goes back to staring into the sink.

Eugene doesn't appear to have the same level of enthusiasm about this plan as Tommy does, which Cal finds interesting. 'No need to be downhearted, son,' he says comfortingly. 'You just ride out the rumours for a while, and things'll be fine.'

Eugene's head snaps around again. 'What *rumours*?'

Cal ducks his head, abashed, like he let that slip by mistake. 'Aw, hell,' he says, grimacing and rubbing the back of his neck, 'nothing you oughta take notice of. People are confused, is all. You just leave them be for a while, and they'll—'

'Confused about *what*? If this is that bullshit about me dumping Rachel, they can all get fucked. Even if I had been, which I *wasn't*, it's none of their business.'

'It ain't that,' Cal says. 'Mostly they're just confused that Rachel didn't call you, before she did what she did. Seems like she woulda.'

'Yeah. No shit. She *should* have phoned me. I'd have been right down to her, I'd have—' Eugene breathes hard and bites down on his lips. 'But obviously she wasn't thinking straight. *Obviously*. What am I supposed to do about that?'

'Nothing you can do,' Cal agrees. 'But there's gonna be folks thinking she must've got in touch with you some other way.

Like maybe you met her that night, or she came over to your place, or whatever. You can't blame them. It's only natural.'

'For fuck's *sake*,' Eugene says, through his teeth. Cal judges that Eugene has had pretty close to enough, all around. 'If I'd seen her, I would have *stopped* her. I was sitting at home all evening, and Rachel didn't come near the place. I have no idea why, because I'm not fucking telepathic, but she didn't. And things are bad enough already without every bored middle-aged cow in this place making up bullshit about me.'

'You might could get your mama and daddy to tell them,' Cal suggests. The outrage sounds real, but that doesn't mean Eugene is telling the truth; he's in the habit of being outraged at anything that doesn't suit him. 'If they were home with you. They could set folks straight.'

'Oh, thanks. Because I hadn't thought of that myself. Yeah, they were home with me. All night, till we went out looking. And no, they're not going to go around explaining that to every bog-monster in town, begging them to please graciously believe us—'

'Hey,' Cal says peaceably. 'Ain't no need to get tetchy with me. I believe you. But if other folks believe you too, then you gotta know they're gonna be saying you and Rachel must've had some kinda argument, or even broken up. Or else she would've come to you.'

The sudden jerk of anger sends Eugene off balance enough that he has to grab the sink to steady himself. 'I can't win,' he says. 'What the fuck. I can't win.'

Cal can see that Eugene means it, but he finds it hard to work up much sympathy for a guy who's had things go his way so often that it feels against God and nature when they don't. 'Well, you can see how their minds would run that way,' he says.

'People around here are fucking morons,' Eugene says. 'I swear to God, this place would be better if we could just . . .'

He makes a loose swiping motion with one arm, and staggers a little. 'Fuck it, clear them all out. Clean sweep. Start over.'

This isn't the sentiment Cal would expect from an aspiring representative of the populace, or anyway not out loud. 'Well,' he says, 'they're mostly not educated folk like you. You can't hold that against them.'

'Yeah, well, if they're not educated, they could at least listen to people who are. No offence, I don't know who you hang out with, but most people around here, their minds . . .' Eugene holds up a finger and thumb, a fraction apart. '*That* fucking size. On a *good* day. The bigger picture? Forget it.'

Cal scratches the back of his neck and considers that. 'You got a point,' he says. 'I guess if you spend your days farming, you gotta concentrate on what's right in front of your nose. You don't get much practice in seeing the big picture.'

'Don't get me started,' Eugene says. 'The biggest thing they can get moving is a fucking combine harvester, and if anyone comes along wanting to do something bigger, they melt *down*. They'll be grateful for it in the end, they always are, but you can't get that through their heads in advance. You just have to put up with their bullshit till everything's done and dusted, and they all come tell you how great you are. My father says it was the same thing when he started the plant. People freaking *out*, oh no it'll taint the water supply or whatever the fuck, and once it was up and running, oh look at all these jobs aren't you amazing. Jesus Christ.'

Cal sends up a prayer to whatever gods are out there that no one will pick this moment to take a leak. Eugene needs to talk, and Cal is safe: he's an outsider. This kid, keeping himself at a genteel distance from peasant doings, hasn't noticed that it's not that clear-cut, these days.

'Rachel seemed like a smart kid to me,' Cal says. He's being very careful. 'Not as smart as you, maybe, but smart enough to see the big picture if you explained it to her. I woulda thought, anyway.'

'Yeah,' Eugene says. His eyes close, which makes him sway worse. 'You'd think. Her family aren't bog-monsters, they can hold an actual dinner-table conversation that isn't about sheep diseases, you'd think, right? And Rachel, a lot of people thought she was just a dumb blonde, but that's because they're morons. She was smarter than all of them.'

'Well, I figured that much,' Cal says. 'I didn't know her too well, but I couldn't see you getting engaged to no dummy.'

'Right. Exactly. People thought, because of the way she dressed and the way she talked . . . But underneath, she had a lot more going on. An actual thought process, with, like, depth, and . . .' Eugene loses his train of thought. His eyes are still closed, and his face is drawn down in tight lines of misery. 'I heard drowning is really peaceful,' he says. 'That could be bullshit, I don't know.'

'But Rachel still didn't get the big picture,' Cal says. Eugene can grieve on his own time.

Eugene jerks with anger again, his eyes flying open. 'So? How the fuck was I supposed to know she wouldn't? She was my girlfriend, I told her stuff. That's *normal*. I'm *allowed* to do that. Like, what's the big fucking deal?'

'Doesn't seem like any big deal to me,' Cal agrees. 'A man telling his woman what's on his mind, that's how it's supposed to go.'

'And we didn't have a fucking *argument*. People pulled that right out of their arses. She was just worried. She would've come round in the end.'

'You figure?'

'Of course she would. She just needed time, that's what she was like, she always needed to think things—' Eugene's knuckles are white on the rim of the sink. 'I told him that. I *told* him.'

'But he didn't agree,' Cal says. He's not about to ask whether they're talking about Tommy. He's had plenty of suspects where Eugene is. Eugene is freewheeling down the tracks under his own desperate momentum, but one wrong touch, even the lightest, and he'll derail.

'I *knew* her,' Eugene says. 'We were together five years, did you know that? Since I was eighteen and she was sixteen. We knew each other our whole lives. If I said to just wait and she'd come round, he should have believed me.'

'Well,' Cal says, 'you can see how he'd be a little bit edgy.'

Eugene looks around sharply. 'What do you even know about it?'

'Hey, I ain't badmouthing nobody,' Cal says, raising his hands. 'Not my place. I'm only saying: when the stakes get high, folks can get a mite twitchy. Am I wrong?'

Eugene blinks hard, trying to focus his eyes on Cal. 'Fuck you,' he says, eventually. 'You don't even know what you're talking about. Just . . .' He rears back from the sink and heads for the door, unsteadily. 'Fuck you,' he says again, over his shoulder. Probably he's trying to make a good exit, but on his way out he gets mixed up with some old guy coming in, and by the time he's disentangled himself, the moment is gone.

Cal does his business and spends a long time washing his hands. He feels a little bit better about Trey's manners, anyway. They may have some inconsistencies, but she's a country mile ahead of the crown prince of Ardnakelty.

In Eugene's defence, he's having a rough month. Eugene thinks Tommy did something to Rachel – Cal figures what he has is a suspicion rather than straight-up knowledge, or he'd be in even worse shape. Eugene may be right or he may not, but either way, family dinner at the Moynihan mansion has to be a real laugh riot these days.

No wonder Tommy is keeping Eugene close to home. It's

got nothing to do with endorsements from Dickie O'Shea and his cheap suit. Tommy wants Eugene under his eye because he's worried Eugene might crack, one way or another. From what Cal just saw, he's right to worry.

The bathroom is cold and smells of some grim industrial bleach. Cal dries his hands and goes back into what feels more and more like the danger zone.

The drink and the chat have smoothed some of the jagged edges off the day. Everyone's posture has loosened; Mel is leaning forward with her elbows on the table, and Phil has given up on sitting like she's wearing a dress, even though she is, and has her knees firmly planted apart. Yvonne is licking her thumb and trying to rub away a drop of vodka and Coke that's landed on her bosom; Julie is passing around her phone to show everyone a selfie Niall just sent her from the balcony of his new apartment. They're able, finally, to start talking about Rachel.

'Niall usedta fancy Rachel,' Julie says. She takes the phone back and gazes at it, slightly unfocused. 'Ages back, when they were fourteen, like. He never said, but I knew. I keep wondering, what if they'd got together? Maybe she'da gone off to Berlin with him. Maybe they'd be sitting on that balcony right now. Having those beers outa massive glasses.'

'She wouldn'ta gone for your Niall,' Mel says. 'She always wanted Eugene. Fuck alone knows why, but she did.'

'I'd say she felt sorry for him,' Yvonne says unexpectedly. She frowns down at her good dress, which is too tight across the bust, and tries to hitch herself into place. 'Rachel was like that: a terrible softie for anything that needed looking after. All them fecking kittens. And that time your Niamh was getting bullied in school, Julie, sure that's how they made friends to start with—'

'Why the fuck would she be sorry for Eugene Moynihan?' Phil wants to know. 'Of all people?'

'She said no one understood him,' Julie says. Phil snorts. 'That's what Niamh said, anyhow. I know he's an awful consequence, but I suppose he's never had much choice, sure he hasn't? With Tommy always at him to be the heir to the throne, whether he wanted to or not. It'd have anyone's head melted.'

'He's still an awful consequence,' Phil says.

'He is, all right,' Julie acknowledges. 'All the same, d'you know what' – she lowers her voice – 'I wouldn't say Rachel was stepping out on him. She'd feel too guilty.'

'In fairness,' Mel says, lifting an eyebrow, 'that's kinda the point people are making.'

'I know, yeah. But still. She wouldn't.'

'*You* wouldn't. You'd never know about anyone else.'

'You were asking around about that,' Phil says, pointing her pint at Lena.

'I was, yeah,' Lena says. She's been waiting for this.

'How come? It's a long time since you gave a shite about anything around here.'

The atmosphere has sharpened. Julie, who always hated arguments, ducks her head and starts picking polish off a thumbnail. It doesn't bother Lena. The sediment of resentment was there all along, the same way it's there in Noreen. She likes Phil for being open with it.

'It's a long time since anyone around here came asking me for help,' she points out. 'Ye all know Rachel called round to me, earlier that night. She was asking about her cat that was hurt, but I felt like there was something else she wanted to say.'

'That's only hindsight,' Yvonne says. 'We're all doing it. There's a fuckin' epidemic of hindsight in these parts.'

'Maybe,' Lena says. 'But once I heard the rumour going round, I reckoned if it was true, that could've been what she had on her mind. I'd like to know. Just to set my own mind at ease.'

'Why would she go to you about that?' Phil says. They're

all keeping their voices low, even Phil, who has five kids and coaches the camogie. 'She hardly knew you.'

''Cause I'm not close to anyone round here,' Lena says. Julie makes an inarticulate noise of protest, but Phil nods. 'So whatever she told me, I'd keep it to myself.'

'Fair enough,' Phil says. 'So what? What difference does it make now?'

'Tell us something,' Lena says. 'How many of ye heard Sean wouldn't let me have friends?'

There's a silence. The women glance sideways at each other, or down at their drinks.

'All of us,' Phil says bluntly. Julie shoots her an agonised look. Phil ignores her.

'I know you did, yeah,' Lena says. 'Did ye believe it?'

No one is sure what the right answer is.

'I don't care either way,' Lena says. 'The point is, it was a loada shite. So I'm not going to believe anything else I hear around the place, not without looking into it myself. Mostly I don't bother my arse, 'cause it's none of my business, but Rachel made it my business this time.'

'Who knows what's true and what's not, at this stage,' Mel says. '*If* Rachel wanted to talk to you, it coulda been anything.'

'Like what?' Lena says. 'You're in the loop; you tell me. What was worrying her?'

'D'you not think we've all been wondering the same fuckin' thing?' Phil snaps. 'I practically sat Louise down and shone a torch in her eyes, asking her had Rachel said anything about anything. I got sweet fuck-all. That's what everyone's got, not just you. Sweet fuck-all.'

'For a while there Michelle Healy was going around saying there musta been some TikTok challenge about drinking antifreeze, for fuck's sake,' Mel says. 'That's how little people have.'

'That's why everyone reckons 'twas her love life,' Yvonne says. 'Not just for the scandal, like. 'Cause there's nothing else it could be.'

'So everyone jumped straight to her cheating,' Lena says, lifting an eyebrow. 'Even if it was her love life, that could be a million things. Maybe Tommy and Clodagh didn't approve, or else they were pushing Rachel to do something she didn't wanta do – go into the family business, let's say, or who knows what. But it can't have been any of that, God no, it hasta have been that Rachel was a slut.'

'Or Eugene was,' Yvonne points out, with a glance around to make sure no one's listening. 'There's plenty of people on that buzz, as well, and that's a lot more likely if you ask me – no one around here would go sticking it in Eugene Moynihan's girlfriend, not if he had sense, but Eugene could get up to all sorts in Dublin, and no one'd have a clue. Look' – she leans closer, across the table – 'Tommy and Clodagh wouldn't be my pick for in-laws, but Rachel was with Eugene years. She knew what she was getting into, Tommy and Clodagh knew what they were getting – and they were delighted with it, from everything I've heard. Why would it all go tits-up overnight?'

She means it. No one has so much as shot each other quick glances, or tightened their lips. There's no warning here. Nothing is being held unsaid; whatever Eugene and Tommy were at, Rachel kept it to herself. Lena could have stayed home today.

'I suppose,' she says. 'Yeah.'

'Either Rachel was doing the dirt on Eugene,' Phil says, 'or he was doing something on her. Whichever one it was, the poor girl's gone; you won't change that. Pick one and leave it at that.'

Lena looks around the table and understands that, for all of them looking back at her, it's that clear because it has to be.

The only way their children are safe is if there's an answer in place, one cleanly confined within the boundaries of Rachel's life. Everything beyond that is barred. Whatever happened to Rachel is being crushed out of existence by other people's needs.

The vodka and Cokes have been wiped away; she's stone-cold sober. Her mouth has the thick, sour taste of a hangover.

'If you go round asking questions,' Mel says, 'all you'll do is start drama. No one needs that. People are up to ninety already.'

'Drama,' Lena says. 'Will I, yeah?'

'We know you wouldn't mean to,' Julie says quickly. Her face is puckered up with worry. 'But we know you, sure. Other people mightn't get it.'

Lena feels herself staked down by their certainty that, after thirty blank years, they know her. She can't tell whether it makes her want to laugh or to walk out.

'What Mel's trying to tell you,' Phil says, 'only she's being tactful, is that people are saying you're nosing around 'cause you or your detective fella reckon 'twasn't suicide. I'm not asking' – she's holding up a hand, although Lena hasn't tried to say anything – 'I don't wanta know. I'm only saying: that's a fuckin' gift to anyone that likes stirring up trouble.'

Here's the warning at last. It's one Lena half expected – Cal's old job has always appealed to Ardnakelty's imagination – but it's not the one she was angling for. 'Well,' she says. 'I've never enjoyed starting drama.'

'Good,' Mel says. 'Then don't.'

Phil examines Lena for a moment and gives her a brief nod. 'You're no fool,' she says. 'You never were.' She tosses back the rest of her pint, to mark the subject closed.

'Hang on,' Yvonne says, blinking. 'If Sean didn't stop you having mates . . .' It's taken her a while to think this out, through the vodka. 'If that was a loada aul' shite. Then how come . . . ?'

'It doesn't matter,' Lena says. She can feel Mrs Duggan's gaze scraping at the back of her head again. She doesn't turn round. 'It made some kinda sense at the time.'

'Was that Sonny McHugh I saw you not talking to over there, bucko?' Mart enquires, as Cal settles back onto his stool.

'I said hi,' Cal says. Someone has got in another prepper-sized bunch of pints. 'He just wasn't talking back. I figure he could have a mood coming on.' Sonny, the loudest and most jovial of the McHugh brothers, is known to have moods. Cal gets the sense that elsewhere the moods might be called depression, but anyone using the word to Sonny would get told to fuck off in multiple creative ways.

Francie snorts into his pint. 'Don't be snorting like a fuckin' bull calf,' Bobby orders him. 'There's no shame in the moods. They could happen to anyone.'

'Doctor fuckin' Phil, is it? Or Oprah?'

'Sure, you're nothing but one big mood,' Bobby tells him. 'A mood in a shirt that needs ironing.'

'Arrah, fuck off and shift your dolly-bird and don't be annoying me. You're pissed.'

Bobby, the resident lightweight, is in fact noticeably drunk. The rest of the guys are a little red around the eyes and a little loose around the neck, nothing that a casual observer would pick up on, but Cal knows the signs.

'Jacks,' Senan says abruptly, standing up and shoving past Bobby.

'See what you done?' Bobby says to Francie. 'Now *he's* in a mood. We'll all be—'

'I done fuck-all. That fella lost a child of his own before. D'you want him to be dancing a jig, on the day that's in it?'

'These last couple of weeks'd give anyone a mood,' Cal says, aiming to restore harmony.

'You've got the wrong end of the stick, Jean-Claude,' Mart

says. 'That's no mood that Sonny's got on him. Tell me something: you were helping the McHughs trim their hedges not long ago, amn't I right?'

'Yeah,' Cal says.

'What about this week, and them pulling down that aul' disgrace of a shed on Con's land? Did they ask you for a hand?'

'Nope,' Cal says. At the time he figured Sonny must have got his cast off, but the cast is still there.

'Watch this, now,' Mart says. A bunch of the McHugh brothers are clustered around a too-small table, their broad shoulders jostling together like bullocks'. Mart keeps his gaze on them till Tadhg McHugh glances around and catches his eye. Mart raises his glass. Tadhg stares for a minute, blank-faced, without nodding or lifting his glass in return. Then he turns away.

'I've known that fella since he was in nappies,' Mart says. 'I banjaxed my shoulder pulling a ewe of his out of a ditch. He helped carry my mammy's coffin. And now I could be bleeding to death on his doorstep, and he'd walk over me.'

Cal, looking out at the crowd, sees it shift and click into a pattern that was there all along, right under his nose. The groupings, and their movement, were never random. The Moynihans' table faces the Holohans', across the room. Around each one, people have ranged themselves. They move around, mingling with the people in the middle, buying drinks and asking after ailments and shooting the breeze, and little by little those people have been shifting their stools, one way or the other.

Cal thinks, *Shit*.

'Father Eamonn wouldn't be pleased at all, at all,' Mart says. 'All that lovely holy advice he worked so hard to give us, and no one heeding a word of it.'

'It'd remind you of a wedding, wouldn't it?' Bobby says. His face is puckered with worry. 'The bride's side over here, and the groom's side over there.'

'I was only ever at one wedding that looked like this,' Cal says. 'It ended in shooting.'

'This might end in shooting as well,' Francie says, with a sudden sharp note in his voice. He puts down his pint and pushes back his stool. 'Look.'

Senan, on his way to the bathroom, has bumped elbows with Long John Sharkey, on his way back from the bar to the Moynihan side of the room. Long John is staring at the splatter of Guinness on his white shirt, and Senan is staring at Long John. Both of them have bad looks on their faces. Their shoulders have rolled into fighting position.

Cal and the others all stand up as Long John says something to Senan, and Senan says something back. Heads have started turning.

'I'll do it,' Cal says. The noise in the room is falling away. Between heads he gets a glimpse of Fintan Holohan's face blank with the overload of despair, beyond even being reached by one more damn thing piled onto this day. 'Sit down.'

Francie is already moving, but Mart puts out a hand to block him. 'Let Jean-Claude sort it,' he says.

Cal moves fast, ignoring the table-corners jabbing him and the handbags snagging his feet. Long John kicks away a stool, making room. Doireann Cunniffe, or someone like her, has started up a high hooting alarm sound. Senan's fists are rising.

Cal reaches Senan just as Long John goes to shove him in the chest, and just as two of the McHugh brothers grab Long John by the elbows. 'Man,' he says, getting an arm around Senan's shoulders in a grip that's tighter than it looks. 'Not here.'

Senan is red-faced and breathing through his nose like a bull. 'I'll have the fucker,' he says. 'Get back.'

He tries to shake off Cal's arm, but Cal holds on. Long John makes another feint at him, and the McHughs drag him back.

Senan laughs and beckons Long John with both hands. Even Doireann Cunniffe has gone silent.

'No,' Cal says, hard and close in Senan's ear. 'The Holohans don't need that. You want to make their day even worse?'

That reaches Senan. After a moment, his shoulders slowly ease under Cal's arm.

The McHughs are already turning Long John away, patting and soothing him like they would an angered animal. He lets them herd him, but he glares over his shoulder as he goes. Senan bares his teeth at him.

'Come on,' Cal says. He steers Senan away, towards their table. Slowly the sound starts to return to the room, a tamped-down frenetic buzz. As Cal passes the Moynihans, he sees Tommy looking him right in the eye, with no expression at all.

10

Mrs Duggan doesn't go upstairs, any more than she goes outdoors. Instead she lives on the ground floor of Noreen and Dessie's house, down the street from the shop. The dining room has been turned into her bedroom; she spends her days in the sitting room, wedged into a massive pink velvet armchair patinated brownish by wear and cigarette smoke, enjoying the wide berth the townland gives her window. Mrs Duggan doesn't have the same kind of power she had back when she ran the shop, but she's adapted.

Lena goes to see her on Thursday morning, when no one else will be home, and she goes a roundabout way so as not to pass by the shop and Noreen's sharp eyes. She's brought a pot of her blackberry jam. She's done this before, and she knows that Mrs Duggan's real currency is less tangible and less innocent; the jam is only a preliminary offering, to open the negotiations.

Cal doesn't know Lena is coming here. Last night – curled up on his sofa with her head on his chest, watching an old cowboy film on the laptop propped on the coffee table – she almost said it to him. Telling Cal things feels natural, these days; when she met him she was out of the habit of telling anyone anything much, but it's become one of her accustomed pleasures, the two of them passing small daily finds from hand to hand for the other to examine. She told him, straight away, what Sheila said – he was the one who asked her to go to Sheila, she had no right to keep the results from him. But Mrs Duggan wasn't Cal's idea, and whatever she comes out with, Lena might not want it handed over to Mart Lavin. She could share it with Cal on condition that he keeps it to himself, but she's not going to do that. Cal's actions are his own; if she makes one move to manage what he can and can't do, it'll alter their relationship beyond repair. Instead she stayed silent and watched the horses gallop across the little screen. Their hoofbeats muddled the steady rhythm of Cal's heart under her ear, till she lost track of it.

Mrs Duggan has filled her sitting room to the brim with herself. Every wall is crowded with ornate brown furniture stuffed with painted porcelain, silver frames, Sacred Heart statuettes; the carpet and the curtains are a tumult of ferocious purple flowers. The side table at her elbow is cluttered with small things, pear drops and dominoes and earrings, all of them wearing the furtively sinister air of amulets that could jinx your week if they found their way into your pocket. Even the air, hot and dry, seethes with the traces of cigarette ash and the faint, high whistling of the gas fire. At the heart of it all is Mrs Duggan, vast and formless in a magenta dress coated with swirls of tiny magenta beads, like one of those underwater creatures that lie wide-mouthed on the seabed waiting to receive anyone and anything that comes their way.

'Well done,' she says, taking the jam from Lena and inspecting it. Her slow, heavy voice raises the hair on Lena's neck. 'I thought you'd find one, all right, if you looked hard enough.'

Lena almost wishes she'd told Cal what she's at. This room feels like the kind of place where you make sure your backup knows you're going in. 'There's this to go with it,' she says, handing over a loaf of soda bread.

Mrs Duggan chuckles, weighing the bread in her hand. 'To save Noreen having to make me some,' she says. 'Aren't you a great sister altogether. Does she appreciate you like you deserve?'

'She does, yeah,' Lena says. Mrs Duggan is scavenging for details of her argument with Noreen. She's not getting them, or anyhow not for free.

'Sit you down,' Mrs Duggan says, pointing to a spindly chair. And when Lena sits: 'Pull it up here, where I can see you. My eyes are going.'

Mrs Duggan's eyes could spot a flinch at a hundred yards. Lena pulls the chair closer, till she stops crooking her finger and nods. Her hair, dyed shiny black and pulled back into a bun, is thinning, and she smells of some heavy floral powder.

Her eyes move up and down Lena, assessing. 'So you're back,' she says. 'You thought you'd never step foot in this room again till you came to see me laid out, didn'tja?'

Lena is used to being tall and hardy, but this room and this woman strip that away and make her feel slight, soft-muscled. She wants to talk, to find solidity in her own strong voice. She understands that this impulse is well-known to Mrs Duggan, and is a dangerous one. 'I'm back,' she says.

'You might as well, sure. I'm not planning on being laid out any time soon.' Mrs Duggan fumbles around the side table for her cigarettes. She shakes one out of the packet and taps its end on the table in a slow, maddening rhythm. 'Go on, so. What is it you wanta know?'

'You're the one that told me to call round,' Lena says.

The corner of Mrs Duggan's mouth curls at that. 'I heard what you've been at,' she says. 'I was watching you, up in the hotel. You want something big.'

'Tommy Moynihan's been trying to run the Reddys outa town,' Lena says. 'I'd like to know why.'

Mrs Duggan blows out a scornful puff of air. 'That's not big. That's a scrap, only. I'd nearly let you have that for nothing, only it'd set a bad example. Let's be having you: what d'you really want?'

'It might be the same thing,' Lena says. 'Or it might not. Tommy and Eugene are up to something that had Rachel Holohan's head wrecked, before she died. I'd like to know what that was.'

Mrs Duggan starts a slow wheezing that gradually builds to a deep, hoarse chuckle. 'You're after letting me down,' she tells Lena, when she can talk again. 'I been sitting here in this window for weeks now, waiting for someone to ask me the right question. When I saw you swanning up to my door, I thought: *Here we go now*. You were always a clever one, I'll give you that; too clever for your own good. And now it turns out all you're here for is shite that anyone coulda thought of.'

Lena says, 'What's the right question?'

Mrs Duggan pushes aside the things on her table till she finds a heavy gold lighter. Her fingers are swollen and stiff, weighed down by rings sunk too deep into the flesh to come off; it takes her a few tries to light up.

'D'you know what ye are, around here?' she says, glancing at Lena over the lighter. 'Ye're a terrible dull lot altogether. I been answering this place's questions since before you were born or thought of, and they're the same questions every time: who's my man doing the dirt with, what way is my mammy leaving the land, is the youngest mine or not. And depending on the answer, there'll be a bit of a spat or else there won't, and that'll be the end of it. I'm sick of the taste of them. I do try to spice things up by having wee bets with myself on who'll do what and when, but I'm right too often; there's no flavour in that.' She breathes out long twin curls of smoke through her nose. 'And the young ones nowadays, they haven't a notion. They think I'm some kinda fortune teller, cross my palm with silver. I'd two of them in here the other week asking how they'll do in their exams.' Her lip rises with disgust.

Lena says, 'What'd you tell them?'

'I took what I wanted offa them,' Mrs Duggan says, 'and then I told them something about their daddies that they didn't wanta hear, and I sent them off. Next time they'll think twice. I'm no one's wee bit of a giggle on a rainy afternoon.'

Lena says nothing. She can't stop herself from sitting with her back rigid and her feet braced on the carpet, ready. Mrs Duggan notes that, and lets Lena see her enjoy it.

'I shoulda made Pateen move away,' she says, 'as soon as we were married. Somewhere bigger, with enough people to keep me occupied. But now 'tis too late for that, so I haveta make do with what I can get around here.'

She fishes for her ashtray, grunting with the effort of leaning over, and drags it closer on the table. 'If someone comes asking me the right question,' she says, 'I'll be that pleased with them for doing something outa the ordinary, I'll give them the answer for free. I'd say I'll be waiting, but. If even Lena Dunne isn't clever enough to get it, there might be no hope. Are you still Lena Dunne? Or did you marry the Yank and no one told me?'

'Not yet,' Lena says. 'You'll hear when I do.'

'If you do,' Mrs Duggan says. 'Plenty of men'd get cold feet around a widda woman whose first man dropped dead outa the blue before fifty.' She leans back in her chair and adjusts the folds of her dress around the folds of herself, getting comfortable. The beads make tiny, dry crunching noises. 'Didja kill the other fella?' she asks, through her cigarette.

This is an easy one, Mrs Duggan warming up her arm. There have always been rumours; Lena knew that already. 'No,' she says.

Mrs Duggan nods. 'I'm playing fair,' she says. 'That's only a scrap of a question, the same as yours. I knew the answer already. But enough people have wondered that I reckoned I'd get it clear for meself, once and for all.'

Lena doesn't ask who's wondered. Mrs Duggan, amused, watches her not asking.

She says, 'Did he kill hisself?'

Lena's mind leaps like a fish inside her, twists, and lands where it was when Sean died, in the dark of their bedroom, reeking of vomit and terror. She can't see. She can feel Mrs Duggan watching, sucking up every drop of this.

She won't give her the pleasure of a long silence. 'I don't know,' she says. She has room for a flicker of surprise at how firm and matter-of-fact her voice comes out. 'The coroner brought it in as accidental.'

Mrs Duggan snorts. 'Anything's accidental if the coroner feels sorry for a poor widda woman. How would you not know? You were the last one that saw him, and the first one that found him. You'd know.'

Lena knows better than to lie. 'Sean drank,' she says, 'and he had medication for when his nerves were at him. He took both at once, when he shouldn'ta, and his heart stopped.' Her mouth forming the shapes of the words feels numb, an alien thing whose movements have nothing to do with her. 'I've no way of knowing whether he did it on purpose, or whether he just lost track.'

'Everyone's always got no way of knowing,' Mrs Duggan says. ''Tis awful convenient altogether. You're no fool. The two of ye were always together. You woulda seen it coming. Didja?'

'I saw it coming for ten years,' Lena says. 'That doesn't mean it came.'

Mrs Duggan's flat pale eyes are on hers, unblinking. Her cigarette is burning away forgotten. 'Did he not leave a note?'

'No,' Lena says. The room feels sealed, like the door vanished when she closed it behind her. 'Nothing.'

'Where was he?'

'In the bed,' Lena says.

'Was he already gone when you found him?'

'He was, yeah,' Lena says. She keeps her gaze blank, but she can feel Mrs Duggan groping through her mind, probing the corners, exploring the silent room where she lay down and held Sean, the same way she had held him thousands of times before, while he turned cold. That room was hers and Sean's alone, and now Mrs Duggan is there too.

At last Mrs Duggan nods, satisfied. She takes a long drag of her cigarette, eyes half closed to savour it. The gas fire sings its shrill single note.

'If I knew,' she says. 'One way or the other. Wouldja ask me?'

Lena says, 'You know nothing about Sean.'

Mrs Duggan chuckles. 'Maybe I do and maybe I don't,' she says. 'Wouldja ask?'

'No,' Lena says.

Mrs Duggan's eyebrows lift. 'You don't want that,' she says, 'but you want all kindsa shite about the Moynihans. What for? Lena Dunne's above this place's goings-on. Why d'you care, all of a sudden, what Tommy Moynihan's at?'

Lena is done. She says, 'You've got all you're getting.'

Mrs Duggan is too expert to try and push someone who's reached her limit. 'For now, anyhow,' she agrees. She readjusts herself to sit up straighter in her chair, in slow, effortful notches, and tamps out her cigarette. Her pleasure is over; she's getting down to business. 'Tommy Moynihan's not trying to run the Reddys outa town,' she says. 'He wants them outa that house, is all. He wants that field, and Rory Dunne won't sell the house out from under the poor fatherless childer.'

Lena says, 'Why would he want the field that bad?'

'That'd be extra,' Mrs Duggan says, 'only for 'tis the same as your other question.' She smiles at Lena. 'We think alike, you and me. I called Tommy in here just a month or two back, to ask him what he wants all that land for.' She chuckles. 'He tried to make out he came outa charity, brightening up a poor old woman's day, but we both knew better. Tommy likes to think he's the one that gives the orders in this place, but when I called him, he came running like a scared pup. He was right to. I'm not fond of being kept waiting.'

Lena's heart is still going too hard. She breathes slowly and pictures Cal, moving about his business in the small warm kitchen, whistling along to Johnny Cash while he peels potatoes.

'Tommy's getting old,' Mrs Duggan says. 'When men start getting old, they do get all in a tizzy about what they're leaving behind. Like a buncha wee dogs running around pissing on lamp posts, 'cause deep down they know all their yapping means nothing, and they're desperate to leave their mark. Tommy wants to make his mark.' Her lip curls in derision.

'He's got the meatpacking plant doing that already,' Lena says.

Mrs Duggan blows out a thin dismissive stream of air. 'Ah, God, that wouldn't do for the likes of Tommy. That's small stuff. You mightn'ta noticed, keeping to yourself the way you do, but Tommy's a man that thinks big. Isn't that a great thing to have around the place?'

Her hand plays in the box of dominoes, picking them up and letting them fall through her fingers with little clicking noises. 'You know there's a factory going up over towards Kilhone,' she says, 'making bits for computers. Everyone knows that, sure. Even you.'

'I heard,' Lena says.

'Here's what most people don't know,' Mrs Duggan says. 'Awful hush-hush, so 'tis. There's men in suits talking about it behind closed doors, but they wouldn't want word getting out to the likes of us. They're after getting more investors in. They want that factory bigger than they planned it. And for that, they need more land.'

She waits, her eyes hooded, stirring the dominoes with a finger, to see where Lena will follow this.

Lena says, 'So Tommy's buying up all the land he can, and then he'll sell it to the factory at a markup.'

'You're close,' Mrs Duggan says. 'Only what would a factory do with the bits he's bought up? A few acres of Bobby Feeney's here, and Fat Pat McHugh's field over there, and a big aul' herd of cattle in between. What use is that to anyone?'

Lena says nothing. Her side of the transaction is done; she's not going to play guessing games.

Mrs Duggan sees that, and is amused by it. 'Let's say Tommy had someone on the county council,' she says. The dominoes tick against each other. 'Someone to guarantee the factory that, if they buy up Tommy's bits and bobs, they'll be able to get compulsory purchase orders on the land in between.'

Lena hears the rush rising in her ears as this floods outwards all around her like dark water, spreading across the townland, insatiable. Probably there are farmers who'll grab at the chance to offload their back-breaking existence of being battered about by the obdurate, unfathomable whims of bureaucracy and weather. There are more who'll go down shooting sooner than give up their land. This is a depth charge; when it detonates, the whole townland will shake.

'Tommy'd be able to name his price, then,' Mrs Duggan says. 'But that's the start of it, not the heart of it. Once the dust settles, Tommy'll have alla the big men behind the factory owing him favours, and the council in his pocket, and everyone that's left round here afraid to say boo to him in case they'd be next out. He'll own this place. He can make it into whatever he wants. If Tommy wants a coupla new housing estates, or a golf club, he'll get them. If someone wants to put in one a them data centres, they'll know who the go-to man is. Tommy'll leave his mark, all right. There'll be nothing left of this townland, only Tommy's mark.'

Mrs Duggan's mouth spreads in a slow, wide smile of

pleasure. 'I'd say that mighta upset Rachel Holohan,' she says, 'if she hadda known about it.'

It fits with what Rachel said, both to Lena and to Sheila. God knows Rachel would have lost friends, if her man was at the heart of something like this. And she was young enough, and naïve enough, to believe there might be some way she could stop him.

Lena says, 'Where's Clodagh in alla this?'

'Clodagh's where she's always been,' Mrs Duggan says. 'Wherever'll get the fanciest crown for her little prince. 'Twasn't her idea – that one never had an idea of her own in her life – but she's well on board.'

'How'd you get all that outa Tommy?' Lena asks. 'I wouldn't say he wants word getting around.'

Mrs Duggan laughs, a low, private wheeze. 'I know that fella since he was born,' she says. 'Him and his mammy and daddy before him. I know a lot more than Tommy likes. He's no fool; he knows better than to say no to me.' The dominoes shift and click. 'And anyhow, Tommy needed me. Same as everyone does, sooner or later. Mick Scully from Kilhone's been on the council for twenty year now, and Tommy needs him gone; Mick wouldn't stand for any compulsory purchases. I told Tommy what to say to him, and now Mick's stepping down at Christmas.'

Lena says, 'Has Tommy been here asking you about Rachel?'

Mrs Duggan pushes the dominoes away from her. 'Let's have a wee guessing game,' she says. 'How many people would you guess have called in to me to ask about Rachel Holohan?'

Lena says, 'A few.' Plenty might want to, but Mrs Duggan is an undertaking that no one enters into lightly.

'Not a one,' Mrs Duggan says. 'You'd think there'd be a queue at my door, wouldn'tja? You'd think this room would be knee-deep in jars of jam and boxes of chocolates. Not a one. No one's asking.' She smiles at Lena. 'Except for you. Asking your wee questions all round the townland.'

Everyone else either believes they know what took Rachel to the river, or doesn't want to know; they've picked the story they need. The exception is Tommy Moynihan, who wants to know something badly enough to try and hire himself a PI, but not badly enough to walk in here and ask.

'That's why I called you in here,' Mrs Duggan says. 'I'd high hopes of you – I still have, sure, even if you're after letting me down today. Now you've got what you came for, what'll you do with it? Will you keep it to yourself, or will you tell the world?'

'You'll have to wait and see,' Lena says. She stands up. She's been bracing her feet so hard that her legs have gone shaky; it takes her a second to be sure they'll carry her.

Mrs Duggan leans back in her chair and chuckles. 'That means trouble,' she says. 'I always knew you'd be trouble. There's you going about all prim and proper, like you only want to be left in peace. I knew better. The first time I saw you, and you a wee baba, I told your mammy: that one's got trouble in her eye. I been waiting a long time for it to come out.'

Lena has her balance back. 'If you go talking like a fortune teller,' she says, 'you can't blame the young ones for thinking that's what you are.'

'I blame no one for nothing,' Mrs Duggan says. 'I'm not in that line of work. I just stay in my place and watch the resta them go about their business. Same as yourself, sure.' She smiles up at Lena. 'Or the same as yourself up until now, anyhow. What changed?'

'Thanks for your time,' Lena says. She resists the impulse to check that no jinxed domino or magenta bead has wormed its way into her pockets. 'I'll see you at Christmas, when I bring the kids their presents.'

'I'll tell you what I'm going to do,' Mrs Duggan says. 'I'm going to have a wee bet with myself, that you won't let me down again.' She reaches, with slow, deliberate movements, for her cigarettes. 'I'll see you soon,' she says.

Lena drives out into the countryside and keeps driving for a long time. This is not, by a long shot, what she thought she was getting herself into. She knows the shapes secrets take, around here. They're dark and jagged, dense enough to wear a hole right through you, but they're small, confined things; they lack scale. This has scale.

She has no idea what she's going to do about it. What's been carrying her along isn't some orderly plan, it's a current, wilful and deep. She has no strategy prepared for this place where it's landed her.

The fields lie neat and empty, ready for ploughing, swept by veils of soft rain. Tall grass and weeds bow on Mossie O'Halloran's fairy hill, never touched even though no one believes in fairies any more. Leaves scud across the roads and pile high against the stone walls; branches of gorse, still lavish with yellow, reach from the hedgerows to skim the car. The houses huddle, smoke drifting from their chimneys, smudges of darker grey against the grey sky. Off in the distance, a man tramps steadily behind a wheelbarrow, his dog running in wide curves around him.

Lena overlays the fields she passes with the map of what she knows: the bits of land Tommy's already bought, the bits he's been sniffing at. The bits in between lie peaceful as churchyards, under the rain.

Tommy can't afford to have his plan get out before he has all the pieces in place: the land bought, Eugene voted onto the council. As things stand, there are plenty of people around here who'll give Eugene their vote, plenty who'll sell Tommy a few acres to build a house for Eugene or an apartment block for the factory workers – doing whatever he asks by reflex, or out of gratitude for everything he's brought to the place, or just to stay on his good side. If his grand plan comes out now, all that will go up in a mushroom cloud. Some people will stick by Tommy no matter what, agreeing with his assessment that whatever a big man wants, he deserves, but plenty of others will feel that what Tommy deserves is to be kneecapped and run out of town for good.

It'll be civil war. Tommy doesn't give a shite about any of that, as long as the explosion doesn't come till it's too late to make any difference.

Rachel was a home bird, she loved this place; Rachel couldn't stand to see anyone hurt. Rachel thought you could always fix things somehow, Rachel didn't know that sometimes there's nothing to be done. Rachel couldn't hold her water, God rest her.

Tommy wasn't hiring Cal to find out what happened to Rachel. Either he assumes the worry was too much for her, or he doesn't care, or he already knows fine well. He was hiring Cal to find out whether Rachel talked, while she had the chance.

Lena has known Tommy and Clodagh all of her life, and Eugene all of his. They've been part of her landscape, taken for granted and navigated by habit like the tricky kink in the road behind Skippy Gannon's farm. The realisation of how little she knows any of them is disorientating, as if she's peered under a familiar hedge and found, as her eyes adjusted, the den of some unidentified savage creature. She has no idea how far any of the Moynihans would have gone to keep Rachel's mouth shut. She pictures Clodagh's pinched smile as she brings Rachel a nice cup of tea, Tommy saying soothing words as he takes her by the elbow and leads her stumbling to the bridge.

Flapper Deery, out in his yard rooting unhurriedly at the same broken-down old van he's been rooting at for ten years, raises a hand as Lena passes, and she raises hers in return. Flapper's two sturdy Connemara ponies watch her solemnly, over the wall.

Gradually it reaches her, with the simplicity of something she's known all along, that she's not going to keep this to herself. The only question is how she's going to get the word out. Noreen would have it all round the townland so fast it'd make everyone's head spin, but Lena isn't going to hide behind Noreen for this.

The rain has eased off to a fine haze; a couple of blackbirds burst out of a hedge and get to work, picking through the fields for worms. Lena finds a gap between overgrown whitethorn bushes and turns the car for home.

Maybe she'll get Noreen to add her to every WhatsApp group in Ardnakelty. Maybe she'll stand up in the middle of Seán Óg's on Saturday night, or in the middle of mass. Maybe she'll hire a plane to trail a banner across the sky. She finds herself grinning. In spite of Mrs Duggan, Rachel, that prick Tommy, civil war, the lot, the biggest part of her is riding high and wild and glorious on the roller-coaster immensity of what she's about to do. She's spent her life fighting Ardnakelty's law book in all the constrained, small-time, pathetic ways she could piece together; she never dreamed she'd get a chance to just blow the little fucker to smithereens. She can't wait to see Trey's face. She hits the pedal and flies down the twisting back roads, puddle-spray fanning from the Skoda's tyres, at a speed that would kill anyone who didn't know this place like the back of her hand.

When Lena sees the black Range Rover pulled up at her gate, her first response is annoyance. She's had her dose of shitebaggery for today, from Mrs Duggan; she's in no humour for a top-up from Tommy Moynihan.

Tommy is out of the Range Rover, leaning back against her

wall, with his hands in his coat pockets and his brown felt hat tipped down over his eyes. Lena pulls up beside him and rolls down her window. The air is chilly and still, dense with the smells of earth and leaves.

'Lena Dunne,' Tommy says, like it's a pleasant surprise to run into her here. 'How's the form?'

'Never better,' Lena says. She doesn't ask him in return.

Tommy watches her with a small amiable smile. His car is blocking the gate.

Lena is used to being on a footing where Ardnakelty, while it can irritate her, has no power to frighten her. It takes her a moment to realise that this has changed.

After a minute, she switches off her engine and gets out of the car. She rests her arse on the bonnet, facing Tommy, and waits.

Tommy tips his hat back so she can see his face. 'You've been asking an awful lotta people about me and my family,' he says.

Lena feels, sharply, how lonely the road is. For miles around, there's no sound but the far-off burr of a tractor and the light wind fingering the hedgerows. She wishes she had brought the dogs.

'I thought I'd save you some hassle,' Tommy says, with a gracious little nod. 'Instead of you wearing yourself out, traipsing around the place trying to pick bits and bobs outa this one and that one, I thought I'd come down here and let you ask me all the questions you like.' He spreads his hands, smiling. 'Go on, then. Fire away. Knock yourself out.'

Lena says, 'I've nothing to ask you.'

'Ah, Lena,' Tommy says, with mild reproof. 'You'd haveta be fierce concerned about my family, to go bothering an old woman like Mrs Duggan for whatever she thinks she knows. I appreciate your concern, and I'm here to put your mind at rest. Sure, isn't that my job around here?'

Lena doesn't know whether he's been having her watched,

or whether someone spotted her at Mrs Duggan's door or window and made a phone call. It doesn't matter. Either way, the message is the same: *Anything you do, anywhere, I see it.*

'My mind's grand,' she says. 'Thanks.'

Tommy cocks his head. 'Is it?' he enquires.

'If there's anything you wanta tell me,' Lena says, 'go ahead and do it. I've to feed the dogs.'

'The dogs can wait a few minutes,' Tommy reassures her. 'They're great little watchdogs, aren't they? They were losing the head when I arrived, but they've settled now.'

Lena feels a more vivid stab of fear: here on his own for God knows how long, he could have put anything through her letterbox. She can hear nothing from the house. Her windows are empty.

Tommy sighs. He takes off his hat and runs a hand lightly over his hair, making sure it's undisturbed. 'To be honest with you, Lena,' he says, 'I've concerns of my own. I can't be having Clodagh and Eugene upset at a time like this. You understand that, don't you?'

He raises his hands like Lena tried to cut in, which she didn't. 'Now, I'm not annoyed with you, nothing like that. I'm worried about you. 'Tisn't healthy, the way you've been obsessing over alla this.'

Lena's eyebrows lift. 'It happens,' Tommy tells her. 'When a woman's got no children or friends or hobbies to keep her occupied, sometimes her mind'd get itself all caught up in some aul' thing, and she'd end up going that wee bit off-piste. D'you remember my auntie Marie? A lovely woman, she was, but she'd nothing to keep her mind occupied. She got it in her head that herself and Father Gerard had been having a mad love affair.' He laughs a little, ruefully, at the absurdity of it. 'No one could convince her 'twas all her imagination. In the heel of the hunt, the poor woman ended up in the mental hospital.'

'Were they?' Lena enquires. 'Having an affair?'

Tommy turns his hat between his hands. Behind his head, clouds shift subtly. 'You're going that wee bit off-piste, Lena,' he says. 'If you'd only take a step back and get a little perspective, you'd see that yourself. You're a smart woman.'

'Thanks,' Lena says. The cold has burrowed through her jacket, and the wetness of the car has soaked into her jeans. She keeps her muscles tight so she won't shiver. Here and there among the hedges, leftover raindrops tick sharply.

'But if a smart woman doesn't mind a bitta advice from a man that's older and wiser,' Tommy says, giving her an avuncular smile, 'that's what I'd advise you to do: take a step back. Give me and my family some peace. Find yourself a hobby, to get your mind back on track. All this great energy you've got, put it into something useful.' He points a finger at her as an idea strikes him. 'You were a grand little camogie player back in the day, isn't that right? Brush up the aul' skills and give Philomena a hand with the coaching. It'll do you the world of good. Before you know it, you'll be looking back on this and wondering what you were thinking, at all.'

I don't give a shite about you, Tommy Moynihan, or your family, or this place. I wouldn't waste another second on any of them if I was paid for it. You leave me alone and I'll leave you alone, how's that for a deal? Lena has spent thirty years constructing the right to say that, and to be believed.

'And we'll say no more about it,' Tommy assures her magnanimously. 'No hard feelings.'

If Lena bows to Tommy, she'll have nothing but that to offer Trey. 'When I want your advice,' she says, 'I'll come and ask for it. Was there anything else you wanted to tell me?'

Tommy nods for a while. He examines the hat he's still turning meditatively between his hands, and flicks a raindrop off the brim.

'I haven't talked this over with anyone else, yet,' he says. 'But if I haveta do that, I'd say they'll think the same way I do: this isn't healthy for you. You're not in a good place.'

'Probably they will,' Lena agrees. 'Some of them, anyhow.'

Tommy shakes his head regretfully. 'Well,' he says, straightening up from the wall, 'you're a free woman; if you don't wanta do what's in your own interest, I can't force you. But I'll keep on doing my best for you, Lena. I promise you that.'

He brushes rain off his hat and adjusts it carefully over his hair. 'All I'm asking in exchange,' he says, 'is that you don't go upsetting my family any more. If you have any more questions, you've no need to go wandering all round the townland. You just come to me. I'm right here.' He looks at her, wearied but keeping his patience. 'Isn't that fair enough?'

'I'll keep it in mind,' Lena says.

Tommy sighs. Lena watches while, at his leisure, he gets back into his car. She doesn't move hers, and Tommy doesn't ask; he manoeuvres the Range Rover neatly past the Skoda with an inch to spare and heads for home at a decorous speed, lifting a hand to Lena as he goes.

Lena stays where she is till he's rounded the bend. Then she goes for the house.

Halfway up her drive, she hears the dogs burst into a joyful welcome. The blast of relief turns her weak. She makes it in the door and slides down to sit on her hall floor. The dogs, delighted with this great idea, swarm over her, licking her face and jamming their paws into her ribs. Lena rubs their warm wriggling bodies and waits for her breathing to slow down.

She set this up for Tommy, all by herself. Each and every thing she's done was a perfect tool for him to turn against her. Lena Dunne's gone obsessed with Rachel Holohan, she's wandering around the townland calling in to people she hasn't seen in years to fire weird questions at them, sure she's at that time of life, she was always odd but now she's finally snapped. She wonders how many of the women she was laughing with yesterday were watching, behind the laughter, for useful scraps they could bring to Tommy.

She tells herself it's not the nineties; Tommy can't have her tidied away into a mental hospital, the way his daddy and Father Gerard did with Marie Moynihan when she stopped being a good girl and keeping her mouth shut. All he can do is put it about that Lena Dunne is losing her mind, which probably half this place has already believed for years. The townland will talk, Noreen will stick up for her, she'll ride it out. That part doesn't matter, or won't in time.

The part that matters is that Tommy's spiked her guns. To plenty of people, anything Lena comes out with now will just be more evidence that she's gone off the rails. A few people will believe her because they hate Tommy's guts, but few enough that he can mock or bribe or bulldoze them out of his way. All Tommy needs to do is ease off the pedal for a little while, till people have time to file this firmly away as just Lena Dunne being mental, and then he can get back to work.

Cal would believe her, no question, but going to Cal would only make things worse. If she tells him this story, he'll bring it straight to Mart Lavin. Mart will use the information in whatever murky, labyrinthine way best furthers his agendas, he'll prove to Trey all over again that this place's will is all that counts, and he won't give a damn if he brings down Tommy's worst on Lena along the way. Cal would fight him on that, of course, if he got the chance, but it wouldn't do any good. Cal has himself convinced that, just because he's formed an allegiance to this place, its allegiance to him is equally strong. He thinks he has weight here; he doesn't understand how Ardnakelty turns people weightless against its own needs.

Trey would believe her, too. This isn't a good thing. Lena

isn't sure what Trey would do with this information, if she knew no one else was going to do anything at all. There's a chance she'd go up against Tommy all on her own, which would do nothing but land her in deep shite. More likely, which is worse, she'd do nothing. Lena hears the flat, final note in her voice: *No point, anyhow. Even if I found out, nothing I could do about it.* Lena feels like the world's biggest fool for ever imagining that might not be true, when it's been true all her life.

Daisy has had enough society for the moment; she gets up, shakes out her ears, and heads for her bed. Nellie takes advantage of the extra space to splay herself, belly up, across the whole of Lena's lap.

Lena needs to get up and bring her car inside the yard, before someone sees it left half-blocking the road, more proof of her craziness. Instead she sits there on the worn tiles of the hall floor, steadily rubbing Nellie's upturned underside, back and forth. A draught flows under the door, lapping cold as river water around her ankles, but she doesn't have the wherewithal to move.

11

Tommy, when he hits, hits home.

Cal and Trey have a wood guy, a rangy, crazy-eyed dude improbably called Sylvester, who lives high on the other side of the mountain with his three rangy, silent sons, his three rangy, muscled dogs, and a pile of logs as tall as his house. Sylvester spends half his time travelling the country collecting tree trunks and the other half turning them into lumber with his sawmill, a ferocious piece of equipment that he treats like an extra dog, a savage but well-trained one that he's particularly proud of. This week he's been all the way to Cork for a two-hundred-year-old walnut that came down in a gale off the Atlantic. Like all artists, Sylvester has his favourite patrons, and when he finds something extra tasty, he phones Cal.

Trey wants to come along and see Sylvester's new tree, so Cal waits till Saturday morning. He figures the kid might be looking for an opportunity to talk about Tommy Moynihan, so he leaves plenty of silences on the way, but Trey's main focus today appears to be the upcoming rematch with Lisnacarragh and how dirty they're likely to play after last time's blow to their self-esteem. Cal listens and concentrates on navigating the roads, which under the never-ending rain are losing their veneer of civilisation and devolving back towards bog. He knows Tommy is in Trey's mind somewhere, but if he's drifted off to the sidelines, Cal isn't about to bring him front and centre again.

It turns out Trey has other reasons for coming along. While

Cal negotiates for a slab of wood and admires the new additions to Sylvester's axe collection, Trey examines the walnut trunk from every angle and picks out a good-looking burl about the size of her head. Sylvester likes Trey, too; he cuts the burl off so she can get a look at the grain, and gives her a good price, which she counts from a squashed wad of cash out of her back pocket. The dogs, big softies around anyone who has Sylvester's approval, nudge at Trey for attention and finally herd her off to climb the log pile with them.

'You got a plan for that burl?' Cal asks, on the drive home. The rain high on the mountain, like Sylvester's dogs, has a different character from the lowland version: less domesticated, more territorial, coming at the car like it's an invader to be driven off. 'Or you just like the look of it?'

Trey shrugs. ''S almost Christmas. Might make someone a present, I dunno.'

Her voice has a self-conscious note, which takes Cal by surprise; he's not used to a self-conscious Trey. It takes a second to occur to him that this might have something to do with Kate. This leaves him with no idea what to say next.

'Well,' he says in the end, 'then we better get it dried out quick. It'll fit in the oven.'

Trey nods, peering out the window at something or other.

Cal wants to ask whether this means she and Kate have managed to ask each other out, whether Kate is going to give her a Christmas present, whether it'll carry the same level of time and thought and craftsmanship as whatever the walnut burl turns into, whether Kate comes anywhere near deserving the kid's scrawny-ass self. 'It'd make a good bowl,' he says. 'Or some kind of box, maybe.'

'I've enough money left for the football boots,' Trey says. 'C'n we go into town later?'

'Sure,' Cal says. 'We can dump this wood at home and head

in there for lunch, get fish and chips at that place you like,' but that doesn't work out because when they get home, there's a marked car in the yard and Garda Dennis is standing on the step, peering forlornly in the window while Rip and Banjo threaten to eat through the door and disembowel him.

'What's *he* want?' Trey demands, eyeing Garda Dennis with disfavour. Trey and her siblings mostly don't play truant these days, but they and Garda Dennis have history, and Trey isn't the forgiving type.

'I dunno,' Cal says. He pulls into the gate and lifts a hand to Garda Dennis, who has straightened up and is looking uncomfortable. The last time Cal saw Garda Dennis down this way, both of them were helping to chase PJ's sheep back in through a broken fence, but this isn't giving sheep-rescue vibes. 'You take the dogs for a walk, lemme find out.'

'He might want me,' Trey says. 'You said Tommy might go after my mam.'

'You been doing anything this guy might be interested in?'

'Nah.'

'Hassling the Moynihans?'

'Nah. Walked the dogs past their place, like I told you, is all. That's not illegal. They didn't even piss on the fountain yoke.'

'So you gotta train 'em better for next time,' Cal says. He lines up the Pajero neatly next to the marked car. 'OK. You just keep quiet and let me do the talking.'

'How come? I done nothing. I can talk for myself.'

'I got a lot more experience dealing with cops than you have,' Cal says, getting out of the car. Trey rolls her eyes, but she quits arguing and follows him across the yard.

'Morning,' Cal says, as they come up to the house. 'Sorry you were kept waiting. Me and Trey here were out buying that.' He nods to the slab of wood sticking out of the back of the Pajero.

Regardless of what Garda Dennis is here for, he's not going to fuss over an open trunk.

'Ah, no problem,' Garda Dennis says. He's gone pink, like they caught him doing something he shouldn't be. 'Sure, I only got here.'

'Well, come on in,' Cal says. Garda Dennis's face hasn't lit up at the sight of him this time. 'Have some tea.'

'Ah, no,' Garda Dennis says hastily, waving both hands. 'I'll come in for a wee chat, just. A few minutes, only.'

Cal knows the drill by now. 'I'm gonna make some tea anyway,' he says, opening the door and giving the dogs' heads a rub to settle them. 'I need it after that drive. Lemme get you a cup.'

'No, no, no,' Garda Dennis says more earnestly, wiping his boots carefully on the mat. 'I'm just after having one, sure. I'm grand, honest to God.'

This can't be good. 'Well, you let me know if you change your mind,' Cal says. He holds the door open. 'Come on in. The dogs won't bother you, but they're going kind of stir-crazy; I was gonna get the kid to take them for a run.'

'Ah, yeah,' Garda Dennis says, relieved. He's giving a dubious side-eye to Trey and her burl, which looks like a cross between an enormous dried cow pat and a troll's head. 'Great idea. They seem like they could use a run, all right.' This eases Cal's mind, at least a little bit. Whatever is going on, it doesn't require Trey's presence.

'Walnut,' Trey explains, hefting the burl in Garda Dennis's direction as she passes. He doesn't look like this makes things any clearer. She dumps the burl on the floor beside the cooker and turns on the oven, low. 'Stick it in once it's ready, if I'm not back,' she says to Cal.

'Yeah,' Cal says. 'Moisture meter's in the back room.' Garda Dennis is starting to look severely out of his depth.

Trey fetches the moisture meter, waves it at Cal and leaves

it on the counter, snaps her fingers for the dogs, and heads out, shooting a dirty look at Garda Dennis's back on her way. Cal puts Garda Dennis at the kitchen table, where he sits like a teenager at Sunday lunch with his new girlfriend's parents: on the edge of his chair, back straight, hands flat on his round thighs. Whatever is going on, he's not one little bit happy about it.

'You've a lovely place here,' he says, the way his mammy taught him to. 'Your missus isn't here, no?' He glances around like Lena might be behind the sofa.

'Nope,' Cal says, hanging up his jacket. 'She mostly works Saturday mornings.'

'Would you mind . . .' Garda Dennis has gone pink again. 'Is it OK if I take notes? No offence, like, just I've a head like a sieve on me—'

'Sure,' Cal says, giving him an approving nod, detective to beat cop. 'Good idea.' He takes a chair opposite Garda Dennis, folds his hands on the table, and looks helpful.

Garda Dennis fishes in his pockets for a very new notebook and a ballpoint pen, and finds himself a clean page. 'Would you be able to tell me where you were last night?' he asks. He's trying to sound official, but what he mainly sounds is miserable.

Cal has always told both Alyssa and Trey, with an intensity rooted in experience, that if there's the slimmest chance you might be a suspect, you don't talk to the cops without a lawyer. But they're in an unusual position here: poor Garda Dennis is looking at Cal as a colleague and as some kind of suspect both, and getting a headache from the double vision. If Cal clams up, he'll tilt them across that line and be a suspect all the way.

'I was right here, mostly,' he says. 'It was raining too hard to do much else. Trey, who you saw there, she came over around four-thirty, after school let out – she spends weekends here, doing some woodworking with me. The two of us were making a nursing chair for Con McHugh.' It's occurred to him to wonder whether Con will still want them making him anything, but until he hears different, they might as well keep on going. 'Around six o'clock, Lena, that's my fiancée, she came over and we ate dinner. I helped Trey out with her math homework, we took the dogs for a walk, watched some Netflix. Lena went home around ten, maybe a little later. Trey went to bed at eleven-thirty, she's got the sofa bed there.'

He nods at the sofa and watches Garda Dennis's gaze move over it. Cal has been aware all along that Trey's living arrangement is a gift to anyone who might be out for his blood. He's relied on the fact that there's no reason why anyone would be.

'I read in my room for a while,' he says. 'Turned off the light around midnight.'

Garda Dennis says, still holding on to his official voice, 'Which of ye brought the dogs for that walk?'

This isn't what Cal was expecting. 'Me and Lena,' he says. 'I can't say exactly what time, but it was when the rain slacked off for a while, so you might be able to narrow it down from that.'

Garda Dennis writes that down. 'Theresa Reddy didn't go with ye?'

'Nope. She wanted to take a shower.' Cal can read his careful printing, upside down: WANTED TO TAKE A SHOWER.

'Where did ye go?'

'Up past Mart Lavin's place as far as the bottom of the mountain road, then back again. About a mile each way. Probably we were out a little more'n half an hour.'

Garda Dennis asks, carefully, 'And how was Missus Dunne? What kinda form was she in, like?'

A spike of fear goes right through Cal. He says, 'Did something happen?'

Garda Dennis's face moves through perplexed to horrified. 'Ah, God, no,' he says hastily. 'Everything's grand – God, sorry, I didn't mean to give you a fright. I'm only asking.'

Cal's heart is hammering. 'She was fine,' he says. In truth, Lena seemed strange all night. She ate the beef stew, took an interest in the nursing chair, discussed what to watch on Netflix, but something about her brushed cold along the back of Cal's neck. She seemed like she was hearing his voice across distance; her eyes, clear and blue as always, were on some horizon more than they were on him or Trey. The remoteness that's surrounded her since Rachel's death has thickened, becoming a miasma that almost hides her from him. He wanted to spend all evening with a hand on her, in case she disappeared altogether, dissolving into that mist and gone.

'Little bit tired, maybe,' he says. 'Everyone's had a long few weeks, around here.'

'Did ye argue at all?' Garda Dennis asks.

'Nope. Mostly we just talked about what sounded good on Netflix. What's going on, man?'

Garda Dennis pokes a hole in the paper with his pen and looks wretchedly uncomfortable. Cal waits, patient but unrelenting, like a teacher waiting for the spitball-thrower to own up.

'I had a report come in,' Garda Dennis says in the end. 'A fella, naming no names, he said he was driving that way yesterday evening and he saw a man and a woman arguing on the road. The man hit the woman an awful clatter. He, this fella that called it in . . .' Garda Dennis shoots Cal an agonised look before ducking his head back down over the notebook. 'He identified the individuals in question as yourself and Missus Dunne.'

Cal knows better than to let his anger show. Aside from the fact that it wouldn't be a smart call, none of this is Garda Dennis's fault. The poor bastard is doing his best with the can of shit Tommy Moynihan has him carrying.

Instead he considers, frowning. 'Shouldn't you be talking to Lena?' he asks, a little reprovingly. 'Before you talk to me?'

'Ah, yeah, no, you're right, I should. I did go over to hers first, like, but she wasn't in, and I thought . . .' Garda Dennis turns up his round, unhappy face to Cal. 'What with you being, you know—'

'Hey,' Cal says, 'it's fine. You gotta use your judgement in this job.'

Garda Dennis looks slightly reassured. 'You don't have to say anything about it,' he says. 'Sure, you know that anyhow. I just thought, maybe you might wanta—'

'Jeez, man,' Cal says, 'come on. Of course I'm gonna talk to you. First off, I've never laid a finger on Lena or any other woman. Second, the only car that passed us yesterday evening was Alice Kelly in her Qashqai full of kids. Somebody's been feeding you bullshit.'

Garda Dennis nods and writes that down, but Cal can tell from his face that something is bugging him. 'There's more,' he says. 'Go for it.'

'When you were in to me the other day,' Garda Dennis says. He's poking a new hole in his notebook. 'You said yourself and the missus hadn't been getting on.'

'Nope,' Cal says firmly. 'What I said was we're not having a lot of laughs these days, what with one thing and another. That's not the same thing.'

'Right. Just, I heard she's been a bit . . .' Garda Dennis trails off. When Cal raises his eyebrows: 'A bit, you know. Off, like. The last while.'

'"Off,"' Cal says. '"Off" like what?'

'I'm not saying she's mental, or anything,' Garda Dennis assures him hurriedly. 'But you said yourself she's been stressed over Rachel Holohan. 'Tis awful hard on a man, living with a woman that's up to ninety.'

'Give me a break, man,' Cal says. 'Damn right, she's been stressed out. I told you that. It didn't make me want to *hit* her. It made me come in to you looking for something to set her mind at ease. You gave me that – which I appreciate – and it calmed her right down. Same as when your wife thought she heard rats, you didn't haul off and slug her, you just climbed on up into the attic. And then everything went back to normal.'

Garda Dennis, scratching his nose with the butt of his pen, still looks troubled. He's been too filled up with warnings, about Cal and Lena both, for anything else to feel reliable.

'Lemme ask you something,' Cal says. 'This guy who called it in. How come he didn't stop, do something about it?'

'The man was on his own, like. He mighta been worried that ye – or the, the couple – would have a go at him. Sure, you know yourself, that'd happen in domestics.'

'Huh,' Cal says. 'How come he didn't call it in right away, before the woman could get beat up any worse? How come he waited till today?'

'He mighta been thinking it over,' Garda Dennis suggests. 'Deciding what to do, like. Around here they don't always like bringing us on board.'

Cal leans back in his chair and rubs his jaw thoughtfully. 'This guy,' he says. 'Don't name any names, now; keep that part to yourself. Just tell me: he the timid type? The type who'd be too scared to pull over, or even honk his horn a coupla times, if he saw a woman getting beat up right there on the side of the road?'

He's banking on Tommy having thrown his own personal weight behind this, seeing as it didn't involve getting his hands dirty. Sure enough, Garda Dennis blinks, wrong-footed. 'I can't give out any information,' he says, falling back on a safe formula.

'Huh,' Cal says, eyebrows lifting. 'OK. How 'bout indecisive, he indecisive? Slow-thinking? Nervous about cops? The type who'd spend a whole night going in circles about whether to call it in?'

Garda Dennis blinks some more. Cal leaves a minute for that to percolate.

'If it doesn't make sense,' he says, 'it's probably bullshit. That's always been my rule.'

Garda Dennis looks at him. 'I wondered about that, all right,' he says simply. 'Sure, we've all had people using us to give each other hassle. There's two aul' lads up in town, every week I've got one or the other of them ringing me up telling me the other fella's dealing drugs outa the house. Neither one of 'em ever went near drugs in his life; they just can't stand each other.' When Cal grins, he looks abashed, suddenly remembering who he might be talking to. 'But this fella,' he says, 'he told me, "I know your man Hooper looks after Theresa Reddy, but he's never laid a hand on her, as far as I know."'

'Well,' Cal says. He keeps his voice even. 'Your guy got that part right, anyway.'

'If he was just aiming to drop you in the shite, but, he wouldn'ta said that. He coulda done a lot more damage the other way.'

A part of Cal genuinely feels for Garda Dennis, trapped trying to deal with two mutually exclusive versions of him at the same time, when all he wants to do is stamp babies' passport forms and reassure little old ladies that the scary noise in their garden is foxes. 'You go talk to Lena,' he says. 'She should be home by now.'

He hates to do this to Lena in her current mood, especially when it won't make much of a difference – domestic violence victims routinely hide the bruises and deny the whole thing, and Garda Dennis knows that as well as Cal does. But none of them have any choice.

Garda Dennis nods. He closes up his notebook and tucks it carefully back into his pocket. He still looks unhappy.

'I just want to say,' Cal says, 'I appreciate the way you're handling this.'

They look at each other across the table, as two cops this time, seeing the ways they both know this could have been done differently.

'I'm doing my best,' Garda Dennis says quietly.

'I know that,' Cal says. 'I'm sorry you got dragged into this.'

He watches Garda Dennis hurry across the yard to his car, chin tucked down against the rain. Cal knew this was coming, but it leaves him sad all the same. He liked Garda Dennis.

The oven has heated up. Cal slides Trey's burl onto the shelf and sets the timer for an hour. Then he sits back down at the table and phones Lena.

'That Guard from up in town is headed your way,' he says, when she picks up. 'O'Malley. He wants to ask you whether I beat you up last night.'

After a moment Lena says, 'That *fucker*.'

Cal takes some heart from the vividness of her anger: she sounds like herself again. 'He's just doing his job,' he says. 'He got a report, he has to look into it.'

'Not O'Malley. He's harmless. I mean Tommy. I oughta go over there and take the head off him.'

Cal says, 'We can't give him anything he can use.'

He listens to the silence roaring like water on the other end of the phone. 'I shoulda seen this coming,' Lena says eventually.

'Yeah, me too. It could be worse.'

'Ah, yeah,' Lena agrees. 'It could.' The anger has dulled out of her voice. She sounds like she's talking to a stranger, about something that has little to do with either of them. Cal has no idea how to reach her. That spike of fear inside him is still there.

'O'Malley can't do anything to me,' he says. 'Just answer his questions and he'll go away.'

'I'll do that. It'll be grand.'

Cal needs to get off the phone before he starts yelling, or something, out of pure desperation. 'Just so's you know,' he says. 'He's probably gonna ask whether you've been stressed out about Rachel Holohan. What I told him is you were a little bit unsettled about being the last person to see her, but now you know there's nothing you could've done, that's put your mind at ease.'

There's another brief silence. 'That makes sense, yeah,' Lena says. 'I'd better go put on decent gear, if he's on his way. Thanks for the heads-up.'

'Come for dinner,' Cal says, 'we're gonna make a stir-fry,' but she's already hung up.

He gets up from the table and walks circles around the room, so he won't throw his phone. He needs to get himself under control by the time Trey comes back with the dogs, but every thought that crosses his mind just makes him angrier. Someone was watching while they walked the dogs last night. Some little shit, Eugene or Donie or whoever else Tommy keeps on a string, watched while Cal tucked Lena's hand through his arm and looked for ways to make her laugh. Probably he was watching the house all evening, while they sat around the table and while Cal and Trey figured out cosecants and while Cal kissed Lena good night on the doorstep, picking out the moment that best served his purpose.

This was a pulled punch, carefully gauged. Garda Dennis has to investigate, but once he gets his full set of denials, he can go away. He doesn't have to bring Cal into the station, put him in the system, interview him under caution, call in various agencies who will never go away, the way he would if Tommy had used Trey instead of Lena.

Cal had it wrong. Trey's living arrangement isn't a gift to Tommy; it's a hostage. This was a warning. Tommy has spelled out his message nice and clear: *Next time, I go for the knockout.*

The back door bangs open, and Trey and the dogs come in on a gust of cold air. 'What'd that muppet want?' Trey demands.

'Nothing much,' Cal says. 'Just shooting the breeze. You want to eat now, or you want to wait till that's out of the oven and we can go into town?'

Trey's eyes stay on Cal for a second and he thinks she's going to push for more, but she just shrugs and squats down in front of the oven to check on her walnut burl.

Tommy, when he hits, hits home.

By Monday afternoon, Cal is going stir-crazy. He needs to do something about Tommy, but he's working in the dark, and he can't think of any action that wouldn't make things worse. Nothing new has happened on the Garda Dennis front, except a text from Lena saying it all went grand and hopefully that'll be the end of that. Cal is less optimistic: every muscle in his body is twitchy with waiting for the other shoe to drop. He feels like he's been stuck in this house, watching rain trickle down the windows and wasting brain cells on a guy he can't stand, for most of his life.

He squelches down to Noreen's, in the hope that she might have picked up some indicator of what Tommy is playing at or at least some inkling of what's going on with Lena. To his irritation, he finds himself bracing for the ordeal of going into his own damn local store. He has no way of guessing who, besides Garda Dennis, Tommy has been talking to; anyone Cal runs into could look at him and see a fiancée-beating psycho. Noreen ought to know him well enough to know that's bullshit, but minds are off balance right now. People are primed to believe that anything, or anyone, is treacherous.

As it turns out, Noreen doesn't appear to have heard any unsavoury rumours, but apart from that reassurance she's not much help to Cal. Noreen is all worked up because someone threw a rock through Long John Sharkey's kitchen window. 'I'm not saying we're feckin' Shangri-la,' she informs Cal, over the angry rhythm of her scrubbing the living daylights out of the shop counter. 'You'd get that kinda thing the odd time, same as anywhere, but it'd be kids, maybe over from Kilhone or down from town, someone robbed someone's girlfriend or there was a row at the disco, kids are feckin' fools and always were. But this fella, 'twas too dark to see his face but Long John says he ran like a grown man. The only grown man round here that oughta be doing something like that is Donie McGrath, and sure if 'twas that lazy lump, Long John woulda caught him and bet the shite outa him before he got to the garden wall. This was someone who should have better sense.'

Noreen gives the counter another vicious squirt of cleaner. Cal moves back a step. 'This is on the back of that loada nonsense in the hotel last week, is what this is. Grown men acting like childer that need a smack. Rachel Holohan'd be horrified, d'you know that? She'd a heart of gold, that girl. She couldn't stand to see anyone upsetted. If she knew people were using the way she died to have a go at each other, she'd— I was going to say she'd die all over again, that sounds terrible, but you know what I mean. She'd never have done it if she'da known it'd lead to this.'

Cal says nothing. Wherever Rachel's death is leading, this is nowhere near the end of it.

'And now Long John'll pick someone to blame,' Noreen says, 'God knows whether he'll get it right or not, he won't give a damn. You tell Senan to watch his windows, and his tyres.' She points the spray bottle threateningly at Cal, like this is somehow his responsibility to fix. 'And then what?' she demands. Cal, aware that the question is rhetorical and that his chances of changing the subject are low, pays for something at random and heads back out into the rain.

By the time he gets home it's dark, the November-afternoon dark that still feels unnatural to him, and all his windows are blazing. Cal turned off all the lights but one on his way out, and locked the doors.

For a moment he stands still, evaluating. Then he moves quietly around the house, keeping a good distance so Rip won't alert, assuming he's able to. He's aware that most likely he's about to feel like a prize dumbass when he finds Lena curled up on his sofa. A few weeks ago he would have taken that for granted and strolled cheerfully up to the door, but these days the townland is something other than its usual self, in ways he doesn't feel safe ignoring.

The kitchen is bright and empty, so is the living room. In the back bedroom Trey is at the worktable, sanding an arm of Con's nursing chair with the same all-out ferocity as Noreen scrubbing her counter.

On Mondays Trey stays at her mama's. Cal hears, clear as day, the neat thud of Tommy dropping the other shoe.

He lets himself in at the back door and makes his way through the dogs' delighted welcome to the workshop. Trey doesn't look up. Sawdust hangs in the air.

'Hey,' Cal says, and waits for it.

'Some little fucker from the council called in to my mam,' Trey says, without breaking her hard rhythm. She's so furious she's practically throwing off sparks. 'Scrawny little specky fuck, I coulda taken him down with one hand behind my back. I shoulda done it.'

'OK,' Cal says. 'What'd he want?'

'Fuckin' *inspection*. On our house. He said 'cause we're only renting, he can swan in and have a look around any time he wants.' A few years back, the kid would have flipped the worktable right about now. 'My mam shoulda told him to shove it up his hole. That's *our house*.'

'Well,' Cal says. He knows where this is going. 'That's meant to be for your good. So the landlord can't rent out some pigsty with no running water to people who can't afford to argue.'

'We've *got* water. We don't need some council shitebag sticking his nose in *for our own good*.'

'OK,' Cal says. He's just as angry as Trey is, but his anger will have to wait till he has hers managed. 'What'd the guy say?'

'There's slates off the roof and there's no carbon monoxide monitor and we've got rising damp in the walls. He was going around with his moisture meter, moving our beds outa his way and all – little prick asked me did I know what the meter was, like I was five.' Trey flips over her piece of wood with a bang and goes at the other side with her sandpaper like she wants to pulverise it. 'And if Rory Dunne doesn't fix the place up, he won't be allowed rent to us any more, and he could get a fine and go to jail.'

'Right,' Cal says. 'Well, that all sounds pretty fixable.'

'Rory already charges us low rent. Now he'll haveta spend a ton on this shite. He's gonna be raging.'

'We'll do it ourselves,' Cal says. 'Carbon monoxide monitor is like twenty bucks, and I meant to take a look at your roof anyway. We can read up on rising damp online. You tell your mama to give Rory a call, say it's all being taken care of.'

Trey stops sanding, finally, and shakes out her cramped hand. She says, 'Then Tommy Moynihan'll find something else.'

'Maybe,' Cal says. He's unclear on whether Rory has been reporting Sheila's rent to the Revenue, and on whether the low amount counts as some kind of gift that someone should be paying tax on. 'Then we'll fix that.'

Trey turns to look at him. 'You said we were gonna do something about Tommy,' she says. 'When?'

'Soon. I just need to know what I'm dealing with.'

'So find out. Do him like you did Donie. Give him a few slaps, make him tell you what he's fuckin' at. Or do Eugene. He'd crack like *that*.'

'Kid,' Cal says, 'I would love to. Believe me.'

'Then *why not*? He's only a piece a shite. We could take him, no bother to us.'

Cal looks at her, her squared shoulders and her furious grey glare all ready to go no-holds-barred, and he wants to sit down. There's too much on the line, it's too heavy. As fast as the kid is growing, this is probably the last time she'll ever look at him and believe he can fix everything, if only he'd try hard enough.

'That's not the point,' he says. 'Point is, we need to win here. That's not gonna happen if we go off half-cocked.'

Trey's fist is clenched around her crumple of sandpaper. 'Then what'm I supposed to do meanwhile? 'S not like I can lay off Tommy and it'll all be grand. We done nothing on him to begin with, and he's still after us. Are we supposed to just leave? Or what the fuck?'

Cal wonders if he ought to say yes. 'No,' he says. 'You're not going anywhere. I'm working on this. Just give me a little more time.'

He half-expects her to throw the sandpaper in his face and slam out, but either she's gotten too big for that or, somehow, that last thread of faith in his omnipotence still holds. Trey lets out an explosive noise of sheer frustration, but her shoulders loosen from their fighting stance. 'Make it quick,' she says.

'I will,' Cal says. 'I promise.'

He makes sure his tone is firm and solid, but he has no idea what he's going to do. Tommy is all around him, immobilising, a straitjacket. Cal realises he was being naïve when he imagined the townland had become something other than its usual self. This has been here all along, a substrate running beneath the land. He just hadn't dug his feet in deep enough to feel it there, till now.

He finds himself a piece of sandpaper and gets to work on the other arm of the chair. Trey goes back to her savage scrubbing. Cal keeps going, steady and even, and little by little her rhythm slows to match his.

Tommy, when he hits, hits home.

Cal spends Tuesday morning at Sheila Reddy's place, putting

in a carbon monoxide monitor and fixing up the roof. He likes roofing. The land around here is flat, with only gentle rolls right up to the sharp rise of the mountain, so even being on a cottage roof expands the view for miles around. Off on the horizon, dark trees blur into the sky like watercolour. The roads follow curves smoothed by centuries, through the web of stone walls dividing the land into swatches of subtly different shades, and the houses are neat and cosy as pottery ornaments carefully placed among the fields. From up here, this looks like the place Cal thought he was moving to.

Sheila, when she gets back from work, climbs up the ladder to join him. This comes as a surprise: Sheila isn't the sociable type. Cal has made sure to maintain some level of regular interaction with her, seeing as he appears to have partial custody of her kid, but the local flair for small talk passed Sheila by, and their conversations have always been pretty minimal. She's loosened over the past year or so, since she moved down off the mountainside, but she's still a hard woman to know, and Cal doesn't fool himself that he's come anywhere close.

He's straddling the roof-tree, working out a nail, when her head appears at the top of the ladder. 'Afternoon,' he says. 'This wasn't as bad as I expected, from what Trey said. Just a few slates missing, few more broken. Another half-hour oughta do it.'

Sheila examines the roof. 'How much were the slates?' she asks. 'And I'll pay you back.'

'No need,' Cal says. 'I had 'em left over from doing my own place.'

Sheila nods. 'I got custard doughnuts,' she says, touching the pocket of her hoodie. 'If you want tea with them, come down to the house.'

'Just doughnuts suits me fine,' Cal says.

Sheila swings a leg over the roof-tree to face him and looks around at the view with a touch of a smile. The breeze catches strands of hair that have escaped from her ponytail. 'I always wanted to get up on the roof of my house,' she says. 'When I was a kid. We never had a ladder long enough.'

'I did it one time,' Cal says. 'My granddaddy whipped my behind.'

'I'da done it anyhow,' Sheila says. 'Nothing stopped me, back then.' She settles herself against the chimney stack, pulls a pink paper bag from her hoodie pocket, and hands Cal a sugary doughnut. 'I talked to Rory,' she says. 'He's not happy, but he'll keep us on, for now anyhow.'

'Well, that's good news,' Cal says. 'Rory have any ideas on why Tommy's hassling you?'

'He reckons Tommy's a prick, is all.' Sheila bites into her doughnut with satisfaction. 'Tommy wanted this field,' she explains, through a mouthful, 'and Rory told him to get fucked – they never got on. Tommy could buy himself another field instead, but he can't stand being told no. He's like a spoilt child.'

'Huh,' Cal says, considering that. He never underestimates the force of offended entitlement, but this explanation seems to leave a lot unaccounted for. 'Maybe.'

'If Tommy goes too far,' Sheila says, 'I'll spread it around that Eugene was beating the shite outa Rachel. I went over and said that to Clodagh yesterday, after your man the inspector finished with us.'

Cal seriously doubts that Tommy will take well to being threatened by the likes of Sheila Reddy. His instinct is to grab Trey and move her into his place full-time till all this is over, but even if she would go, that would just give Tommy more ammunition. 'What'd she say?' he asks.

Sheila shrugs, turning her doughnut to get the bite she wants. 'Not much. Pinched up her mouth and bugged out her eyes at me, like I was after spitting on the carpet, and then said she wouldn't recommend that. I said that's grand, and went home.'

Sheila looks nothing like Trey, but sometimes Cal sees a strong resemblance all the same, not necessarily in a good way. The two of them sit in silence, eating their doughnuts and watching the townland go about its business at a pace that, from up here, has a dreamy, leisured air. Two tweenage girls are cantering ponies around a field, their calls rising thin and sweet as lambs' through the distance.

'Trey said something about quitting school after this year,' Cal says. 'Doing an apprenticeship up in town. She mention anything to you?'

Sheila sucks sugar off her thumb. 'She said that, all right. Sam Murray.'

'Yeah,' Cal says. He's on delicate ground here; he has no idea what Sheila might consider to be overstepping. 'You figure maybe she should finish school first?'

Sheila looks at him. Her eyes are still beautiful, a blue that's the most vivid thing in all this muted landscape of greys and greens. 'I don't stand in that one's way,' she says. 'She's got plans.'

'Right,' Cal says. He supposes that much is definitely true, for better or worse. It's not that he really expected to find an ally in Sheila, whose approach to child-raising has never been what anyone could call hands-on, but he feels let down and frustrated all the same. 'Just in case her plans change somewhere down the line, though.'

Sheila thinks this over. 'Has she a fella?' she asks.

'Nope,' Cal says. He's not going to tell Sheila about Kate, not that he has anything to tell. 'I'm pretty sure.'

Sheila nods. 'That's grand, so,' she says. 'As long as she doesn't turn up pregnant, she can always change her plans if she wants.'

She crumples up the paper bag and tucks it back into her pocket. 'Thanks,' she says, nodding at the roof, and she swings herself back onto the ladder and leaves Cal to it.

He finishes up the last few slates with the enjoyment gone out of the job, and heads for Seán Óg's. Sheila's roof is ready for Tommy's tame inspector, and Cal feels he's earned a pint. If anyone gives him hairy looks for being a wife-beater, he can sing intimidating folk songs at them.

No one does, though. The pub is quiet, just the permanent-installation pensioners stretching their pints thin to cover a few hours' company. They nod peacefully to Cal as he comes in, and he gets his pint of Smithwick's from Barty and settles into the alcove to watch the racing on the TV.

He's halfway down his pint, and the cold of the rooftop is thawing out of his feet, when the door opens and Bobby Feeney peers around the pub. His round face is puckered with what looks like worry, but he perks up when he sees Cal.

'There you are,' he says, rubbing his hands together. He's rosy from the cold, right up to his bald patch. 'I was hoping I'd find you in here; I saw your car down the road there. What'll you have?'

'Nah, I'm good,' Cal says. 'Gotta drive home.' He catches Barty's eye and points to Bobby. Cal and Bobby don't mostly hang out solo, but he's pretty sure he knows why Bobby wants a private conversation. He feels like Bobby's picked the wrong time, or maybe just the wrong guy, to ask for romantic advice, but he supposes he can probably be more helpful than, say, Mart.

'How's Róisín doing?' he asks, once Bobby's got his pint and drawn a careful smiley face in the head.

Bobby lights up like Cal gave him a present. 'Ah, she's amazing,' he says. 'Honest to God, these relationship yokes, they're only brilliant; even better than I expected. I always thought the bit of a kiss and a cuddle'd be great, and they are, sure' – he goes even pinker – 'but no one tells you about the talking. Myself and Róisín, we could talk all day and never get bored. I didn't even know I had anything in my head that was worth talking about, but I have.'

'Here's to Róisín,' Cal says, clinking his glass against Bobby's. He keeps his voice extra cheerful because Bobby is making him, somehow, unaccountably sad. 'We gonna meet her someday?'

Bobby's little mouth sets stubbornly. 'I won't have them dirty fuckers slagging her,' he says. 'You heard them. They're filthy animals, so they are. If one of them says something about Róisín, I'll have to put manners on him.' He clenches a fist to demonstrate.

'Lemme talk to them,' Cal says. 'I'm not saying I can get them to back off altogether, but I can probably get them to dial it down enough that you won't have to kick anyone's ass.'

Bobby brightens. 'They'll listen to you,' he agrees. 'If I tried, it'd only make them worse. Would you have a go?'

'Sure,' Cal says. 'No problem.'

''Cause I'd only love to bring her here. I'm sick of driving all that way every weekend, and nothing but video chats in between, and the connection always dropping right when we're at an important bit. I'd only love to, you know . . .' Bobby is turning bright red. He glances over his shoulder, to make sure none of the old guys are listening in, and leans across the table towards Cal. 'You know. Marry her, like. Sure, why not? I know the lads'd slag me, getting mixed up in that class of carry-on at my age, but they do slag me anyhow. It'd be worth it, to have her there the whole time.'

Cal thinks of Lena's remoteness, dense as the silence prisoned under deep water. *Don't do it*, he wants to tell Bobby. *Don't change a damn thing. Just freeze it right here, today, while everything's great.*

'Go for it,' he says. 'Mazel tov.'

'That's the thing, but,' Bobby says, worried again. 'I wouldn't know how to go about it. I wanted to ask you that. You've got experience with the aul' proposals; how did you do it?'

'You've got experience,' Cal points out. He does kind of

sympathise with the guys: it's hard to resist teasing Bobby. 'You asked Lena to marry you, before I came along and got in your way.'

Bobby blinks and flaps a hand at Cal, embarrassed. 'Ah, no, that didn't count. That wasn't a proposal; I thought we'd get on grand, is all. This has to be . . . you know. Romantic.'

'I dunno how much help I'm gonna be with romance, man,' Cal says. 'I just asked.'

'See, that's what I thought,' Bobby says, pointing a finger earnestly at Cal. 'I thought all I hadta do was get a ring and go down on one knee. But then I looked online – just for a few tips, like – and, my God. People have photographers, and crowds singing songs, and trained doves, and fuckin' *helicopters*. I wouldn't know where to get a helicopter, and Róisín's not mad about loud noises anyhow.'

'Listen,' Cal says. 'I don't know who these helicopter guys are – they sound like douchebags to me – but Róisín doesn't want to marry any of them. From what you say, she wants to marry you. If just getting down on one knee in her living room is your style, then it's gonna be hers.'

Bobby thinks that over, picking bits off his beermat. Then he glances up at Cal with a shy smile. 'I'm going to do it,' he says. 'Whenever I can get my courage up. Will you be a groomsman? If she says yes, like.'

'Sure,' Cal says, touched. 'I'd be honoured.' He hopes to God that Róisín says yes.

'I oughta invite Tommy Moynihan,' Bobby says, a little defiantly. 'I know there's people that's got a grudge against the Moynihans these days, but I owe the man.'

Cal doesn't particularly like this line of thinking, and he especially doesn't like what will happen if Bobby airs it around the rest of the guys. He's almost impressed by the amount of damage Tommy is strewing around this place, grenades going off right and left, land mines under lifelong friendships, fuses merrily burning away. 'You figure?' he asks.

'God, yeah. If he hadn't bought that field off me, I'd never have gone to France. And then I'd never have met Róisín.' Bobby is round-eyed with the horror of the thought. 'I owe that fella . . .' He gets stuck for words. 'Everything,' he concludes simply.

'Well,' Cal says carefully. 'Maybe, maybe not. You and Róisín only live a couple of hours' drive apart; it's not like she's in Australia. You would've met one way or another.'

'Like Fate,' Bobby says, struck by the idea. He thinks it over. 'Fate,' he repeats, warming to it. 'D'you reckon?'

'Sure,' Cal says. 'Tommy just happened to come in useful. If he hadn't've bought your land, you'd've met her at someone's wedding, or her car would've broke down when you were passing by, or something.'

'I'd rather 'twas Fate,' Bobby confides. 'I'm not mad about Tommy.'

'Nope,' Cal says. 'Me neither.'

Bobby settles back on the banquette, looking happier, and sinks a couple of inches of Guinness. 'D'you reckon you and Lena were Fate?' he asks. 'And that's why she turned me down?'

Cal doesn't believe in Fate, and right now he doesn't know what he and Lena are. 'Sure,' he says. 'Probably.'

'That's what I came in here about,' Bobby says. His face, when he glances over at Cal, is suddenly troubled. 'Then we got onto Róisín and all. But I was looking to talk to you about Lena, like.'

'OK,' Cal says. He remembers Bobby's quick blink when Lena's name came up. He knocks back a fair amount of his own pint and prepares to explain calmly that he doesn't beat Lena. 'Shoot.'

'Sure, 'tis only a loada aul' shite,' Bobby assures him. 'I just thought you'd wanta know all the same.'

'Yep,' Cal says. 'What'd you hear?'

Bobby looks like he'd rather be anywhere else in the world, but he's determined to see this through. 'You know how Rachel Holohan went to Lena's house,' he says. 'That evening.'

This is not what Cal was expecting. 'Yeah,' he says.

'And you know what people are like round here. Sure, they'd say anything.'

'I noticed that,' Cal says. He sits still and waits for yet another damn shoe to drop.

'There's a few of them saying . . .' Bobby has gone back to picking his beermat apart. 'You know all that talk about Rachel, that she was doing the dirt on Eugene? I'd say there's nothing in it, she always seemed like a lovely girl, but—'

'Right,' Cal says. 'People'll say anything.'

'Yeah, but Lena going around asking people about it . . . that's not like her. Sure, you know yourself, she wouldn't be the nosy type.'

'Nope,' Cal says. He had no idea that Lena was doing any such thing. 'So people, what? They have a problem with that?'

'Not a problem, just . . . why would she care who Rachel was riding, like? Unless . . .' Bobby shoots Cal a glance of pure appeal, like he's begging Cal to finish the sentence for him.

Cal says, 'Unless what.'

'There's people saying Lena got it in her head that Rachel was . . . you know. With, with you. Not saying it was true, like,' Bobby adds hastily, when Cal's shoulders move, 'just that Lena thought it.'

Cal notices he's gripping his glass much too hard. He carefully lets go of it and folds his hands together on the table.

'And so she got Rachel over there,' Bobby says, to the beermat, 'and she said to Rachel that she was going to tell Eugene. And that's why Rachel done it.'

Cal bites down before he can say *What the fuck*. He catches Bobby's quick glance, like he's afraid Cal might flip the table.

'And,' Bobby says, taking a deep breath and speeding up to get it over and done with, 'there's a few people saying it was true all along, 'cause why would Rachel have kilt herself if it was all a loada shite? And that's why Lena's been asking around, to find out who else knew.'

Cal realises that his whole body is ready to punch someone in the face, and that it probably shouldn't be Bobby. He concentrates on sitting still and listening to the commentator's voice jabbering endlessly from the TV.

Bobby is watching, his face crunched into a tight knot of wretchedness, to see how Cal is taking it. 'Maybe I oughta have kept my mouth shut,' he says. 'I didn't wanta upset you, but . . . in case someone came at you or Lena, saying things, like, or looking at you funny, and you didn't know what they were on about. If it was me, I'd wanta be told. Should I have stayed quiet?'

'You did right,' Cal says. 'Thanks.' He doesn't bother to ask Bobby who's saying what. He already knows the part that matters. 'Just so we're clear: that's the biggest load of horseshit I ever heard in my life.'

Bobby looks up at that. 'You don't haveta convince me,' he says simply. 'Sure, everyone with a titter of sense knows Lena wouldn't hurt a fly. She's kind. When I asked her would she ever marry me, that time, she coulda laughed in my face and told the world I'd made an eejit of myself, but I knew she wouldn't. That's why I done it. I thought to myself, *I wouldn't mind spending the rest of my life with someone that's kind.*'

'She's a good woman,' Cal says.

'And you'd never play offside on her. Specially not with some young one that's barely older than your Trey. I told people that.'

They look at each other. 'Thanks,' Cal says gently. He has just room enough in his mind to understand what Bobby was doing, by asking him to be a groomsman. 'I appreciate that.'

"'Tis all just shite talk,' Bobby says earnestly. 'It won't last. Sure, there were rumours about you before, d'you remember? And then they blew over, and everything was grand.'

'Right,' Cal says. 'Yeah.'

"'Tisn't personal. Everyone gets a bit of it. When I was only a little young lad, back in school' – Bobby leans in closer, turning his shoulder to the bar – 'some fucker put it about that I was shagging the sheep. I never did, like,' he adds, for clarity. 'But I was getting terrible slaggings all the same. It got that bad, I thought about doing myself in. Only that woulda upset the mammy, so I didn't do it, and in the end everything blew over.'

He sits back and gazes hopefully at Cal. 'Things mostly do,' Cal says. He stands up. 'I gotta get going.'

Bobby looks alarmed. 'Don't worry, man,' Cal says, laying a hand on Bobby's shoulder as he passes. 'I'm not gonna kick anyone's ass or anything. Small town like this, people make shit up, whatcha gonna do. Right?'

'You're right, o' course,' Bobby says, looking at least half reassured. 'There's some awful eejits out there; you wouldn't want to mind them.' He moves up to the bar, to watch the racing and swap the occasional peaceful comment with the old guys while he finishes his pint.

What's enraging Cal is the ease of this, casual and quick as a man whacking misbehaving puppies on the nose with a rolled-up newspaper. Trey sassed Tommy, Cal refused him, Lena poked around: out comes the newspaper, *no, no, no, bad dogs*, and they're all cringing in their corners. Bobby is right that rumour is one of Ardnakelty's primary weapons, the glinting flip side of its dark silences, and that Cal has been on the wrong end of it before, but that was different. The rumours about him, like the hints about Eugene cheating on Rachel, were collective, co-alesced almost unconsciously out of the place's communal need.

This is one man's cold, deliberate strategy to show his power over all that, by taking an expert grip on the townland's weapon and aiming it at his own personal targets. Cal drives home very carefully, thinking of Eoin Duggan, and the Boss Moynihan's woman, and all the other people who have lived out their lives here feeling this same rage and unable to do a single thing about it.

He leaves the Pajero at home, gets Rip, and starts walking. It's not raining, but clouds hang heavy and the air has a hard damp chill that digs through his jacket. Rip, aware that something is wrong, sticks close and trots to keep up.

Cal can't imagine why Lena would have been asking around about Rachel Holohan's love life. He figures this has to be connected to her weird mood, but he can't see how that would work, either. Whatever her reasons, she's given Tommy everything he could want. Not that that makes much difference. Tommy is an expert in his field; regardless of what he was given, he would have found something to use.

Cal finds himself heading for the riverbank, like it's a crime scene that might yet offer up some overlooked scrap of evidence to make everything crystal-clear. Brambles drag grimly at his pants, and trees dump their loads of rain down the back of his neck. The place where they dragged Rachel from the water is still a brutal mess, branches snapped and layers of leaves scrabbled up all around. It looks like the scene of a brawl, or a fight to the death between wild animals. In summer, new growth would be smoothing the scar by this time, but nothing is growing now.

Bobby is right, this will blow over, but the dust of it will stick. Cal grew up in the backwoods, he knows how small places roll. Whenever people look at him and at Lena, they'll see this, whether they believe it or not. The place where they've lived till now is gone; Tommy Moynihan has transformed it to suit himself.

Normally the bridge looks like something off an old postcard, but today it has a sly air, too low-walled and too slippery, hunched waiting for a traveller it can pitch into the water below. The rain has swollen the river to a thick brown muscle, humped up in the middle by its own force; its roar, crammed with variations too quick for the ear to catch, makes thinking difficult. Cal has fished this river maybe a hundred times, by himself or with Trey, when they're in need of peace – the river, if it's in the mood, can come up with a couple of perch at any time of year. He has a hard time imagining ever fishing it again.

He starts searching, beginning at the bridge and working his way back along the path Rachel would have taken to get there. He shoulders through snarls of branches, shines his phone light into bushes, gropes in tree-trunk holes, rakes up layers of dead leaves with his hands, hunting for an antifreeze container or a note or a message carved on a tree or whatever the fuck. He's aware that he looks like a crazy man, crashing through brush, down on his knees among the creepers wrist-deep in muck with twigs in his hair and scratches on his face, but the thought only makes him work harder.

He ends up with a disintegrating cigarette packet, a bedraggled fishing lure, and a little kid's rubber boot. Rip, trying to help, rustles around in the undergrowth and digs out a chewed-looking tennis ball. A rich smell of rot rises from beneath the raked-up leaves.

The light through the branches has been dimming, so gradually that Cal didn't notice until he finds himself standing, breathing hard, in half-darkness. His fingernails are broken and his feet are numb with cold. All around him and high above his head, everything is as still as if it's been frozen in place; anything alive in there is watching him. Only the river keeps endlessly charging on.

Pushing his body this hard has cleared his mind. It comes

to him, for the first time, that Tommy shouldn't be doing this. Siccing the inspector on the Reddys and Garda Dennis on Cal, sure. But Tommy should be aiming to move people on from Rachel as fast as he can, not stir them up even more. If Tommy is pushing a brand-new high-scandal story to explain why Rachel died, it's because there's something he needs it to paper over; something he's afraid Lena might have dug up, while she was asking questions.

For the first time Cal thinks, as a plain clear statement rather than as a flicker to be brushed off: *Tommy killed Rachel Holohan.*

He feels like a part of him has been waiting for this ever since Mart's phone call. The cop in him said suicide; it was straightforward, it all added up. But somewhere along the way, the patterns of Ardnakelty, strange intricate weaves invisible or meaningless to any outsider, have embedded themselves in his mind, twisting through the neat cop-think grids. He felt the snag in the pattern, the web tugging around it, and he knew.

If he had a badge and an interview room and a tech department at his disposal, he has no doubt that he could slap a pair of handcuffs on Tommy before Christmas. But he's not a cop any more. The part of his mind reaching for cuffs and badges is a vestigial thing.

Tommy may not have done it himself. Tommy operates at a CEO's remove from the manual labour; he could have delegated the messy stuff. Regardless, this is his work.

Cal needs to find out what the hell Tommy is playing at that would give him a motive to feed young girls antifreeze, but there's no one to ask. Noreen and Mart between them know everything around here, but neither of them knows this. Tommy is running his game on some level to which they have no access.

What Cal wants to do is waylay Eugene and beat the tar out of the little shitbird till he comes clean, and maybe for a while after that. If he does it, he'll come home to Child Services on his doorstep, Trey will come home to an eviction notice, and God only knows what Lena will come home to.

Rip, uneasy, nudges his nose into Cal's hand. 'Yeah,' Cal says, taking a breath. He rubs Rip's ears. 'Good boy. Let's go home.'

They start walking, their feet sinking into the wet leaves.

Cal is going to have to talk to Lena. She has a right to know this. He badly wanted to have something more to offer her, some answers or a plan or some kind of hope, before he dumped this reeking mess in her lap.

12

Cal seldom comes to Lena's house. Without knowing or needing to know his reasons, she appreciates this. Her house has had too much in it; her relationship with Cal needs a barer place in which to unfurl. He's never been in her bed.

When he shows up at her door, it's because he's bringing something special. A few weeks after she gave him Rip, he called round with a pair of bookends for her – simple ones, since he was only starting out at the woodworking back then, but made from old oak with a grain she's run her hand over a hundred times. He's brought the first ripe hazelnuts from his trees, a tiny belligerent toad he found in the middle of the road. Last year, after she told people they were engaged, he showed up with a look halfway between sheepish and mischievous, and a sapphire ring. The sight of his Pajero turning in at her gate has come to bring with it a sense of expectation; it readies her to smile.

This time, when she lifts her head from the washing-up and sees the Pajero, she knows it's not hazelnuts. She stands still for a moment at the sink, looking out through the morning mizzle. Then she dries her hands, takes the ring from the windowsill and puts it back on, and goes to the door.

The air outside is thick with damp and with autumn smells. The blur of rain has brought the horizon closer; only a few fields away, nothing exists. Cal kisses her too briefly and too hard.

Lena brings him into the kitchen and sits him down at the

table – if they have to do this, they might as well have a cup of tea to go with it. The dogs, sluggish with the cold, lift their heads to greet Cal and then go back to dozing in their corner, twitching and snuffling through their dreams.

Cal is so careful and delicate about how he tells her, it would break Lena's heart, except that she finds it hard to focus on what he's saying. She's been expecting this; the only faint surprise is how thorough Tommy's been, how he's gone above and beyond just saying she's mental, to offer the place something skilfully concocted to catch at their taste buds so irresistibly that it'll never fade. The rest flows past at such a distance that only some of the words reach her. Instead she watches Cal while he talks. His crow's-feet have got deeper, and his brown beard has speckles of grey. For the first time she realizes what it means that the pair of them are middle-aged; that, from now on, their changes are unlikely to be in their favour.

'I'm gonna do something about it,' he says, when he's picked his way through it all. He's watching her, too, with worry he's trying to hide.

Lena raises her eyebrows. 'I don't see much that needs doing,' she says. 'If Tommy takes it any further, then maybe, but it sounds like Sheila's after putting a stop to his gallop, and I laughed in that Guard's face; he won't be back to you. The rest is small-town shite. There's not a lot you can do, only leave it till everyone gets bored.' She finds a touch of comfort in the fact that she can sound so perfectly like her usual self.

Cal says, 'This isn't your average small-town bullshit.'

'I've heard worse,' Lena says. 'So have you, sure.'

Cal stands up fast and starts pacing circles around the kitchen. 'If people think I'm a sleaze,' he says, 'I'm gonna run into trouble about Trey.'

Lena hears the things running beneath his voice, the anger and the fear and the urgency, but she can't feel them; they slide over her without touching. Only the thought of Trey reaches her. Regardless of where it leads, she has to talk to Trey.

Cal says, 'And I'm not gonna let people go around saying that shit about you.'

'You could challenge Tommy to a duel,' Lena suggests helpfully. 'With hurling sticks, like. Beside the grotto in the village. You'd make a fortune on tickets.'

That gets half a grin out of Cal, but it's gone quickly. He stops pacing and leans back against the counter. After a minute he says, 'You were asking people about Rachel cheating on Eugene. I figure that got Tommy's back up because there's something he doesn't want coming out.'

'Probably,' Lena agrees. 'I'd say Tommy mostly has something he doesn't want coming out.'

Cal says, 'How come you were doing that? Asking around?'

For a moment Lena remembers how she loved telling Cal things; how it felt like a breathtaking surprise gift, after all those years of guarding against telling anything to anyone. And now, if she told him this, the only thing it would do is damage. She wants to close her mouth and never open it again. All that talking she did with half the women in the townland, all that talking with Mrs Duggan, and none of it did any good in the end.

She says, 'I shoulda known better.'

Cal waits. When she says nothing more, he asks, 'What'd you find out?'

'Clodagh started the story,' Lena says.

'Surprise,' Cal says, with a grim twitch in his jaw. 'Anything else?'

'No,' Lena says.

Cal watches her. She knows he doesn't believe her, but it doesn't matter. Their tea mugs sit there, untouched.

He asks, 'You turn up something bad?'

'No,' Lena says.

After a minute Cal says, 'You're not worrying over that crap about me and Rachel. Right?'

'I am not,' Lena says, with all the force she has – she owes him that. 'Not in a million years.'

'And you know I don't believe that bullshit.'

Lena says, 'I never thought you did.'

Cal says, 'So what's wrong?'

Lena tries to remember the feel of his skin under her palms. All she can find is Sean's cold cheek. 'Nothing's wrong,' she says. 'It's a hard time round here, is all.'

Cal nods for a while. His hands are scraped up; there's a plaster around one thumb, and he rubs the end of it, smoothing it down. In the end he says, 'I think Tommy killed Rachel Holohan.'

'He might've,' Lena says. 'Yeah.' It makes no difference, because they can't do anything about it, but she doesn't try to get that across to Cal. Even if she found the words, he would try to go out and fix it; that's how he's made. She thinks of Sheila saying *A grown woman knows sometimes there's nothing to be done, so you do nothing.*

Cal starts to say something and then stops. Lena waits, but he just stands there, leaning against her counter, by the sink full of half-done washing-up.

The rain makes soft, unhurried rustles against the windowpanes. Outside, the horizon has come closer again, hanging in the field just across the road, patient. Lena thinks of the women in the stories her grannies used to tell, swapped by the fairies for changelings who sat unmoving and empty-eyed by the hearth till they withered away to husks, or until someone decided to burn the strangeness out of them. She reckons this is the reality running under the stories: women whose own home places were the creatures that scooped them out of themselves and took them away somewhere unreachable. She's become a thing out of a story no one bothers to tell any more.

After a while Cal sits down at the table again and reaches a hand across to her. 'I'm gonna do something,' he says.

Lena takes his hand. She's drowning, with Cal right there by her side. She wonders if this is how Sean felt.

Trey is considerably less tactful than Cal. She bangs on Lena's door after school and says, when Lena opens it, 'Some fucker's putting it about that you made Rachel Holohan kill herself 'cause she was riding Cal, and he found out and bet you up.'

'I know, yeah,' Lena says. 'Is that how you got that?' Trey has an impressive lump, gashed and purple, above one eyebrow.

'Yeah. This prick Jayden Crilly, he said it to me so I hit him, so he hit me and I kneed him in the balls.'

Trey used to get into fights at school on a semi-regular basis, but it's been a long time since the last one. She looks like she's holding herself back by sheer willpower from bursting into flames. 'You've still got blood on you,' Lena says, stepping back from the door. 'Come in here and get cleaned up.'

Trey makes a *pfft* noise, but she follows Lena through into the kitchen and dumps her schoolbag on the floor. 'Jayden's thick as fuck,' she says. 'He didn't come up with that himself. Someone said it to him.'

Her fury clears Lena's head till things feel almost real. 'Here,' she says, handing Trey a swathe of kitchen roll.

Trey wets it at the sink. 'This is Tommy fuckin' Moynihan,' she says. 'Again.'

'It's got that smell, all right,' Lena agrees.

Trey leans over the sink and uses the kitchen window, already dark, as a mirror to go at the dried blood on her forehead. ''M not letting him away with it,' she says. She's scrubbing hard enough that it has to hurt. 'He's not gonna call Cal a fuckin' sleaze.'

Lena says, 'What are you going to do about it?'

'I'm gonna prove he kilt her himself. Or Eugene did, whichever. Me and my mates, we're gonna get Eugene and beat the bollocks outa him till he talks. Cal keeps saying wait, wait, don't go off half-cocked— I *been* waiting. I'm not letting them away with this.'

Only a week ago, this was all Lena wanted: to see this fight in Trey. Now she's terrified by it. She's fought against Ardnakelty's current for thirty years. When she was young she welcomed the battle, just like Trey does; there was a fierce secret joy in the way it used all she had. She had never found anything else that would do that – only, later, her battle for Sean. Now she's not young any more, and she's worn out. Her fight for Sean is lost, and it's been brought home to her that this one was always unwinnable. The most she could ever have hoped for was to reach the end of her life before she could lose.

'Listen to me,' she says. She feels a surge of solidity that she knows is limited and specific, just enough to carry her through this conversation. 'I'm serious: you pay attention.'

Trey turns from the sink to look at her.

'Forget Tommy and Eugene,' Lena says. 'Forget those fuckers ever existed. And' – she raises her voice over whatever Trey is trying to say – 'the same for Sam Murray and his apprenticeship. Forget him.'

'Cal already *gave* me hassle about staying in school. What's that got to—'

'I don't give a shite about school. Get yourself an apprenticeship tomorrow, if you want. But you get it in Dublin, or Wexford, or anywhere that's far enough that you'll haveta live there. Me and Cal and your mam, and your mates, we'll come visit you. Don't come back.'

Trey stands still. She says, with no expression at all, ''Cause this was my fault. Tommy's going after you and Cal 'cause I fucked with him. If I'm gone, he'll lay off.'

'What?' Lena says. 'No. Jesus, no.' She had forgotten the extent to which teenagers are the centre of the universe.

Trey's face doesn't change: she thinks Lena's lying to her. 'I'm gonna sort it. I don't haveta leave. Once we get Eugene to—'

'No. Nothing like that. I swear.'

'Then *why*?'

'Because,' Lena says. 'This place is fucking lethal.'

Trey says, very levelly, 'I know that.'

They look at each other, across all the things Lena knows and guesses about Trey's life. She realises, with a strange jolt of perspective, that for the first time they're looking at each other not the way an adult and a teenager do, but as two women.

She wants to somehow inject into Trey's head all the vast parts that she doesn't know. Understanding this place's dark streak is only the first step. Trey has no conception of what it means to live out your whole life side by side with that.

'Listen,' she says.

She gives Trey the whole story: her pathetic detective work, Mrs Duggan, Tommy showing up at the gate. She has a vague memory of how she imagined handing this over, as the magic talisman that would cancel out all the damage she's done and let Trey live here unscathed. Somehow it's been turned into the opposite: the one thing that might get Trey out to safety.

Trey listens without moving. She's come to take after Cal; she listens like him, leaning back against the counter with her head down and a twitch of concentration between her eyebrows. There are still speckles of blood on her cheek.

'Fair play to you,' she says, glancing up, when Lena stops talking.

'Thanks,' Lena says. 'I did no good to anyone except Tommy, but thanks all the same.'

Trey says, 'I'm gonna get him for this.'

'No,' Lena says. 'You're not. That's what I thought I was

doing. I went out there guns blazing, all ready to take him down. Look at me now.'

'He's a fuck,' Trey says, but abstractedly, by reflex. She's unfolding and refolding her wad of kitchen roll, thinking. 'I toldja Rachel found out something.'

'You can't do anything about him,' Lena says. 'And doing nothing'll take you to pieces. Go home and look up apprenticeships. I'll lend you the money for a flat.'

'Nah,' Trey says. She turns back to the window and gets to work on her face again, tilting her head to peer at her reflection. 'Thanks,' she adds, as an afterthought.

'You're not still going after Eugene,' Lena says. 'Right?'

Trey blows out a scornful puff of air, like that's baby stuff. 'Nah. Don't need to bother with that.'

'Then what?'

Trey looks at Lena, over her shoulder, like she's the thickest thing alive. 'Gonna tell Cal,' she says.

'*No*,' Lena says. She feels like banging her head off the wall. 'No. That won't do any good. Did you not hear a word I just said?'

'Yeah. Cal knows how to go at this stuff, but, from his job. He'll sort it.' Trey gives her face one more perfunctory scrub and throws the kitchen roll in the bin. 'He was only waiting 'cause he'd nothing to go off. Now we know the story, he'll be all on for doing something.'

'He will, yeah. And Tommy'll find a way to use it against him or me or you or all three of us. Do you want that?'

She's hoping the thought of harming Cal will get through, but Trey just shakes her head. 'Cal's not thick,' she says. 'We'll keep things tight, make sure nothing gets out, nothing gets back to Tommy that he can use.'

This is a level of Ardnakelty that Lena never thought she'd hear out of Trey Reddy's mouth: keep things tight, let nothing out, nothing anyone can use. She should have found a way to get Trey out of here years ago, while the place still despised her, before it revised its views and took possession. Instead she got comfortable and left it too late.

Trey is giving her a curious look. 'It'll be grand,' she says, almost gently.

Lena doesn't answer. She's exhausted, the kind of bone-crumbling exhaustion that used to hit her out of nowhere in the months after Sean died.

Trey grins at her, on the way towards the door. 'Motherfucker's goin' down,' she says.

Con McHugh hasn't been in touch about the nursing chair in a while. Normally Cal would just keep working on it, on the grounds that anything going on inside Con's head isn't his problem unless he's told otherwise, but somehow every head in this townland appears to have become his problem these days. He has no idea what to do with himself instead. He's walked the back roads till his legs ached and even Rip started lagging. He pokes around on the internet for a while, researching what to do about rising damp, but his connection is being shitty and he stops when he realises he's in danger of throwing the laptop. He actually considers kicking in a cupboard door, just so he'll have something he can fix.

Tommy Moynihan is good at this. He's left things perfectly poised, so finely balanced that Cal can't touch them. He can't do anything because he doesn't know what's going on, but he can't move to find out without hitting a tripwire. If Tommy had taken one step farther, Cal would have had no choice but to fight back; but Tommy's stopped just short of that, holding that one more step like a grenade whose pin he can pull any time. The only thing Cal can do is sit still, with his head down, and let Tommy have his will.

He can't remember ever feeling anger like this, sealed-in and unstoppably corrosive. He wishes he were a cop again, but he knows it's probably a good thing that he's not.

The evening is dark and gusty, wind growling in the treetops and slamming against the windowpanes at irregular intervals that make it impossible to be at rest. Cal sits at the kitchen table and tries to work on a present he's making for Lena, a trefoil knot whittled from a block of Sylvester's walnut tree, just on the off chance that the two of them are still together come Christmas. This morning he held her hand for so long that his arm went to sleep, but he couldn't feel her there. She held his and barely looked at him.

He knows he's missing something, because he can't for the life of him see what could have made this change. Lena has never given two shits what people say about her; Cal finds it hard to believe that she would be this shook by some dumbass rumour, and anyway her strangeness started before the rumours did. He's considered that she might be pissed off with him for getting mixed up in this mess and bringing Tommy down on them, but that doesn't seem like enough to warrant this reaction, especially considering that she's been deliberately getting mixed up in this mess herself. And Lena isn't the kind to fool around with the silent treatment and guessing games; if she had a problem with something he'd done, she would tell him, or leave him. He wonders if that's what she's working her way towards.

He could head down to Noreen's and ask whether Lena seems OK to her, which might at least give him some hint of whether the problem lies only between him and Lena, or whether it's a broader thing. He rejects the idea as soon as it enters his mind. Noreen, wound tight as she is, would go into a frenzy of worry and start bombarding Lena with attempts to find out what's going on and smack it back into shape, which would just make Lena withdraw farther into whatever distant place she's occupying.

Cal has always known that Lena's chosen weapons are barricades, not artillery, but he never thought she would use them against him. Last night he dreamed that he found her house abandoned, leaves blowing in through broken windows to scud across the kitchen table, and when he went to Noreen's looking for her, Noreen gave him a funny look and didn't know who he was talking about.

His fingers are clumsy today, and one wrong cut could fuck up the whole trefoil, a three-pointed endless knot that he currently feels like only a fool would try to carve out of wood, so he's working at the speed of molasses and getting more frustrated by the minute. Mostly he has music on while he works, but he doesn't like the thought of missing something, whistling away to Nathaniel Rateliff like a dumbass while Tommy's boys close in around the house. What with the wind, he misses Trey's approach anyway; when she slams the door open, he and Rip both jump a mile.

'Jesus, kid,' Cal says. His heart is pounding. 'Can't you open a door like a human being? What happened to your face?'

'That *fuck* Tommy Moynihan,' Trey says. She fires her schoolbag across the room like she's shot-putting, and lands it on the armchair with so much force that the chair rocks.

'He did that?' Cal says. He's out of his chair.

'What? Nah. That was school. Listen to this.'

She's so triumphant and so furious that it takes a few tries before Cal gets her story straight. 'That's why the fucker wants us out,' she finishes. 'For the land. And that's why he kilt Rachel: 'cause she was gonna say it. I knew she didn't do it herself. *Fuck* him and Eugene and the whole lotta them.'

'Hold on,' Cal says. He's still standing at the kitchen table; Trey's flood of info came at him too hard and fast to let him move. 'Back up a minute. Where'd you get all this?'

'Lena. She got it offa Mrs Duggan. And that's why Tommy's telling everyone she's mental, so no one'll believe her.'

'Lena,' Cal says. He starts moving in circles around the living room. As far as he knows, he has never once given Lena any reason not to trust him.

'Now we know what he's playing at,' Trey says, 'we can get him. Take him to fuckin' pieces. Put him in jail for the resta his life.'

'No life sentences here,' Cal says automatically.

'So twenty years or whatever. Poncy twat like that, he'll get the shite bet outa him. See does he still think he's great when some skinhead's knocked his teeth out.'

'All that stuff with the land, that's all legal,' Cal says. He's still moving, to help himself think this through. 'Probably some bribes here and there, but we're not gonna prove that.'

'What about Rachel? That's not fuckin' legal.'

'There's no evidence he ever did anything to Rachel. What you and me think isn't evidence.'

'Then *get* some.'

Trey is still standing in the middle of the floor, messy-haired from the wind, her triumph dimming fast with frustration and bafflement. She came in here all ready for Cal to catch fire with her excitement, and instead he's wrecking it.

'Kid,' he says. He wants to head out the door right now, in his sock feet, come back to her laden with armfuls of evidence so they can mount Tommy Moynihan's head over the fireplace. 'If I was a cop, then maybe. If I could pull location histories on Rachel and Tommy and Eugene, go through Tommy's phone to see who he was in touch with around then, pull location histories on them. Or if I could bring Eugene in, go at him hard enough. But I can't.'

'You can still go at him hard,' Trey points out. 'Harder. We'll help, me and the lads. It'll take about a minute.'

'Right. And then I'm in jail for assault, Eugene says he was just telling me whatever would make me back off, and we've got Tommy on our asses even worse.'

Trey says, with the weight and the force of a wrecking ball, 'I'm not letting him away with what he said about you.'

'I'm not gonna let him get away with any of this shit,' Cal says. Things rise up at him, Lena's cold hand in his, Claire Holohan's destroyed eyes, Senan's shoulder taut under his grip; Rachel's face, secretive in death, upturned to the sky. He feels like he's lifting off the floor with fury. 'Not any of it.'

'So what do we do?'

Cal has been trying to find some way around this. When it comes to shit as serious as this, his instinct is to turn to the law; it's always seemed to him the best way to make sure things hold together, instead of disintegrating into an unholy mess. That's what he wants to be telling Trey right now: *We'll take this whole hell-brew to the police, they'll set everything straight.* But if Garda Dennis and the home inspector are any indicators, the law around here has no intention of setting anything straight, even if they had the raw materials to do it. All the borderlines have got mixed up; the patterns Cal understands have been shaken like a kaleidoscope and come down unrecognisable. He's thought about going higher up, talking to the brass, but the brass seem almost unimaginably remote; he can't picture this story making any kind of sense to some suit in an office in Dublin.

If he knew Rachel's father, he'd be bringing all this to him. Probably that would be a terrible idea, but the man has a right to know what happened to his girl, and to decide what to do about it. But Fintan Holohan doesn't go to the pub – he has a name for being a quiet man, a homebody – he's not a farmer, he works up in Kilcarrow; Cal has barely spoken to the guy. If he showed up on the Holohans' doorstep with this wild story, Fintan would more than likely kick his ass to the kerb.

He says, 'We're gonna need to call in the cavalry.'

Trey gives him a blank look.

'I need to talk to Mart.'

Trey's face shuts down. Trey doesn't like Mart one bit, or this townland, or their methods of dealing with problems. She has every reason not to.

She says, 'You and me can handle it ourselves.'

'Kid,' Cal says. 'Tommy's got his pockets full of Guards, inspectors, probably Child Services, who knows what-all. If you and me go up against him, he can take us down in a heartbeat.'

He doesn't want to look at the blank disbelief on Trey's face. The kid brought this to him taking for granted that he could fix it. It comes even harder than he expected, admitting to her that it's beyond his power.

'What can Mart fuckin' Lavin do that we can't?' she demands.

'He's got plenty of backup,' Cal says. 'And he knows how this place works, better'n I do; better'n anyone. He'll come up with something.'

Trey is still looking somewhere between outraged and crushed, but now that the decision is made, Cal finally has enough clear space in his mind to take in how much has transformed in the last ten minutes. 'Hey,' he says. 'Kid. This is great. You did great. I've been sitting here going out of my mind, climbing the walls, 'cause I couldn't do one single thing about any of this. Now we can.'

After a moment, Trey nods.

'We just need to make sure we do something that's gonna work. Now that you've got us a shot, I'm not gonna waste it.'

Trey says, 'You seriously reckon Mart can take Tommy down?'

'No,' Cal says. 'Not Mart all by himself. Mart and you and me and your buddies and Mart's buddies and whoever else he brings on board: yeah.'

He watches Trey turn inwards, sharp and alert, while she examines this and its implications. Both by nature and from experience, she fights shy of community projects. She's come to a wary acceptance of her standoff with Ardnakelty, at a mutually agreed distance where she does her finest woodwork for them and charges full price, and they invite her to Halloween parties safe in the knowledge that she won't come. This will shift that balance beyond reversal.

'Guess themens have a right to be in on it,' she says, after a minute. 'Since Tommy's planning on fucking them over as well.'

'Well, he is that,' Cal says. He wishes he had some way of knowing whether what's happening is a good thing for Trey or not. Lena would consider it a bad one, but Lena isn't here.

Trey draws a fast breath. She says, 'I'da rathered do it ourselves.'

'Yeah,' Cal says. 'Me too. But this is what we've got.'

In the end Trey looks up at him and nods. 'Yeah,' she says. 'You gonna go talk to Mart now?'

'Wednesday evenings he mostly goes to the pub. First thing tomorrow, I'll talk to him.' Trey's face has a look Cal hasn't seen on it in a while, the stretched-thin look kids get when the day has held too much for them to take in. 'Meanwhile,' he says, 'let's you and me get some food inside us.' He's suddenly starving; it occurs to him that he hasn't eaten all day. 'We can throw on some hamburgers.'

Trey pulls off her jacket and hangs it up. She says, 'Gonna text Lena to come?'

'Not tonight,' Cal says. He sweeps his wood shavings off the table into his hand and takes them over to the garbage.

Trey watches him. She says, 'You and her breaking up?'

'Not that I know of,' Cal says. 'Where'd that come from?'

'Then what's wrong with her?'

Trey has never before appeared to pay the slightest bit of

notice to anyone's emotional state, including her own. Cal, while he's delighted to see her maturing up, wishes she had picked another day or another way to do it. 'Kid,' he says, 'I have no idea.'

'So text her.'

'Nah,' Cal says. He goes to the sink to wash the sawdust off his hands. 'This here that I'm working on, this is her Christmas present; she can't see it. You want onions on your hamburger?' He doesn't want to invite Lena. He doesn't want to see the text marked as read, and the long blank after that.

13

Cal finds Mart up his attic ladder, with only his legs visible, banging something metal and singing 'Come Out Ye Black and Tans' into the attic at the top of his lungs. Kojak, determinedly staying put at the foot of the ladder in case he's needed, gives Cal an imploring eyeroll. Cal has to shout three times before Mart hears him.

'Ah,' Mart says, when he's reversed his way down the ladder till he can twist his head around to see Cal, a manoeuvre complicated by the fact that he has a frying pan in each hand. ''Tis yourself. That fucker's back.'

'Squirrel?' Cal says. Mart's battle with the squirrel is an annual event, as reliable a part of the calendar as the National Ploughing Championships or the little old ladies' springtime novena at the village grotto. The squirrel, when the weather turns cold, feels that Mart's attic is an ideal place to spend the winter; Mart disagrees. According to him, the war has been going on for fifteen years and counting. Cal has pointed out that squirrels only live a few years and this is presumably a hereditary feud, but Mart is having none of that. In his view, this is personal.

'Raffles himself,' Mart says. He drops the frying pans, which thud onto the congealed brown hall carpet, and comes down the ladder after them. His fleece has a fresh layer of dust and cobwebs, over its usual decorations of mud and tractor grease. 'D'you know what that fucker's after doing? Yesterday, while myself and Kojak were out on the farm doing a dacent day's work, he strolled into our kitchen, as bold as brass. Et the food right outa Kojak's bowl and done a shite on the table. That's a declaration of war.'

'You sure it's not a rat?' Cal asks. He picks up the frying pans, to spare Mart's joints, and hands them over.

Mart snorts. 'Rat, me arse. I know this fella's work when I see it. What I oughta do, if I was a man of leisure, is lie in wait for the bastard. Spend the day sitting in my kitchen with my rifle, and when he shows his face' – he mimes firing the frying pans – 'go ahead, punk, make my day. D'you fancy taking over the farmwork for tomorrow, Jean-Claude?'

'You're turning into Yosemite Sam here, man,' Cal says.

'That rabbit was a fuckin' amateur,' Mart says darkly, picking a cobweb out of his eyebrow. 'This fella's the real thing. A stone-cold professional.'

'You're gonna end up burning the house down or something,' Cal says. Things have never escalated to flamethrower levels yet, but it appears to be a matter of time.

'A man's got to do what a man's got to do,' Mart says. 'One year I tried rat bait, and d'you know what he done? Took it outside and dropped it around the yard. That cute hoor tried to poison my dog. I can't let that slide.' He shoots the ladder back into place and slams the attic trapdoor closed. 'All that noise oughta have scared him out for now, but he'll be back. We'll go have a look for where he's getting in.' He hands Cal one of the frying pans. 'If you catch sight of the fella, give him a skelp with that. See can you get him over the wall.'

They circle the house, their boots sticking in the gravelly mud, Kojak trudging behind them with a long-suffering air. The day is cold and windless. The rams have been turned out with the ewes, for spring lambing; their deep calls carry faintly, muffled by the low mist hanging over the fields. Every half-minute Mart whips around to scan the trees that edge the yard.

Now that he's here, Cal finds himself putting it off a little longer, like he could just do this: help Mart fix his lintel or his vent or whatever, maybe even agree to do some farmwork tomorrow while Mart hides in the kitchen playing *Caddyshack*, and then go home, taking his grenade with him. Once he pulls the pin, he has no idea what the blast radius is going to be.

'Hey,' he says, pointing his frying pan up at the eaves. 'That a hole, right under there?'

Mart squints at the tiny dark patch in the soffit. 'By George,' he says, 'I think he's got it. Isn't it a great thing to be young and have good eyesight?'

'You want me to go up there, take a look?'

Mart shakes a finger vigorously at Cal. 'Ah, no, no, no. This is between Raffles and myself. If I go bringing in backup, he'll take it as a sign of weakness. If you're in a helpful humour, but,' he adds, 'are you any good at the aul' auto repairs?'

'Not my department,' Cal says. 'That rustbucket finally give up on you?'

'That classic vehicle,' Mart informs him with dignity, 'will be riding the range long after yourself and myself are dead and gone. No: someone took a crowbar to Senan's car. Bet the living shite outa it. That yoke wasn't going to win any prizes to start with, but the state of it now: if 'twas a horse you'd shoot it. Senan's bulling. And he can't go through the insurance without making a police report, so he's stuck paying for the whole thing outa pocket.'

Cal doesn't need an explanation. Senan will leave the police out of this, both by reflex and because he doesn't want them keeping an eye on what might come next. He says, 'Long John?'

'Who knows, Sunny Jim,' Mart says. 'Who knows. Long John'd be the obvious suspect, all right, but it never pays to go after the obvious around here. There's plenty of other people besides Long John that have strong opinions, these days.' He narrows his eyes at the eaves, scratching his jaw. 'While we're on the subject,' he says. 'Did you ever find any of that clarity you were looking for?'

'Yeah,' Cal says. 'About that.'

Mart turns to look at him.

'Word is,' Cal says, 'that factory over towards Kilhone is gonna want more land than they thought. If Tommy buys up enough parcels here and there and sells them to the factory, and if he gets Eugene onto the county council, the factory can get compulsory purchase orders on everything in between.'

There's a silence. Mart says, 'Where'd you get this?'

'Lena got it from Mrs Duggan,' Cal says. Mart's voice, its complete lack of any expression at all, chills him.

Mart nods a few times. 'That means 'tis likely true,' he says. 'I'll say this for Dymphna: her prices are high, but she delivers the goods.'

He stands still, thinking, his eyes on nothing. Back on the job, that particular stillness would have had Cal reaching for his gun.

'It'd work out, all right,' Mart says. 'Tommy already has a few of the council in his pocket, one way or t'other. If he gets Eugene in there to run the show, they'll do anything he tells them.'

'Why would anyone want that much land?' Cal asks. It's the one thing that's been making him doubt this story. 'How big is this factory gonna be?'

Mart smiles, a small grim smile out to the fields. 'That's the beauty of it, Sunny Jim,' he says. 'Once the land is theirs, 'tis theirs. Whoever's behind that factory can have a change of heart any time they like. Maybe it'll dawn on them that they don't need all that land for the factory after all, but they can get the council to re-zone it, not a bother on them, and they've developer pals who think a housing estate'd go lovely right there. Or a tourist village, maybe, or a data centre. Or they can sell the whole lot to one a them megafarms. The world's their oyster, or anyhow this townland is.'

Cal says, 'They don't have to sell it back to you guys if they change their minds?'

Mart's smile widens. 'Ah, God, no. A few years back, there was people trying to get that rule brought in, but your woman that was Minister said we didn't need it; sure, she said, that'd never happen. Whenever a politician starts promising that something'll never happen, boyo, that's when I start the countdown.'

He's still looking out at the fields. PJ is out on his land, poking at something with the toe of one boot, a big yellow bucket hanging from his hand. Behind him, the mist blurs trees to huddled ghosts; stone walls hang unmoored. The fields eddy like water.

'Everything in between,' Mart says.

'Bobby,' Cal says. 'Rory Dunne. Lena.' He recalls Tommy, way back in Noreen's shop with Rachel Holohan outside the window, nudging to find out whether Lena would be moving to his place.

Mart nods. 'Flapper Deery. The McHugh lads. Ciaran Maloney.'

The names fall like a list read over a tolling bell. 'Not this side,' Cal says. 'Not you and me and PJ.'

'Not yet,' Mart says. 'But it will be. I'd say it'll be one a them megafarms; all investors behind it, not a farming man or woman among them – and we all know who one of the big investors'll be. And that'll be the young fellas around here scuppered. If I decide to sell up tomorrow and spend the rest of my days cruising the Caribbean – which I'm considering, if 'tis the only way to escape that Raffles fucker – then some young lad whose father hasn't enough to share between all the brothers could buy my land. But once one a them megafarms comes in, land prices'll shoot up till no one else can afford to buy.'

He smiles that small grim smile again. ' "I own this town," the Boss Moynihan usedta say. Tommy's after taking that awful literally.'

Cal recognises that Mart's feeling for this land is outside his understanding. Cal grew up among folks whose grip on their land was given a hair-trigger savagery by the fact that they had nothing else; when he first came here, he was wary of asking directions at a strange farm in case he found himself on the wrong end of a shotgun. When he realised that he could knock on just about any door in the townland and be met with not only directions but a cup of tea, he thought people here held their territory in lighter hands. It took him a while to start understanding that their tie to their land is different not in its intensity but in its nature: rooted thousands of years deep, through strata of dispossession, famine, bloody rebellion. This land has been reclaimed, not claimed, and that changes things. The ferocity of their possession may not display itself in brandished shotguns and yelling dogs, but it's built into every cell, latent and ineradicable, ready to rise when it's needed again.

'We can make an objection,' he says, hearing the weakness of it as he says it. 'Or take them to court, or something.'

'Oh, there'll be plenty of objections along the way,' Mart agrees. 'And plenty of courts, and plenty of lawyers getting richer, right up until all of us little fellas run outa cash. But we all know who'll win in the end.'

'I'm not gonna sit back and let Moynihan do whatever he wants,' Cal says. 'And I don't believe you are either. So don't give me that bullshit.'

Mart turns to look at him. Cal almost takes a step back at the violence in his eyes.

'I could have the man dead in a bog by morning,' he says, 'and no one would ever know what happened him. Is that what you want?'

Cal says, 'I've thought about it.' He didn't intend to say that out loud, to anyone, let alone Mart.

Mart nods. 'I wouldn't blame you. I heard what Tommy's been spreading around.'

'Yeah,' Cal says. 'I figure most people have.'

Mart's blue eyes, watery from the cold and infinitely patient, are level on Cal's. 'And what did you decide?'

'No,' Cal says.

'Why not?'

'Few different reasons,' Cal says.

'That's a good choice,' Mart says. 'There's plenty of people that'd have every right to put Tommy in that bog. And if I thought 'twould sort the situation, I'd get it done. But it wouldn't sort a bloody thing.'

'It'd sort out most of my problems,' Cal says.

Mart shakes his head. He looks like himself again; the violence has gone out of him, put to one side for now to let him think. 'We need Tommy, boyo. He's started this off now, and we've no way of knowing how far it's gone; for all we know, if he was outa the way, it could just keep on moving ahead without him. Getting rid of him won't get rid of wee Eugene, or alla them big investors up in Dublin. We need Tommy to pull the plug. Our job is to explain to him that it'd be in his best interest to do that, before things go too far.'

'I need to be careful,' Cal says. 'Tommy's been loud and clear that if I give him any trouble, he's gonna fuck up Trey and Lena and me pretty good.'

Mart gives Cal's arm a tap with the frying pan. 'That's why you were right to come to me, Jean-Claude. Strength in numbers. Tommy can bring out the big guns against one family, but he can't bring them out against half the townland at once.'

Cal says, 'Half?'

'More than that, maybe. But we might as well go into this

with our eyes open: there'll be plenty who'll find reasons why Tommy oughta have anything he wants.'

'Including their land?'

'Not everyone's a farmer, man. And even the ones that are: *Sure 'twill be grand, you're only making a loada fuss over nothing 'cause you're jealous of the man, 'twon't be my land anyhow, doesn't Tommy deserve a bitta payback after everything he's done for this place . . .*' One corner of Mart's mouth twists drily. 'You wouldn't credit it, wouldja? But I told you before, sunshine: we're a terrible place for the forelock-tuggers. You can blame it on the Brits getting us in the habit, if you like, or the Church; take your pick. But the minute a man's got a bitta power, there's some people that reckon saying no to him is the same as saying no to God Almighty.'

Kojak is still waiting resignedly, at Mart's heel, for them to start moving again. Mart whistles a sharp note between his teeth for him to sit, and bends to rub his ears. 'But Tommy'll need more than just the hardcore forelock-tuggers to get Eugene onto the council,' he says. 'No wonder he had his knickers in a knot when people started blaming Eugene over Rachel Holohan. That could make a big difference: if Eugene's in the bad books around here and he doesn't get the votes, Tommy might not get his compulsory purchase orders. His big investors wouldn't like that one wee bit.' He glances up from Kojak. 'I wondered about that: why wouldn't Tommy just forget about this election, send Eugene back up to Dublin till it all blew over, then have him run next time round instead? But it all adds up now. If he done that, he might miss his big chance. And the stakes are awful high.'

'From what I've gathered,' Cal says, 'Rachel was planning to make a difference, all right. Eugene told her what him and his daddy had in mind. And Rachel didn't like it one bit.'

Mart's eyebrows lift. 'Wouldja look at that,' he says. 'Columbo's been out there getting the goods. Tommy was right to try hiring you, bucko.' He straightens up, in increments, and scratches thoughtfully at his white stubble. 'I'm not surprised Rachel was having none of it,' he says. 'The Holohans are dacent people, always have been; there's no notions about them. This wouldn't be their style at all, at all.'

'She was looking for ways to stop Tommy and Eugene,' Cal says. 'I don't know what she had in mind, exactly. I get the feeling she might've been thinking about warning people what they were up to.'

Mart tilts his head, unconvinced. 'That wouldn'ta done the job. It'll pack a fair aul' punch now, with the poor girl dead and people already blaming Eugene, and the blood up all round. But back then, sure, most of the place wouldn'ta believed her, even. *Ah now Tommy's a great lad, where would we be without him at all, he'd never do the likes of that. That Rachel one musta had a row with Eugene and now she's looking to make trouble, disgraceful carry-on, I'da thought better of her.* No: if Rachel wanted to scupper Tommy's plans, she'da needed a better strategy than that.'

'Rachel was just a kid,' Cal says. 'Sweet-natured, too, from all's I hear. She didn't have your resources.'

'I'm sweet-natured,' Mart says, offended. 'I'm only saying: telling the world woulda done fuck-all. And wee Rachel may have been sweet-natured, but she was no thick.'

'Even if that's all she could come up with,' Cal says, 'seems like, as high as the stakes are, Tommy might not have wanted to run any risks.'

Mart's eyebrows go up again. He ruminates over this, scraping something off his frying pan with a thumbnail. 'You might have a point there,' he says. 'Tommy's after getting awful outa hand.'

'Tommy's a piece of shit,' Cal says.

'True enough,' Mart agrees. 'But 'tis a bit more complex than that, Sunny Jim. Tommy always did find ways around the rules, but you mighta noticed, we're fans of people that get around the rules.'

'I picked up on that,' Cal says.

'You can blame that one on the Brits as well, while you're at it. There was plenty of centuries where the rules were only made up to keep us down and take what was ours. Why wouldn't we prize the people that could find ways around them and get away with it? So when Tommy handed around a few brown envelopes to get the factory up and running, and when he sorted out a few inspectors now and then so he could cut some corners, everyone thought he was a great fella altogether, not letting themens up in Dublin get the best of him. And sure, who'd turn down the chance to get a speeding ticket squared, or the re-zoning sorted?'

He glances up from the frying pan to meet Cal's eyes. 'But there's other rules, boyo,' he says, 'as well as the ones that get made all the way up in Dublin.'

'Yeah,' Cal says. 'I picked up on that part, too.'

'With all them pats on the back Tommy gets, and all them lickarses telling him anything he does is pure gold, that fella's after losing the run of himself. We shoulda put manners on him a long time back.'

The sheep are still calling. Mart turns his head to watch them, pale smudges in the mist, moving in their own mysterious, restless patterns. 'I shoulda seen this coming,' he says. 'I blame myself for that. I never liked the fucker, but I thought there was lines he wouldn't cross. 'Tis a long time since I felt like an innocent, Sunny Jim, and I don't like the feeling one wee bit.'

'If Tommy was to get arrested for murder,' Cal says, 'or even just questioned, his big-shot investors wouldn't like that. They're not gonna pump millions into some project when their fixer might land in jail any minute.'

Mart gives Cal a look like he suggested enlisting the Tooth Fairy. 'Tommy's not getting arrested for anything, bucko. He's got the Guards around here in his pocket. I thought you'd spotted that.'

'There's other Guards besides the ones around here. Some detective up in Dublin doesn't know Tommy Moynihan from Adam. He doesn't give a shit about the meat-processing plant.' Cal still can't picture himself explaining this situation to a Dublin detective, but it seems to him that someone should at least try.

'This is a small country you're in, sunshine,' Mart says gently. 'Dublin feels awful far away sometimes, but a man down here can pull a string up there, no problem, if he's got the string ready in place. Tommy's donated plenty to Dickie O'Shea, and whatever he's concocting, I'd bet my life Dickie's got in on the ground floor. Let's say you convinced some detective to go sniffing around Tommy, on nothing but bitsa suspicion. Tommy'd hear all about it, from his pocket policemen. Then Tommy has a word with Dickie, Dickie has a word with one of the high-ups in the party, the high-up has a word with a high-up in the Guards, and next thing you know . . .'

He mimes blowing the whole thing off his hand into the air, like a piece of thistledown. 'Gone,' he says. When he sees Cal's face: 'I'm not saying Tommy couldn't get in hassle, if he done anything on Rachel. He might, or then again he might not. But there'd haveta be some solid proof, before we'd have a chance in hell; something that couldn't be brushed off as just locals getting themselves in a tizzy. And the aul' solid proof's a wee bit thin on the ground.'

He smiles at Cal, all his wrinkles creasing up. 'No: we're better off leaving the Guards outa this. We mostly are, sure. I can't remember the last time bringing the Guards on board improved matters.'

'OK,' Cal says. 'OK. So what do we do?' He doesn't notice the *we* until he catches the flicker of a grin on Mart's face.

'You do nothing,' Mart says, 'and say nothing. I know that's not your style, but don't be worrying: 'twon't be for long.'

'If you want me to wait around,' Cal says, 'Tommy needs to lay off Lena. And Trey. Starting now.'

'I'll do what I can,' Mart says. 'But we might as well be honest with ourselves, man: things could get worse before they get better.'

'No,' Cal says.

Mart watches him. This time Cal recognises the patience in his eyes: the underdog's patience, made endless by necessity. 'If you go rogue,' he says, 'you'll only do more harm than good. You know that as well as I do, or you wouldn't be here. Stick to the plan.'

Cal says, 'What is the plan?'

He doesn't expect an answer – Mart's core protocol is never to tell anyone anything unless he has no choice – he's just registering his opinion that he has a right to be kept up to speed. To his surprise, Mart cocks his head to one side, considering him.

'Tell me something, Jean-Claude,' he says. 'If Tommy hadda had the good sense to leave you and your family alone, would you have brought this to me anyhow?'

Cal feels the weight of the question land on him. It seems like a long time ago that Mart warned him about crossroadses, and they just keep on coming.

'Yeah,' he says.

'And let's say we'da needed a hand from you to deal with it. Would you have been on board?'

Cal says, 'Yeah.'

Mart nods for a long time. 'I thought that, all right,' he says. 'Well: we've a few angles at our disposal, boyo. I'd say we'll start with the direct route. Sure, you know I've always been the straightforward type.'

'What's the direct route?' Cal asks. He can't imagine what

Mart's definition of the term would look like. He isn't sure he's ever seen anyone around here, except Trey and Lena, go at anything direct.

'I'll spread the word to the right people,' Mart says, 'build up a bitta momentum, and half the townland can explain to Tommy that if he keeps on going with this loada shite, he'd wanta have his holiday home abroad bought and paid for, because Ardnakelty won't be an option for him. Clodagh wouldn't like that,' he adds, parenthetically. 'She's awful fond of being the queen of the canapés around here; I wouldn't say she'd fancy starting over from scratch, even in Puerto Banús.'

Cal says, 'Explain to him.'

'We'll use small words,' Mart says. 'That fella's not as bright as he thinks. The direct route might do the do, and it'll be great if it does, but I'm not getting my hopes up too far. If that doesn't work out for us, then we'll haveta get a wee bit more subtle about it all.'

'What kinda subtle?' Cal asks.

'God almighty, cool the jets there, Speedy Gonzales,' Mart says, giving him a reproachful stare. 'You're only after dropping the bombshell on me five minutes ago. I haven't had time to consider our options in detail.'

When Cal keeps looking at him, he sighs and rubs his fluff of grey hair to help himself think it over. 'Offa the top of my head,' he says, 'something might come out about Eugene – maybe Rachel stumbled on the stuff he was looking up on the internet, and that's what sent her into the river. That oughta keep him off the council.'

'I was talking to Sheila Reddy,' Cal says. He has that feeling again, like he's back on the job working out a case strategy with a partner, only upside down and backwards in some bizarre mirror. 'Tommy gives her any more trouble, she's gonna spread it around that Eugene was beating Rachel.'

Mart considers this, intrigued. 'That's not bad,' he says. 'There could be mileage in that.'

Cal says, 'This is gonna get messy.'

'Oh, God, it is,' Mart agrees. 'Wear your wellies for this one, boyo.'

'If you hassle Tommy, he's gonna whip up some momentum of his own.'

'He'll do that, all right,' Mart says. 'And we can all have a good look at whose momentum is bigger. I'm betting on mine, but sure, doesn't every man?' He gives Cal a sharp glance. 'Are you getting cold feet on me, Sunny Jim?'

'Nope,' Cal says. 'Just want to be sure we're all clear on where this is headed.'

'Sunshine,' Mart says drily. 'I been living here since before your daddy had his first impure thought about your mammy. I'm clear as crystal. If there was a nice civilised way to get this done over a cuppa tea and a biscuit, I'd be only delighted, but there isn't.'

Cal says, 'And you figure your way can do it.'

Mart looks at him. He says, 'Tommy shoulda known better.'

Behind him the low layer of mist shifts over the fields, so they look like they're slowly twisting, pulled by unknown gravities. Cal feels in the back of his neck the two kinds of power unfurling across them: Tommy's, suited and badged, sleek with money and assurance and legal phrases; this other thing, rising up wordless and bare of any outside weaponry, smelling of earth and blood.

'Man,' he says, 'I hope you know what you're doing.'

'We'll find out soon enough, sure,' Mart says. 'Till then, you'll just have to trust me. Can you manage that?'

'I don't have much choice,' Cal says.

'Ah, that's lovely, so 'tis,' Mart says, smiling up at him. 'I'm honoured. For now, anyhow, all you have to trust me to do is have the chats with the right people. Is that fair enough?'

Cal says, 'I'd rather you didn't put it around that this came from Lena.'

'I'm not planning to, Jean-Claude,' Mart says gently. 'I've no wish to drop your missus in the shite. And above and beyond that, the pair of us know Lena's as reliable a source as you could wish for, but not everyone does.'

'Right,' Cal says. 'Yeah.'

'I'll say it came from Dymphna Duggan, is all. Even His Lordship knows better than to go up against that one. But before I get stuck into that nonsense,' Mart adds, on a different note, 'I'm going to seal up them eaves tighter than a duck's arse, and see what that Raffles fucker makes of that.' He holds out a hand for his backup frying pan. 'D'you know what you oughta do? You oughta train them rooks of yours to hunt squirrels. They might as well come in—'

Midway through turning back towards his front door, he freezes like a pointer dog, his whole body aimed at an oak tree in the corner of the yard. A grey squirrel is spreadeagled halfway down the trunk, head lifted to stare at them.

'Wouldja look at that, Sunny Jim,' Mart says, barely moving his lips. 'He's been watching us this whole time. I shoulda brought my rifle.'

He takes one slow-motion step towards the tree. The squirrel cocks its head and lets out a sharp, insulting chatter.

'Get ta fuck!' Mart roars, brandishing the frying pans. His voice spreads like a shock wave over the silent fields. The squirrel turns and whisks up the tree trunk to disappear among the branches, waving his tail at them all the way like a big furry middle finger.

14

Unsurprisingly, Trey isn't one little bit impressed by Mart's plan. She shows up at Cal's straight from school, while Cal is working on the trefoil knot for Lena. He can't bring himself to put it aside, even though it's come to feel as dumb and delusional as working on Con's nursing chair.

He should update Lena. She won't like what he has to say, but she has a right to know, and Cal feels he has a right to ask her why she kept this from him. That isn't a phone conversation, so he manned up and texted her to invite her over for dinner, earlier, and endured the silence before his phone beeped: *Bit wrecked today but thanks.*

Cal's first instinct was to text her back, *Tomorrow? We need to talk about what's going on.* He didn't do it. He's already got his answer, not with Lena's usual clarity, but in full oblique Ardnakelty style. Pushing would do no good; deflection comes to this place with the effortlessness of reflex. Cal is accustomed to it from Mart and everyone else. He doesn't want it from Lena.

Get rest, he texted instead. *See you soon. Love you.* A long time later the reply came through, from a million miles away: *Love you.*

He wants to go over to Lena's house, fast, before it becomes too late, and haul her free of whatever dark current is pulling her away from him. He's stopped by the fact that he doesn't know how; he has no idea what this current is, or whether she even wants to be freed. He carves doggedly away at the trefoil instead, and pictures himself laying it on her doorstep, Christmas morning, and walking away.

At least Trey doesn't ask where Lena is, this time. She's too busy demanding to know what Mart said, and then objecting to it.

'Hang on a fuckin' second,' she says, when Cal finishes. Across the worktable she's taut with outrage, ready to overturn her chair and go kick ass, Tommy's or Mart's, Cal can't tell. 'So all the Moynihans haveta do is quit buying land, and they're just gonna get away with it. Rachel and everything. And what they said about you. The *fuck*?'

'Well,' Cal says. 'Not get away with it scot-free. Once the dust clears, I don't think Tommy Moynihan's gonna be Mr Big around here any more. I figure there's a better-'n-even chance he'll have to find somewhere else to live.'

'He's not gonna go to *jail*. He's not even getting bet *up*. He's getting away with it.'

'I don't like it either,' Cal says. This has been on his mind; not just all that Tommy is going to get away with, but the ease with which he himself fell into line with this plan. Cal has always aimed to live by a moral code that doesn't allow for letting shit-birds kill young girls and walk away based on their level of local clout, but apparently that's shifted while he wasn't looking; everything Mart said sounded not just rational but unarguable. He feels like he's been drinking the water around here for too long, or something. 'But I don't see any way around it.'

'Kill him,' Trey says promptly.

'No,' Cal says.

'Why not?'

'You can't go killing people just because they deserve it.'

Trey looks unconvinced. 'Plus,' Cal says, 'that wouldn't fix the stuff he's been spreading around. Miss Lena has to live here.'

'She doesn't give a shite what themens say,' Trey says, but she glances at Cal like it's a question.

A few weeks ago, Cal would have thought the same thing. Now he has no idea. 'Maybe not,' he says, 'but it can still make her life harder, and I'm still not gonna stand by while they say it. I don't need Tommy dead. He's no good to me that way. What I need is him tarred and feathered and run out of town on a rail, with every man and woman in this place lined up to spit on him along the way, 'cause they all know he's a piece of shit and so is everything that comes outa his mouth.'

His voice has a rising savagery he didn't intend. Trey considers this and nods, with some reluctance.

'Besides,' Cal says. He focuses on smoothing a curve of the trefoil, and on bringing his voice back to normal. 'Tommy's the only guy who can stop this crap with the factory. We need to keep him around and arm-twist him into doing it, or a lot of people around here are gonna lose their land.'

Trey gives him her best blank stare. 'So? Fuck 'em.'

'Well,' Cal says. He turns the trefoil to work his knife, delicately, deeper into a corner. 'There's that. But I don't have the right to go, "Hey, fuck all y'all, I do what I want" to this whole townland.'

'Yeah you do. Why not?'

'Nope. I came to live in this place, by my own free will. If you do that, you owe the place something.'

Trey blows this away with a derisive puff of air. 'I never came to live here,' she points out. 'Just got stuck with it.'

'Yep,' Cal says. 'You can take off the minute you finish school, if that's what you choose. Then you won't owe a thing to anyone here.'

He shaves away tiny curls of wood and watches Trey from under his eyebrows. He has no idea what he's hoping she'll say, or how he should respond, either way. Somehow, with the kid getting older, every decision she makes seems to have taken on such weight that he can hardly breathe, in case he somehow steers her wrong and her whole life crashes and burns. She listens to him, at least sometimes; she might listen to him in this, and the possibility is terrifying. Cal doesn't want her binding herself to a place that's done her wrong, and that responds to just about any situation by producing elaborate new layers of darkness, purely because she's got herself a girlfriend, or because of him; but then again, he doesn't want her ditching everyone who cares about her and taking off into the world half-cocked, just because she knows this place's flaws and doesn't understand that no other place is innocent either. He made the mistake, when he came here, of thinking he'd found a place that was innocent. He's learned how that story goes.

Trey's first rush of outrage has faded. She's playing with a curve of scrap wood, leaning her elbows on the worktable and balancing the wood on one finger. She says, 'Lena said to do that. Clear out, don't come back.'

'Huh,' Cal says. He shoves down a helpless, painful anger at Lena, for playing at whatever the hell she's playing at, and for shutting him out of it. He has no practice being angry at Lena, and he hates it. 'That what you want to do?'

Trey shrugs. 'Nah.'

After a second Cal says carefully, 'I didn't think you liked this place enough to stick around.'

Trey glances up at him, the curve of wood neatly poised on her fingertip. 'You think I should go, too?'

Her eyes are intent on his. 'I'm not saying that,' Cal says. 'All's I'm saying is, I wasn't sure what to expect.'

Trey spins the piece of wood on her fingertip, digging around for words. 'I usedta be set on leaving,' she says. 'But I done a load around here. Feels like I earned this place.'

'You don't need to decide anything now,' Cal says. 'You've got time.'

That gets him another quick glance. 'You do think I oughta go.'

'I don't think anything,' Cal says. 'I just want you to be sure.'

Trey doesn't answer this. 'Needs more off there,' she says, pointing her piece of wood at an angle of the trefoil.

She wants to drop the subject, which is fine with Cal. 'Quit kibitzing,' he says. 'You want to work, get out your own stuff and let me do mine in peace.'

'I was thinking about a cabinet yoke,' Trey says. 'Outa that bitta walnut. Like, leave the outside the way it is, so when it's hanging on the wall it just looks like a burl, only then you open it up on hinges and the front half's all little drawers inside. Seen it on the internet.'

'Jeez, kid,' Cal says. 'Your life too easy, or something?'

Trey shrugs. 'Make a good showpiece. When I'm going for the apprenticeship.'

'Finish school first,' Cal says automatically. It occurs to him that one reason he's set on her finishing school might be so the heaviest decisions can wait, just till she's a little bit older. Trey rolls her eyes extravagantly and heads for the shelf where she left her walnut burl.

They take an inch-thick slice off the raw side of the burl, to make the back wall of the cabinet where the beauty of the grain will be on show, and then start measuring and planning how to carve out the main chunk. Cal manages to persuade Trey away from drawers and on to cubbyholes, seeing as Christmas is only a month away, but even so, the planning takes them long enough that she decides to stay the night. They're cleaning up and aiming for bed when Rip lifts his head and lets out a bark.

For one heartbeat Cal thinks it's Lena, but the steps

crunching on the drive are too heavy, and there's more than one set of them. 'Wait here,' he says to Trey, throwing his handful of shavings into the garbage can, but she follows him to the front door anyway.

It's Mart and PJ and Senan. They stand on the doorstep, bundled to the ears against the cold.

'And you're still up,' Mart says with pleasure. 'That's great; I woulda hated to catch you in your negligée. Evening, young one. I've to borrow this fella here for a while.'

Trey watches him, unsmiling, from behind Cal's shoulder.

'I've a fancy for a game of cards,' Mart explains. 'But sure, you can't work up any excitement with only three. We need a fourth.'

'Mart,' Cal says. 'The kid's the one who told me what Tommy's up to.'

Mart's eyebrows go up and he examines Trey with new interest. She gives him a blank stare back.

'Ah, well then,' Mart says, his face crinkling into an approving grin. 'Fair play to you, young one. See? You weren't wasting your breath. We're heading over to Tommy's now.'

Trey shrugs.

'Here you go, Sunny Jim,' Mart says. He digs in his jacket pocket and hands Cal a black wad that turns out to be a beanie, sliced in three spots to make a balaclava. 'To cover up the head on you,' he explains, 'so you don't give anyone a shock, with the state of that beard.'

Anything requiring balaclavas doesn't meet Cal's definition of a direct route. He says, 'While we do what?'

Senan and PJ move on the doorstep, shoulders rolling, boots shifting.

'Nothing dramatic,' Mart assures Cal. 'Or that's not the plan, anyhow. Just a bitta explaining, like I told you. If we're in luck, Tommy'll be in a direct humour as well: he'll be on for a nice chat, and we'll have everything straightened out in time to get a good night's sleep.'

Senan grunts cynically. Mart smiles at Cal. 'I haveta admit,' he says, 'I'm not feeling lucky. But either way, Sunny Jim, the message'll get through loud and clear. And then we'll see what we'll see. Wrap up warm; we could be a while.'

'I'll come,' Trey says. 'Got another one a them yokes?' She points to the balaclava.

'No,' Cal says, pulling on his boots. 'You're staying here.' He doesn't like leaving her alone, on a night that has this in the air. But just because Mart's not planning on drama, that doesn't mean no one else is.

Trey's chin is out. She says, 'Tommy fucked with us.'

'If I know anything about you, young one,' Mart tells her, 'you'll get your chance, or make one. This isn't it. Adults only, tonight is.'

Trey says, 'I don't take orders offa you.'

'You'd get on with my Finbarr,' Senan tells her. 'He's a cheeky little fuck as well.'

'Kid,' Cal says. 'Do me a favour. Stay here.'

Trey eyes him for a moment, but in the end she nods. She retires to the far end of the room, taking Rip with her, and rubs behind his ears while she watches Cal tie his bootlaces.

'We oughta ring Bobby again,' PJ says. He sounds like he's saying it for the fifth or sixth time.

'Fuck him,' Senan says flatly. The set of his jaw says he's pissed about something, above and beyond the obvious.

'I s'pose,' PJ says. He's fidgeting his feet, troubled. 'But he oughta be here.'

'He oughta be,' Mart agrees, 'but he's not. Another phone call won't change that.'

'Have a guess where that fat little fuck is right now,' Senan says to Cal. 'Go on, guess.'

'Róisín's place?' Cal says, throwing on his jacket.

'That'd be understandable,' Mart says. 'I wouldn't mind that. You can't keep a bull from the heifer.' PJ shoots Mart a horrified look and jerks his head at Trey.

'That wee shite,' Senan says, 'is at home in his bed. He says he's got no love for Tommy Moynihan, but he owes Tommy for giving him the cash to meet Whatshername, so he can't go up against the man. Did you ever hear such a loada – fuckin' rubbishy—' Words fail him.

'So tonight's just us four?' Cal asks.

'God, no,' Mart says. 'I toldja: momentum.'

'Lock the door,' Cal tells Trey. He stuffs the balaclava in his jacket pocket. 'And call me if you need me.'

'Smash his fuckin' face in,' Trey says.

No one talks as they start, shoulder to shoulder, down the long road towards the village. The cloud is high tonight, letting through a haze of moonlight here and there so that streaks of fields rise ghostly out of the darkness, and the air has an icy bite that burrows to the bone. The silence is so powerful it comes at them like an attack.

As they near a side road, there's movement: crunch of dirt, rustle of jackets. Mart stops at the turning, and they wait while two men take shape out of the dark: Francie and his cousin Skippy. Up ahead, down the road, there are more footsteps.

All the way to the village, men come out of gates, out of side roads, in twos and threes, to join them. Some of them have brought things with them: tyre irons, lump hammers, crowbars. They go down the main street thirty strong, with the near-soundless, purposeful surge and patter of a wolf pack. The shops are dark and shuttered tight, Noreen's, the ladieswear boutique, Seán Óg's. In the houses, windows are still lit here and there, but no one moves behind them.

The Moynihans' house is on the edge of the village, just far enough out that the view doesn't get cluttered up by common people going about their business. The garden is walled in by high concrete blocks. As Cal and the guys come closer, shadows peel off from the walls to meet them.

No one talks. Mart pulls another makeshift balaclava out of his pocket and works it down over his face. Small movement ripples along the road as other men zip fleeces high, pull down hoods, arrange home-made balaclavas of their own. In the turns of heads Cal catches flashes of Halloween masks, Frankenstein, Wolverine. He pulls on his balaclava and feels something shift, his own outline wavering as he blurs into this thing that's happening. He can hear the other men's breath all around him, the hiss of their jackets as they move, the gritty sounds of their feet on the road; he can smell their shared scent, hot and angry like a burner left on too long.

Mart turns his head, faceless, to scan the assembly. Then he nods, and steps through Tommy's gate.

The security lights snap on, a brazen white glare that floods the yard from every direction at once. The shadows it throws are stark and strange-angled, so each thing stands out separately, like stickers slapped onto a background: pagoda-shaped water feature, palm trees, glossy trio of cars. Forty or fifty men follow Mart through the gates and into the glare. They spread out across the smooth gravel, work boots crunching, and keep on spreading, onto the fake grass and the groomed flower beds, around the fancy conservatory, encircling the house. Cal recognises a few, by their jackets or their walks or Dessie Duggan's snowman build, but most of them could be anyone. Ardnakelty is made up of related guys with worn clothes and worn bodies; there's nothing distinguished about any of them. They wait, silent in the white dazzle, breath smoking in the cold air.

In a front bedroom, a light goes on.

Somewhere a deep voice rises, pitched to carry across fields, or through triple-glazing: 'Hands off our land!'

The curtains don't move. Presumably Tommy doesn't need to look out the window; he can inspect them all, and record them, from some app on his phone. Cal turns his blank black face up to the camera above the front door, straight to Tommy Moynihan, and points two-fingered to his own eyes and then to the lens: *I see you.* Very few men in this townland are as tall and as broad-built as he is, but he doesn't care.

Another voice, off behind the house, calls, 'Hands off our land!'

Other voices pick it up, ragged and overlapping at first, then condensing into a hard, rhythmic chant. The sound floods out to fill the vast night silence, ruling the fields, the village street, the invisible mountainside. Cal doesn't realise he's chanting too till he hears his own voice, full-throated, pulled from deep in his belly by the voices rising all around him. He feels the wild freefall of the fact that this fury isn't his sole possession, or contained within his bounds; it's a thing held in common, surging from him and every man with him, from their women and their children and their dead.

The curtains don't shift, no more lights come on, the front door doesn't open. Inside the house, Tommy Moynihan is realising that his cover is blown, and evaluating what to do about it.

A new sound has started, a low dark pulse running beneath *Hands off our land*. It takes a few beats to rise up into clarity: *Out out out out out.*

The flare of the security lights means Cal can't see if there's movement behind the windows. He can only sense it, the frantic scurry within the house, the dashes that meet the same faceless anger on every side. Men are pounding weapons on the ground and stamping in time, the earth shaking with their drumbeat, *Out out out.*

Cal has stopped existing, dissolved into this. He's not cold any more. He understands now why Mart called this the direct route, how the meanings here are different from any he's known. Faceless, nameless, he and every man here is charging on Tommy stripped naked, all their trapped and swollen rage laid bare to the night sky. Cal feels it lifting him, he knows he could keep roaring into this dizzy mix of darkness and white glare all night long, and he wonders who'll break first, Clodagh or Eugene, or the walls of the house crumbling to dust under this barrage.

Mart was right: Tommy isn't going to come out. Cal is hit by a blast of savage exultation at what must be going on in Tommy's mind right now. Tommy is slick, Tommy is rich, Tommy has everyone who matters in his pocket and he always gets his way, but none of that is any kind of armour against this. They could storm this house, smash every window and every stick of furniture, beat Tommy and Eugene to bloody pulp, and torch the place to ashes. No one could come in time to stop them. No one would have seen a damn thing.

The thought is circling the house, leaping from one man to the next like electricity. Men are shifting their grips on the handles of their tools, getting ready. One guy – young, by his shape and swiftness – picks up a rock from the edging of a flower bed.

Mart, next to him, catches his arm as it rises and holds it down. For a second it looks like he's going to pull away, and a surge of motion ripples outwards from him, weapons rising, the circle breaking forward. The chant is speeding up, building like a great wave ready to smash down, *Out out out out.*

In the splinter of a pause between beats, a siren whines, far off.

The pause holds too long; the chant breaks apart and falls away. Men stop moving and listen, heads turning. The siren whines on, still distant but coming closer.

Mart's voice – pitched to carry, but with no urgency and no fear – calls, 'Time to go, lads.'

For a long minute no one moves. Then they melt away, without hurry, over the walls and out the gate. In seconds the white expanse of the garden is empty. As Cal turns at the gate to look back, he thinks he sees a curtain lift, in an upstairs window.

Lena's alertness to the townland has stopped being a pleasure. In Ardnakelty's winter silence, the scatter of remaining sounds travel farther, and have a sharp edge of warning. Ciaran Maloney's oldest practises the flute, a faint broken thread of notes like the soundtrack to a stealthy approach. The smells that drift on the cold air – tractor exhaust, cooking meat – feel like deliberate intrusions, reminders that her territory is anything but impregnable.

She's sitting on the kitchen floor, running Nellie's soft ears between her fingers, when she hears the sound. At first it's only a faint jag in the silence, so far off and ragged that it could be a car stereo pumping, or teenagers having a party. Then it coalesces and takes shape: voices, going on and on, for too long.

Lena goes to the front door with the dogs close at her heels. Her yard is dark and empty. In the cold air the sound reaches her more clearly: men's voices, a crowd of them, raised in a hard savage chant. They're too distant for her to make out the words, but the anger charges the air like coming thunder.

It hits her with a primal flare at the back of her neck: they could be coming for her. Scraps of half-forgotten granny stories rise in her mind, long-ago bad women driven from the townland for sins that were only hinted at, running bruised and wild-eyed for the river or the mountain, one slip of a foot and gone. For a moment of pure animal terror she almost follows them: grab the car keys, grab the dogs, drive.

Then she sees the patch of white light in the sky, off beyond the village, cold and ghostly on the cloud. Her mind is still flying for the hills and for a spinning second she thinks of Bobby Feeney's aliens, before she realises what it is: security lights, triggered by motion.

Lena stands in the doorway, palming back the uneasy dogs and forcing her mind to lay hold of sense. Only one house around here has security lights on that scale. This mob isn't out for her blood; she's nothing to them. They're after Tommy.

When she understands what Cal's done, it reaches her like something she knew all along. He took everything she found and brought it to Mart Lavin.

She tried to warn him, but even after everything he'd seen, he took this place too lightly. *This isn't some big deal, I'm not gonna let Mart get me into anything.* Now he's out there amid the roaring men and the white light, subsumed into them, unreachable. This place has eaten him, the same way it's eating Trey.

Somewhere far away, a siren starts up its banshee wail. The chant is still going, a throb in the night air, so faint that it feels like it's inside Lena's skull. Tommy is going to come after her.

She could still grab the dogs and drive, but she has nowhere to drive to. She's left it thirty years too late.

The dark of the road is like blindness, after the white light. It's full of movement, quick deft rustles and crunches. Small sounds scatter out across the fields, men moving along tracks they know by heart towards wherever they're supposed to be tonight. Cal feels something like dizzy; it takes him a minute to get his bearings and turn for home. His ears are still ringing.

He and Mart and Senan and PJ find each other along the way. Mart has rolled his balaclava back into a beanie; in the bleary moonlight, his hair sticks out like dandelion fluff around the edges. 'There's yourself,' he says to Cal. 'I was worried the big bad Moynihans had got you and they were holding you for ransom. I can't afford you.'

'Nope,' Cal says. He pulls off his balaclava and hands it back to Mart. His throat is raspy from shouting. His heart is still going hard, to the rhythm of *Out out out out*.

'Well,' Mart says, clapping his gloved hands together as he sets off up the road again. 'That's a job well done, lads. I'm not saying we got the result we were looking for, but that woulda been too much to ask. We done the job we went out to do. Tommy heard us, loud and clear.'

He reminds Cal bizarrely of a coach giving a post-match pep talk. Somewhere behind them, the siren is still coming closer, endless and mindless.

'I never thought he'd call the Guards,' PJ says. He's clomping along at his usual pace, shovel-feet slapping down steadily, but to Cal he seems subtly changed. All of them do.

'You already knew he was a fuckin' traitor, sure,' Mart points out reasonably. 'That's old news.'

'He's a fuckin' coward as well,' Senan says. His voice is hoarse too; he sounds like a stranger. 'Any man with a pair of balls on him woulda come out to us. Even just to tell us all to get fucked. If I'da had any respect for him before, it'd be gone now. Hiding behind the curtains with his missus and his child—'

'Calling the fuckin' *Guards*,' PJ says, with bottomless disgust.

'We shoulda done the house,' Senan says. He's still keyed up, whipping his beanie back and forth in his hand like a weapon.

'No,' Mart says. 'We gave the man a chance. That's good strategy, is what that is. If he doesn't take it, he's got no one but himself to blame, and no one can say the poor cratur got no warning.'

'He didn't take it. I toldja: that fella doesn't need a chance. What he needs is a root up the fuckin' hole.'

'If Tommy's wise,' Mart says, 'he'll send someone to talk to me tomorrow. What he oughta do is come to me his own self, but he won't stoop that low. He'll send someone.'

'Or else he won't,' Senan says grimly. Before anyone can answer, he turns in at PJ's gate, where his battered car is listing to one side in the drive. PJ follows him, still shaking his head over Tommy's iniquity.

At his own gate, Cal lingers for a minute. He feels like he should be saying something, or asking Mart something, but he can't figure out what. The whole evening feels like it broke away from reality, somewhere in there, and he's having trouble finding his way back. The cold has hit him again; he's shivering, from deep down inside.

Mart cocks an eyebrow at him and smiles. 'What I'd prescribe for you, Jean-Claude,' he advises, 'is a nice drop of hot whiskey to get the cold outa your bones. And then a good night's sleep.'

'Right,' Cal says. 'Yeah.'

'And remember: yourself and myself and Senan were over in PJ's house all night long. Why we chose PJ's I don't know, with his place in tatters and your lovely hacienda just waiting to host a gathering, but sure, we can't deny him his turn just 'cause his housekeeping's not up to par.'

He touches his beanie in a salute and heads off up the road. Beyond the village, Tommy's security lights are still blazing, a small unearthly patch of white against the cloud.

Trey hears Cal's steps on the driveway and is at the door to meet him, electric with impatience. 'You give them the slaps?' she demands.

'Nope,' Cal says.

'*Why?*'

'It wasn't that kinda night,' Cal says. He drops onto the sofa and starts unlacing his boots. His fingers won't work right.

'Then what fuckin' kinda night was it?'

'Kid,' Cal says. He can't begin to describe tonight to her. He's glad she wasn't there. 'I wouldn't want to be Tommy Moynihan right now.'

Trey scans his face intently for a minute. Whatever she sees there apparently satisfies her. 'OK,' she says, and she goes to the kitchen and switches on the kettle to make him a cup of tea.

15

All the next day, Cal finds reasons to be out on his land or at his front windows, which needed cleaning anyway. All he sees is Mart, trundling around on his patched-up tractor or stumping across the fields, head bent against the drizzle, to examine a limping sheep that Kojak cuts neatly out of the herd. The odd car goes past, without slowing.

By night-time, he's not watching for an emissary any more. Tommy has no intention of negotiating, let alone surrendering. Cal is watching for the counterattack.

He doesn't know where he ought to be. The expanse outside his windows hums with danger, on every side; he has no way to tell where it'll condense itself. He wants to grab Trey and Lena and gather them in under his roof, but neither of them would come. He has to stop himself from driving around in circles on the muddy roads like a crazy guy, rifle on the passenger seat, trying to keep an eye on everyone at once.

Mart is the most likely target, so Cal makes himself stay home and keep an eye on Mart's place, and try to trust that Trey or Lena will call him if they need him. He texts Lena – *Everything OK? Love you* – and watches the check marks turn blue when she reads it, and then stands in his kitchen looking at his phone for a long time until she goes offline. He sits up most of the night in his living room, with the lights out, listening to the fitful rain against the windows and watching the blank darkness outside.

Running underneath everything he does, he misses Lena. Their relationship, which neither of them planned on, has always been a serene thing, holding no surprises except for its existence. Cal put that down to them being middle-aged, having too much experience to either expect or want the flashy stuff, the fireworks and transformations and revelations that his younger self considered essential to romance; what they looked for was a steady mutual happiness, a warming and brightening of both their lives. He loved the thought of the two of them continuing this way, greying and unwavering, into old age. Now – assuming they're still together, which is unclear – things have shifted; the steadiness he loved, once cracked, might be mended somehow but can never be taken for granted again. He feels, with a combination of deep grief and outrage, that somehow both of them are being robbed; and, at the same time, that Lena isn't doing her share to prevent the despoiling.

On Saturday morning his patience runs out and he heads over to Mart's, to see if he can get some sense of what the fuck is going on. He finds Mart in his sheep shed, bending over a ewe he's got trapped in an undignified sitting position between his knees. Even near-empty, the shed has a placid, comforting smell of wool, straw, and sheep shit. A thin greyish light filters through the high roof windows, catching on specks of dust that hang motionless in the air.

''Tis yourself,' Mart says, looking up from the ewe. He waggles her hoof at Cal, like she's waving. 'Have a look at this, now. D'you know what that is?'

Cal steps over Kojak, who's lying across the entrance to the pen waiting to be needed, and bends to inspect the hoof. Mart watches him with the encouraging smile of a teacher supervising crayon ABCs. Between the toes, the hoof is moist and reddened, oozing white. The ewe stares blankly past Cal's ear, apparently unaware of his existence.

'Scald?' Cal says.

'We'll make a sheep farmer of you yet,' Mart says. 'That's scald, all right. I've been waiting for it, with the fields wet as bog for months, and here it is. She's the third one this week. Pass me that bottle there.'

Cal hands over the hoof gel, and Mart deftly pinches the ewe's toes apart and squirts it between them. The ewe gives a convulsive start and then, when Mart grips her tighter between his knees, relapses into her trance.

'How's the squirrel doing?' Cal asks.

'Pacing,' Mart informs him, rubbing the gel into crevices with a thumb. 'All night long, up and down my roof. I've got the measure of that fucker. He wants me to know he's not giving up. He's working out his next move.'

'I dunno if squirrels pace,' Cal says. 'Maybe your house is haunted.'

'I wouldn't mind that,' Mart says. 'A poltergeist'd be a bitta company, and when I got bored of his antics, I'd sell the telly rights for millions and live out my old age in me lavish on a beach in the Bahamas. No: 'tis Raffles, all right. I know that fella's style. But I won't be bested by a fuckin' rodent. If he finds another way in, I'll be waiting for him.' He hands Cal the bottle, pulls a roll of green tape out of a pocket, and starts winding it between the ewe's toes. 'Didja come here to ask after Raffles?'

Cal catches the ewe's other front hoof and squirts gel between the toes. 'Nope,' he says. 'I came to ask if there's been any movement, after the other night.'

'Movement,' Mart says, his face creasing up in a smile. 'That's a lovely way of putting it; very elegant altogether. You could say there's been movement, all right. Long John's car went on fire last night; 'tis only by the grace a God and the rain it didn't spread to the house. Someone's after spray-painting "TRAITORS OUT" on Tommy Moynihan's wall. Izzy O'Connor minds

Pauline McGinty's little fellas while Pauline works at the plant, only Izzy said the plant should have a walkout and Pauline told her she oughta be ashamed of herself, so now Izzy won't mind the childer any more, and Pauline's going mental trying to find someone else. Cara Deery was walking back from Noreen's with her shopping, and Mouth McHugh went by in the tractor and swerved straight at her; she hadta jump into the ditch, shopping and all.' He rips off the tape and pats the end into place on the ewe's ankle. 'I mighta missed something – the grapevine's suffering from a bitta network overload – but that's the guts of it. Give or take the odd gate left open, like, or the odd man that's not welcome at his card game any more. Is that enough movement for you, Jean-Claude?'

Cal thinks about the pretty country road he walked to get here, all flanked by soft fields, the whole picture delicately framed by a horizon of lacy trees. It seems to him that the dogs should have been hurling themselves against doors and howling to the grey sky, cows kicking down walls to run for the mountains before the lid blows off the whole place and everything underneath rises up, merciless.

'How many people are on Tommy's side?' he asks.

''Tisn't even that they're on his side, half a them,' Mart corrects him. ''Tisn't that they want the land taken over. They just don't believe that's on the cards, 'cause if they believe it, they'll haveta change their way of thinking, and maybe even stand up to the big man. 'Tis easier to just not believe a word. Like I told you: *Tommy wouldn't do that, are you mad, Mart Lavin's losing the plot in his old age, he's gone paranoid, he'll be saying the CIA has his phone tapped next* . . .' He takes the second hoof from Cal and starts taping it up. 'What were you expecting, Sunny Jim? We went looking to stir up trouble, and we got it.'

'Except it's the wrong kinda trouble,' Cal says. He moves on to the ewe's rear hooves; she doesn't appear to notice. 'This isn't getting us anywhere. People aren't turning against the Moynihans; they're getting more and more pissed off at each other, is all. This keeps up, someone's gonna get killed.' It hits him that he's hoping Mart will say all of this is exactly what he expected, it was in the plan and will inevitably lead, in some way that a blow-in like Cal can't see, to Tommy getting his comeuppance. He's come here looking for reassurance.

'I toldja before, boyo,' Mart says. 'We need momentum. 'Tisn't easy for people round here to go up against Tommy. 'Tis one thing for the likes of you, but we've been bowing and scraping to the Moynihans all our lives. People need to rev the engines a while before they can break outa that habit. Once the blood's up, then we'll give people something useful to do with it.'

He bends, with a grunt as his joints snag, to catch a rear hoof for taping. ''Tisn't the bitta trouble I mind,' he says. 'Will I tell you what's worrying me about all this?'

'I wouldn't even know where to start,' Cal says.

'The scale,' Mart says. 'Whatever else about Tommy, and there's plenty else, the man has scale. What's happening around here is all wee bitsa nonsense; the likes of what you'd get in an argument over someone moving a boundary stone, or a dog worrying someone's sheep. Small-time carry-on, that's what it is. Where's Tommy?'

'Tommy doesn't like getting his hands dirty,' Cal says. He caps up the hoof gel.

'True enough,' Mart agrees. 'Tommy was always one for leaving the wet work to the minions; if I caught him sticking his own neck out, I'd know his back was well against the wall. But mostly, Sunny Jim, Tommy'd be the ideas man. He'd come up with the plan, he'd issue the orders, and then the minions would go out and do what they're told. This foostering about burning cars and swerving tractors, those don't smell like Tommy's ideas to me. D'you see what I'm getting at?'

'So maybe he's holding his fire,' Cal says. 'Hoping we'll all be so busy spray-painting shit on each other's walls, we'll forget about him.'

'Not Tommy,' Mart says. 'He's the big fella. That's his stock in trade, sure. He hasta be seen to do something, or otherwise the peasants'll lose faith in him. We upped the ante there the other night; if Tommy wasn't going to fold his hand, he shoulda upped it right back at us. I've been waiting for some inspector to turn up at my door and tell me my sheep have some fancy new disease and I've to cull the whole herd, or this shed doesn't comply with EU regulations and I've to take it down and start over.'

'I've been waiting for the tax man to give me a call,' Cal says. He doesn't like where this is taking them. 'Or Child Services to show up at my door.'

'That kinda thing,' Mart agrees. 'Only I'da bet it'd be me, not you, on the wrong end of it all. No offence, sunshine, but as far as Tommy's concerned, you're small potatoes. He may be outa touch with the lower orders, but he knows enough to know that people around here listen to my opinion – God help them, says you.' He smiles at Cal. 'If Tommy puts me back in my box, that'll give plenty of people enough of a fright that they'll back off. Then he can mop up the stragglers in his own time.'

He straightens up and shoves the roll of tape into his pocket. 'Only he's not putting me back in my box,' he says. 'And maybe this sounds mental, Sunny Jim, but I don't like that one bit.'

Cal knows he's right. Tommy has to be afraid; what came at him the other night ran deeper than any man's courage or arrogance. Faced with that, no man would hold his fire, or fool around with pissant little popguns, when he has buffalo rifles at his disposal. Tommy is at work.

"'Tisn't all action that's going on, now,' Mart adds, with a sideways glance at Cal. 'There's been plenty of talk as well. The rumours flying around about wee Eugene, God almighty, you'd want to wash out your ears with holy water after hearing them.'

Mart has stopped waiting for the emissary, too. The direct approach didn't work out; he's moving on. 'I bet,' Cal says.

Mart fishes a red paint stick out of another pocket and pulls off the cap with his teeth. 'Not all the rumours are running our way, now,' he says. He marks the ewe with two neat swipes: the forehead to show she's been treated, the lame leg to show which one it was. 'There was one I meant to mention to you, the next time I saw you.'

'Yeah,' Cal says. He knows what's coming. 'I heard stuff, along the way.'

Mart releases the ewe, who wriggles to her feet in a clumsy flurry of legs and flounces off to a corner of the pen to figure out what just happened. 'The way this one goes is,' he says, 'your Lena thought you were riding Rachel Holohan, whether you were or not. So she started giving Rachel hassle – following her, like, blocking her way, calling her a slut. Rachel said it to some of her pals, but they told her not to worry, Lena Dunne was harmless—'

'Right,' Cal says. The story is expanding nicely, from a shard of scandal to a full-sized edifice with fancy curlicues all over. He was expecting that, but the surge of anger rocks him all the same. 'That one's been going around for a while.'

'That part has. The rest is new. D'you wanta hear this or not?'

'Why not,' Cal says. He's pretty sure he doesn't. 'Go for it.'

'So,' Mart says. He caps the paint stick and tucks it neatly back into his pocket. 'So when your missus asked Rachel to call round to her place 'cause she wanted to hear Rachel's side and get it all sorted, Rachel went, not a bother on her. Your Lena gave her a cuppa tea fulla antifreeze, and the poor girl headed off to the bridge to meet Eugene. Only she was staggering about from the antifreeze, and in she went.'

Cal realises that his muscles are about to take him out of the shed, down the road, and straight to the Moynihan place. He stands still and counts the empty sheep pens.

'And then Lena panicked,' Mart says, 'so she's been going all round the place trying to find out who knows what. And she's made up this story about Tommy Moynihan in order to take the attention offa herself.'

Being a cop has left Cal with at least one useful skill: he's good at sounding calm when he wants to rip someone's head off with his bare hands. He says, 'Do people believe that shit?'

Mart is watching him, gauging his reaction. 'If someone said that about Noreen,' he says gently, 'or about Angela Maguire, they'd be laughed out of it. But your Lena's a bit different, if you don't mind me saying. There's not many people that'd owe her, or that'd need her, or that'd know her well enough to be sure what she would and wouldn't do. If it takes a lotta effort to believe rumours about Tommy, it doesn't take much to believe them about your missus.'

'Right,' Cal says. This isn't just an expertly calculated counter-attack, undermining the land-grab story and deflecting focus off the Moynihans; it's also revenge. Somehow or other, Tommy knows Lena was the one who let the cat out of the bag. Cal feels Tommy like a cold swirl all around, rising up at his shoulder, streaming across the fields, curling around window frames. Tommy has eyes and ears everywhere. Mart, all the time he was assuring Cal he'd keep Lena out of it, must have known that.

'I can see why you'd be bulling,' Mart says, 'but if you look at it right, sure, 'tis a kinda compliment. You don't see anyone accusing me of seducing gorgeous young ones in my spare time.'

'I don't need that kinda compliment,' Cal says. 'Specially not from that shitbird. And that's not the part that's bothering me.'

'I wouldn't say anyone enjoys hearing his woman called a murderer,' Mart agrees, 'but to be honest with you, sunshine, this doesn't smell like Tommy to me, either. Clodagh, maybe, or just some bitchy one that's not fond of your missus. In my experience, rumours about riding is usually women. You wouldn't think it, wouldja? Here's yourself and myself raised to keep our filthy talk away from their delicate ears, and all the while, what they're saying amongst themselves would blister a bishop.'

'No,' Cal says. His voice comes out hard enough that Kojak lifts his head from his paws. 'This isn't Clodagh bitching. This is Tommy. And I'm gonna bet he's not just aiming to make people doubt the land story. He's aiming to get Lena arrested. That's why he hasn't come for you: he's got Lena in his sights.'

He's hoping Mart will laugh his ass off and tell him to quit being a drama queen, but Mart's eyebrows lift. He thinks it over, absently wiping foot gel off his hands onto his work pants.

'That'd be Tommy's scale, all right,' he says. 'And it'd do the job. For anyone that's on the fence and dithering, or that doesn't wanta get involved one way or t'other, that'd be the perfect excuse: sure, you can't be giving them poor Moynihans hassle, after all they've been through. And for everyone that's against Tommy, that'd be a warning: you don't wanta go messing with me. That'd be the last word, all right. There'd be a lovely long silence after that.'

'Yeah,' Cal says. He takes a breath and tries to engage whatever's left of his cop mode. 'Only I don't see how he's gonna make it work. Maybe Tommy's got the Guards in his pocket, but he doesn't have some big-shot Dublin prosecutor. No matter how many strings he pulls, they can't charge someone with no evidence.'

Mart smiles a small grim smile. 'If Tommy wants evidence

bad enough, Sunny Jim, there'll be evidence. There'll be nice respectable witnesses that saw Rachel leaving your place at disreputable hours, or that she told all the details of your mad passionate affair – excuse me being indelicate,' he adds, when he sees Cal's jaw tighten. 'There'll be people who saw Lena following her, or stopping her to call her names – half of them won't even be lying, sure; once that rumour's had a bitta time to simmer, they'll have themselves convinced that was what they saw. There'll be people Rachel told that she was afraid of Lena, and that Lena wanted to have it out with her once and for all. There'll be someone to say Lena called round to their house to borrow antifreeze. There'll be—'

'Right,' Cal says. He can't listen to any more of this. 'Whatever. That's all talk, not facts. Fact is, Lena headed straight over to my place after Rachel left hers, and the postmortem says Rachel didn't drink that antifreeze till hours later. Tommy's not God, even if you people all act like he is. He can't make the medical examiner rewrite the goddamn postmortem.'

'There's ways round everything,' Mart says. He watches the ewe lifting her hoof, testing the strange sensation of the bandage. 'Not to pry into your intimacies, but did Lena stay the night?'

After a moment Cal says, 'She went home.'

'Well then,' Mart says. 'Maybe a coupla them witnesses saw Rachel knocking on Lena's door again, later that evening.'

'Them saying it won't mean shit. If this turns into a murder investigation, the Guards are gonna pull location records off Rachel's phone. They'll be able to see that she never went back to Lena's.'

'Or she didn't bring her phone with her,' Mart points out. 'Or maybe those witnesses saw Lena heading off to wherever Rachel's phone says she was, instead. Or—'

'Yeah,' Cal says. 'I get it.' His voice comes out harsher than he expected. He feels like a fool, looking for reassurance from Mart, of all people, when deep down he knew there was none to be had.

'Them's the facts, Sunny Jim. No use shooting the messenger.' Mart throws Cal an enquiring slantways look. 'Are you having second thoughts about putting Tommy in a bog? Just outa interest, like, so I know what's what.'

'No,' Cal says. It takes him a second to make himself say it. 'I need him gone, but not like that. What I need is the same thing you and the rest of the guys need: for people around here to quit buying into Tommy's bullshit and run his uppity ass out of town.'

'Well, that's great news,' Mart says happily, giving Cal a clap on the shoulder. 'Isn't it a beautiful thing when everyone's on the same page?'

'Yeah,' Cal says. 'We're not gonna get it done by spray-painting shit on walls and telling people Eugene has a phone full of underage nudes.'

Mart smiles at him. 'Then we'll get it done some other way. Don't worry, Jean-Claude: we've got your missus's back.'

'You said that before,' Cal says. 'You said no one was gonna find out that story came from her.'

Mart regards him steadily. The smile has fallen away. He says, 'I told no one.'

'Yeah,' Cal says. 'But Tommy found out. And you knew he would.'

'I knew he might,' Mart agrees. 'But 'twas spread the word or else sit back and let that fella sell off this townland to the highest bidder, so I took the chance. Nothing personal; sure, I'da done the same if 'twas you in the firing line, or meself, or Bobby or PJ.'

His voice is tranquil and inexorable. Small echoes eddy in the high corners of the sheep shed. 'I know you're thinking you'da done different,' he says. 'But that's an easy thing to tell yourself, when you're not the one holding all that in your hands.'

Cal says nothing. Probably he should be heading to Lena's, but he can't make himself go to her with nothing but this shitpile to offer. *Hey honey, guess what, this whole town is saying you're a psycho killer, that sucks huh?* He would be failing her, starkly and irredeemably, at a level that might well crack them apart beyond repair. If he's going to give her this with one hand, he needs to have a way of fixing it ready in the other.

'And anyhow,' Mart adds, in a different tone, 'this is what you'd call a temporary nuisance. We'll get that fucker outa Lena's hair; you've got my word on that. For better, for worse, isn't that it?'

'You're not married to her,' Cal says. 'You don't even like her.'

'I never said that,' Mart corrects him. 'She doesn't like me, is what I said. I'd call her a woman of poor taste, only that'd be impolite to present company. Either way, but, she's your woman, bucko. We won't stand by and see her hauled off to jail, and you after treating my ewe's scald. On top of everything else.'

The words hit Cal strangely. Mart could be bullshitting to keep him on side, but he doesn't think so, not this time. He feels some change in himself, or in his place within the sweep of fields and houses and rain that spreads all around the quiet shed: a new weight, a gravitational pull that he didn't know he had.

'OK,' he says. 'Good to hear.'

'D'you know what I'd love, Sunny Jim?' Mart says. He fishes around in his pants pocket for his phone, a battered old model with hairy Scotch tape over the cracks, and checks the time. 'I'd murder a nice toastie. And a pint or two on the side. Will we head down to Seán Óg's for our lunch?'

'Go for it,' Cal says. 'I got stuff to do.'

'No you don't, sunshine,' Mart says. 'You don't fancy sitting in the pub wondering who there believes you're a dirty aul' man, and I don't blame you: that'd curdle your pint, all right. But 'tis no use hiding away. We've got work to do, so you'll drink your sour pint and like it. I'm paid up with Barty; how about yourself?'

Barty lets regulars run tabs, but as the tab rises his attitude gets correspondingly saltier, until people can't take it any more and pay up, which hits the reset button. Anyone who's too far in the red isn't getting any toasted sandwich. 'Close enough,' Cal says.

'Then we'll head down to Seán's,' Mart says, 'and I'll see if a few of them other reprobates fancy joining us.' He opens the pen and gives the ewe a nudge with his toe, to start her heading back where she belongs.

When the knock at Lena's door finally comes, it's almost a relief. She's been moving on autopilot, going to work, doing her shopping in town, dressing and eating and washing when she's supposed to, waiting for the axe to fall. Her limbs feel numb and heavy, like she's moving under cold water, and her muscles are so tight that sometimes it's hard to breathe. No one at work seems to notice anything amiss. Lena thinks probably she should be glad of this, but in fact she finds it terrifying. It feels like she's moving on a parallel plane to everyone else, already a ghost.

The only person who's come to the house is Trey. Lena didn't open the door, and in the end she went away again, with Banjo trailing despondently behind her. Noreen and Cal have texted, and Lena's left the texts unread. Nothing else has happened. All she can do is await Tommy's pleasure.

Before she answers the knock, she shuts the dogs in the kitchen, with the back door left a crack open. 'Stay,' she tells them. If she doesn't come back, it could be a while before anyone notices she's gone. The dogs will find someone who'll look after them.

When she opens the front door, she finds a Garda car in her yard and Breege, the friendly Guard who came to ask her about Rachel, on the step. 'How's it going?' Breege says cheerfully. 'Can I come in for a few minutes?'

Lena sees Cal's face. Her heart rises and crashes down. She says, 'Did something happen?'

'Ah, no,' Breege assures her, hands going up. 'Everything's grand; I'm only here for a wee chat. Can I come in?'

After a moment Lena stands aside. 'That's the worst of this job,' Breege says, as she follows Lena into the kitchen. 'Everyone thinks you're bad news. Honest to God, sometimes I wish I'd gone into plumbing; everyone's always delighted to see a plumber. And I wouldn't be out and about on a Saturday morning.'

'Bed,' Lena says to the dogs, shutting the back door. She watches Breege's eyes move around the kitchen, a Guard's eyes, noting everything from the toast left uneaten on the table to the heap of washing she hasn't ironed. 'Will you have a cup of tea?'

'Go on, so,' Breege says, grinning at her. Breege has her thick brown hair up in a bun, and no make-up except a smudge of concealer on a spot. Lena reckons her face – good-natured and able for anything, the face of the neighbour you automatically turn to in trouble – must be worth its weight in gold on the job. 'That's a great pair of dogs you've got there.'

Nellie and Daisy have gone to their corner, but they can feel Lena's tension and they're watching, on the alert. 'They're good dogs,' Lena says. She flicks the kettle on and gets out the teapot and mugs.

Breege pulls out a chair and makes herself comfortable at the table. She has the kind of sturdy, generous figure that automatically looks at home; on her, even the uniform is cosy and reassuring. 'I've a greyhound,' she says. 'I thought I'd get in shape, giving him all that exercise, but you can see how that turned out.' She laughs and slaps one broad thigh. 'Come here, actually, have you lost weight since the last time I saw you?'

Lena has. All her clothes are loose. 'God, I wouldn't have a clue,' she says, putting the mugs on the table and taking the breakfast things away. 'I don't keep track.'

'Last time I was here, it was about that poor girl in the river,' Breege says. Her eyes are still doing their work, but now they're on Lena, scanning her hair, her clothes, her hands. 'How've you been getting on since?'

'Not too bad,' Lena says. She gets the milk out of the fridge and is relieved to see that it's in date. 'It's been a tough time round here, but we'll get through it.'

'Tougher on you than most. It's not easy, being the last one to see a person alive.'

The kettle boils. 'I didn't know Rachel well,' Lena says, pouring. 'I knew her mother, back in school. I'm upset for her, mostly.'

Breege cocks her head, waiting for more. When Lena outwaits her, she says, 'You've got people worried about you, girl.'

Lena starts to see what Tommy has sent her. She says, 'Who's worried?'

'Sure, if I told you that, it'd only lead to awkwardness,' Breege says reasonably. 'It doesn't matter, anyhow. They want to be sure you're OK, just.'

She's right, it doesn't matter. Tommy didn't do the job himself. Probably he, or more likely Clodagh, got a woman to do it; someone who would carry conviction, because she could convince herself she was genuinely worried. Lena thinks of the women she drank and laughed with at the funeral, and wonders which one.

'Why would I not be OK?' she asks, baffled.

'You haven't been acting like yourself, is what I've heard.

You've been awful worked up about what happened to Rachel. And you've been saying a few things that have people concerned.'

Lena brings the teapot and the milk over to the table, and sits down opposite Breege. She doesn't ask for details. Some of it will be true, the stuff she handed Tommy like a gift; some of it will be made up, but she has no way of proving that. She can feel Breege assessing her: what kind of woman she is, what kind of crazy she is, what strategies will work best here. It's like having hands all over her.

'I'm acting the same as I always do,' she says, pouring tea. Her hand is neat and steady, like nothing important is happening. 'Going to work, walking the dogs, going over to see my fella. Maybe I've been a bit more sociable than usual, 'cause at a time like this you want people around you, but I don't see how that would worry anyone. D'you take milk?'

'Just a drop. That's loads; thanks.' Breege takes the mug and settles back in her chair. 'We don't want any harm coming to you, is all,' she says. 'That's what I'm here for. See if you're OK, and what I can do to help out.'

Lena has almost nothing left, but she has this: her thirty years of ruthless training in being pleasant and blank to people who want to delve around inside her. This is lucky, since it's the only thing that might save her, but it seems grotesque that this should be what's left of her when everything else is gone.

'Harm?' she says, eyebrows up. 'What kinda harm?'

Breege takes a swig of her tea. She says, 'I don't want you hurting yourself.'

'Jesus,' Lena says, taken aback. 'Whoever you were talking to, they're after getting themselves in a right state. I suppose it's nice of them to be looking out for me, but there's no need. I'm grand. Thanks, though.'

'Listen,' Breege says, pointing her mug at Lena. Her tone is good, matter-of-fact, not too delicate or sympathetic; Lena is a run-of-the-mill problem that can easily be solved if they work sensibly together. 'If you're having a bad patch, you'd be better off with people to look after you and help you get through it. I can bring you somewhere, if you want. They'll have you back on your feet in no time.'

'A hospital, like?' Lena says, amused, her eyebrows still up. 'Seriously?' And when Breege nods: 'God, no. There's nothing the matter with me that a sun holiday wouldn't fix. Have you got one of those on offer?'

'Here's how it works, yeah?' Breege says. Apparently she's decided that Lena will respond best to straightforwardness. 'If I think there's a serious risk that you could harm yourself, I need to bring you somewhere you'll be safe. But it all runs a lot smoother if you go on your own. What do you reckon?'

Tommy is so expert at what he does, he's got such an army, Lena can't believe she ever thought she stood a chance against him. There she was reassuring herself: *It's not the nineties, he can't have me put away*. Tommy can do anything he wants.

'Come here,' she says. She puts down her mug and faces Breege squarely, across the table. 'Do you honest-to-God reckon I'm a risk to myself? Never mind whatever you heard off people I've barely seen in years. You're sitting here talking to me. Do I seem to you like I'm off my head and about to fill myself up with paracetamol?'

It won't do any good, in the long run. All Lena can do is buy herself a few more days or weeks, until Tommy comes up with something too heavy for her to push away. The fight she's putting up isn't because she thinks she can win. It isn't even a doomed gallantry, a determination to go down swinging; it's just a meaningless reflex. She supposes she's glad this is the other thing that's left of her.

'It doesn't always show, sure,' Breege says. 'Are you?'

'No,' Lena says, exasperated. 'I've no intention of doing

anything to myself. Except maybe taking myself for a good long walk with these dogs and waving like a big eejit at everyone I see, so they'll all know I'm alive and well.'

Breege creases up her forehead, trying to make sense of things. 'What would've given people that idea, so? Can you think of anything you said – even just joking, maybe, and someone might've taken you up wrong? Or maybe you were a bit down one day, and someone thought it was more than that?'

Lena isn't stupid. She doesn't think Breege is, either. Breege is from Kerry, by her accent, and not Tralee or any of the big towns; she's from somewhere like this. Lena wonders what would happen if she told Breege the whole story; whether she'd be willing to recognise its patterns for what they are, or whether it would just add a reflexive intensity to her need to lock this whole thing safely away.

'Listen,' she says drily. 'You know small towns as well as I do. Either someone's got themselves worked up over nothing, or else someone's pissed off with me and wants to give me a bitta hassle.' That gets a flicker of recognition; Lena was right, Breege knows the score. 'I never in my life said I was suicidal, or anything close to it. Why would I be ready to kill myself over a girl I hardly knew?'

'From what I've heard,' Breege says, 'you were having a few problems with Rachel Holohan. Her dying could've hit you harder because of that.'

She drinks her tea, settled comfortably in the worn kitchen chair, and watches Lena to see how she reacts.

If Breege likes straightforwardness, Lena can give her that. She says, 'Is this the rumour about Rachel riding my fiancé, is it?'

Breege says, 'That's the one.'

'Feck's sake,' Lena says, with a touch of eyeroll. 'That's pure foolishness all round. For one thing, Cal's not that kinda man. And for another, everyone knows Rachel was mad about

Eugene; she wouldn't have looked at any other fella, let alone some middle-aged lad with a belly on him. I think Cal's drop-dead gorgeous, o' course, but I can't see her agreeing with me.'

That gets a smile out of Breege, although not one that lasts. 'And another thing,' Lena says. 'I never heard a whisper of that story till a few days ago. If you ask me, neither did anyone else. It's a fairy tale made up after she died, 'cause people wanted an explanation.'

'Rachel didn't mention it when she was here, no? The night she died?'

Breege's face is too steady and too neutral, and that's when Lena finally understands. She's looking straight down Breege, like a gun barrel, into Tommy Moynihan's eyes. Through the mouth of this woman who knows nothing about him, Tommy has spelled out his message clear as day. Lena has a choice. She's mad, or she killed Rachel; pick one, or he'll pick for her.

She says, 'Nothing like that. Like I told you before, all we talked about was her cat. If you wanta check, have a look at the cat; I wouldn't say anyone's had a chance to get that ringworm sorted yet.'

Breege says, 'And you're telling me you wouldn'ta been one bit bothered if you'da heard that story earlier? Water off a duck's back, yeah? 'Cause I'm telling you, I wouldn't be happy. No matter how much I trusted my fella.'

Lena shrugs and makes a wry face. 'I wouldn'ta been over the moon about it,' she says. 'I don't like people making Cal out to be a hoormaster and me to be some poor sap that's been played for a fool, and I don't like them talking shite about a girl who's not around to defend herself. But I'm used to this place. I know what it's like for the rumours. We'll just haveta wait it out, me and Cal. By next week there'll be something else.'

Breege gives Lena a half-convinced face and waits to see what that gets her. In their corner the dogs are shifting, troubled.

'Look,' Lena says firmly. 'All I can tell you is I'm grand, I've no intention of doing myself any harm, and I never took that rumour serious for a second. Probably you'd expect me to say that either way, but there's not a lot else I can say.'

She sits back in her chair, done with this nonsense, and drinks her tea.

Breege looks at her for a few more seconds, weighing Lena against the things she's been told. 'Fair enough,' she says in the end, with a nod. Her Guard face gives away nothing. 'I'm going to leave you my card, OK? If you decide you need a bitta help, or just someone to talk to, give me a bell. Any time.'

'I will,' Lena says. She doesn't pick up the card. 'If you seriously wanta help me out, you could take a jar of blackberry jam with you. I made too much this year; I'm trying to get it off my hands.'

A faint part of her mind is proud of this touch. It provides a sensible, sane explanation for her round of visits, and a woman who makes her own jam can't be too far off the rails.

'Ah, no, thanks, I can't take gifts,' Breege says, waving the offer away. 'And God knows the aul' thighs don't need it, hah?' She laughs. Lena can tell she's one notch more at ease with her decision. The jam has done its job.

'Where are you from?' she asks, on the doorstep.

'Outside Killarney,' Breege says, zipping her jacket against the cold. 'A little place in the back arse of nowhere; you wouldn't know it.'

Lena says, 'You did right to get out.'

They look at each other. 'Everywhere's got its downsides,' Breege says. 'I'll call in to you again soon, see how you're getting on. Look after yourself.'

'I'll do that,' Lena says. 'Thanks for checking in.' She stays on the step, lifting a hand politely, while Breege turns the car and drives off. She doesn't look around to try and spot who's watching, from some field or hedgerow, to report back to Tommy.

16

Seán Óg's is its usual Saturday-lunchtime self, unless you look more closely. Beneath the peaceful rhythms of conversation and the smell of toasted cheese, it has the edgy air of a place under a conditional truce. A clump of the McHugh brothers are hunched protectively over their pints; all the voices are running a notch too low, tucked away under the TV football commentary like their talk needs to be kept close. The families who would normally stop by for lunch after the weekend shopping are missing; only men are here. Only some of them nod to Cal and Mart as they come in.

Senan and Francie and PJ are in the alcove, around a table of pints and toasted sandwiches. Bobby isn't there. Cal doesn't ask.

'I shouted ye these,' Senan says, pushing glasses and plates across the table. 'If ye didn't want ham and cheese, tough shite.'

'Myself and the big fella'll eat anything,' Mart says, pulling up a stool. 'You don't complain about the toastie fillings at a council of war. Tommy Moynihan's after putting it about that Lena Dunne kilt that poor young one. He's aiming to send her to jail for it.'

Francie's overgrown eyebrows go up, which is as far as Francie goes towards showing emotion. 'Ah, now,' PJ says, shocked, putting down his toastie. 'That's dirty, that is.'

'Angela heard that, all right,' Senan says. He's lowered his voice. To Cal: 'I'd say that fucker's in your bad books now.'

'He already was,' Cal said. 'But yeah, I'm not gonna take this.'

'Damn right,' Senan says. 'We shoulda sorted that fella a long time back.'

'Will we burn him out?' Francie asks.

Cal finds himself genuinely touched by the offer, which he knows to be sincere. He raises his pint to Francie.

Mart is less impressed. 'We're not burning him out,' he says, opening his toastie to squeeze a mayonnaise packet carefully onto the ham. 'Wouldja ever think things through, for fuck's sake? What'll that do, only get Tommy a loada extra sympathy and a big aul' insurance payout? And that's the best-case scenario. Worst case, the man gets some kinda evidence and we're all up for arson. Maybe you've got no better way to spend the next ten years, but I do.'

'Then what's your fuckin' plan?' Francie demands.

'That's what we're here for, sure,' Mart says, gesturing expansively at the company with the mayo packet. 'Brainstorming. Blue-skying. Thinking outside the box. Implementing solutions.'

'I'll tell you what I figure we do,' Cal says. His mind cleared, back in Mart's sheep shed, as that shift within him and around him clicked into place. For the first time in weeks, he's thinking not in caged circles, but in patterns that lead somewhere. He's been turning this over all the way to the pub, while Mart drove with one hand and used the other to point out various issues with the state of the fields they passed. 'I figure we get loud.'

'He's already loud,' Francie says, pointing his chin at Senan. 'You're halfway there.'

'I haveta be loud,' Senan says, 'to get things through your thick head. What're you on about?'

He's asking Cal. All of them have leaned in tighter, around the table.

'Eugene told Rachel Holohan what him and his daddy had

planned,' Cal says, 'and Rachel wasn't happy about it. I know that part for a fact. I think she was gonna try and stop them, so Tommy killed her to shut her up.'

There's a silence. PJ's mouth is open.

'You're not the only one who's thought that,' Senan says.

'Yeah,' Cal says. 'That's my point. You bet your ass plenty of people are thinking the same thing, only they're all scared to say it out loud. Maybe some of them know something solid, and they're scared to say that, too.'

'How would anyone know anything?' Francie demands.

'This place?' Cal says. 'I can't buy low-fat butter without half the townland asking me if I got cholesterol. Someone knows something.' Francie tilts his head, reluctantly acknowledging the justice of this. 'I already got one person who Rachel told that she was gonna try stopping the Moynihans. I'd bet cash money there's more out there.' Cal is stretching it a little bit – Rachel didn't get that concrete with Sheila – but he doesn't care.

'That won't prove Tommy done anything on her,' Senan says. He's listening intently, watching his pint glass as he turns it in slow neat circles on the table. 'If he did, he won't be shouting it from the rooftops. He's no fool.'

'Tommy's not some evil genius supervillain,' Cal says. 'I've seen guys a lot smarter'n him do bad shit, and every one of them fucked up somehow. Maybe Tommy dropped hints about what he did, to scare someone into line, or Eugene got sloppy drunk with his buddies. Or everyone keeps telling me Tommy doesn't do his own dirty work; maybe he got someone to do this for him, and that guy isn't as careful as Tommy.'

''Twould be like him, all right,' Mart agrees. 'Keep talking, Jean-Claude. I'm enjoying meself.' He takes a huge bite of toastie and watches Cal like he's the best show on TV in a long time.

'From all's I hear,' Cal says, 'Rachel was a really good kid. People cared about her. If anyone knows anything, they're not thinking, *What the hell, good riddance.* They're out there wishing they could do something about it.' That gets nods of agreement from Senan and Mart. 'Right now, there's nothing they can do. They're not gonna go to the police. They're not gonna do anything to put themselves on Tommy's shit list. But if we start telling the world straight out that we reckon he killed Rachel, there's something they can do. They can bring what they've got to one of us, and let us take it from there. We're the ones on the shit list.'

There's a silence. Senan sinks half his pint; Francie stares moodily into his. PJ, his long legs twisted around the legs of his stool, is working away absently at his toastie and trying to puzzle this out. Mart licks mayonnaise off his fingers and watches them all with interest. When he gets to Cal, he throws him a big cheerful wink.

Cal drinks and waits. He knows just how deeply he's going against the grain. Centuries where the only safe way was the hidden way have bent this place's DNA like hard prevailing winds bend trees; Ardnakelty has been formed to the circuitous, the elliptical, the plausibly deniable. Working in the open goes against every instinct, on a level as fundamental as poking yourself in the eyeball.

'You won't put Tommy in jail,' Francie says. 'Whatever you get, he'll have a dozen witnesses to say it's all bollocks.'

'I can live without him going to jail,' Cal says, 'and so can you. What we need is him out of our business. We just need enough solid stuff that we can go to Moynihan and say, "Hey, motherfucker, back off, or else we take this to the Guards, and you can deal with them while your investors run for the hills." Like you said' – he nods to Mart – 'the guy's got scale. He's long-sighted. He's not gonna go all in on a losing hand just 'cause he started. He's gonna fold while he's ahead. Drop the compulsory purchases, drop Lena, get us off his back. Then get Eugene on the council, build houses or some shit on the land he's got, and wait for some other chance to crown himself king of this place.'

'Now this,' Mart says, leaning back on his stool and pointing at Cal like he's a prize ram, 'd'ye see this? This is why we need a bitta new blood around here, every now and then. Don't be telling me any of ye woulda come up with this, 'cause I know fine well ye wouldn't.'

'Tommy won't lie back and take it,' Francie says. 'He'll do something.'

'Yeah,' Cal says. 'No point pretending he won't. So we need to get the word out as loud and as fast as we can. Once we've got enough on Tommy, he can't do a damn thing to us. Up until then, though: yeah, he's gonna do plenty.'

Senan is turning his glass carefully between his fingers again. 'If you put that around,' he says, 'it'll get back to Claire and Fintan.'

'I know,' Cal says. This has been on his mind, too. The Holohans have too much to bear already. 'I'm barely acquainted with them, but someone who knows them should go talk to them. So this doesn't hit them out of the blue.'

All four guys recoil. 'Jesus, Sunny Jim,' Mart says, shocked. 'Are you outa your head?'

'No fuckin' way,' Francie says.

Cal expected this reaction, but it irks him anyway. 'OK,' he says. 'Then what did you have in mind?'

'Claire and Fintan'll have to manage the best they can,' Mart says gently but inflexibly, both to Cal and to Senan, 'the same as the rest of us. They've more right to know the story than anyone, sure, and the likes of me showing up at their door to break it to them won't make it any easier to take.'

Senan glances up from his glass. 'What if there's nothing out there to get?' he asks. 'Say we're wrong, and Tommy never done anything on Rachel. Then what?'

'Then we're in deep shit,' Cal says. 'But I don't think we're wrong. Eugene thinks his daddy did something to her, and he oughta know.'

'Go at Eugene, so. Instead of bringing Tommy down on us.'

'I'm gonna talk to Eugene,' Cal says. 'Just not yet. If I rock up with nothing and go, "Gee, Eugene, how come you think your daddy killed your girlfriend?", he's gonna tell me to go fuck myself. If I want to make that conversation work, I need to bring something good with me.'

'Then get it on the QT,' Senan says. 'We'll all go out and have a few chats, feel out who knows what, subtle-like. Then you can go in and get the goods. You were a detective, for fuck's sake; no better man for the job.'

'We can't afford subtle,' Cal says. 'How long would it take us to even get a lead on who's got what we need? Once we do, how long is it gonna take me to convince them I'm not Tommy's stooge, sniffing around so I can rat them out? Even say I manage that, how do I convince them they'll be safe talking to me, if I'm so scared of Tommy I'm sneaking around in corners dropping hints? By the time we get even halfway there, Tommy's gonna hear about it, and he's gonna come down on us like a ton of bricks, before we've got one thing to fight back with.'

Senan is staring down into his pint, his mouth set in a stubborn line. Cal doesn't know how to show him what he's seeing, the generations' worth of extravagantly tangled thickets that, if they try to navigate a way through, will snag them and hold them trapped for Tommy to pick off; how their only chance is to charge at the whole damn mess, full speed, and try to leap it. 'We gotta be loud,' he says. 'No one's gonna bring us squat unless we're shooting our mouths off like we don't give a shit.'

'I'm bored of being subtle,' Mart says. 'This'll rattle Tommy's cage, all right. No one's ever returned fire on the man before;

it'll be a new experience for him. I'm interested to see how he takes it.'

Senan's eyes are still on his glass. Francie is leaning back on the banquette and drinking, dour and unreadable. PJ, troubled, looks from one face to another.

'We tried your kind of direct,' Cal says. 'Now let's try mine.'

'Exactly,' Mart says, raising his pint in approval. 'Time to mix it up a wee bit. Shock and awe, motherfuckers.'

Senan glances up again. He says, 'I've Angela and the kids to think about. Tommy fights dirty.'

'I know that,' Cal says. 'If you want to stay clear, no one's gonna blame you. Get up like I pissed you off, call me a couple of names, walk out, don't hang with us till this blows over. It'll be fine.'

They look at each other, across the table.

'Desperate times call for desperate measures, boyo,' Mart says. 'Watch this.' He twists around on the stool. 'Hey! Bernard! Sonny! Alla ye lickarses! The whole lot of ye oughta be ashamed of yourselves, talking shite about a widow woman who never done anything on anyone, when everyone knows 'twas Tommy Moynihan that fed Rachel Holohan the antifreeze and threw her off the bridge.'

Every head in the pub rises and turns to Mart. He pops the last hunk of toastie in his mouth and looks back at them, chewing, unfazed. There's a silence, while the room receives the fact that the terms of engagement have been transformed.

Bernard McHugh puts down his glass. Bernard is a square-set, quiet guy, known to be the brains of the McHugh family. In Tommy's plant, he's worked his way up to be some kind of manager; he always smells clean, a marker that has meaning in this place full of farmers and meat-workers. Cal, going mainly by the fact that Bernard keeps trying to get Trey on the GAA team he coaches, has always liked him.

'The hell are you at, man?' Bernard asks, a little reproachfully.

'That's what I'm asking you,' Mart says, pitching his voice to keep everyone's attention, not that they need any encouragement. 'Lena Dunne's got her wedding to organize, to this fine specimen here; she can't be dealing with your nonsense. And here's you trying to put her in jail to cover Tommy Moynihan's fat arse. If your mammy finds out what you're at, she'll take the wooden spoon to the lot of ye.'

Bernard gets up, brushes down his pants, and comes over to the alcove. Every pair of eyes watches him all the way.

'Mart,' he says, deliberately lowering his voice to turn this into a private chat. He glances at the banquette, but no one moves to let him sit down. 'I know you've doubts about the factory coming in. That's only natural, sure. But this isn't the way to go about it.'

'I haven't a doubt in the world, man,' Mart assures him, happily and loudly. 'I'm not having the council take my land off me to give to Tommy and his golf pals, when that wee hoor's-melt should be rotting in jail for murder.'

It strikes Cal that for someone with no practice being up-front about stuff, Mart is taking to it remarkably well. As far as Cal can tell, he's having the time of his life.

'Ah, for God's sake,' Bernard says. 'Have some decency and leave the poor girl out of it. If you've problems with Tommy, go talk to him. Don't be dragging in some young one that should be left to rest in peace.'

'I'm not the one that dragged Rachel into this,' Mart says. 'I hardly knew the girl. I'da been only delighted to leave her outa things, if Tommy had.'

Cal is watching the pub. The initial identical stunned looks are starting to separate themselves and take on form. Some of the faces are puffing up with outrage at Mart's nerve; some are avid for the coming explosion; some look just plain scared.

Others are intent, quick-eyed, absorbing the change and assessing its meaning. Old FX Deery, clasping his pint in both shaky hands and turning his good ear to catch the words, looks like all his remaining Christmases just came at once.

Cal is watching the alcove, too. Senan and Francie and PJ are less easy to read. Since Mart started shooting his mouth off, none of them have moved.

Bernard sighs, exasperated, and runs a hand over his neat hair. 'Look,' he says. 'No one's taking anyone's land. People have themselves worked into a state about compulsory purchases and megafarms, but that's all shite talk. Maybe there'll be the odd CPO on an acre here and there, so the factory can get up and running. That's not the end of the world. It happened with the plant, sure, and everyone survived. The rest is rumours. Pure fuckin' imagination.'

'We're all just a buncha foolish yokels getting ourselves in a tizzy over nothing, is it?' Mart enquires. 'And we oughta go back to our sheep and not worry our simple wee heads?' Somewhere across the room, there's a low mutter of anger.

Mouth McHugh has followed Bernard over and is standing in the entrance to the alcove, thick arms folded like a bouncer, chin tucked into where his neck ought to be. Mouth is Cal's least favourite of the McHugh brothers. He once told Cal that he almost went into the Guards, and Cal knows exactly what kind of cop he would have made.

'I have it straight from the horse's mouth, man,' Bernard says. 'Our Con got himself so worked up he couldn't sleep, thinking his farm was going to be taken off him. In the end I said I'd go ask Tommy straight out, just to put the young fella's mind at rest. You coulda done that yourselves, any one of ye, if ye wanted to know the facts. That's the kind of man Tommy is.'

'Ah, God, isn't he a great fella altogether,' Mart says. 'Making time for the little people.'

Bernard ignores that. 'D'you know what Tommy did, when I asked him? He laughed his arse off and told me whoever came up with that one would wanta lay off the poteen. Everyone's overwrought right now, is what he says, so they're getting hysterical about nonsense they wouldn't give a second thought to any other time. No one's coming for this townland, man. I've Tommy's word on it.'

'And d'you know what I have?' Mart says, grinning at him. 'I've a bridge to sell you. A lovely big one, all covered in diamonds. I'll take cash.'

'I've had shites that were worth more than Tommy Moynihan's word,' PJ says, good and loud, and looks astounded at himself. Somewhere there's a snort of laughter, and somewhere else a growl.

'You,' Mouth says, pointing at PJ. 'Have some fuckin' respect.'

'I never had any respect for the Moynihans,' PJ tells him. 'They're like big babas, throwing things when they don't get their way. Grown men shouldn't behave like that.' Cal wasn't sure PJ even knew how to get loud, but apparently he's had a gift for it all along, just lying latent until the moment came.

'Mart,' Bernard says, silencing Mouth with a raised hand and moving closer to the table. His tone has shifted; he sounds like he and Mart are alone, sitting together late into the night with a bottle of whiskey between them. 'Think long-term for a minute. This was always a one-horse town, and the horse is on its last legs, man. The post office is gone. The hardware shop's gone. Lydia's talking about closing the boutique. Farming's getting tougher every year – sure, who am I telling? The young people get out as soon as they're able, 'cause there's nothing here for them. Look around you: the place is dying. Is that what you want?'

'Well, holy God,' Mart says to the pub. 'Here we are, dying, and no one told us; we thought we were doing grand. Musha,

God love us, what'll we do at all? Thank God we've Tommy to save us.'

'Tommy's going to bring people to this place, man,' Bernard says. 'Young people. Families. He'll bring it alive again. Even if it did take more than a few acres, don't you wanta see that?'

'And instead of this street,' Mart says, smiling sweetly at him, 'we can have Moynihan Plaza, with a McDonald's and a multiplex and a phone shop, and a big gold statue of Tommy where Our Lady is now. It'll be only gorgeous. I'd say you'll leave flowers in fronta the statue every day, will you?'

Someone snickers. Mouth shifts his weight ominously. Bernard throws him a quelling look and takes a breath to keep his patience. 'I'm grateful to Tommy,' he says. 'I'm not ashamed to say it. He's given this place a lot. There's no harm in him getting something back.'

'So 'cause he gets the potholes fixed,' Francie says, 'I'm meant to hand over my fuckin' land. Have I got that right?'

'Look, man,' Bernard says, turning to him. 'Progress isn't a bad thing. You've no kids, it's no skin off your nose if this place dies a death, but I want mine to have something to stay for. Jobs, and houses, and maybe the odd shop or the odd café to go into. What's wrong with that?'

'I've kids,' Senan says. He's sprawled on the banquette with his legs splayed wide, in a pose that looks casual but isn't. 'I want them farming our own land that my father and my granddad farmed before me. Not hiring themselves out to break their backs for Tommy Moynihan's fuckin' city pals. Away you go and pimp yours out if you want, but keep your hands off mine.'

'You,' Mouth says, unable to stay silent any longer, pointing a thick finger at Senan, 'get fucked. When you've done something for this place besides sitting in here complaining and scratching your fuckin' hole, you'll have a right to give out about the Moynihans. Till then, shut your gob.'

Senan turns up his hands and grins: *Come and make me*. Barty has moved out from behind the bar.

Cal wants his mark on this conversation, before matters progress past that point. 'You wanna kiss Tommy Moynihan's ass,' he says to the McHughs and to the pub at large, 'I can see why. Rachel Holohan went up against him, and look what happened to her. But I'm not some kid he can take down easy, and I don't kiss any man's ass.'

He's talking like a blow-in, and he's doing it deliberately. Every man in this room needs to be clear that Cal, at least, is bound by none of their hereditary tangles of laws and fears. Off in the far corner, old FX Deery's face splits into an incredulous grin of pure glee, before he wipes it away with a fast hand.

Mouth turns his stare on Cal. 'There's Don Juan,' he says. 'Lock up your daughters, lads.'

Cal puts down his glass. He says, 'You got something to say to me?'

'Mouth,' Bernard says.

'Let him talk,' Cal says. 'I want to hear this.'

'You're a dirty fuckin' hoormaster,' Mouth says. 'If Lena Dunne wasn't mental, she'da poisoned you instead.'

Cal says, 'You sure you want to bring Lena into this?'

Bernard says, '*Mouth.*'

'Watch how you eat her cooking,' Mouth says. 'Look what happened her last fella.'

Cal realises, with enormous relief, that he finally gets to punch someone. Mouth's face just has time to register that Cal is out of his seat and shouldering Bernard aside, before Cal's fist gets him right under the jaw.

Mouth staggers backwards. Barty is shouting something. Bernard grabs Cal's arm, but someone pulls him off. Cal lunges after Mouth and lands a gut-punch, Mouth gets hold of his collar, and together they lurch into a table, sending pints flying.

All around him, Cal hears the explosion of shouts and crashes as everything goes all to hell.

The brawl, in a place that size and that crowded with people and furniture, is chaos. Cal and Mouth are grappling, trying to hammer each other, but other bodies slam into them, sending them careening down the length of the pub, and neither of them can find room for a decent swing. Cal manages to get Mouth in a headlock, but Mouth is strong and unwieldy and he can't land a blow. Everyone is shouting. Glimpses flash past Cal on all sides: PJ planting a neat right hook, a table going over, Skippy Gannon's face streaming blood, a man on the floor straddling another and punching; someone up on a banquette, kicking out, dragged down flailing; Senan, wide-mouthed, bellowing in mid-charge.

Cal's feet get tangled up with a stool, he takes someone's elbow to the head and sees stars, but he hangs grimly on to Mouth. Mouth is nothing, but he's the closest Cal can get; Cal feels like if he can just hit him hard enough, hit him into silence, out of existence, he can make a clear space where Lena is safe and he can find her again. He lands a punch in Mouth's ribs, with all his strength behind it, and hears the grunt of pain.

Someone big gets shoved into them, Cal's hold slips, and then Mouth is gone and somehow Cal is blocking a swing from a skinny guy whose face is frozen in a snarl of fury. The floor is slippery with drink and crunching with glass, there's no solid footing, but the skinny guy is no fighter and Cal fends off his whirling arms easily. He ducks a swipe from someone, grabs the skinny guy around the middle, and body-slams him onto a banquette. Then he turns, panting, to look for Mouth.

The fight seems to have thinned somehow; the noise has lessened and he can't find Mouth, can't see Mart or PJ. He feels someone behind him, spins, and then strong hands grab him under the armpits and he's hauled backwards. 'Out!' Barty roars in his ear. 'Get ta fuck!'

Cal tries to twist free, but there are two guys holding him: Barty has deputised Fergal O'Connor, who's young and big and the obliging type. They bum-rush Cal straight through the remaining action to the door. On his way out Cal catches a glimpse of FX Deery, clutching his stick in both hands and joyfully whacking someone across the back with it.

Barty's final shove sends him reeling halfway across the street; he has to grab hold of the lamp post to steady himself. There are other men out here, and Cal looks around wildly for Mouth, but instead he catches the astonished stare of Doireann Cunniffe, agog on the sidewalk with her shopping trolley frozen in mid-roll. They look at each other. Cal can't think of a single thing to say.

Barty launches Senan out of the pub, Fergal shoves the skinny guy after him, and FX Deery totters out under his own steam, grinning and brandishing his stick high. 'Ye're all barred!' Barty shouts after them. 'The lot of ye!' He slams the door, and Cal hears the bolt shoot home.

There are maybe fifteen or sixteen of them on the street, red-faced and breathing hard in the fine rain. Everyone glances around, ready to roll if someone else starts up again, but no one does. The sudden change of scene has taken the momentum out of things. Mrs Geraghty's grandkids are pressed up against her sitting-room window, wide-eyed.

'I'll fuckin' have you,' Mouth says to Cal. He's holding his ribs and wheezing.

'Any time,' Cal says.

'Come on,' Bernard says sharply, getting Mouth by the elbow. Bernard has a black eye coming up and a lot of beer on his ironed shirt, and he doesn't look happy with anyone. 'You've done plenty. Let's go.' He herds the rest of his brothers towards their cars. Doireann Cunniffe comes out of her trance and zips into Noreen's, to be first with the oven-fresh gossip.

Gradually men move off, in twos and threes, sending dirty looks over their shoulders and throwing the odd insult. For a fight that brief and that cramped, a lot of damage got done. Tadhg McHugh looks dazed, holding his head and leaning on one of his brothers; Skippy Gannon's cheek is still pouring blood from a gash that looks like someone glassed him. Fights are inevitable, among men tied together this tightly, and Cal has seen a few break out before, but those were scuffles: shoving, shouldering, a couple of token punches, to establish hierarchies or to clear a disagreement. This was entirely different.

Cal and his buddies gather at the grotto, where PJ is sitting on the wall, rolling up his pants leg to inspect his shin. His pants are soaked and smell strongly of beer. 'Someone turned over a table,' he explains. His shin has a purple line across it and is swelling rapidly. 'It caught me on the way down.'

'Didja enjoy yourself there, boyo?' Mart asks him.

PJ glances up. He's still wearing the same astounded look he had before the fight broke out. 'I can't tell,' he says. 'I never done anything like that before.'

'You've done it now, boy,' Mart says, 'and you done it like a pro. You're a man of hidden talents, is what you are.'

'Fuck me sideways,' Senan says, flexing split knuckles. He's grinning like a teenager who just scored with the prom queen. 'That was deadly.'

''Twas fuckin' gorgeous,' Francie says. For the first time since Cal's known him, his long melancholy face is lit up, exhilarated. He has a fat lip, but he doesn't seem to have noticed. 'The faces on people, man, when this fella' – Mart – 'said his piece. I thought someone'd take a heart attack.'

'That fuckin' eejit Larry McGinty, didja see him? Face on him like a cat's arse. I thought he was going to cross himself.'

'I sorted Larry, boy. I fetched him such a kick up the hole, he flew halfway across the pub.'

'I knew ye'd get into the swing of it,' Mart says, grinning back at them. He has a graze on one cheekbone, and his hair is standing out in all directions, but apart from that he looks unscathed. 'Ye just needed a wee nudge, is all.'

'We're in the swing of it, all right,' Senan says. 'No going back now, man. Was that loud enough for you?'

'Loud and clear,' Cal says. 'That was beautiful.'

'D'ye know something?' PJ says. He unfolds himself from the grotto wall and stands on one lanky leg like a flamingo, shaking the sore one experimentally and looking around at the rest of them with surprised pleasure. 'I did enjoy that.'

'There you go,' Mart says, smiling at him and giving him a clap on the shoulder that nearly topples him. 'Now you've started, there'll be no holding you.'

'I don't give a damn what Tommy does,' PJ announces firmly. 'I'm sick of tiptoeing around that shower.'

'Tommy can go and shite,' Senan says. He's rolling one sleeve to try and hide a rip in his fleece. 'The one I'm worried about is Angela. She's only after buying me this yoke. I'm a dead man.'

'Let him work away and be damned to him,' PJ declares. 'If he comes at me, sure, I've my shotgun.'

'The hell are you on about?' Francie demands. 'He's not going to show up at your door looking for a fuckin' *gunfight*.'

'I know that, sure,' PJ explains, with a harassed look at Senan, who's started singing the theme tune from *The Good, the Bad and the Ugly*. 'I only meant—'

'In a cowboy hat and chaps, is it? He'll be lovely.'

Senan is doing a spraddle-legged cowboy walk, unholstering double finger-pistols. Mrs Geraghty's grandkids are giggling in the window. He tips an imaginary Stetson to them. Cal and Mart have started laughing.

'I only said *if* he—'

'On a fuckin' mustang, yeah?'

Mrs Geraghty has joined her grandkids and is staring, open-mouthed. Senan tries to trot a mustang for her, but he's laughing too hard. Francie cracks up too, and then even PJ joins in at his own expense, and the five of them stand there in the middle of the street laughing their asses off. Mrs Geraghty gives them a tentative polite wave, but that only makes them laugh harder.

Cal is in Mart's car, heading home, before it occurs to him to check out his injuries. The main ones are a tender lump above his ear, where he got elbowed, and a sore neck from him and Mouth hauling each other around. He has a few random bruises and scrapes thrown in, but nothing feels serious enough to need attention, and none of it detracts from his mood, which is better than it's been in a long time. He knows any kind of victory is a long way off and by no means certain, but the rules of engagement are no longer Tommy's rules, which in itself counts as a win.

'I do love a good roola-boola,' Mart says happily, shifting up a gear as they leave the village behind. 'I haven't had one a them in years. I was worried that I'd got too old, but wouldja look at that, Jean-Claude: I've still got it. Bernard McHugh's eye can vouch for that. He won't look very managerial in work on Monday.'

He glances sideways at Cal. 'Did I take you by surprise back there, starting shite?'

'Little bit,' Cal says, twisting his neck to test it out. 'I figured we'd at least wait till the guys had made up their minds.'

'If I'da waited,' Mart says, 'them lads woulda gone on dithering till Christmas. Sometimes a decision looks awful complicated till you're dropped into the middle of it, and then 'tis all crystal-clear. I was just providing a bitta clarity.' He slants Cal a wicked look. 'And anyhow, don't you be lecturing me about patience, and you the one that resorted to violence.'

'Sorry I got you guys barred,' Cal says.

'That won't last,' Mart says, waving the idea away magnificently. 'If that fella bars the lot of us, he'll be outa business. We'll be back in by Thursday.'

'You reckon that was a bad call?' Cal asks. 'Hitting Mouth?'

'Ah, God, no,' Mart assures him, taking a hand off the wheel to dig out his tobacco pouch and rummage in it for a rollie. 'You saw the lads: they're only over the moon with themselves. They needed that. And no one'll hold it against you for giving Mouth a few skelps; sure, we've all had the urge. He's some gowl, that fella.'

He waits for a pothole-free stretch of road and flicks his lighter. 'And it stopped Bernard talking,' he says, through his rollie. 'I appreciated that.'

'Bernard's an OK guy,' Cal says. 'He wasn't trying to start anything.'

'Exactly,' Mart says, aiming his cigarette at Cal like Cal just said something profound. 'That's the problem with Bernard, bucko: the man isn't just some lickarse that thinks anything Tommy does is holy. He's a dacent lad, he's thought this over, and he has a point. I don't agree with it – as far as I'm concerned, he can shove it up his hole – but 'tis a point. That's what I don't like.'

'He was talking quiet,' Cal says. 'Nobody much heard him.'

Mart shakes his head impatiently, like Cal missed his meaning. His glee over the fight has dropped away; his profile, against the hedges speeding by, has an intent, inward focus that Cal can't read.

'I'm getting old, Sunny Jim,' he says. 'Regardless of Bernard's eye, and although I hate to admit it. I've always had a terror of getting old.'

Cal has never heard Mart confess to any fear of anything except cauliflower. He wonders if Mart is about to reveal something terminal. The thought hits him harder than he would have expected.

'You look like you're in pretty good shape to me,' he says. 'No worse'n you were when I got here, anyway.'

Mart blows that away with a scornful snort. 'I'm not talking about the aul' aches and pains, man. I'm fulla those ever since I was a lad of thirty; I don't pay any notice to them. But I never wanted to be one of them aul' fellas whingeing and whining about how things were back in their day. What's the point of them? They're not in the world at all; they're getting no sense outa it, nor it outa them. To all intents and purposes, Sunny Jim, they're dead men walking.' He rolls down his window to flick ash. 'I've always made an effort on that,' he says. 'I read the internet, when the aul' connection doesn't give up on me. I take an interest in what the young people do be saying, seeing as I've none of my own to keep me up to date. I've a favourite Taylor Swift song.'

'Which one?' Cal asks. He's not clear on where this is going.

'"Shake It Off",' Mart informs him. 'That's beside the point. What I'm saying is, even if I listen to Tay-Tay all day long and read the whole of Reddit, I'm still getting old. Maybe Bernard's right: this place needs progress, and I'm just another aul' fella throwing a wobbler 'cause the world's moving on.'

'No,' Cal says.

Mart cocks an eyebrow at him. 'No?'

Cal doesn't know how to find words for what he means. The things he's come to prize in this place are not, mostly, the ones he moved here in search of. The beauty is all there and more, but he was also picturing simplicity and peace, maybe even innocence, none of which showed up in any noticeable quantity. Instead he's found the intricate webs, constructed over centuries, that bind people to one another, to their land, and to their past. He's under no illusion that these bindings are simple or innocent, either. They've sliced people to the bone, scourged them out of town, choked them to death. But alongside all that, they've held the place together, steadfast in the face of time, dark happenings, rifts, attacks, and sieges. The things under threat from Tommy wouldn't hold any weight in a corporation's profit-and-loss projection, or meet government criteria on innovation and sustainability; by any standard that has power, they're worthless. Their currency has value only to its holders. But it seems to Cal that dismissing them as disposable because of this would be some grievous kind of sin.

'Bernard's got a point,' he says. 'Not one that's good enough.'

Mart nods, accepting that. 'I'm not against this place changing,' he says. ''Tis no fuckin' paradise, whatever the tourist board likes to say; there's plenty of things that could do with a bitta change. But we oughta be the ones doing it. Not a buncha suits ripping the guts outa the place and building it back whatever way'll fill up their bank accounts.'

They've reached Cal's gate. Trey won't be there – Aidan's parents are out of town for the weekend, so everyone is heading over to his place to do unspecified stuff that Cal assumes will include the kind of party that would give him nightmares. For once, he's glad of her absence. He's not in the right frame of mind for explaining why he gets to kick ass and she doesn't.

Mart pulls in at the side of the road, but he doesn't turn to Cal; he's still looking out the windshield, one hand on the wheel, a thread of smoke curling from the rollie between his fingers. The car is cold and has a comforting smell of tobacco, rain, and dog.

'Will I tell you something, Jean-Claude?' Mart asks. 'Something I haven't said to anyone else?'

'Go for it,' Cal says.

'All this that we're doing,' Mart says. 'Gathering at Tommy's place the other night, and shouting from the rooftops, and getting ourselves barred from Seán's. 'Twon't make a blind bitta difference.'

Cal is startled. 'Hey,' he says. 'We got this.'

'Quit being American, for fuck's sake,' Mart says. 'You'll give me the sick. You're in Ireland now; follow the local customs. We don't give fuckin' pep talks.'

'I'm just saying,' Cal says. 'We've got plenty more left in the tank.'

'Ah, we do,' Mart agrees. 'I'm not saying we'll get nowhere. We'll get Tommy off your missus's back, one way or another. We might beat him back off the land, this time; I wouldn't put a bet on it either way, but we might. But Tommy's a long-sighted man. He'll give people a coupla years to simmer down. He'll do some good deeds for the townland meanwhile – pull a few strings and get the aul' post office reopened, maybe, or bring in more school buses. And then he'll start over.'

'So we're gonna have to get thorough,' Cal says. 'He can't get the post office reopened from Puerto Banús.'

Mart leans back in his seat to draw the last out of his rollie, and regards Cal steadily. 'You're not taking my meaning, bucko,' he says gently. 'Tommy looks like the problem, but he's not. I'm going after him 'cause he gives us something solid to fight against, and we need that. But if Tommy doesn't get the job done, then sooner or later, someone else will. 'Tis happening here and there, all round the country. There's plenty of farming men getting old, Sunny Jim, and getting old alone, with no childer to take over the farm. When they retire, or die, in come a buncha investors to snatch up the land, at prices the young men can't match. Next thing you know, there's a megafarm, sucking up everything around it and getting more mega every year.'

He nods dispassionately at his own knobbly knees, in their

stained pants. "'Tis only a matter of time before these joints of mine won't get me through the day's work. PJ and Bobby and Francie and plenty of others, they're no chickens either; they won't be able for this forever. Whatever buyers Tommy's lined up, if they've enough patience, they won't even need fancy schemes and compulsory purchase orders. All they'll haveta do is wait us out.'

He throws his rollie butt out the window, into a puddle. 'You came here just in time, Jean-Claude,' he says. 'Look at that.'

Cal follows his look. All around them, the stone walls spread out in a pattern as individual and intimate as a fingerprint. The rain has faded; under the low-hanging cloud, the greens and tawny-golds of the fields have a strange rich glow, like they've been infiltrated by some other self from a memory or a dream.

'In ten or twenty or thirty years,' Mart says, 'that'll be gone. Them walls'll be cleared away, to let the big machinery through for the large-scale tillage. Mosta the hedgerows'll haveta go, as well – some a them are here since the Stone Age, didja know that? but sure, you can't let sentiment get in the way of business. The houses'll be bought up with the land, and people moved into nice new estates named after the developers. Instead we'll have livestock sheds the size of airport terminals. There'll be no cattle out to pasture; they'll be housed year-round – you can fit more on the same land that way, d'you see. Take a good look while you can, boyo. That's the last of it.'

The fields around here have names. Cal has learned them one by one, along the way: Garrybrock, Thady's Acre, the Furze Field, the Five Rood, the Liss, the Stray Field, Tobardove, the Far Curragh, Gannon's Kesh. A kesh, according to Mart, was a causeway made of sticks across boggy land. It vanished before living memory, along with Garrybrock's badger and the Tobardove black well; no one remembers who Thady was, and no one gets led astray by fairies any more, but the footprints of all these things still run easily through every day's pub talk, directions, anecdotes. None of them are gone.

Maybe Tommy will get one of the developers to name a row of identical cardboard houses Tobardove Terrace, to show how much he respects local heritage. His tenants can show their kids photos of drystone walls, and tell them how cows used to graze free where they park their cars.

Small with distance, Mary Ann Gannon and one of her sons tramp across their land, where the causeway used to run, with heavy sacks slung over their shoulders and her red wax jacket bright against the grass. Richie Casey is moving sheep, swinging his crook and signalling to his dog with whistles sharp enough that flickers of them carry all the way to Cal's ears. These people and their way of life are turning into myth in front of his eyes.

'If you figure we won't make any difference,' he says, 'then what the hell are we doing?'

Mart turns to look at him. 'What I just said to you,' he tells Cal, 'I wouldn't say to any of the lads. And I expect you to keep it to yourself, as well. You can handle it; 'tisn't your home place on the line. But it'd take the heart outa the lads. That's all I'm doing, Jean-Claude: I'm keeping the heart in people. So that when alla this is taken off us and changed, we'll know we fought like fuck, and we'll have a bitta heart left in us for whatever comes next.'

He smiles at Cal and lifts his chin, dismissing him. 'Go on,' he says. 'You done a good day's work. And you never got to eat your toastie. Go get some food into you; you'll need your strength.'

Cal gets out of the car. Mart lifts a hand and drives off, spray flying up from his tyres as he bumps through potholes.

17

Cal wakes up feeling both the fight and his age: he's sore in places that haven't even occurred to him before. Senan has sent him a gif of two penguins having a slap-fight, which Cal takes to be himself and Mouth. He sends back one of Russell Crowe yelling, 'Are you not entertained?' Then he showers away some of the aches, makes himself breakfast, and gets ready to wait.

This being Sunday, Trey will presumably show up at some point or other, depending on how late and how wild Aidan's party got. Cal finds himself hoping she won't come. Probably anyone with information to share will go to Mart, who not only has status around here but has firmly established himself as the guy leading the charge; but there could be someone out there who has a complicated generational grudge against Mart, or a special appreciation for Cal punching Mouth, or who would just be more at ease unburdening himself to a man with a comparatively uncluttered outlook. Any such guy is likely to be scared shitless, liable to shy away if he's faced with an unexpected teenager. Cal almost texts Trey to say he's come down with some bug and she should stay clear, but he can't bring himself to do it. The kid has always been furiously sensitive to any hint that she might not be wanted, and she's moving away from him fast enough as it is; he can't make himself do anything that might push her farther and faster.

Not much is likely to happen today, anyway. Anyone calling on Cal, at least for helpful reasons, is likely to come in darkness.

He makes himself accessible, just in case, by finding random shit to do in his front yard – his car could use a wash. It's not raining, but the cloud thickens both the light and the cold so that it feels like dusk, a dusk that stretches on and on unchanged.

Mart and Kojak, up in their back field, are steering another ewe towards the shed; even at this distance, Cal can see the limp that says she's picked up the scald. PJ is clipping hedges and singing – PJ has a fine tenor voice which he mostly uses for melancholy folk songs and Mario Lanza, but today's number, although Cal can't hear the words, has a more martial sound. Apart from PJ's song choice, everything is exactly, impeccably its usual self.

The rooks are delighted to see Cal; fucking with him is one of their favourite pastimes, and in winter they don't get enough opportunities. At least a dozen of them swoop over to explore his possibilities. They warm up by perching on the wall for a while, making rude remarks about the state of his car and cracking up when he insults them back; when that gets stale, a few of them start trying to lure him away from the Pajero, by waving mysterious objects and hassling Rip and whacking rocks on his kitchen window, so their buddies can steal his sponge and scrabble all over the parts he's just washed. This field where Cal's house stands is called Derryrucach, the rooks' oak. His rooks have been hanging out in that oak tree since before English took over from Irish on people's tongues.

It occurs to him for the first time to wonder what he'll do if Tommy's buddies take his land away. The threat doesn't seem to be immediate, but Mart was very sure that it's on the way.

Mart was right, this doesn't hold the same weight for Cal as it does for the rest of the guys. He feels like it shouldn't hold any weight at all: given what's going on both with Lena and with Trey, there doesn't seem to be any real reason why he shouldn't just up sticks and go, anywhere that will take a middle-aged

American and a dog, and maybe even has sunshine. But somewhere along the way, he stopped thinking in terms of moving on from Ardnakelty, and now he doesn't know how to get back into the habit. He had come to believe that Ardnakelty, like Lena, was his final love, to be valued all the more for being unexpected and unsought.

Trey shows up around eleven, swinging through the gate on her bike, with Kate cruising along beside her. 'Brought Kate,' she says, unnecessarily, as they pull up next to the car.

Both of them look reassuringly un-hungover. Also reassuringly, they're not wearing the kind of clothes Cal associates with nightmare-fuel parties. He's not sure what teenage girls wear to go wild these days, but he doubts it's baggy jeans and hoodies.

'Hey,' he says. Trey has never brought her friends over before. 'How's it going? You guys need some breakfast?'

'Nah,' Trey says, leaning over to give Rip's head a rub as he wriggles and wags. 'We crashed at Aidan's, so we et there. Thanks,' she adds, as an afterthought.

'Right,' Cal says. He wonders if something horrifying happened at the party and they need him to get them out of trouble – Aidan's dad is known to be a hard man – but they don't have that air. 'How'd it go? Aidan's house still there?'

''S grand,' Trey says. 'Lauren O'Farrell got sick all over the cooker, but it's electric so it wiped off easy. And Ross broke an umbrella 'cause him and Callum Bailey were doing lightsaber fighting, but Aidan's gonna say the dog done it.'

'That's how come we're this late,' Kate says. Rip, who knows her from rides to football matches, is jamming his nose into her hand in welcome. 'We stayed to help Aidan clean up. His mam and dad won't even know there was anyone there.'

'Good call,' Cal says. Even with everything that's going on, he can't help feeling the lift of this small, pure triumph: Trey, doing dumb shit with her buddies at parties like any teenager, and even having the manners to stick around and clean up afterwards. 'This what people wear to parties these days?' he enquires.

Trey and Kate look at themselves and then at him. 'Yeah,' Trey says. 'What?'

'Fancy,' Cal says. 'You sure know how to dress to impress.'

'What'd you wear, back in the eighteen hundreds? A suit and tie, yeah?'

'Sure. And the girls wore ball gowns. You oughta get one. Bright pink.' Trey mimes gagging. 'You guys have a good time?'

'Yeah,' Trey says, dismissing the party. 'You said I could tell Kate what's going on. With Moynihans and all.'

Cal says, 'Right.' He drops his sponge into the bucket, dries his hands on his pants, and braces himself.

'So me and Kate, we done something about this shite. Seeing as ye were doing fuck-all.'

Cal should have known, when she agreed to stay home and let the grown-ups fix it. He thought she was getting old enough to accept solid reasoning, but Trey has never, since he first met her, been docile about doing nothing. The part that comes strangely to him is Kate. Half the reason he couldn't make himself turn Trey away, when she first showed up here, was her air of savage solitariness, an isolation forced on her so ruthlessly that it had become part of her nature. The kid had no one and trusted no one, including him; anything she did, she did alone. She and Kate stand there astride their bikes, shoulder to shoulder like partners, looking at him.

'OK,' he says. 'Come on inside, fill me in. I can finish this up later.'

'It'll go sticky if you leave it,' Trey says, nodding at the Pajero.

'It's gonna rain anyway,' Cal says. 'It'll be fine. Come on.' Whatever they have to say, he doesn't like the thought of them saying it out here in the open. All morning, he's felt watched. It could be just the rooks, or his own raised level of alertness, or the fact that the whole townland is on the watch, but he wants the kid inside his walls.

He's not sure whether he's supposed to offer them tea, or coffee, or cookies, or whether any or all of those would turn out to be somehow wrong and terminally embarrassing, so he just puts them on the sofa and sits himself in the armchair to listen. Rip, making up for Cal's failure of hospitality, brings over an old sneaker of Trey's and shakes it at them, looking for tug-of-war. 'Nah,' Trey says, shoving the sneaker away. 'Sit.' Rip gives her a wounded look, but she rubs under his jaw to settle him, and he flops down on her feet to chew the unappreciated sneaker.

'That night Rachel died,' Kate says. 'Me and Trey and the lads, we were down in Mossie O'Halloran's byre. You know that, right?'

'Trey told me,' Cal says. He finds himself watching Kate with new attention, and liking what he sees: the easy way she sits, with her feet planted firmly and her elbows on her knees, the straight way she meets his eyes. He likes her voice, too, clear and clean of any shrillness or affectation. This only eases his mind a little bit. Even if what he sees is what Trey gets, that's not enough. From all Lena said, Kate is a good kid from a healthy family; she has no way of understanding what Trey's life has been, or what it's built into her.

'Like I said,' Trey tells Kate. 'He's grand.'

Kate nods. ''Cause it was Saturday night,' she explains to Cal. 'That's what everyone does, goes and hangs out somewhere. We'd mostly go to Mossie's, 'cause me and the lads are from Knockfarraney, so it's halfway between. It's miles from the river, but, so we wouldn'ta seen anything to do with Rachel.'

She pauses to check that Cal is following. He nods. The kid appears to be more at home with the concept of communication than Trey is, which is probably a good thing.

'But there's other places,' Kate says. 'Closer to where she went in the river. Like, you know Casey's boreen, yeah, that goes down to the old bridge? There's a house—'

'That one we went into that time when we were fishing and it started lashing,' Trey tells Cal. 'With the weird pink wallpaper, and the nest in the sink.'

'I know it,' Cal says. The townland is scattered with these places, homes emptied by famine in the 1840s, orphaned by emigration in the seventies, left behind in the millennium rush to easier city jobs. Mostly no one bothers to knock them down, whether for complicated zoning reasons or complicated sentimental reasons or just because there's no particular need, who knows. They get left for nature to repurpose in its own time: a map of small, bitter lost battles, forgotten now.

'So last night at Aidan's,' Kate says, 'we asked around, found out who was where that night. Then we talked to anyone that was near enough to the river or to Moynihans' place, asked did they see anything. Most of 'em didn't, but—'

'We were careful,' Trey reassures Cal. 'We waited till everyone had a few drinks in them, and we made it sound like just gossip and shite. You know, "I heard Chelsea Moylan and Callum Bailey were in that house down Casey's boreen and they heard someone screaming," and then people were like, "Nah, Chelsea had a free gaff so her and Callum went there, it was Zoe Greaney and her lot that were in the house."'

'You, gossiping?' Cal says. 'People fell for that?' He didn't know Trey was capable of this kind of subtlety. He's caught between being proud of how she's grown and being suddenly sad, missing the half-feral little kid who had no strategies beyond charging at things head-on.

That gets him a grin from both of them. 'People are thick,' Trey says.

'So then,' Kate says, 'we went to Zoe and we were like, "Ohmygod, someone said you heard screams," and Zoe—'

'Zoe's *seriously* fuckin' thick,' Trey puts in.

'—Zoe was like, "That's stupid, why would anyone scream when they killed themselves, and anyhow no one screamed, we woulda heard." So we went, "Didja see her go past?" and Zoe went, "No, she musta come the other way, we saw no one only—"'

'Listen to this,' Trey says. She's grinning again.

'"—only Tommy Moynihan,"' Kate says. 'Zoe and her mates, they saw Tommy Moynihan go down the road towards the old bridge that night.'

They both look at him, triumphant, stepping back to let him admire their kill.

'Well,' Cal says, being gentle about it, 'a lot of people were out looking for Rachel that night. And Eugene was supposed to meet her at that bridge. Nothing weird about Tommy thinking to look for her there.'

'Nah,' Trey says. Her grin has widened. 'We asked Zoe what time they saw him. Guess what she said.'

'Half-nine, about, or a little before,' Kate says. 'Zoe's positive. Hannah Lynch was late getting there – she was minding her brothers, so she couldn't come out till her parents got home. So when the four of them heard someone coming, they thought it was Hannah. They hid behind the wall by the road to scare her, and Tommy nearly caught them.'

'You got that call at like half-three in the morning,' Trey reminds Cal. 'No one was out looking for Rachel at half-nine.'

And Eugene said he and his parents were home together all night, till the search began. In his head, Cal runs over his timeline. Somewhere between seven o'clock and eleven, Rachel drank antifreeze. Somewhere between eight and midnight, she went into the water. Sometime that night, she might or might not have had plans to meet Eugene at the bridge. Cal can't think of a single harmless reason why Tommy should have gone to that meeting instead of Eugene.

For once, Tommy didn't send a minion to do his dirty work. Tommy did it himself this time.

He says, 'They didn't tell anyone about this? The police, their parents, no one?'

'They'd said they were at each other's,' Trey explains. 'So they'da been in shite if anyone found out where they went. Zoe's dad already said if he catches her drinking again, he's gonna send her to boarding school.'

'And that house's meant to be dangerous,' Kate says. 'The ceiling's falling in, like. We're not supposed to go in there. So they'da got in hassle for that as well.'

Cal says, 'Any chance they're making it up?'

'Nah,' Trey says. 'Zoe's mates are even thicker than her. None a them even copped it could have anything to do with Rachel. They just thought Tommy had a one somewhere that he was going to see.'

Cal is heartily thankful they got this story when they did. By the end of today, when the news of last night's pub goings-on has spread, even dumb Zoe and her dumb buddies will see things very differently. Either the story will expand into a lurid epic full of bloodcurdling screams and daring chases and people fainting from terror, or it'll disappear altogether.

'It was pretty dark out there,' he says. 'They sure it was Tommy?'

'I thought of that,' Trey says proudly. 'I was like, "No way was it Tommy Moynihan, he's fuckin' ancient, he's not going out looking for the ride. Coulda been anyone, in the dark." Zoe got all snotty—'

'She gets snotty with everyone,' Kate tells Cal. It takes him a second to realise she's reassuring him that this Zoe kid isn't picking on Trey.

'She was like, "*Hello*, I'm not *blind*, I was like this far from him, and he had his phone light on so he could see where he was going. It was Tommy. Is that OK with you?" She's positive.'

'Well,' Cal says. He looks at the two of them, vivid and alert as a pair of young hunting dogs, pulled forward on the edge of the sofa by their own eagerness. He was a fool to forget about teenagers and their world, a separate layer underlying the adult world and invisible to it, the way wild creatures' networks of roadways and meeting-places underlie human ones. 'Look at that. I think you got something.'

They're both grinning, lit up by their triumph. 'Yeah we did,' Trey says. 'Someone hadta.'

Cal asks, 'Could Zoe and her buddies see the bridge?'

'Nah,' Trey says. 'There's trees in the way.'

'They see where Tommy went to? See him coming back?'

'Nah,' Kate says. 'I asked. I was like, "Oh my *God*, who's Tommy riding, didn't you watch and see where he went?"' Her voice has turned high-pitched and breathless. Trey is laughing. Cal likes the way she is around Kate, too. Trey is wary of humans; her default is to withdraw into watchful silence. Here, next to Kate on the sofa, she's at ease. 'But Zoe went, "Ew, no, who gives a shit, we were freezing, we just went back inside and texted Hannah to see where the fuck she was." But there's nothing down that road, only the old bridge. He hadta be heading there.'

'*Now* can we get him arrested?' Trey demands.

'Nope,' Cal says. And when Trey stiffens, ready to explode into outrage: 'Kid. If some Guard shows up to interview Zoe Whatever and her buddies, they're just gonna say they don't know what he's talking about, they were never there, you made the whole thing up. And even if he pushes them hard enough that they come clean, then he goes to Tommy, and Tommy says he doesn't know what they're talking about, he was never there, they made the whole thing up. And Clodagh and Eugene back him.' As he says it, he realizes he has a question mark over Eugene. 'Who do you figure the Guard's gonna believe? A bunch of teenagers who keep changing their story and who were probably drunk or stoned or both, or the Moynihans?'

'Fuck's *sake*—' Trey throws herself back on the sofa hard and furiously enough that Rip lifts his head. 'You said we'd no fuckin' evidence, we *got* fuckin' evidence, now you're like, "Nah, doesn't count"— What do we haveta *do*?'

'You already did it,' Cal says. Kate is watching both of them, withholding any reaction till things become clearer. 'You did great. We can use this. Just not to put anyone in jail.'

'Then how?'

Douche or not, Eugene genuinely cared about Rachel. And back in that hotel bathroom, at the funeral, he was showing signs of having had enough of bowing to Daddy's say-so.

'I'm gonna have a talk with Eugene,' Cal says. 'One-on-one.'

'What for?'

'Eugene knows something. I don't know how much, but something's been eating him. I can use what you got to pull it out of him.'

Trey accepts that with a sharp nod. 'Then what?'

'First let's see what he's got,' Cal says. 'Then we decide.'

'How're you gonna get him on his own?' Kate asks. 'Eugene won't be going anywhere by himself, these days. Too scared he'll get hopped on.'

'I don't blame him,' Cal says.

'Send him a note,' Trey says. 'Tell him you know something, meet you at—'

'No,' Cal says. 'You think he's gonna show without backup?' Trey tilts her chin, acknowledging this. 'Eugene's gotta get a little bit stir-crazy every now and then, cooped up in that house with his mama and daddy. He'll come out.'

'We'll keep an eye on the house,' Kate says. 'If he goes out on his own, we'll text you.' Trey nods.

'You've got school,' Cal reminds them. 'Remember that?'

'Fuck school,' Trey says promptly.

'Maybe,' Cal says, 'but you playing hooky gives Tommy ammo.' He can't find a delicate way to point out that it would probably be good if Kate's parents don't get the impression that Trey is a bad influence. 'I'll keep my own eye on Eugene.'

'You'll get caught,' Trey tells him. 'Someone'll see you, and Tommy'll call the Guards, and you'll get done for trespassing or stalking or whatever. If someone sees us, no one gives a shite about kids mitching.'

They have a point. 'Where you planning on watching from?' Cal asks.

The two of them look at each other, consulting some shared inner map. 'Not Geraghty's hill,' Kate says. 'The dog'll lose its shit, and then Red Geraghty'll lose his shit.'

'Yeah,' Trey says. 'Fuck it, we'll go right next door to Moynihans': them trees on the ridge behind Nance Maguire's. We'll be able to watch the back of Moynihans' as well as the front, and no one'll see us in among the trees. Nance's half blind anyhow.'

They both look at Cal. 'If she catches us,' Kate says, 'we'll say we're monitoring bird movements for a school yoke.'

'And we'll get there from the other side,' Trey says. 'From the lane, up the back of the ridge. So no one'll see us coming.'

'OK,' Cal says, not that he has much choice. 'You go ahead and watch today, and we'll hope you get lucky. Tomorrow you've got school.'

They humour him by not arguing. 'Cool,' Trey says. 'Let's go.' She starts easing her feet out from under Rip.

'If you're gonna sit out there in the cold all day,' Cal says, 'you need some hot food inside you, and sandwiches or something to take along. You want to eat here?'

'I haveta go home,' Kate says, standing up. 'Show my mam I'm not dead or pregnant after last night.'

Trey snorts; Kate's mam's worries are apparently a familiar theme. 'I'm not dead or pregnant,' she tells Cal.

'Congratulations,' Cal says.

'Meet you at the top of the lane in like an hour and a half,' Kate says to Trey. To Cal she says, 'We'll text you. And we won't get caught.'

Trey walks Kate out. Cal, at the kitchen window, watches for anyone watching them as they stand talking in the day that's still unchanged, stagnant in its cold grey dusk. After a minute or two Trey nods, and Kate swings herself onto her bike and heads off.

'What do you want to eat?' Cal asks, when Trey comes back in.

Trey leans against the counter. She says, 'Heard there was a fight in Seán's last night.'

'Yeah.'

'About what?'

'What you'd expect. Some people like Tommy Moynihan's big plan, some don't. Mouth McHugh was running his mouth, I shut it for him, other guys got involved.'

Trey says, 'There's people saying Lena gave Rachel the antifreeze.'

Cal opens the fridge to see what he has to feed her. He says, 'I know that.'

'That why you hit Mouth?'

'Pretty much. Yeah.'

'Mouth didn't start that. That was Moynihans.'

'Yup,' Cal says. He finds eggs and sausages. He can feel Trey watching him and wanting something from him – solutions, justice, revenge, who knows. Whatever it is, he doesn't have it.

'That why Lena's head's wrecked?' she says. ''Cause there's people shit-talking her?'

'Dunno,' Cal says. 'You should ask her.'

'How come you don't ask her?'

Even with his back to the kid, Cal can feel the tension humming off her. Him and Lena having a minor disagreement was enough to send Trey out the door; whatever's going on between them now would send her into a wild animal's silent panic. He feels a rush of helpless anger, at Lena and at himself. If they can't keep the kid in school and can't keep her away from Tommy Moynihan's bullshit, the least they could do is keep themselves from fucking up whatever belief she has that the world might hold a few safe places.

'Don't you worry about me and Lena,' he says. 'It's a weird time, is all; everyone's feeling nervy. It's all gonna be fine.'

'How's it gonna be fuckin' *fine*? Her sitting over there like a fuckin' emo, "Oh what's the point of anything," not even talking to you – when was the last time she was round here? And you're like' – Trey does jaw-dropped vagueness – ' "Duh, not gonna *do* anything, except maybe I'll beat someone up, that oughta sort it—" The pair of ye need a good kick up the hole.'

'Kid,' Cal says, turning around to her. He's at the end of his rope. 'I'm doing everything I can.'

Trey receives that with a long silence. 'Rooks are sticking something up your exhaust,' she says in the end, turning away from him to get out plates. 'Think it's your sponge.'

If anyone is going to flush Eugene out of cover, it's Clodagh Moynihan. Clodagh is a scrawny, sharp-nosed, tight-lipped woman who, once she lights on a tender spot, can't stop herself from pecking frenetically away at it; Cal would bet she's been following Eugene around the house, asking whether he needs to see a grief counsellor, listing breaches of etiquette she spotted at the funeral, tapping on the bathroom door to make sure he hasn't drowned himself in the bath, and suggesting eligible candidates for his next girlfriend. In Eugene's shoes, after weeks of this, Cal would need a lot of bourbon on the rocks and a lot of long drives, or long walks, or both. He hopes Eugene is going heavy on the bourbon and light on the driving.

Apparently Clodagh takes Sundays off, though. While Cal pries the sponge out of his exhaust and finishes washing his car, Trey and Kate report the Moynihans coming home, presumably from mass and lunch in town, and then staying home. Three women who all look like Clodagh arrive in fancy cars, and leave a couple of hours later. Nothing else happens. Trey keeps Cal updated via increasingly bored texts: the Moynihans' conservatory sofas are the colour of shite, Red Geraghty's ram isn't doing his job and she and Kate reckon he's gay, they've found an emoji wearing Tommy Moynihan's hat. Cal isn't sure what to make of this. He's seen Trey go after things she cared about before, and she was trained on her target like a rifle sight, no room for anything outside her crosshairs. She sure as hell wasn't sending him hat emojis.

This being Sunday, Cal phones Alyssa, once Seattle is awake. Alyssa is buoyant with a work project that she's finally managed to get off the ground – it means changing her flights, but she's coming on the twenty-second, and what does Trey want for Christmas? She asks Cal how things are going on his end, and he tells her about Con McHugh's nursing chair, and how Trey's rematch against Lisnacarragh got postponed because the pitch was too wet. They have a laugh about Irish weather. Cal imagines trying to explain what's actually been going on around here, and the disconcerted silence he would get in response, like he was speaking an unfamiliar language. Alyssa seems so terrifyingly far away that he wants to reach through the phone and grab her into a hug, but a part of him feels like he should be telling her to cancel the trip. This doesn't seem like somewhere he wants Alyssa to be.

When it starts getting late, he convinces Trey and Kate to go home, or at least to tell him they will. Then he turns off all his lights except the living-room lamp and pulls the armchair in front of the window, where he can keep an eye on his front yard and where any visitor will see him awake and silhouetted against the light. When he lets Rip out before bedtime, he stands in the cold on his back porch and sees all Mart's windows lit.

The night brings nothing. A few sets of headlights pass along the road, but they don't slow down. Rip, in his bed by the fire, lifts his head occasionally, raising an ear to some sound too faint for Cal to hear, but he never goes to alert. Cal dozes off and on in the armchair, jerked awake by loud dreams that are gone before he can catch them.

It's early days; people need time to think things over, build up their courage. Cal tells himself there's no rush – Tommy's plans clearly don't include going anywhere near Lena himself, and it's not like he can have her in handcuffs before the day is out. All the same, Cal can't tamp down a rising sense of urgency, like something terrible is happening somewhere out there in the darkness, and he should be running flat out to stop it. Too much is under way, unseen, among the peaceful spread of fields.

Regardless of Trey's helpful relationship advice, he still hasn't updated Lena. He has no way of telling what might drive her farther away, to a distance they'll never be able to cross. He texted her – *Good night. Love you* – and then put his phone away, so he wouldn't watch for the reply that isn't coming.

He's always known she had rooms he couldn't enter. This never felt like a problem before – the spaces she let him into were broad and generous, and he loved them – but now it seems fatal. Something has shifted her geography: the locked rooms have expanded, till the ones where he was welcome don't exist any more.

He wonders whether it would have made any difference

if they had gotten married, like Noreen and everyone wanted them to. He knows better than many that marriage is no guarantee of permanence, but it would at least be something solid binding them. As it is, Lena isn't his wife, Trey isn't his kid, his land may not be his land much longer, everything he's built here has no more solidity than mist over the fields.

Lena has started sleeping in the sitting room. Her bed feels unsafe; she might sleep too deeply, miss something coming closer until it's too late and she's trapped. Instead she piles duvets on the sofa and curls awkwardly under them, fully dressed, in the dim light of a corner lamp and the dying fire. Even with the fire, the room is never warm enough, but Lena prefers it that way: the chill keeps her in the shallows of sleep, ready. In their corner, the dogs twitch and sigh.

Sean had a shotgun, for vermin. Lena has taken it out of the gun safe where it sat untouched for six years, cleaned it and loaded it and put it under the sofa where she can reach it quickly. She's out of practice, but she knows better than to let anyone see her getting her eye back in. She doesn't expect the shotgun to make any difference, anyhow. She just wants the knowledge that she's done everything she can.

When Daisy lets out a huff of a bark, deep in the night, Lena is awake instantly. Both dogs are half out of their bed, bodies taut and stretched towards the front door. The lamplight catches in their eyes; the fire is only a red pulse in the grate.

Lena sits up, very carefully, and listens. Outside the front of the house, something moves, a scrape and a rustle. Daisy starts a low, slow growl.

'No,' Lena says, in an undertone. Daisy quiets, but she stays tense, quivering with alert.

Inch by inch, Lena takes the shotgun from under the sofa and stands up. She doesn't go to the window; if she moves the curtain, she'll be clear against the lamplight. The spare bedroom is at the front of the house, but she doesn't know how many of them are out there; she could look out the window and find herself eye to eye. She stands still, holding the shotgun, feeling the chill swirl around her ankles, waiting for whatever comes next. Nellie lets out a suppressed little moan.

Something heavy gives one thump, loud and deliberate, against the front door. Both dogs flinch. After a moment there's the rhythmic crunch of gravel as someone big walks away, in no hurry, down the drive.

Lena goes into the spare bedroom and makes herself put her eye to the crack between the curtains. Down by the gate there's movement, a thicker dark against the darkness, shifting and then gone. After a while a car starts up, around the bend, with no lights. Its sound fades away towards the village.

Lena waits a long time before she goes to the front door. The dogs try to come too, but she sends them back to their bed. She opens the door with the shotgun in her other hand.

No one's there. In the light from the doorway she can see the broad footprints tracking their way through the gravel, straight up the drive and back again. On the doorstep is a litre bottle of antifreeze, and beside it a bowl, neatly half filled.

Lena understands both messages. The bowl is to tell her that they can get the dogs any time they like. The bottle is for her.

It would be the simplest way to clean up this mess. Women lose hold every day; a few of them kill their rivals; some of those can't live with what they've done. The story would be clear and convenient, and over. The wave of sympathy for poor Eugene, victim of a slut and a mad bitch, would carry him onto the council and wash away any objections to Tommy's plans. The infighting and tension would ebb, and everyone would keep moving on.

She doesn't want to touch the antifreeze, but a fox or a

hedgehog could pass by. She takes the bowl into the kitchen, pours the antifreeze down the sink, and throws the bowl in the bin. She leaves the bottle where it is.

Far off through the townland's winter silence she can hear the river, endless and relentless. Its silt smells rich and cold at the back of her nostrils. She thinks of men dragging the water, and of the hordes of souls who would come up, howling, on the dragging hooks.

18

When Cal lets Rip out again at dawn, Mart is in his yard tinkering with something, his blue beanie a bright spot against the grey day. He raises a hand to Cal, but doesn't come over. The night brought him nothing either.

Cal is having concerns about women. When Rachel needed help, she turned to women: Sheila, Lena. She might have turned to others, and told them more. Ardnakelty tends to segregate its socialising along gender lines; Cal is on terms of amicable small talk with most of the women, but no closer than that to any of them, with the exceptions of Noreen and sort of Sheila Reddy. When it comes to Rachel's friends, he doesn't even know who they are; he hasn't differentiated the small flock of leggy, fast-talking girls who zip back and forth between Ardnakelty and courses or jobs in Athlone, Galway, Limerick. He can't picture one of them turning up on his doorstep, or on Mart's, with something she's been afraid to share. His plan made no provision for them.

Angela Maguire is probably their best hope. Angela and Senan, together since schooldays, are known as a solid couple who stand united on anything important; Angela is on good terms with most people, and has the wry, generous common sense required to put up with Senan for thirty-some years. A woman might go to her.

Or a woman might go to Lena, if she had knowledge that Lena was being dragged into this unfairly. Cal has no idea what

Lena would do with that. He's had her in his arms hundreds of times, but now he's not sure he ever touched her. He calls Rip back in and heads for bed.

Clodagh Moynihan comes through for him late that morning. Cal has caught a few hours of actual sleep, and is trying to wake himself up with too much coffee, when his phone beeps. It's Trey.

Eugene gone out their back gate turned left onto lane past nance maguires. Could go straight towards kilhone road or turn off to river

Another beep: *Wearing poncy black coat. Cant follow him not enough cover*

On my way, Cal texts back. *Good work both of you. Go to school.*

He throws on his jacket without waiting for the beep of the eyeroll emoji. 'Come on,' he says to Rip, who's already bounding for the door.

There are guys who would be haunting the riverbank, but Eugene isn't one of them. Eugene is irritated by things that have the audacity to upset him; he won't seek them out. Cal heads for the Kilhone road, driving too fast.

The back lane Trey is talking about is a long one, twisting between fields, and not much used except by the odd farmer moving stock or equipment. Eugene is looking for privacy, which is nice, because Cal is too. He leaves the Pajero on the shoulder at the entrance to the lane and starts walking towards Tommy's, with Rip happily investigating the hedgerows and marking his presence. The day is cold; branches drip leftover rain, and beneath them hoofprints have sunk deep into the waterlogged ground.

Cal is listening for the crunch of footsteps, so he hears Eugene coming a bend away. He calls Rip to heel with a finger-snap. Then he moves to the bend, very quietly. He waits in the shelter of the hedge for the crunching to come close before he steps out, face-to-face with Eugene.

Eugene stops dead, and Cal sees the flash of fear. The kid looks like shit. He's managing to keep his sharp shave in place, and he's probably not drunk right now, but his eyes, red and saggy, say he had a few last night. He looks like he hasn't been sleeping much.

'Morning,' Cal says.

'What do you want?' Eugene demands. He's going for his usual arrogant tone, but he glances around too fast. There's no one in sight. The hedges, still unclipped on this half-forgotten lane, are tall on both sides, ragged limbs reaching out over the road.

Cal says, 'I've got something I need you to hear.'

'Not interested,' Eugene says. He wheels around and heads for home at a smart pace.

Cal stays right by his side, in step. 'That's fine,' he says. 'I don't need you to be interested. All I need you to do is listen.'

Eugene speeds up, but Cal has five or six inches on him and keeps the pace without effort. Rip, understanding that this has stopped being an ordinary walk, sticks close at heel and puts on his attack-dog hunch, ready to eat Eugene for lunch if Cal gives the word. 'Do I have to call the Guards?' Eugene snaps.

'Son,' Cal says, 'we can do this the stupid way if you want. I can tackle your ass and hold you down while I tell you what I've got to say; I got nothing to lose. Or you can quit scurrying down this road like a scared bunny rabbit, stand still like a grown-up, and listen, and we can both go home with our clothes clean.'

That pricks Eugene's pride. He stops and whips around to face Cal, taking a step back so he won't have to look up too obviously, just like Daddy does. 'All right. Get it over with. You've got five minutes.'

Cal isn't aiming to antagonise Eugene more than necessary, which probably rules out giving the little shit a good spanking. 'Sit,' he tells Rip, who sits promptly and dedicates himself to staring Eugene into submission. To Eugene he says: 'You remember that talk we had, back at Rachel's funeral?'

Eugene shrugs. 'Not really. You weren't exactly top of my priority list.'

'Well, you were high up on mine, son,' Cal says. 'I remember every word.'

'Good for you. So?'

'So,' Cal says, 'for instance, I remember you telling me that the night Rachel died, you were home with your parents all evening, till you got the call that she was missing.'

'For fuck's sake,' Eugene snaps. 'I'm not going back over that night.'

'Just bear with me a minute, son,' Cal says. He's staying good and leisurely; Eugene doesn't get to set the pace here. 'That's what you told me. Right?'

'Are you *interrogating* me?'

'Just getting things straight,' Cal says mildly. 'You got some problem with that question?'

Eugene takes a breath through his nose, keeping his patience. 'No, I don't have a problem. Yes, that's what I said. Yes, that's where I was. OK?'

'That's where you were,' Cal says. 'That's not where your daddy was.'

He catches the quick spark of wariness, but Eugene fields that one easily. He raises his eyes to heaven. 'Oh, for God's sake. Don't even try that. We were home.'

'Eugene,' Cal says. 'I've got four witnesses that saw your daddy out and about that night.'

'*Witnesses?*' Eugene asks, eyebrows up, doing Cal's accent badly. 'Um, this isn't court? You're not a cop here?'

'People,' Cal amends, agreeably. 'You'll have to excuse my language; old habits die hard. Four people saw your daddy that night. A little before nine-thirty. That ring any bells?'

Eugene snorts. 'Yeah, of course they did. Look: some people around here have some weird obsession with my father, in case you haven't noticed. He's successful, they can't handle that, they decide he needs putting back in his place or something – I don't know what's going on there, I'm not a psychologist, and I don't care. You're new around here, you don't get it, but you should know better than to fall for that shit. You could probably find four *witnesses* who'd claim they saw him shoot JFK.'

'Nope,' Cal says. 'These aren't people who've got anything against your daddy. They don't give a rat's ass about him one way or the other.'

'Right. Who are we talking about, exactly?'

'Come on, son,' Cal says, amused. 'I don't think so.'

'Well, *if* they exist, I guarantee you they have an opinion about us. Everyone around here does. That's not arrogance, it's just a fact.'

'Not these people,' Cal says. 'Their only opinion is, they saw him. And if the Guards do end up getting involved in this situation, one way or another, it's gonna look pretty strange. Not that your daddy was out and about, but that he made such a big deal about keeping it under wraps. Why would you lie your ass off about it, if he's got nothing to hide?'

Eugene sighs noisily, up at the sky, and re-evaluates. 'No one's keeping anything under *wraps*,' he says. 'Jesus. Not everyone lives at your level of drama. My father has no problem telling the Guards anything they want to know, but he doesn't have any duty to give a bunch of bored housewives something to gossip about. Is that OK with you?'

'Meaning he went out that night,' Cal says. 'You know where he was headed?'

Eugene gives him a cold stare. 'Is that your business?'

'You're misunderstanding me, son,' Cal says. 'I'm not asking you to tell me where he went. I'm asking whether you know.'

'Why would I? Even *if* he went out, we're all adults; we don't keep tabs on each other.'

Eugene isn't as bright as he thinks, but he's no dummy; he's leaving the slate blank for Tommy to fill in whatever story he picks. 'Lemme guess,' Cal says. 'He said he was just going out for a walk. Or maybe he'd dropped something earlier on, his glove or his keys or whatnot, and he wanted to go find it before it got rained on. Something that nobody would be able to contradict, if any questions got asked down the line. Am I close?'

'Like I said. He doesn't need an excuse note.'

Cal says, 'You want to know where he went?'

Eugene whips out the cold stare again. 'Not particularly.'

'Just before nine-thirty that night,' Cal says, 'your daddy was heading down Casey's boreen towards the old bridge.'

He's watching very carefully to see whether this is news to Eugene. It is. Just for a second, Eugene freezes straight through, wide-eyed with shock, like a little kid who got slapped right across the face.

Then he says, 'That's *bullshit*.' His voice is rising; the second of horror has left him furious. 'I know you're going around saying – which is slander, by the way, and we're considering taking legal advice – you're saying my father did something to Rachel. If you actually had *witnesses*, you'd have gone straight to the Guards. You've got *nothing*.'

'I've been here longer than you think, son,' Cal says. 'And I learn fast. I don't take stuff like this to the Guards any more.'

'Then what the actual fuck are you trying to accomplish here? Is this you trying to *blackmail* us? Or are you hoping I'll, what, break down in tears and confess to—'

Eugene has forgotten all about the height difference and is right up in Cal's face. Rip is starting a growl; Cal lifts a hand to keep him in place. He says, 'I'm telling you this because you think the same thing I do. You think your daddy did something to Rachel.'

'*No I fucking don't.* Who do you think you—'

'Yeah you do. You told me straight out, back in the hotel. You let Rachel in on your daddy's plan, she didn't like it, you said if he just waited she'd come around, but he wouldn't wait. That's what you told me.'

'No. I didn't. I was probably talking all kinds of shite that day, *unsurprisingly*, with everything that was going on, and then you cornering me to *harass* me, but I never said any of that.' Hearing all these things he doesn't want to hear has sent Eugene into full fight mode. He's got a finger in Cal's face, and he's one step away from a chest-shove. 'Prove it. Go ahead, prove it.'

Cal doesn't budge. 'Eugene,' he says, unhurried and unfazed. 'You gotta remember, this is new territory to you, but it's not to me. I've seen plenty of people in your shoes. I know exactly how this plays out. You loved Rachel. You were all set to make a life with her. Right about now, you guys oughta be tasting wedding-cake samples together.'

That stops Eugene. His eyes flinch shut against it. 'Tell me something,' Cal says. 'You still carry the engagement ring around with you, just in case this was all a bad dream? You got it in your pocket right now?'

Eugene doesn't answer. All the lines of his face are drawn down by misery.

'Your daddy took all that away,' Cal says, 'sooner than just listen to you for once in his goddamn life.'

Eugene's eyes, bloodshot, open. He stares at Cal with no expression at all.

'That's not gonna stop eating at you,' Cal says. 'You're not the kind of limp-dick who can let that slide just because Daddy says so. Probably you think you are, 'cause you've been letting him boss you around your whole life' – Eugene tries to break in, but Cal spent half his night in the armchair working out this little speech, and he's not letting it go to waste – 'but you're a grown-ass man now, and he's gone way over the line. You're trying hard to be Daddy's good little boy, but take it from me: sooner or later, you're going to snap and do something. Hell, you've already thought about it. I get that right?'

Eugene, breathing hard through his nose, presses his lips tight. 'I figured,' Cal says. 'I told you, son, I know how this story goes. But I've got more news for you: you won't do it. You're not a killer. And you're not a suicide, either. What you'll do is cut and run. You'll have a big blow-up with your daddy, maybe throw a few punches, tell him to shove his council election up his ass, and then you'll flounce off and find yourself a job in London or somewhere.'

That hits home. Eugene's eyes flicker away. 'And your daddy'll pick out someone better-behaved to be his little bitch on the council,' Cal says, 'and he'll keep right on going with his big plan. You and Rachel both: thrown away like you never existed.'

Eugene is working hard to look like this whole conversation is beneath his notice, but he doesn't have enough left in him to pull it off. 'So,' Cal says, 'I'm gonna give you another option.'

That gets a hard little snort. 'Oh, wow. Aren't you amazing.'

'You know something, Eugene,' Cal says. 'Something beyond what you already told me.'

Eugene says, 'There's nothing to know.' All his muscles are so tight that he can barely get the words out.

'Yeah there is. Something your daddy said, or did. You weren't sure till today, but there was something that had you worrying from the get-go. What was it?'

After a moment Eugene says, without looking at him, 'And then what? If there was something. You go to the Guards?'

Cal says, 'Is that what you want me to do?'

Eugene makes an angry twitch, halfway between a shrug and a spasm. Cal understands why it isn't a simple question. All his life, Eugene has been defined by his standing within this place. He's been raised despising its people as dumbass yokels; probably this is the first time it's ever occurred to him that he needs them, not just for practical purposes, but for everything he is, inside and out. Without their esteem, he's an office drone in a big city where the name Moynihan means nothing to anyone. If Tommy gets deposed, by the law or by the townland, then Eugene dissolves, just more mist over the fields.

'I won't know the answer till I hear what you've got to tell me,' Cal says. 'But I guarantee you I'll do something. I can't promise your daddy'll get what's coming to him, but I can promise he won't get away with this scot-free.'

For a second, Eugene could go either way. All the massive weight of grief and of years' pent-up rebellion is surging against his walls like floodwater against a dam; Cal, watching his face, sees its force buckling him from inside. When he catches his breath like it hurts, Cal thinks he's going.

The Moynihans build their dams heavy and thick. In the end, Eugene reverts to what he knows how to do. He sticks his chin up and manages to give Cal the look of disgusted disbelief that Tommy Moynihan's son and heir is supposed to give to some uppity blow-in who doesn't know his place.

'You've got some fucking nerve,' he says. 'That or you've lost your fucking mind. If you come anywhere near us again, I'm calling the Guards.'

'You do that, son,' Cal says. Unlike Eugene, he's under no illusion that this is the end of the conversation. That weight isn't going anywhere, and the cracks are only going to keep growing. He just hopes Eugene's dam breaks before everything else around here does. 'I said what I've got to say. If you change your mind, you know where to find me. Meanwhile, you go home and ask your daddy why he was heading for the bridge that night. See what he says.'

Before he's finished talking, Eugene whips around and strides off. Cal stands at the bend and watches him try to keep up an outraged dignity while dodging puddles, till another twist in the lane takes him out of sight behind the ragged hedges.

Cal's phone beeps. Trey: *Whatd he say*

She and Kate are still hanging out on the ridge behind Nance Maguire's, watching Eugene flounce home. Cal texts back, *Nothing good yet but we're close. Any chance you guys can keep an eye on that house tonight? Let me know if anyone goes anywhere?*

Dont know bout that its a school night we should be in bed

Yeah right, Cal texts back. *Thanks.* Trey sends him a thumbs-up emoji.

Rip shoves his nose into Cal's hand, looking for some appreciation of his restraint in not eating Eugene. 'Good boy,' Cal says.

Around lunchtime it starts raining hard. Lena has called in sick to work. She sits at the kitchen table, feeling the cold numb her hands and listening to the rain striking her house on all sides. She thinks of Sean; how this weather, waterlogging the fields to uselessness, would have sent him half-wild with fear, and how she would have worked day and night to draw him out of it. She tried everything she had to keep him with her, and never understood till now why none of it made a blind bit of difference.

The dogs are restless, from lack of exercise and from her strangeness. Nellie tries to play with Daisy, Daisy skulks away into corners and finally gives Nellie a nip, Nellie yelps extravagantly and looks to Lena for redress. 'No,' Lena says, to both of them. She should give them to Cal or to Trey, but she needs them here. They'll have to take whatever comes, alongside her.

The dogs hear it coming first, and lift their heads, their

fractiousness instantly forgotten. It takes a moment before Lena catches, through the relentless battering rain, the swish of a car turning in at the gate. She knows it's Breege, come back to get her, one way or the other.

The second car brings the dogs to their feet. 'Sit,' Lena says, but they don't hear her, or maybe she didn't say it. They strain towards the door. The third car sets off a low moan deep in their throats.

Lena stands up and, through the rush of lightheadedness, goes to the sitting room and finds Sean's shotgun. She can't tell what she's going to do with it. The rain roars all around her like the river in flood, but the crunch of footsteps and the jumble of voices in her front yard rise up through it, coming for her. The dogs keep up their tense, warning moans.

She stands at the end of the hall, watching the front door. The hall looks strange, too long and too dim; the door is tiny, wavering a million miles away. The gun in her hands is the one solid thing.

The banging on the door, when it starts, doesn't make her jump. She hopes if she closes her eyes and lets herself fall, the roaring water will sweep her away before they can get her.

A woman's voice, with a laugh breaking through, shouts, 'Jesus, Lena, would you ever let us in, we're drowning here!'

Lena is dizzy. She bends over till her eyes clear. Then she puts the shotgun back under the sofa and goes to the door.

It's Sheila Reddy and Yvonne McCabe and Julie Quinn, all of them crowded onto Lena's step to shelter from the rain. 'About feckin' time,' Yvonne says, and then they're in the hall, shaking the rain off their jackets and wiping their faces and making a fuss over Nellie, who's practically bending herself in half with joy at all the attention. 'Why's this on your step?' Yvonne asks, waving the antifreeze bottle at Lena.

'Someone left it there,' Lena says. She can't see them straight, through all the movement and the noise. She's not sure they're really there.

'Ah, for fuck's sake,' Yvonne says, indignant. 'Who was it?'

'I didn't see,' Lena says. 'It was dark.' Someone shoves something into her hands. It's a bottle, a different one, not antifreeze. She doesn't understand what's going on.

'Dirty little gurriers,' Yvonne says disapprovingly. She heads into Lena's kitchen, dumps the antifreeze bottle in the bin, and dusts the whole business off her hands.

'I'm frozen,' Sheila says. 'Here.' She thrusts something else at Lena and follows Yvonne. 'I knew themens would bring booze, so I brought that instead.'

'You're making us sound like a pair of alcos,' Julie protests.

'If the shoe fits, girl—'

'I'm not even *drinking*, I've to drive ye all home, I only brought it for the rest of—'

'You did, yeah, o' course you—'

'Did anyone remember tonic?'

Lena looks down at the things in her hands. She's holding a bottle of gin and a plate with a clingfilmed cake on it. 'Where d'you keep your glasses?' Yvonne calls from the kitchen.

Lena goes after them. Julie is piling wet coats on a chair and giving out about her feet being cold, Sheila is reaching down glasses from a cupboard, Yvonne is pulling more bottles out of a shopping bag and saying something about ice, everyone is moving and talking and Nellie is prancing between the lot of them with a tug-of-war toy, looking for takers. Someone has switched on the lights.

Lena says, 'What are you doing here?' She doesn't have the thoughts to put it better.

'Sure, you called round to us,' Julie says. She whisks a couple of leftover mugs off the table and dumps them in the sink. 'With the jam. It's our turn.'

'I hadn't seen you in forever,' Yvonne adds. 'If we left it any longer, you'd only feckin' vanish again.' She waves her bottles. 'Look, I've tonic *and* Coke. And vodka. We're sorted. I'm not sure these exactly go with cake, but like Charlie Sheen says, fuck it, let's do it all.'

Lena looks at Sheila. 'Trey said you were in shite form,' Sheila says. 'And I oughta call round. I brought these two while I was at it.'

Lena says, '*Trey?*'

'I know, yeah. She never gave a toss about anyone being in bad form before. You oughta be honoured.'

Faintly, through everything else, Lena feels the prick of anger. She's no one's charity case, to be coaxed out of her bad mood with cake and sympathy. 'There's nothing wrong with me,' she says.

'Well, tough shite,' Yvonne says, plunking the bottles on the table, 'we're here now, and I'm not going out in that rain again without a drink inside me. D'you want gin or vodka?'

'I'll have tea,' Julie says. 'Or I can just have Coke, if you're not boiling the—'

'Ah, Jesus, have the one,' Yvonne says. 'You can't be sitting there with a cuppa tea while we're—'

'No,' Sheila says. 'We're going to be pulled over, leaving.'

There's a beat of silence. Yvonne nods, acknowledging that.

Lena starts to understand what this is. It's not a charitable intervention; it's an act of alliance and defiance, carefully thought through. These women know what Tommy Moynihan is aiming at her. They drove here separately so they can leave two of their cars in her front yard to tell his watchers: *You thought Lena Dunne was easy prey, the lone animal cut off from the herd, to be taken down at your convenience. Let's see you come for her now.*

She says, 'Tommy'll go after you.'

Yvonne flaps a hand and makes a *pfft* noise. 'I'd say I'm in his bad books anyhow. Mark was out with that crowd making a ruckus around Moynihans' the other night. He had a scarf pulled up over his face, but d'you know what he was wearing, the feckin' eejit? That red puffy jacket he got in Canada. No one else has a jacket like that. We're on Tommy's shit list, right enough, but so's half this townland; it'll take him a while to get to us.'

'I already was,' Sheila says. She's found a knife for the cake. 'And you said you'd back me, if I needed it.'

'Yeah,' Lena says. 'I would.'

'I was worried,' Julie confesses. 'Just at first, like.'

'She's always worried,' Yvonne says, conquering the stiff cap of the vodka bottle. 'Nothing personal.'

'But then I thought,' Julie says, giving Yvonne a smack on the arm for that, 'he can't do anything to the kids. They're outa the country. We all act like Tommy's the king of the world, but no one in Berlin or Birmingham ever even heard of the man. So if I don't wanta do what he says, I don't haveta.' She looks happily surprised at herself.

'And Clodagh ratted me out in the exams in fifth year, when I'd the dates written on my leg,' Yvonne says. 'What I'm saying is, basically, fuck the Moynihans. Have you got any ice?'

'Right,' Lena says. 'OK. Fair enough.' She puts the bottle and the cake on the table, and goes to the freezer. 'I'll have a G and T.'

She rummages for ice and tries to clear her head; it's smeared and rocking, like she's either dreaming or just waking up and she can't tell which. The room where she was sitting five minutes ago has evaporated. Julie is filling the kettle and complimenting its colour, Yvonne is explaining to Nellie why she can't have any vodka no matter how much she begs; even Sheila, who was made of iron-weighted silence for decades after she married Johnny Reddy, is telling everyone that her Maeve made the cake, so if they don't like it they can keep that to themselves.

Lena says, 'Is this place freezing?'

'Just a teeny bit subzero, yeah,' Yvonne says. 'Few icicles forming here and there. D'you get the hot flushes? Mel keeps her place bleedin' Baltic 'cause of those, I wear three jumpers if I'm calling over to her.'

'I'll light the stove,' Lena says, handing her the ice cube tray. By the time she gets back to the table, Yvonne has the drinks ready, Sheila is slicing cake, and everyone's found a chair. Someone has brought paper plates and napkins left over from Halloween, with carnivorous-looking pumpkins on them. Nellie is sprawled under the table, to gnaw her toy in the centre of the action.

'Chocolate and orange,' Sheila says, pushing a plate towards Lena. 'Maeve's baking all the time now. She was never interested in anything before, only Snapchat and make-up, so I've to eat my head off. Just to encourage her, like.'

'That's great and all,' Yvonne says, 'and I'll help encourage her any time, but this is a war council here. We'll get to the kids later.' To Lena: 'You know what Tommy's spreading around, yeah?'

'More or less,' Lena says. She takes a big drink of gin and tonic, and feels it hit her right between the eyes. 'He sent a Guard over here, to see could she put me in a mental hospital or arrest me for killing Rachel. So I got the gist of it, like.'

Julie, pouring milk into her tea, gasps and spills it. 'The cheeky *fuck*,' Yvonne says, her glass coming down hard.

'Tommy's a fool,' Sheila says, taking a big slice of cake for herself. 'You couldn'ta killed Rachel. You were over at mine that evening.'

Lena looks at her. Sheila cocks an eyebrow and gives her a grin.

'I was there as well,' Julie says, mopping up milk with her napkin. 'We'd a lovely night. It was great to catch up.'

'I couldn't make it,' Yvonne says, through cake, ''cause the kids know I was home all night, except when I went to pick up Sophie. But Julie told me all about it the next day. I'm raging I missed it. I love a bit of do-you-remember.'

Lena is so startled she can't talk. She never in a million years expected this.

'Not just do-you-remember,' Sheila says. 'Rachel'd called over to me earlier, all in bits about how Eugene was treating her. So I was asking ye should I do anything about that.'

'We won't use that bit at first,' Yvonne says. 'Keep that in the back pocket, whip it out if we need it.'

Lena manages to bring her mind to bear on this. She doubts it will hold up if the Guards do any real digging, but that doesn't seem to matter. The danger may not be gone, but it's been transformed beyond recognition. It was a dark sediment thickening at her windows, seeping into the air she breathed, targeted and unstoppable. Now it's a solid shared annoyance, something large and smelly plopped down on the table for them to work on together.

'Thanks,' she says, looking around at their faces. 'That's great. Thanks.'

'It doesn't even matter whether we can prove it,' Yvonne says. 'All we haveta do is say it to the world, and make sure they feel like eejits for believing all that soap-opera crap, and then everyone'll shut the fuck up about you. And I seriously doubt Tommy'll be arsed going any further with the Guard shite, if he knows no one's falling for his bolloxology.' She raises her glass to them all and takes a neat sip, closing the door on that. 'Which would be lovely,' she says. 'For you, obviously, but for everyone else as well. Didja hear about the fight in Seán's?'

'I haven't heard much about anything,' Lena says, 'this last week or two.' The cake tastes more vivid than normal, like cake used to taste when she was a little kid. She can feel the sugar speeding through her blood. She's not sure when she last ate.

'Oh, Jesus,' Julie says. 'You've a load to catch up on. I shoulda brought another bottle.'

'So Mart Lavin,' Yvonne says, propping her bosom on the table to lean over it and wave her fork at Lena. 'D'you know what he done? You're not going to believe this.'

'I think he's gone mental,' Julie says. 'Honest to God.'

'Mart Lavin's not mental,' Sheila says, and Lena hears the echo of that old iron silence under her voice. Sheila has no love for Mart. 'That fella knows what he's at.'

'Saturday afternoon, right,' Yvonne says. 'The pub's packed. No one's feeling the friendliest, we'll put it that way. And Mart turns round and tells the whole place, at the top of his lungs, that Tommy Moynihan kilt Rachel 'cause she tried to stop him taking people's land.'

'Right,' Lena says, eyebrows up. 'Didn't see that coming.' She knows as well as Sheila how Mart Lavin works: slantways, coded, everything concealed behind layers of mazes and elaborate false doors. This doesn't sound like his style at all. Like Sheila, though, Lena also knows that Mart always has a plan.

'See?' Julie says. 'It's been too much for him. I'm not surprised.'

'So Bernard McHugh starts doing his voice-of-reason bit,' Yvonne says, 'only Mart and your Cal and all those lads tell him to get fucked. And then Mouth McHugh—'

'He's disgusting,' Julie says. 'He put his willy on Mattie Carroll's neck when we were like ten, remember?'

'He doesn't do that these days,' Yvonne says, 'as far as I know. But he brought out the rumours about you' – Lena – 'and your Cal hit him, and that's when it all kicked off. Sharks versus Jets, murder on the dance floor, please don't shoot at the piano player. Half the fellas in this townland have black eyes on them.'

This time the anger reaches Lena more clearly. She doesn't want Cal using her as a reason to throw himself deeper into this place's dealings.

'And now,' Yvonne says, 'there's people saying Tommy done it, and people saying you done it, and people saying Rachel done it herself, and people who just wanta forget the whole thing and "move on", God bless their little hearts—'

'That's Mel,' Julie tells Lena. 'That's why she's not here.'

'—and every lot is going apeshit at all the other lots,' Yvonne says, 'and it's all gone to shite. So if we can dial everyone down a wee bit, chill pills all round, that'd be our good deed done for the day.'

Lena has no desire to do any good deeds for this place. 'Right,' she says. 'And then what?'

'Not sure about that part yet,' Yvonne says. 'I'm living life in the moment right now, if you know what I mean. But at least that oughta make people pull their heads in a bit while they think twice about believing every word outa Tommy Moynihan's mouth, and we'll have a better shot at making it through the week without anyone else ending up dead. Speaking of which, do you reckon Tommy actually did something on Rachel? Or do you reckon Mart's only saying that to stir people up against him?'

'I think he did,' Lena says. Probably she shouldn't say it, but she doesn't care. 'Yeah.'

There's a brief silence. Yvonne takes a breath and nods. 'God,' Julie says softly. 'Tommy Moynihan, like. Of all people.'

'Makes sense, actually,' Yvonne says, 'if I'm honest. Tommy's always got what he wanted, and all of a sudden there was Rachel getting in his way. He'da been a lot more pissed off about it than you or me or anyone that's used to the idea.'

'I wouldn't say he kilt her,' Sheila says.

Lena turns sharply to look at her. Sheila knows, better than any of them, how killing can come up on someone out of the blue. Lena thought she was the one who would have the easiest time taking this on board.

'Why not?' she asks.

Sheila looks back at her out of tranquil blue eyes. 'He might as well take the blame anyhow,' she says. ''Twas his doing, one way or another.'

'Is that why you were asking around about Rachel?' Yvonne says to Lena.

'No,' Lena says. 'Back then, I thought she done it herself.'

'Then what? Don't be telling me you were just nosy, 'cause I won't believe you.'

Lena takes herself aback by realising that she wants to explain. It's not just the gin and the sugar spinning her off balance; it's the way things have transformed, her kitchen glowing sweet and safe as a storybook picture, the warmth and the brightness and the talk melting her from the inside out. If Tommy's minions are heading this way for an attack, they'll take one look at the drive full of sturdy, mud-splattered cars and back the fuck off. Yvonne's snub nose and Julie's wet tendrils of hair have a beauty that could break her heart.

'It was 'cause of Trey,' she says. 'Right from the start, she thought someone kilt Rachel. But she was there taking for granted that that made no difference to anyone. Whatever story suited this place best, we'd all just haveta bite our tongues and go along with it, no questions asked; no choice. Trey wants to live here. I couldn't let her go the rest of her life thinking like that.'

She's watching Sheila for any sign that this is overstepping, but Sheila is just listening, chewing on an ice cube. 'I didn't even think there was anything much to find out,' Lena says. 'I just wanted to find it, whatever it was, and tell the world. To show her she doesn't always haveta bow down to what this place wants.'

She's almost afraid to look at Yvonne and Julie, in case now they think she's mental, but both of them are nodding too, unsurprised. 'They're a right pain in the hoop all the same, aren't they?' Yvonne says. 'Kids. All this shite that you'd never do for yourself, not in a million years, 'cause it's too hard or too dangerous or . . . But there's the bloody kids, needing it done. And away you go.'

'When mine said they were leaving,' Julie says, glancing around like she's confessing something terrible, 'I was glad. I mean I wasn't, I was in bits, I still bawl my eyes out, but a part of me was only delighted they'd be starting out fresh, somewhere they knew no one. None a this.'

'I wish Trey hadda wanted to leave,' Lena says. 'I wouldn't be in this mess.'

'That one never bowed down to anyone unless she wanted to,' Sheila says, fishing another ice cube out of her glass. 'She's getting the hang of this place, is what she's doing; learning how to work it. She'll be grand.'

'*No*,' Lena says. 'God. The last thing I ever wanted was her getting the hang of this place.'

'That's you,' Sheila says. 'You go on and live here your way. She hasta do it hers.'

They look at each other. Lena thinks of everything she did to get here, all the jam and the careful questions and the funeral and Mrs Duggan and facing down Tommy Moynihan. She can't tell any more how much of it was ever for Trey's sake.

They sit silent for a little, drinking their drinks. The room has warmed. Julie catches Yvonne's eye, and a little wry smile passes between them as they remember something together; Sheila cuts Lena more cake. The wind blows long, steady gusts of rain against the windowpanes.

'Fair play to you,' Julie says to Lena, in the end.

'Not really,' Lena says. 'Look where it got me. And I never even did what I was after.'

'Yeah, about that,' Yvonne says. 'I've a favour to ask you.'

'Go on,' Lena says. A part of her feels like she should be wary, but she can't find it in herself.

'OK,' Yvonne says. She blows out a quick breath and takes a sip of her drink to brace herself for this. 'The night Rachel died, yeah? Like I said, I'd to pick Sophie up from her pal's that evening – she passed her driving test, did I tell ye?' Yvonne adds parenthetically, 'but I didn't want her driving in the dark, in that weather. So I was going through the village, around seven, maybe a bit after. And Rachel was there. Knocking on Noreen's door.'

Julie's mouth is open in surprise; she didn't know this story either. 'I reckoned she was calling in to Noreen's Ella,' Yvonne says, 'or else Claire had sent her to drop something round, 'cause she was holding something, like a box or something. And I thought they shoulda texted first to check, 'cause I knew Noreen and Dessie and the kids were after going into town to the cinema, so there'd be no one home only Mrs Duggan, and she doesn't answer the door. But I didn't really think about it, d'you know the way? All I thought was Rachel was after going out in the rain for nothing and she hadn't even brought the car, and I couldn't give her a lift home 'cause I was going the other way.'

'You never said that to me,' Julie says.

'I know, yeah. I never said it to anyone, 'cause afterwards I thought I musta got it wrong. 'Cause when Noreen rang me later, right, to say Rachel was missing, I said to her, "Wasn't she at yours? I saw her outside your door earlier." And Noreen said no, sure Rachel knew from Ella that they were going to the cinema, and anyhow, Mrs Duggan woulda said if she'd come to the door. So I thought it musta been someone else. Sure, the girls all have the same hair these days, and half of them have that same jacket; it coulda been anyone. Maybe I shoulda said it anyhow, but . . .' Yvonne glances around the table, troubled.

'God, no,' Julie tells her. 'You were right. Sure, it's not like you were talking to her and she said something that coulda been important. All you'da done is start a loada rumours and send everyone off down the wrong track.'

'I'da done the same as you,' Sheila says.

Yvonne nods, but she's looking down into her glass, not comforted. 'I wish I'da given her that lift,' she says quietly. 'I was running late, so I didn't even think . . . It wouldn'ta done Sophie any harm to wait a few extra minutes.'

'How were you supposed to know?' Julie demands, leaning across the table to squeeze Yvonne's arm. 'And sure, it probably wasn't even her.'

Yvonne shakes her head. 'No, it was her. I couldn't swear to it in court or anything, but I'm sure in my own head.'

It was Rachel; and Lena, who knows how Rachel was spending her evening, knows what she was doing there. She didn't miss Ella, or Noreen. She deliberately waited till she knew they weren't home, and left her car behind so no one would see it outside the door. When neither Lena nor Sheila gave her what she needed, Rachel went to see Mrs Duggan, looking for something that would stop the Moynihans, and then she died.

'Only now,' Yvonne says to Lena, 'if your Cal thinks Tommy done something . . . He was a detective, sure; he'd see clues where we wouldn't notice them. It could mean something to him, Rachel being there.'

'Yeah,' Lena says. 'It could, I suppose.' Cal would find some use for that, all right, or Mart Lavin would once Cal turned it over to him. Deep down, Mart is no different from Tommy, doing whatever it takes to get his way, using anything or anyone he can get his hands on.

'I don't know him well enough to turn up on his doorstep – I've barely even talked to him, only "God, it's awful rainy, isn't it?" down in Noreen's. He wouldn't know whether I'm reliable or whether I'm Doireann Cunniffe, like, making up bollocks to be important. Would you say it to him?'

Out of nowhere, Lena finds her hands shaking with rage. 'The girl's dead,' she says. 'Can no one even leave her that? She was meant to have a whole life, and that's been taken off her. Her death is all she's got left. And here's Tommy Moynihan trying to rob it off her to use for his land deals, and Mart Lavin wanting it for himself so he can scupper Tommy's plans. And I was as bad, wanting it to use for Trey.'

Yvonne's eyebrows are up in surprise; Julie's face is puckered with unhappy bewilderment. Lena can't tell if she's making sense, or if the gin's taken over, or if Tommy has got to her and her mind is gone. She's seeing the bodies, leathered and twisted by thousands of years, that turf-cutters find in the bog a few times a century. They come up hands tied, hearts stabbed, heads split, ropes or willow rods still round their necks from when their deaths were offered in exchange for a good harvest, an end to plague, victory in battle, some communal need long forgotten and gone. Since before history started, this place has never changed.

'I'm saying nothing about Rachel to anyone,' she says. 'I'm leaving her be.' If any of them hint that she owes them a hand, that she's being ungrateful, she'll throw them all out of her house and take her chances with Tommy and Breege and the shotgun.

'Right,' Yvonne says, after a second. Her eyebrows are still up. 'If I'da known it was this big a deal, I wouldn't've asked.' She takes a sip of her drink.

'If Tommy Moynihan kilt me,' Julie says tentatively, 'I'd love if someone used that to get him.'

'That's you,' Lena says. 'It wouldn't be me. And it mightn't be Rachel. I've no way of knowing. None of us do.'

'Being blunt about it,' Yvonne says, 'it's not like you can do her any damage either way.'

The wall of incomprehension on her face and on Julie's makes Lena's anger rise higher. She looks to Sheila for backup. If anyone should be on her side here, it's Sheila.

'When Johnny needed stopping,' Sheila says, 'I done it. A child woulda sat there saying she wouldn't do it 'cause it'd upset her feelings. Or a man, maybe. We're grown women.'

'*No*,' Lena says. 'That's not the same. Johnny was your man. Tommy Moynihan isn't my problem. You said you'd never lift a finger, remember? You said themens could look after themselves.'

'I did, yeah,' Sheila agrees. 'Only then Tommy went after you, and Trey started going on at me, and look at me now.'

'I never fuckin' asked for any of this,' Lena says. Her voice is rising. 'All I ever wanted was to be left to mind my own fuckin' business.'

Sheila shrugs. 'I know, yeah. You're here now, but.'

Lena comes up against that hard enough to jolt her right out of her anger. She stares at Sheila. Sheila looks back, eating cake, her blue eyes untroubled.

Lena feels like the room has gathered itself together, given itself a shake, and thumped into solidity. This isn't a fairy-tale haven. The warm glow of it is real, and so is everything else it carries, the ties and the weights. No one dragged her here. By whatever strange knotted route, this is where she's come to.

'Right,' she says, after a minute. 'Right; fair enough. I'll tell Cal.'

Things are rearranging themselves in ways that are going to take her a while to absorb. This should feel like defeat, but it doesn't. It only feels like a change, as matter-of-fact as the changes in the season or in her own body. She thinks she might be starting to understand, only a small bit, how Trey can live here.

'Great,' Yvonne says briskly. 'Thanks. It's probably nothing, anyhow, but just in case.' She reaches for the gin bottle to top up Lena's glass. 'And while we're here,' she says, 'we've a ton of catching up to do. Noah has my fuckin' head melted, and if I don't get it off my chest I'll have a stroke or an aneurysm or something, so ye can listen whether ye like it or not.'

'Oh Jesus,' Julie says, her face scrunching up in sympathy. 'Did he get another detention?'

'They're not human beings at that age,' Yvonne says. 'Honest to God, they're not. They're bloody – baboons or something. The school rings me up, right, and says they caught him sniffing glue—' Julie claps a hand to her mouth. 'No, hang on. So I'm practically having a panic attack, I'm picturing him expelled, brain damage, rehab, the lot. Only then I say, stupid question but I'm freaking out enough that I don't even know what's coming outa my mouth, I say, "What kinda glue?" And the teacher says' – Yvonne shuts her eyes for a second before she can make herself come out with it – ' "Pritt stick." The little *gobshite* was picking bits off his glue stick and snorting them up his nose.'

All four of them burst out laughing. '*Why?*' Julie wants to know.

'Don't ask me. Maybe he heard about glue-sniffing and he wanted to look like a hard man for the other lads, or maybe he was just bored. Now he's not allowed have glue any more, he has to ask the teacher if he needs some, and they're all calling him Sticky.'

'He'll never shake that,' Sheila says. 'He'll be Sticky McCabe when he's eighty.'

'I know, yeah. You might even say he's stuck with it.'

'Speaking of kids,' Lena says to Sheila, through the laughter. 'The cake's gorgeous.'

Once the rain clears, Cal climbs over the wall to Mart's place. Mart is in his near field, replacing the ballcock on a water trough, observed by a clump of mildly interested sheep. 'Jean-Claude,' he says, raising his head to nod to Cal. 'I hear your car was loitering on the Kilhone road this morning. Tell us: did it go for a stroll all on its ownio, or didja have business there?'

Cal updates him. Mart doesn't stop working, but his eyebrows do go up once or twice.

'Wouldn't that warm your heart,' he says, when Cal's finished. 'The young one following in your footsteps, like a wee duckling.' He tightens the ballcock another fraction and considers it, head on one side. He's used what looks like a worn-out grinder disc for a washer. 'What's your guess?' he enquires. 'Will the bold Eugene hand over the goods?'

'Maybe,' Cal says, 'or maybe he'll go running to Daddy. Or both, if he runs to Daddy and doesn't like what he hears. Either way, we're gonna get some movement.'

Mart glances up and smiles at Cal. 'I'd say we'll get that, all right,' he agrees. 'Sure, isn't that what we were looking for? The aul' movement.'

'You got any thoughts on what kinda thing we should be watching out for?' Cal asks.

Mart examines his handiwork and gives the ballcock an experimental wiggle. 'D'you know what Senan reckons?' he says. 'He reckons that stylish hairdo of Tommy's is a toupee. Would you say he's right?'

'Can't say I ever had the urge to look that close,' Cal says. He gathers that he's not getting an answer.

'I'm not in favour of the notion,' Mart says. ''Twould be awful hard on the aul' self-esteem, to find out I spent all this time tiptoeing around some gowl with a dead hamster stuck to his head. I won't believe it unless I've proof. Could your Theresa put that next on her list to investigate?'

Before it gets dark, Cal bites the bullet, gets in his car, and drives over to Lena's. His reluctance doesn't matter any more:

he's poked the bear good and hard, and he has no way of guessing what Tommy might come up with in response. He's not sure what he's planning to do at Lena's – even if she opens the door to him, he can't imagine she'll agree to come over to the safety of his place – but at least she should have some warning about what they're dealing with, and the offer of company while they wait for it to come knocking.

It turns out Lena already has company. There are two extra cars in her front yard: Sheila Reddy's beat-up silver Hyundai, and a red seven-seater that Cal recognizes as Yvonne McCabe's.

Maybe Sheila and Yvonne are bringing Lena up to speed, or maybe they have some crucial piece of info to pass on, or maybe she just feels like shooting the breeze with them. Regardless, Cal is clearly surplus to requirements. He keeps driving, and hopes no one happened to be looking out the window to see him pass.

That night he does the same as the night before: leaves his living-room lamp on, and himself silhouetted in the window. This time he has his Henry rifle across his knees, out of view. Mart's lights are off tonight, but Cal knows he's not asleep.

He texts Lena: *Keep an eye out. If you have any problems let me know and I'll be right there.* It sounds stilted and wrong, like he's talking to someone he's never met, but it's the best he can do. He doesn't expect an answer, but after a few minutes Lena texts back: *Will do. Thanks.*

The night is still, with faint shifting patches of moonlight amid broken cloud. The cold reaching him through the glass has a new arrogance. The change is subtle, but Cal has been here long enough to read the place's shorthand: winter is coming in. Some morning soon, he'll open the door for Rip and find the fields white with frost. Outwintering cattle will breathe big, sweet-scented puffs of fog; farmers, wrapped up warm, will start their ploughing; Noreen will plaster the shop in an explosion of Santas and elves and tinsel. Later the ewes will be housed for early lambing, the winter wheat that lay dormant under the cold will unfurl its first green from the soil, and spring will rise all over again.

It's past two o'clock when Cal's phone beeps. Trey: *Someone left out the back. Not sure who secrity lights turned off but too tall for cloda. Heading other way on lane this time up towards village. Gonna try n follow*

Whoever it is, they're not aiming for Lena's, anyway. That lane weaves at its leisure among the fields behind the village and eventually comes out on Cal's road, right about opposite Mart's far field.

OK, Cal texts back. *Doesn't matter if you lose him. Just don't scare him off. Keep me updated.* He doesn't like any of this being in writing, but they can't exactly do it out loud. Sound carries for miles, on a night like this.

Mart answers his phone on the second ring. 'You'd better have news for me, Sunny Jim,' he says. 'You promised me movement, and I'm dying of boredom here. I've read the whole fuckin' internet, trying to keep myself occupied, and just to save you time, there's nothing on there only eejits having a go at other eejits. I had faith in them Moynihans to come up with something interesting, after your wee expedition today, but they're after letting me down something fierce.'

'I reckon they're coming through,' Cal says. 'Either Tommy or Eugene left their place a few minutes ago, headed our way on the back lane.'

'Well, glory be to God,' Mart says. 'That's an improvement. Fair play to him. Are you ready, Jean-Claude?'

'Yeah,' Cal says. 'You?'

'I was born ready,' Mart informs him. 'And I'll let PJ know the score; not that I think there's anything coming his way, but still. Catch you on the flip side, Sunny Jim.'

Cal waits in his armchair for twenty minutes before his

phone beeps again. *Defo Tommy. Had his phone light on we saw his face. Carrying sthing could be a gun. Couldnt stick close wo getting caught lost him but headed your way*

Tommy wouldn't do his own dirty work unless he was on the ropes. Eugene went to Daddy looking for answers, and wasn't happy about what he heard. The rage that was battering at Tommy's house the other night has broken through; it's inside his walls now.

Good work, Cal texts Trey. *I'll take it from here. You guys go home so you don't get in my way.*

He turns off his living-room lamp. Then he texts Mart: *Tommy. Maybe armed maybe not.* That part might as well be down in writing; it could come in useful someday, depending on where this night ends. Mart texts back a thumbs-up.

With all the lights off, the darkness outdoors slowly takes on form. The trees, branches bared for winter, spread like river tributaries against the sky. In the patchy moonlight the road has a pale cast; on its other side, the stone walls are veins of denser darkness against the fields, so faint that Cal can't tell whether he's actually seeing them or whether he knows them so well that his memory overlays them on the night.

Rip's head goes up. 'Stay,' Cal says.

Outside the window, nothing moves. He goes quietly to the back door, cracks it an inch, and puts his ear to the ribbon of cold air. His land is silent. Far off at Mart's place, Kojak is barking.

Cal texts Mart: *All OK?*

Bloody dog, Mart texts back. *Someone was headed this way. Now Id say hes after scaring them off.*

Cal texts: *They could come back.*

Not tonight. Have to start all over tomorrow. If I knew this was a full time job Id of turned it down.

Mart is likely right, but Cal stays in his chair anyway, in case Tommy takes advantage of that thinking. Trey texts him: *Story*

Nothing, Cal texts back. *Kojak scared him off.*
Nah. Watch that fucker
I am. Go to bed.

The night, silent and with no stars to mark time passing, goes on and on. Its scent of earth, leaf mould, and vast cold space seeps in at the cracks of the house. Cal thinks about all the smells that he used to take for granted, back in Chicago, and that vanished from his life overnight: traffic fumes and alleyway piss, lavish riots of spices curling out of restaurants, deep snow, damp coats steaming on the L train. So many things didn't occur to him, when he decided to move here.

When the sky finally starts to pale, he walks his land, keeping Rip to heel, looking for anything Tommy might have left behind, either accidentally or on purpose. The fields are still grey with dawn. Feeding rabbits scatter at their approach, and under the hazel trees a squirrel is hunting for any last nuts. Cal's boots swish steadily in the dew-wet grass. He thinks of how Mart said he should give his place a name, and wonders whether, if he did, it would go ignored and dissolve into nothing, or whether it would trace a trail through the maps of this townland's conversation, for however long Ardnakelty lasts.

Mart is out in his near field, checking that the repaired water trough is working. He's blurred to the ankles by the layer of mist over the grass, so that he looks like a ghost rising up out of the earth, summoned by some signal.

19

The dogs, after so long without a proper walk, are riotous with joy at being out. They bound like puppies, find sticks for tug-of-war, plunge into ditches and come out muddy and delighted. Lena takes the longest way, down every back lane and detour, not just for their sake but for her own. She feels like she's getting over a bad dose of the flu; her body has that unpractised, tentative quality that's not a frustration to her but a pleasure, as it claims back all its resurgent heft and strength. She's enjoying her muscles as much as the dogs are; she'd walk all day, if she didn't have business that needs doing. The rain, so light it hangs suspended in the air, has a full, nutty smell of turf and gorse.

The townland looks different, in ways she can't pin down. Part of this, she knows, is in her own eyes. The distance from which she's seeing this place has changed, whether she likes that or not; it's going to take a while for her focus to adapt to the altered perspective.

Part of it is real. Men and tractors are moving at a rhythm that's one beat too fast and grim; even people working side by side aren't talking. The place has its head down against itself, the dark fissures spreading through its soil.

Lena isn't headed for Cal's place, or not yet. She gave her word that she'd talk to him, and she'll do it, although she's not sure what she's going to say. He texted her early this morning – *All good?* – and she texted back: *Yeah all grand*, but no more than that. Her anger at him is still there, but it's changed too. Cal, like her, brought himself to somewhere that has its own demands, and barring the doors against those hasn't turned out to be as simple a thing as she believed. She wants to sit somewhere for a long time, unseen, and watch him go about his business until his unhurried rhythms clear her mind.

There's someone else she needs to talk to first. She told Julie that no one knows whether Rachel would want her death used against Tommy Moynihan. It only came to her afterwards that there's someone who might know. *I been sitting here in this window for weeks now*, Mrs Duggan said, *waiting for someone to ask me the right question.*

The village street has a weary, down-at-heel look, oil stains rainbowing on the wet tarmac, stray bits of soggy paper scattered from an overturned bin. The shop is empty except for Noreen, looking up from a column of figures at the ding of the bell. On the radio a woman's voice sings something low and melancholy.

Lena says, 'Can I leave the dogs here for half an hour?'

She watches while Noreen almost says several different things, and stops herself from saying any of them. In the end she says, 'Yeah, no problem. Put them in the back room, where they won't be sniffing at things.'

Lena takes Nellie and Daisy into the little back room, which is stuffed with cardboard boxes, filing cabinets, tea-making apparatus, and bags that Noreen's going to take to the charity shop when she gets a chance, and finds a bowl to give them water. When she comes out, she half-expects Noreen to have turned up the radio and buried herself in her figures, but Noreen is waiting for her.

Noreen says, 'Yvonne McCabe was in earlier.'

'Yvonne's sound,' Lena says. 'So are Sheila and Julie.'

'They are, yeah. You're lucky to have them.'

'I know that,' Lena says. Noreen's face has sagged, just in the last few weeks.

'You don't deserve them. I was ringing you. I was texting you. You coulda at least bothered your hole answering.'

'I don't deserve you either,' Lena says. 'How many people are you after barring for talking shite about me?'

'No one talked shite about you to me,' Noreen says. 'They know better. All anyone did was hint; a wee hint here and another one there. I barred them anyhow.' She presses a finger and thumb into her eyes like they're tired. 'Probably they went off and said I done it for no reason at all, and the whole family of us are after going mental.'

'Well,' Lena says, 'you'll be able to let them back in now, once Yvonne sets them straight. Or will half the place be heading to town for the rest of their lives, every time they want a loaf of bread?'

That gets a startled sound, almost a laugh, out of Noreen. 'Ah, I'll let them off,' she says, after a moment. 'The ones that apologise, anyhow. I might make Laura Barry work for it; I never liked her.'

'Neither did I,' Lena says. 'Sure, her business won't make or break you either way; she never eats anything only SlimFast shakes.'

This time Noreen does laugh, but there's a crack in it. 'Jesus, Helena,' she says, on a long shaky breath. 'You had the life frightened outa me there.'

'I know,' Lena says. 'I wasn't enjoying myself either. I'll aim not to do it again, how's that?'

'You'd better not, my feckin' heart won't take it. Jesus.' Noreen has a hand to her chest. 'Go back out there and make us a cuppa tea, go on; I need one. The biscuits are in the second drawer of the grey filing cabinet, Cliona found where I had them hid before, that one's got some kinda radar for sweet stuff, she'd ate sheep shite if I sprinkled sugar on it.'

'I've to get something done first,' Lena says. 'I'll come back for a cuppa tea after.'

For a moment Noreen looks like she might ask questions, but then she nods and bends over her figures again. 'Them dogs better not do their wees on my floor,' she warns, as Lena heads out.

Mrs Duggan is playing solitaire, but she feels Lena's shadow block the light in her window. She looks Lena up and down, with a slow smile growing. Then she considers the card in her hand, lays it in its place, and crooks a finger to beckon Lena in.

The house is silent; Lena picked her time right, Dessie and the kids are out about their various business. In Mrs Duggan's room, the light is on against the dimness of the morning and the haze of cigarette smoke. Mrs Duggan's dress is pink today, a thick hot pink churning with big purple flowers. Her worn slippers poke out from under the hem, but she gives no impression of having been caught unprepared. Her eyebrows are pencilled in, and her hair is pulled back in its tight bun; she's ready and waiting.

'I toldja I'd see you soon,' she says, without looking up. She moves a stack of cards onto an empty space.

'You did,' Lena says. 'And I'm here.'

Mrs Duggan deliberates and shifts a queen onto a king. 'Where's my jar of jam? I'm almost finished the other one.'

'I brought nothing,' Lena says. 'You said if anyone asked you the right question, there'd be no charge.'

Mrs Duggan looks up. Her eyes, unblinking on Lena's, slowly light.

'Sit you down there,' she says, nodding to the other chair. She sweeps her cards into a pile. 'And pull it close.'

Lena does as she's told. The room is too hot. The gas fire sings its monotonous note, almost too high to hear, like Mrs Duggan has a swarm of insects trapped in a jar somewhere among the clutter on her shelves.

'If you get it wrong,' Mrs Duggan says, 'I'll charge you extra, for wasting my time.'

'I don't have it wrong,' Lena says. She has no fear that Mrs Duggan will lie to extract payment. That would take the spice out of things.

Mrs Duggan nods. 'Go on, so,' she says. 'Let's be having you.'

Lena says, 'What did you and Rachel Holohan say to each other, the night she died?'

Mrs Duggan leans back in her armchair and starts to laugh. It's a deep, hoarse wheezing that goes on and on. Lena waits.

'I knew it,' Mrs Duggan says in the end, wiping her mouth. 'I bet myself that you'd get there in the end, and I win. Reach down that bottle a sherry off the shelf, and go get glasses outa the kitchen. We'll celebrate.'

Lena finds the bottle and goes to fetch the glasses. The kitchen is all Noreen: big and airy, smelling of toast and cleaning spray, cheerful colours and fruit patterns and kids' fleeces everywhere. Lena takes two glasses from a cupboard and goes back to the front room.

'You'll have to do the honours,' Mrs Duggan says, nodding at the bottle. 'My hands haven't got the strength.'

Lena opens the bottle and pours. The sherry sends out a sweet, thick reek like decaying fruit.

'Here's to you,' Mrs Duggan says, raising her glass.

'I'll save mine,' Lena says.

That gets a chuckle out of Mrs Duggan. 'Are you afraid I'll poison you? Don't be worrying; I wouldn't waste you.'

Lena says, 'I'm waiting to see do I have anything to celebrate.'

Mrs Duggan shrugs. She takes a drink of her sherry,

half-closing her eyes while she lets the taste of the triumph move around her tongue. 'Now,' she says, lowering the glass. 'Here's your prize.'

Up until this moment, a part of Lena was afraid she was missing the mark – Rachel and Mrs Duggan said nothing to each other that mattered, and she would leave here holding less than she came with. By the pale shine of Mrs Duggan's eyes when they open, she knows she didn't get it wrong. Whatever Mrs Duggan gave Rachel, it was big enough that Tommy killed her for it.

'That Rachel one waited till your sister and alla them were away to town,' Mrs Duggan says, 'and then she came to me. A wee box of shortbread biscuits, that was all she brought, like something her mammy had in the press for visitors. I mighta told her to come back with something better, only for she was in bits. Make-up all down her face, and snivelling outa her like a child after a bating. So I said she could sit down.'

Lena is under no illusion that this was kindness, and she knows no illusion is intended. A distraught woman offers much more than the same woman the next day, when things will have subsided back into some kind of proportion.

'She told me what Tommy was at,' Mrs Duggan says. 'She tried dancing around it at first, till I got bored of watching her dance and told her I already knew. I coulda taken offence that she thought I wouldn't, but I'm not easy offended.'

There's a quick beat of footsteps outside and the light shifts as someone passes by the window, but Mrs Duggan doesn't turn her head. She's been waiting for her chance to tell this story.

''Twas horrible, that wee girl said, what Tommy was aiming to do; horrible. 'Twasn't her Eugene's fault – she was fulla excuses for him; he just wanted a better life for the two a them, he was usedta taking his daddy's word as gospel, he was under his daddy's thumb, he hadn't thought through what it'd do to the place . . .' Her thin mouth curls in scorn. 'Women'll tell themselves every lie in the world about a fella they fancy. But she couldn't find a lie to tell herself about the rest. There'd be people dead, she said; people killing each other, or themselves. I said likely there would be, all right. She said everyone'd hate her and her precious Eugene both, and I said plenty would, all right. She said even if she threatened to leave Eugene, 'twould make no difference 'cause he'd always do what his daddy told him, and I said he was in the habit of that. She said she couldn't do without him, she'd never imagined any life for herself that didn't have him in it, and I said that was a terrible predicament altogether. She said if she did leave him, Tommy'd go after her guns blazing, in case she talked, and I said 'twould be like him. Then I asked her what she wanted outa me. And she said she wanted a way to scupper Tommy's plans.' She glances at Lena over the rim of her glass. 'Did she come asking you for the same thing?'

'You said no charge,' Lena says.

Mrs Duggan grins. Her swollen fingers probe among the objects on her table, trawling for something. The array of things has changed since the last time Lena was here: the playing cards, a jar of mint humbugs, scissors, tangled spools of coloured thread.

'I thought at first she was one a them fools that take me for a witch woman,' she says, 'and she was looking for me to put a curse on Tommy. I do get plenty of fools wanting curses, and love charms. Not just young ones; you'd be surprised how many aul' lads come looking for a charm to make sure some foreign young one offa the internet loves them forever, instead of till the money runs out.' She extracts her cigarette packet from among the spools. 'How about you?' she asks, her eyes moving up to Lena. 'Would you take a love charm, if I had one handy?'

Lena doesn't blink. 'Not my style,' she says.

The corner of Mrs Duggan's mouth lifts in amusement, like

that told her all she needs to know. 'Wee Rachel looked like that kind,' she says. 'But I had her wrong, and she had me right. She was no fool, and she knew I'm no witch woman. What she wanted was muck. Something she could bring to Tommy and say, "Wind your neck in, or I'll tell this to the world."'

'I'd say you've plenty of muck on Tommy,' Lena says.

Mrs Duggan holds out the cigarette packet. 'Get one a those out for me,' she says. 'My hands is bad today.'

She waits, sipping, while Lena takes out a cigarette and passes it over. 'I could fill a slurry pit with the muck I've got on Moynihans,' she says. 'Only 'tis all stuff that the world knows already. They mightn't know who Tommy bribed or what dirty deals he done, but they know he done plenty, and they think he's a great man altogether, in spite of it or because of it or both. None of that woulda been any use to the girl. There's things he coulda done that mighta stuck in people's throats, maybe, but he never done any of them. He's fierce careful, that fella.'

Lena says, 'So you said to Rachel there was nothing she could do. Is that what you're telling me?' She doesn't believe it for a second.

Mrs Duggan hooks her gold lighter from under a tissue packet and holds it out to Lena. 'Light that for me,' she says.

Lena has to move in close to do it. Mrs Duggan takes her time fitting the cigarette in her mouth and bringing it to the flame, her pale eyes holding Lena's all the way. Under her floral powder there's a smell like hot tar. The end of the cigarette glows red as she takes a long, slow drag.

Then she settles back in her chair, releasing Lena, and lets smoke seep from her mouth. 'You're getting wrinkles,' she says.

'I am, yeah,' Lena says, putting the lighter back on the table. The nearness has sent adrenaline gunning through her. She doesn't let her hand shake.

'It does go awful fast from there on in. Before you know

it, you'll be eighty-two and stuck in a chair all day. The young people don't believe 'twill ever happen to them, but you're old enough to know it will.' Mrs Duggan takes another long drag on her cigarette. 'And that's if you're lucky; lucky and tough. Tell us, Missus Dunne: d'you fancy your chances?'

Her eyes are still on Lena, sifting at their leisure through what the last few weeks have been. She knows more than Noreen, or anyone, could have told her. Nothing comes free here. Mrs Duggan may not have the pleasure of forcing Lena to hand over payment, but she's taking it anyway, pulling threads of it from Lena's face and voice. 'I'm tough enough,' Lena says.

'Maybe you are,' Mrs Duggan says, 'and maybe you're not. Just 'cause you're able to start trouble, that doesn't mean you're able to see it through. But we'll say you'll make it this far.' She nods to herself, the chair and the body. 'What'll you do to amuse yourself then? When you can't go walking the roads, or playing about with horses, or making jam, and your fella's dead and buried, and half the time your hands is too sore even to do a bitta embroidery. There's a terrible lotta hours in the day. What'll you do with them all?'

'Who knows,' Lena says. Out of nowhere, she pictures telling Sheila and Yvonne and Julie this story: *And then she said, she did not, oh God she gives me the willies, pass Lena the gin she's earned it, did I ever tell ye what that aul' weapon said to me once?* 'By that time I'll probably be able to do alla that stuff online. And have a virtual fella to do it with me.'

'I'll tell you what you'll do,' Mrs Duggan says. 'You'll take whatever comes your way, and you'll take whatever amusement you can get outa it. And if you get a chance to make a bit more, you'll do it.' She smiles at Lena, through her cigarette. 'You're telling yourself that's all a loada shite, isn't that right? Lena Dunne's too good for that carry-on. You'd never lower yourself.'

'Hadn't thought about it,' Lena says.

'Wait,' Mrs Duggan says. Her voice falls heavy as a stone. 'You'll lower yourself, all right, when 'tis that or go mad. A fool might be grand sitting and playing dominoes all day, but you've brains. If you don't occupy them, they'll turn on you. You'll take what you can get.'

Lena, suddenly, is having none of this. 'You were amusing yourself the same way when you were forty,' she says. 'You could be helping the grandkids with their homework, if all you wanted was to keep your brains occupied. What'd you say to Rachel?'

Mrs Duggan's thin eyebrows go up. 'Wouldja look at that,' she says. 'Maybe you're tougher than I thought.'

'Maybe,' Lena says.

Mrs Duggan leans her head back in the chair to blow smoke upwards, and watches as it spreads out across the ceiling. 'Wee Rachel wanted a way to stop Tommy,' she says, 'and I gave her one. I done right by her, I didn't cheat her; I told her the truth. It'd take something big, I said. A death on his hands. And any death wouldn't do. A good one, it'd haveta be; one that packed a punch. Someone that was well liked, so that everyone'd be up in arms. Someone that was young and innocent, so no one could say they went looking for it.'

Her eyes slide to Lena. 'And what did I do then?' she asks.

In that overheated room, Lena is cold right through. She says, 'You tell me.'

'Then,' Mrs Duggan says, 'I told wee Rachel where Dessie and Noreen keep a coil of rope, out in the shed, and a jug of bleach, and a bottle of antifreeze, and anything else that might take her fancy. And I told her where Noreen keeps pen and paper in the kitchen, for to write herself notes. And I told her to let herself out, and she did.'

Lena sits still, feeling the breath go in and out of her. Mrs Duggan, sipping, watches her face and enjoys it.

'I had that girl wrong,' she says. 'I don't know the young people the way I'd like. I thought 'twas a hundred to one against her doing it; more, maybe. I thought all she wanted was for me to tell her there was nothing she could do, so's she'd be off the hook. I said to myself, says I, at them odds, if she goes through with it I'll have Dessie go into town and buy me a bottle of the best sherry he can find.'

She shifts her bulk forward, with effort, and finds a space for her sherry glass on the table. 'Fill that for me,' she says. 'And drink up.'

Lena says, 'I'm not celebrating.'

Mrs Duggan's lip lifts in scorn. 'You came looking for it,' she says, pressing out her cigarette in the ashtray, 'and now you've got it, you don't like it. You're awful squeamish for a woman your age. Whether it turns your stomach or not, I was right: Tommy wouldn'ta been stopped any other way.'

Lena says, 'He doesn't look stopped to me.'

'Not yet, but he will be. Am I wrong?'

'I've to head to work,' Lena says. She stands up.

'That young one made a hames of it, mind you,' Mrs Duggan adds. 'She shoulda pinned it on Tommy good and proper; left her mammy a note, or put something up on the internet. I won't hold that against her, but. It's been better entertainment this way.'

She pours herself more sherry. The heavy bottle wavers in her hand, but she doesn't spill a drop. 'Away you run, so,' she says, leaning back with her glass. 'I'll be watching to see what you do with this. I'll enjoy that, whatever it is. And I'll tell you what I'll do in exchange: I'll leave you this chair in my will.' She runs her palm down the chair's tarnished velvet arm. 'So's you'll have somewhere to sit and take your amusement where you find it, if you make it this far.'

★

Cal is dragged out of his catch-up sleep by knocking. It takes him a minute to work out where he is, and why his heart is slamming like he might need to spring into action. He has no idea how long he's been asleep; the grey line between the curtains tells him nothing except that it's not night.

The knocking comes again, a timid tap at his front door. Cal wants to stick a pillow over his head and ignore it – whatever byzantine bullshit this place has come up with now, it can take care of itself for a few hours; even if this is Eugene coming over to the dark side, Cal is in no condition to handle the onboarding delicately. But Rip is starting up his ferocious guard-dog rumble, and Cal can't stifle the hope that this might be Lena. He struggles out of bed and puts his pants on. His phone says it's ten-thirty in the morning.

It's not Lena. It's Bobby, turning his flat cap nervously in both hands, his bald spot pink from the cold.

'Hey,' Cal says.

'If you're not talking to me,' Bobby says humbly, 'you can say it. Or, I don't know, shut the door.'

'Why wouldn't I be talking to you?' Cal asks. He feels like he should know this, but he's not awake enough. He has no idea how anyone keeps track of this place without an incident-room corkboard covered in sticky notes and pieces of red string.

'Senan isn't,' Bobby says. He looks miserable. 'Or Francie either, or PJ. Mart is' – he gives a harried glance towards Mart's land, but the little red tractor is trundling across the far field, a safe distance away – 'only all he does is give out and call me an arse-licking peasant. 'Cause I didn't come with ye to Moynihans' the other night.'

'Right,' Cal says. He tries to flatten his hair. 'Come on in.'

The look Bobby gives him, as he wipes his boots on the mat, is pathetically grateful. Cal sits him down at the kitchen table and sets about making the strongest coffee his machine can come up with. He lets Rip investigate Bobby's boots and bring him toys meanwhile, so he won't have to start this conversation till he's got caffeine at the ready.

'Sit,' he says, when he brings the mugs over to the table. Bobby glances up like Cal might mean him, and then realises when Rip obediently sits down. 'Milk? Sugar?'

Bobby, a tea man, looks unsure. 'Ah, no,' he says in the end. 'I'm grand.' He gives his coffee a dubious look, sips it out of politeness, and blinks hard.

'So,' Cal says. 'How's things?' He sinks half his coffee in one slug.

'I wanted to talk to you,' Bobby says. He takes a breath; apparently this isn't going to come out easy.

'Go for it,' Cal says. He hopes Bobby doesn't want more romantic advice. He misses his favourite diner in Chicago, which offered a caffeine overdose called the Jumper Cable for days like this. He can't remember what he's doing here.

'D'you know how I was telling you, down the pub, that there was people . . . you know. Saying things about Lena?'

'Yeah,' Cal says. 'I appreciated that.'

'That's all over now, but,' Bobby reassures Cal hastily. 'Everyone knows 'twas bollocks. Sure, Lena and Julie Quinn were over at Sheila Reddy's all that evening; she couldn'ta been giving Rachel antifreeze.'

'Well,' Cal says. 'That's good.' He has no idea where this came from – he's not sure who Julie Quinn even is, let alone what she's doing in the middle of this – but here's another reason why Tommy has turned desperate enough to get his hands dirty. His scapegoat has been taken away.

And no wonder whatever Tommy had in mind last night was aimed at Mart or at Cal. Lena is no use to him any more. Somehow or other, she's safe. Cal knows it shouldn't come as a blow that he wasn't the one to save her, but it does. That was the hope he was holding on to: if he could do that, he might be able to reach her again.

'I hadn't a clue,' Bobby says, leaning across the table with the urgency of it. 'That Tommy was behind it, like, or that he was going to say Lena kilt Rachel. And I wasn't spreading it around; I never said a word to anyone but you. I swear on my mammy's life.'

'I know that,' Cal says. 'I never thought you did.'

Bobby blinks at him. 'You didn't?'

'Nope,' Cal says.

'Everyone else does. They all reckon I'm one of Tommy's men, and I was helping spread them rumours for him. Noreen threw me outa the shop yesterday. I only went in for a Turkish Delight bar, and she told me they're reserved for people that don't go slandering her sister. I tried to tell her different, but . . .' Bobby spreads his hands helplessly.

'Yeah,' Cal says. He can picture Bobby trying to tell Noreen different when she's mad. The blast would have blown him out of the shop and right down the road.

'And Tadhg McHugh came up to me to say I'm a sound man and he'll buy me a pint once Barty lets him back into the pub. He patted me on the back and all.' Bobby is turning red with outrage. 'That fucker usedta call me Ralph Wiggum. I don't want him *patting* me.'

'Tell him to stick his pint up his ass,' Cal says. He appreciates the update, but he needs Bobby out, to make room for Eugene or someone with something useful to offer.

'I did. He just laughed – he thought I was trying to cover up, like. I was never on Tommy's side; I just didn't wanta be ungrateful. But I don't know how to prove it. I thought maybe I could do something on him, like maybe . . .' Bobby stops, stymied. 'Spray something on his wall?' he hazards. 'Only I wouldn't know what to say. And anyhow no one'd know 'twas me. Or I could call him a prick next time I see him in Seán's, only he hasn't been in.'

Tommy won't be in Seán's for a while. 'Just hang in there,' Cal says. 'You'll have plenty more chances to get in on the action.' He thinks of Tommy, in the winter dark, coming out from behind his high walls to prowl the edges of Cal's and Mart's land. 'This shit isn't over,' he says.

'Ah, I know it's not. Only no one'll want me in on it, if they think I'm Tommy's man. In case I go squealing to him. Like no one texted me to go down to Seán's, the other night.' Bobby blinks wretchedly up at Cal. 'Could you tell them?' he asks. 'Senan and Mart and alla them. And Noreen.'

'I guess,' Cal says, taken aback. 'I don't know that they'd listen to me, though.'

'Why wouldn't they?'

'You guys have all known each other since you were in diapers. If this whole thing has them so wound up that they won't take your word, they're not gonna take the word of some guy that just jumped off the last bus.'

'You're not a blow-in,' Bobby says. 'You're not *local*, like, but you're . . .' He gestures vaguely, trying to find the right term. 'You were at Moynihans' with the rest,' he says. 'You were in the roola-boola down the pub. How would they not listen to you?'

'Right,' Cal says. 'OK.' He feels again the gravitational pull that he felt back in Mart's sheep shed, shifting the balances all around him. 'I'll talk to them.'

Bobby lets out a breath of relief. 'That'd be great,' he says. 'I kept thinking . . . Here's me hoping I'll be getting married next year, you know? Imagine themens not being there. I don't know if I'd have the guts to stand up there at the altar, without . . .' His voice falters.

'Hey,' Cal says. He figures Tommy Moynihan deserves to be ridden out of town on a rail for this alone. 'They'll be there. You think Senan's gonna miss that kind of opportunity to give you shit?'

Bobby manages a smile. 'Would you say it to Lena, as well? I'd hate to have her think I was talking bad about her.'

'Lena knows you better'n that,' Cal says.

'So do the rest, sure,' Bobby points out mournfully, 'and they still think it. Wouldja say it to her?'

'I haven't talked to Lena in a while,' Cal says. He drains the rest of his coffee.

Bobby is staring at him, startled and unsure. 'Why not?' he ventures.

'Dunno,' Cal says. 'She doesn't want to talk to me.'

Bobby struggles to make sense of this and come up with something helpful. 'One time my mammy wouldn't talk to me for a week,' he offers. 'I hadn't a notion why. In the heel of the hunt, it turned out I'd broke her St Anthony statue. I didn't even know I'd knocked it over. I got a new one in, and we were grand. Didja break something?'

'Not that I know of,' Cal says. Bobby, deflated, retreats into his coffee.

Cal asks, 'What would you do?'

Bobby pops up out of his mug and gives Cal a round-eyed stare of pure astonishment. 'Me?'

'Yeah,' Cal says. 'If it was Róisín.' He's not sure how he's ended up asking Bobby for relationship advice, except that he apparently needs to ask someone, and all his other options are a lot worse.

'You don't wanta know what I'd do,' Bobby assures him, alarmed. 'Sure, I haven't a notion about women. Whatever I'd do, 'tis bound to be the wrong thing.'

'Well, then you gotta tell me,' Cal says. 'So I can be sure and not do it.'

Bobby still looks dubious, but he creases up his forehead and gives the question his full attention. 'I wouldn't say Róisín'd be into that,' he tells Cal, after a few moments' thought. 'She's a great one for the chats. If something was up, I'd say she'd tell me all about it before I even knew to ask.'

'Yeah,' Cal says. 'That's what I thought about Lena. She's pretty chatty, too. Normally.'

Bobby goes back to thinking. His face is puckered with trouble; if Cal the expert can't keep a relationship afloat, clearly a beginner like Bobby is screwed. Cal wishes he had kept his mouth shut.

'What I'd do,' Bobby says eventually, 'is I'd go over to her place and I'd sit there, on the step. Not hassling her, like; just waiting. And either she'd come out and tell me to fuck off – not like that, 'cause Róisín doesn't use language, but you know what I mean – and then at least I'd know where I was. Or else she'd come out and talk to me.'

'What if she didn't?' Cal says.

'Then I'd keep waiting,' Bobby says. He gives Cal a shy sideways glance. 'That's probably wrong,' he adds humbly. ''Tisn't subtle, or anything. But 'tis the best I can do.'

Cal hopes Róisín appreciates Bobby the way he deserves. 'It sounds pretty good to me,' he says.

'Ye'll be grand,' Bobby assures him, from the heart. 'I was only saying to Róisín the other day, no word of a lie, I'd rather we were like the two of ye than any other couple I know; the way ye just trot along together, no drama, happy out. Lena's head's just melted by alla this that's been going on. Once that's sorted, ye'll be right as rain.'

'Well,' Cal says, 'thanks. I hope you're right. You ask Róisín to marry you yet?'

'Not yet,' Bobby says. 'But I bought a ring,' he adds, glancing at Cal to see if he's going to get a ribbing for this. 'Your man said I could swap it if she doesn't like it, or if she says no.'

'Tell me something,' Cal says. He's not sure how to word this, but he feels like the issue needs addressing. 'You gonna take her out looking for aliens?'

Bobby blinks, wrong-footed, and hides in his coffee. 'I never seen any aliens,' he corrects Cal. 'Lights, only.'

'OK,' Cal says. 'You gonna take her looking for UFOs?'

Bobby looks up at him. 'There was never any aliens,' he says, simply and a little sadly. 'I'd say half the time them lights was just Malachy Dwyer and the other mountainy lads taking the piss outa me. And the rest was bog-lights or satellites, that kinda stuff.'

'Could've been,' Cal says gently.

'It was,' Bobby says. 'I'd say I knew that all along, underneath. But the nights woulda got awful long with nothing to go looking for.'

'That's the truth,' Cal says. 'You could've done a lot worse than aliens.'

Bobby smiles a little bit at that. ''Twill be strange, without them,' he says. 'It's a change.'

'Well,' Cal says, 'you can't get away from those.'

'I never had any before, but,' Bobby explains, 'not since my daddy died and I took over the farm. I stopped looking for any. I thought I'd keep jogging along the same way as always, till I dropped dead. I'm not complaining,' he adds hastily, in case the universe should take umbrage at his ingratitude. 'I'm over the moon with myself. Only every now and again it feels awful strange, d'you know the way?'

'Yep,' Cal says. He does. He has a feeling that he strayed into the same illusion as Bobby, and with a lot less of an excuse.

'Come here to me,' Bobby says, struck by an idea. 'D'you know that holy water bottle I brought you from Lourdes?'

'Got it right there,' Cal says, nodding to the mantelpiece.

Bobby looks gratified. 'I put a drop of mine on the ring,' he says. 'For luck. You oughta do the same: put it on yourself, before you go see Lena.'

'Good idea,' Cal says. He finds himself actually considering it.

'I'll show you,' Bobby says, seizing the chance to offer something useful. He goes to the mantelpiece and brings back the Mary bottle, holding it carefully upright. 'Now,' he says, uncapping it and handing it over. 'Just put your thumb over the top and tip it up, and then rub the drop of water on your forehead. Normally you'd make the sign of the Cross, but Protestants mightn't be allowed, I don't know.'

He gazes hopefully at Cal. Cal gives up and does what he's told, smearing his thumb down his forehead between his eyebrows. The water leaves a cold streak where the air hits it. He knows it's meant to be a blessing, but it feels like some older and fiercer ritual, an anointing for battle.

Once Bobby heads home, looking a lot happier, Cal spends the remainder of the morning getting so restless he could bite himself. He needs to talk to Mart, but he can't see Mart anywhere – presumably he's doing something in his bottom field, hidden from Cal's view by the slope of the land – and he doesn't want to go out looking. He's reluctant to leave the house. Somewhere out there are Tommy and Eugene, both of them pushed to the edge, right where Cal wants them. If either of them should come calling, Cal can't afford to miss him.

In the end he heads out back, to collect the last of the oak leaves and add them to his compost pile – this doesn't particularly need doing, but it'll prevent him from chewing the furniture and let him keep an eye out for Mart. A few rooks swoop back from the day's business to see what he's doing with their oak tree; they hang around, competing to see which of them can find the most unhelpful stuff to drop in the wheelbarrow. Maybe they've caught what's in the air, because today their screwing around has an ugly edge. Among their usual contributions of rocks and discarded plastic, Cal picks out lumps of what smells like fox shit and something that turns out to be the leftovers of a finch, head and one wing ripped off, delicate claws curled.

He's turning the wheelbarrow towards the compost pile when, somewhere, a howl rises through the cold grey air. After the first frozen second Cal knows it has to be a dog, but it sounds like no dog he's ever heard; this is a death cry or a war cry, as savage and desolate as a wolf's. The hair lifts on his neck.

Beside him Rip is hunched, teeth bared. When the sound ends, the air stands still. Even the rooks are silenced.

The howl rises again. This time Cal realises which way Rip is pointing, and then he's dropped the wheelbarrow and he's running.

He vaults his wall without breaking stride and goes flat out for the crest of the slope that hides Mart's bottom field. He's walked this land a hundred times and never realised the breadth of it, how long it takes to cross. The howling goes on and on, closer now.

Halfway across the bottom field, Mart's little red tractor is on its side, revving hard, with its tyres pointing uphill towards Cal. Beside the tractor Kojak stands with all four paws braced, nose to the sky, howling. Sheep have clustered in the field's far corner, unsettled, watching.

'Sit,' Cal says to Rip. 'Stay.'

When he rounds the tractor, Kojak cuts off in mid-howl and spins to face him. His eyes are white-ringed and he shows his fangs. Mart is on the ground, lying on his side with his back to Cal. His blue beanie is too bright, unnatural, against the faded grass. The lower half of him is pinned under the tractor.

Cal moves forward very slowly, holding out one hand and saying soothing words of some kind: *Hey boy it's me, you know me buddy, everything's OK* . . . Gradually Kojak's hackles go down, and the hunch of his spine eases. He starts up a high wild whine. 'Good boy,' Cal says steadily. 'You did great. Now you just sit a minute and I'll fix it all up.' He moves towards the tractor, and Kojak lets him.

He has no doubt that he's kneeling to a dead man. He almost leaps out of his skin when Mart's eyes open.

'Jean-Claude,' Mart says. His voice is thin, but it's clear, and his eyes are focused on Cal's. 'The very man I was hoping to see.'

The relief almost drops Cal. The earth, boggy from all these weeks of rain, must have cushioned the worst of it. He can't see any blood; the angles of Mart's neck and back are natural, not distorted, and he lifts one hand in something like a wave. Cal knows what tractor accidents can do, but everyone has a story about the guy who got lucky.

'Don't try to move,' he says. He gets down on the ground and reaches to turn off the tractor, and its angry roar fades into stillness. 'I'm gonna get PJ. He's got a winch. You just hang tight and we'll get this off you.'

'Don't be a fool, man,' Mart says. 'I can't feel a thing below the waist. I'm not complaining, 'cause this'd be awful sore otherwise, but on the other hand, the bottom half a me is porridge.' He has to take a new breath after every few words. 'This tractor's the only thing holding me together. If you lift it offa me, I'll bleed to death before you can put it down.'

'OK,' Cal says. 'OK.' Mart is right. God only knows what's ripped apart inside him, sealed off from bleeding by the tractor's weight. 'OK. I'm gonna get you an ambulance.'

'You do that, Sunny Jim,' Mart says. 'I'd say they'll get here too late for the action, but we'll give it a go. Take your time; I won't go anywhere.'

Cal's cop voice gets the call-taker's attention, but it can't do much more than that. She'll get an ambulance to them as soon as possible, she can't give him an ETA, he should keep his friend warm and not try to move him.

'They're on their way,' he says, when he hangs up.

Mart's eyes crease in amusement. 'They are, o' course,' he agrees obligingly.

Cal tucks his jacket around Mart's body, as well as he can. He takes off his sweatshirt and folds it up. 'I'm gonna stick this under your head,' he says. 'Keep your face out of the dirt.' Probably he shouldn't do it, spine injuries or whatever, but there's no one here to do better. Mart's face tightens in a grimace when Cal lifts his head, as gently as he can, but he relaxes again when Cal lowers him onto the makeshift pillow.

'That's lovely,' he says. 'Sure, you wouldn't get better in a fancy hotel.'

Mart's tractor has always looked like a dinky little thing, but now, shadowing them both, it's immense, a brutal hunk of metal weight. It's as old as Mart is, and has the safety features to match: no cab, no rollover bar. Cal has called it a death trap before, but Mart just laughed at the city boy and pointed out that he never died yet.

The bale of silage that he was taking to his sheep has tumbled away and lies on the grass. 'What happened?' Cal says. 'Silage too heavy?'

Mart manages a snort, although it's a wisp of his normal one. 'Don't be insulting me. That's what the investigators'll put down on their wee notepads: wasn't he very foolish altogether, driving the tractor on the slope, and the ground this wet and the silage on the front. But you oughta have better sense than that. I've driven this same path on this same tractor since before you were born. I don't make fuckin' mistakes.'

He takes a minute to get his breath back, but when Cal starts to say something, Mart raises a hand to stop him.

'Hold your whisht and listen to me,' he says. 'When you lift this tractor, you'll find a hole in the ground under that front tyre. I felt it; felt the tyre go into it. It'll be small enough that the investigators won't get their suspicions up, with the ground all boggy and the rabbits everywhere, but 'twasn't there when I drove this path yesterday. That hole was dug. Someone came out here last night and dug it, and laid the sod back down over it so I'd see nothing till 'twas too late.'

Carrying sthing could be a gun. Trey guessed wrong. Tommy, at bay, brought an older weapon to battle, and worked in dirt and darkness with his bare hands, to the sound of his own hard breathing. Not a gun; a spade.

'It mightn'ta worked,' Mart says. 'That's the part that annoys me. The tractor mightn'ta tipped right over, or I coulda been thrown clear. I don't appreciate dying just 'cause that fucker got lucky.'

Cal wants to say *You're not gonna die*, but Mart wouldn't thank him for cheap comfort. 'Wait for the ambulance,' he says. 'Don't talk too much. You gotta save your strength.'

Mart ignores that. 'There's one silver lining,' he says. He's turned his head, with some difficulty, so that his watery blue eyes can hold Cal's. 'This could come in fierce useful. Don't you let it go to waste. I hate waste.'

'I'll use it,' Cal says. He can't afford his anger at Tommy right now; he's keeping it for later. 'You got my word on that.'

'You're the one that'll haveta get the job done, Jean-Claude,' Mart says. 'The resta them reprobates are grand men in their way, but there's not a one of them that has a head for strategy. That's what Tommy's banking on: without me, they'll all be running around like headless chickens. He hasn't bargained for you.'

'That's a mistake,' Cal says.

Mart nods, satisfied. 'Your Theresa was out on the prowl last night,' he says. 'Amn't I right? She's a good girl. I'd say she saw something.'

For a reflexive second Cal baulks at dragging Trey into this, till he realises there's no such thing. Trey lives here now; this is her fight already. 'She probably did,' he says. 'You ever think you'd be grateful for a Reddy?'

Mart's laugh is an effortful wheeze that costs him. When it stops, he's panting.

'I don't know about you,' he says, 'but I need a drink. Go on up to my kitchen. There's a bottle of whiskey in the press above the kettle.'

'I'm gonna stay here a while,' Cal says.

'Get ta fuck with that. I need a drink to get me through this. That's not a lot to ask. Get me a fuckin' drink.'

He's working himself up. 'I'll call PJ,' Cal says. 'He can bring us something.'

'You will not. By the time you get this explained to PJ, we'll all be dead. Just fetch the fuckin' bottle. I'll still be here when you get back.'

Cal finds himself standing up. The air is cold, biting through his T-shirt like it's not there. 'You want me to call anyone else?' he asks.

'If you ring Father Eamonn,' Mart says, 'I'll come back and haunt you right outa Ardnakelty. I don't want my sins forgiven, and I'm not having that Jabba the Hutt head be the last thing I ever see.'

'I meant friends,' Cal says. 'Relatives, I dunno.' Mart has brothers somewhere, if they're still alive, and cousins scattered around, but Cal doesn't know whether he even has their phone numbers, let alone how to get hold of his phone.

'What for? I haven't time for all that fussing and foostering, and I'm not the famous-last-words type anyhow. Just get that dog over here, before you go. I don't like the look of him, and I haven't the volume to do it myself.'

Kojak is crouched a few yards away, ears flat and tail tight between his legs. Cal coaxes him, and in the end he slinks close enough to sniff Mart's hand, and then his face and chest, lip drawing back at the wrongness in the scent. 'That'll do,' Mart says, and Kojak folds to the ground, into the curve of Mart's body.

'About fuckin' time,' Mart says. He puts a hand on Kojak's head. 'Get a move on,' he says to Cal.

Once Cal is out of Mart's line of sight, he runs. It feels like running in a nightmare, slow motion through an endless landscape of empty fields, under a flat grey sky and a silence thick enough to choke him. The only sounds are his own panting and the squelch of his boots in the muddy ground. Rip runs by his side, silent.

Mart's house is dark. The kitchen smells faintly of frying bacon, and breakfast things are still on the table, plate, mug, Mart's Dalek-shaped teapot. The whiskey is where he said it would be, a bottle of Powers, three-quarters full.

Cal finds Mart's bedroom after wrong turns into two spare rooms where stripped beds and dark wood furniture lie under a thick film of dust. Mart sleeps in a single bed, below posters so old their colours have faded: *The Magnificent Seven, Charlie's Angels*. Cal rolls up the duvet to fit under his arm. There's a worn blue fleece at the end of the bed, and he pulls it on; it's several sizes too small, but it'll be enough for the time he needs it. 'Stay,' he says to Rip, on his way out, and shuts the door on him.

He can't run any more, cumbered by the bottle and the duvet; he crosses the fields in a ludicrous clumsy jog. When he gets back to the tractor, Mart and Kojak haven't moved, and Mart is still alive. 'That's lovely on you,' he says, when he sees Cal wearing his fleece. His face is whiter. 'You can keep it, as a souvenir. Where's my whiskey?'

Cal steadies the bottle as Mart drinks. A little bit dribbles down the side of his face, and Cal wipes it away with the cuff of the fleece. Mart's skin is clammy and too cold. Kojak watches, only his eyes moving.

'That's the stuff,' Mart says, when he's had enough. Cal spreads the duvet over him and Kojak both. Mart grins when he sees it, but can't laugh.

'Have a sup yourself,' he says, nodding to the bottle. 'I'd say you need it.'

Cal takes a swig. The whiskey turns his stomach, but when it hits his blood it braces him up.

Mart's hand, with a shake in it, moves on Kojak's head. 'Bring this fella down to PJ, after,' he says. 'I'd let you have him, only he'd never be happy without the sheep.'

'He's a working dog,' Cal agrees. He figures he'll end up having to do Kojak a mercy.

'I've left the farm to Senan's young lad,' Mart says. 'The second one; Ruairi. That way Senan won't have to split his land. And I've no need to worry that the young fella'll sell up to the likes of Tommy Moynihan and his pals. Senan'd rip the head off him and shove it up his hole.'

His sentences have more gaps for breath now, and the lines of his face have tightened. 'You got any pain?' Cal asks.

'You couldn't do anything about it if I had,' Mart says, 'so don't be annoying me. Just give us another sup of that.'

Cal steadies the bottle for him again, and wipes his face. 'Ruairi's a good kid,' he says. He's talking to stop Mart talking. 'He goes out with Noreen's girl, right? The oldest one. Ella. After all your fighting and fussing with Noreen, her grandkids could end up running your farm. Bet you would've got yourself a wife if you thought that was in the cards.'

He expects that to get a grin, but Mart isn't paying attention; he's looking past Cal, out over the fields. Cal thinks maybe he's starting to wander, but his eyes are focused. He's scanning the land with a farmer's purpose, with intimate, fine-grained knowledge of each stretch of earth, each wall, each animal, in all their history and their worth and their needs.

'Tell Ruairi about the scald,' he says, after a minute. 'He'll need the footbath.'

'I'll do that,' Cal says.

'Senan's raring to give Bobby a few skelps. This'll make him worse. Don't let him do it.'

'Bobby's back on board,' Cal says. 'He came over to my place this morning, to tell me he's had enough of Tommy Moynihan and he's not gonna stand aside any more. I was gonna come tell you.' He'd forgotten all about that – it feels like it happened in a different world – but he's glad Mart reminded him. It's something Mart should know.

'Better late than fuckin' never,' Mart says. 'Them sheep are still waiting on that silage.'

'Me and PJ'll see to it,' Cal says. 'Don't worry.'

Mart nods. His eyes close.

'Mart,' Cal says. He doesn't get an answer.

Cal works a hand carefully past Kojak and feels at Mart's throat till he finds a pulse, faint and very fast. 'Mart,' he says again, louder. Kojak's eyebrows twitch. Mart doesn't move.

Cal sits with his back against the tractor. He has the impulse to say a prayer, but he can't think of any that would fit. He takes another drink of whiskey.

The sheep, losing interest in a situation beyond their understanding, have started to graze. In all these fields, nothing moves except animals meandering through their steady patterns; in all this silence, there's no distant wail of a siren coming. All he can do is wait there while Mart's life ends.

After a minute or two, Kojak lets out a wrenching sound between a howl and a whine. When Cal looks, he sees that Mart is dead.

20

The ambulance, when it finally comes, comes fast and silently, with no lights or sirens. Cal is so cold and so stiff that when he stands up to wave, his legs almost go out from under him. The sky is too dark for mid-afternoon; against its bruised grey the paramedics stride briskly across the fields, neon-yellow, snapping on gloves, shouldering their bags of delicate sharp tools. Kojak rises up to guard against them, with a low warning snarl, and it takes Cal a long time to persuade him away and get a grip on his collar so they can bend over what they've come for.

In spite of its discretion, the ambulance has been noted. From every direction people move in, across fields and along the road, to stand at a distance. PJ brings his tractor with its winch, and he and a couple of other men weave straps through Mart's tractor, tug at clasps, squint to check angles. They say a word or two here and there. Their faces wear no expression. The paramedics have pulled up the duvet over Mart's head.

When the tractor is raised and steady, the paramedics move in with their stretcher. Cal turns away, so as not to see what they're lifting and covering. All around, the treelines have closed in, intent and watching; farther off, the mountain is hidden by cloud, so that the world ends at its slope.

People cross themselves as the stretcher passes. The small sharp sound of the ambulance door slamming carries across the fields. As the ambulance starts back towards the main road, more slowly now that there's no hurry, the watchers turn for home.

Cal and PJ and Senan are left. They unhook the winch rope and disentangle the straps from Mart's tractor. 'Leave it stand,' Senan says. 'The oil needs to settle.'

Cal's jacket and sweatshirt and Mart's duvet lie tangled on the grass. The hole in the earth is there, but Mart was right: blurred by the ground's sogginess and by the tractor, to the Guards and the inspectors it could pass for something dug by rabbits or badgers. Cal pulls out his phone and takes photos, before he treads on the edges a few times just in case. He has to cast around for a while before he finds the heap of dark dirt tucked away discreetly at the foot of a wall, and takes photos of that too. He catches Senan's head turned towards him.

'Come over to my place,' he says, when he gets back to the tractor. 'When you're done here. And get Francie.'

PJ winds his winch rope back in and loads the silage onto his tractor to feed the sheep – they turn noisy at the sight, and jostle around their trough. Senan takes charge of Kojak while Cal trudges across the fields, with the duvet under his arm, to retrieve Rip from Mart's house. Kojak is obeying commands docilely now, but he still has a wild creature's eyes; if he finds Rip alone in his home, he'll kill him.

Cal is the kind of cold that feels like nothing will ever thaw him. He folds away his jacket and sweatshirt and Mart's fleece in a corner of his bedroom, and layers himself in sweaters. Rip trails him around the house, making anxious beagle conversation; he's happily impervious to most things, but today has left him cowed. Outside, in the stillness that's too heavy for a workday, the news is flying.

Cal's mind goes to Lena, but he can't do anything about her right now; he has other business that needs dealing with first. His thinking has a strange, rhythmic clarity, like it's being paced by a drumbeat he can't hear. He washes his hands, scrubbing tractor grease and mud out of the cracks in his skin. He finds a bottle of bourbon and a handful of glasses and mugs, and sets them out on the kitchen table. His phone is full up with frantic texts from Bobby, who's heard some version and is afraid to come near in case he gets run off. Cal texts him back: *Come over to my place.*

The other men won't welcome that, but Cal figures he might as well find out straight away whether Bobby and Mart were right about people listening to him. And if he wins this fight, Bobby will take his side, out of gratitude, in any others that might come up. He needs to start thinking this way. He goes to the workroom and brings out his spare chair.

Senan and PJ and Francie arrive together. Kojak slinks to a corner and lies flat, but no one else can settle; they move around Cal's kitchen and his living room, shoulders rolling, breathing like bulls. The house feels too small for them. It smells powerfully of sweat, mud, rage.

'Now,' Senan says. 'What's the fuckin' story?'

'Mart drove that path every day of his fuckin' life,' Francie says. 'He didn't roll that tractor. Tommy Moynihan's at the back of this.'

'Bobby oughta be here any minute,' Cal says. 'We'll talk then.'

All three of them wheel to face Cal. 'Fuck Bobby,' Senan and Francie say at the same time. PJ is open-mouthed.

'The man's a fuckin' traitor,' Senan says.

'Bobby's changed his views,' Cal says. 'He's had enough of Moynihan's shit.'

Francie lets out a harsh snap of a laugh. 'Bit late for that, hah?'

'If he walks in that door,' Senan says, 'I'll punch his teeth out for him.'

'Nope,' Cal says. 'Bobby never did one thing to help Moynihan out. All he did was take a while to get his priorities straight.'

'"Cause he's a waste of fuckin' space,' Francie says.

'Maybe,' Cal says, 'but if you cut him out, you're doing Moynihan's work for him. That's what he wants: everyone pissed off with everyone else, so we won't team up against him. We've been playing his game long enough.'

'The man's right,' PJ says, to all of their surprise. PJ takes so little part in arguments that people tend to factor him out altogether, but apparently the other night's foray into loudness had a lasting impact. 'Bobby's sound as a pound. You're only sore 'cause he didn't do what you tolt him for once. Now he's doing it, what more d'you want?'

'I want the little shite outa my sight,' Senan says. 'Today of all days.'

'I been pals with Bobby since school,' PJ says, unbudged. 'I'm not having Tommy fuckin' Moynihan decide who my friends are.'

'What d'you want that gobdaw for, anyhow?' Francie asks Cal. 'I can get you a dozen men that'd be more use.'

'Tommy's got sources,' Cal says. 'He's gonna know exactly who's been on board with us all along, and who was staying clear of the action up until now. I want to show him that people are done with staying clear.'

They look at him, registering that he has some plan in mind, weighing the value of that. Cal looks back at them.

They could, with reason, turn on him. They did things his way before, and now Mart is dead. All of them know that Mart never in his life did anything except by his own choice, but these men have more anger than they can hold, and they need somewhere to lay it.

'It's your house,' Senan says, after a moment. 'You can invite anyone you want.'

'I'm warning you now, but,' Francie says, 'if that *amadán* comes out with any shite about giving Tommy the benefit of the doubt, I'll fetch him such a kick up the hole, he won't sit down for a month.'

This is as near to capitulation as Cal could hope for. 'If he does that,' he says, 'I'll kick him up the ass myself. But he won't.' Francie snorts, unconvinced, and sheers off to pace the living room again. Rip, further unsettled by Kojak's strangeness, is watching him warily; Kojak lies like none of them are there.

The tap on the door is so timid that Cal only hears it because he's been listening for it. Bobby is a mess, pale and red-eyed, his sparse hair sticking up at frantic angles. When he sees the others, he freezes.

'Come on in,' Cal says. And to all of them: 'Have a seat.'

Senan and Francie eye Bobby, who blinks hard but keeps his chins up. No one says anything.

Cal sits down at the table and starts pouring bourbon, with a generous hand. PJ folds his lankiness into a chair. After a long second, the others follow.

Senan takes his glass and raises it. Cal thinks he's going to say *To Mart*, but instead he clears his throat suddenly and fiercely, and says nothing at all. The rest of them lift their glasses to match, and drink hard.

Cal knows the evening they should be having: more drink, anecdotes about Mart, more drink, dark stories about other farm accidents, more drink, songs to fill the place of the weeping they won't do. This death requires a different kind of tribute.

'I seen that hole,' Senan says, putting down his glass. 'Under the tyre. That's what rolled the tractor.'

'Yeah,' Cal says. 'Mart was awake when I got there. Awake and talking.' He sees that reach them, what his day has been like. 'He said that hole was dug last night. And the sod was put back over it, so's he wouldn't see it.'

No one meets that with any surprise. All it gets is a slow,

grim tightening of the anger around the table. ''Twouldn't be hard,' PJ says, 'and the ground this wet.'

'There's tyre-tracks worn in the grass,' Francie says, 'where Mart took the same route every time. All anyone'd have to do is pick a spot on one a them tracks, and they'd have him.'

Senan nods, and keeps nodding. 'Tommy's a dead man,' he says. 'We'll head over there tonight and take him up the mountains.'

Cal drinks and keeps quiet. He knew this was coming. It needs to have its time.

'You oughta stay out of it,' PJ says, to Senan. 'You've Angela and the kids.'

'The kids won't know. And Angela'll say nothing.'

'Ah, I know that, sure. But if we get caught, like.'

'I'm not fuckin' staying outa anything,' Senan says. His voice is flat and final. To Cal: 'How about you? You've Lena and the child. D'you wanta stay outa this?'

All of them are looking at Cal. 'Whatever we decide on,' he says, 'I'm in.'

There's a brief silence, and a scatter of nods around the table. Cal reaches for the bottle and tops up the glasses.

'I've zip ties,' Francie says.

'I've duct tape,' Senan says. 'And I'll find an aul' feed sack.'

'We oughta leave it till late,' PJ says. 'I'd say everyone'll be awful nervy tonight. They mightn't go to bed on time.'

'Half-three,' Francie says. 'Home before it starts getting bright, or before anyone's out on the land.'

'Meet in the lane behind Moynihans',' Senan says. 'We'll go in by the back, through that fuckin' conservatory. Take him out the same way, have the car waiting.'

'I'll drive,' Francie says. 'That yoke of yours is on its last legs. The rest of ye walk there, and take the back roads. No torches.'

It rises up as powerful and vivid as a memory, spreading in

the air between them. The dark of the lane between the hedges, breath rising in the cold; tinkle of breaking glass, grunts of a struggle; and then the car bumping over potholes all the long twisting way up the mountain, the weight of a man lifted between them and the smell of his fear, and the high calls of night birds over the bog.

Cal lets it fill the air for a long moment, but he can't give it more than that. Any time now, the Guards will come looking for accounts of what happened today, and there's work to be done before he and the other men can be ready to provide those. He says, 'What about Tommy's security system?'

'Fuck the security system,' Senan says. 'We'll get out them balaclavas again, and say we were home the whole time. They can't prove different.'

'He's gonna have one of those alarms that call the Guards if there's a breach.'

Everyone snorts. 'By the time the Guards get up off their holes,' Francie says, 'we'll be home in our beds.'

Cal says, 'Tommy's got half the Guards in town living up his ass. He's got phone numbers. We take him, Clodagh makes a call, and we're done: if they don't pick us up on the way out, they'll get us on the way back.' He leaves a second for that to sink in. 'Or were you planning on taking Clodagh and Eugene, too?'

'Ah, no,' PJ says firmly. 'This was Tommy's doing.'

'Then what are we gonna do with them?'

'We could leave them tied,' Francie says.

His voice lacks conviction, and no one nods agreement. No one likes the thought of binding and gagging a woman.

'We could,' Cal says. 'But odds are they're gonna be able to identify at least one of us, just by build.' This is unarguable: he's too big to be confused for anyone else, PJ is too lanky, Bobby is too little and round. No one responds to this, either; no one is on board for making sure Clodagh and Eugene can't identify them. 'And that's before we even get started on camera footage. And tyre tracks, and footprints, and—'

'Then we get Tommy on his own,' Bobby says. It's the first time he's spoken; his voice is thick and hoarse. Cal sees Senan's glance flick to him. 'He hasta go out sometime. We'll get him then.'

'We gonna have eyes on him twenty-four seven?' Cal says.

Senan says, 'We'll take shifts.'

'Hanging around outside his house?' Cal asks. 'Shadowing him every time he leaves? You think that won't get noticed? This place, everyone sees everything.'

'They might see it,' Francie says. 'They won't say it.'

'Maybe they won't, or maybe they will. Depends who it is.' Cal lets that land. Ardnakelty doesn't talk to cops, but even that has shifted under Tommy's hand.

'That gobshite Long John,' PJ says, with disgust. 'He'd rat. So would Mouth McHugh.'

'Even if no one does,' Cal says. 'Say I spot Tommy going out by himself: I gotta get in touch and let the rest of you know. The Guards are gonna track where Tommy's phone went, find out mine was near it, find that contact with you, track where your phones went—'

'So we'll leave our phones behind,' Senan says, throwing himself back in his chair. He's losing patience with Cal's roadblocks.

'How? Think it through, man. How do I keep the rest of you guys updated on where Tommy's heading, where to meet, if nobody's got their phones?'

PJ is starting to look baffled by all the permutations; Bobby has his mouth set mulishly, rejecting what he's hearing. 'Then whoever gets the chance does the job on his own,' Francie says. 'Luck of the draw.'

'This isn't a one-man job,' Cal says. 'Tommy's gonna be on

his guard; he won't go down easy. And he's too heavy for one guy to haul into a car, out of the car, into the bog; that's gonna need two pairs of hands, maybe three. And we need someone to take his phone in the wrong direction meanwhile, dump it in the river or—'

'Shoot the fucker and leave him in the road,' Francie says. His voice is gathering danger. 'He'll go down easy enough with a bullet in his head.' The table feels crowded with elbows planted wide, heads lowered for battle. The guys don't like where this is going.

'Your gun registered?' Cal asks. "Cause mine is. It'll take the Guards about a day to match the bullet. It's not gonna work.'

Senan's eyes are steady and bleak on his. 'Man,' he says, 'you don't get it. My granddad usedta tell me stories about the shenanigans himself and Mart's granddad got up to.'

'One time,' Bobby says, and clears the roughness out of his throat, 'one time a heifer pinned my daddy against the wall of the crush. He woulda been kilt, except Mart's daddy got her away. That's back in the sixties, like. I wouldn'ta been born only for him.'

'Mart's granny got TB,' Francie says. 'She hadta go into a sanatorium. My family took in the kids, till she was better.'

Cal understands what they're telling him. These aren't just bittersweet anecdotes. These men's lives have been knotted together with Mart's since centuries before they began. They can't be disentangled at will.

'Mart's brothers is all gone,' PJ explains. 'He's got cousins over to Gorteen, but they're not close, like. There's no one to get the job done, only us.'

'If what I said won't work,' Senan says, 'you find something that will. You're the cop.'

'I was the cop,' Cal says, 'so that's how I know there isn't any safe way. Too many things come down to luck. All it takes is one of 'em going wrong, and we're screwed.' Senan starts to say something, but Cal keeps going. 'If we take Tommy out, we'll end up in prison.'

'Don't be telling me Tommy Moynihan can get away with murder and we can't,' Senan says. His voice is rising; he's hunched like he might overturn his chair any minute. 'That prick's sitting in his conservatory right now, with a big smirk on him, thinking he's warned us all off and he can do what he likes. We've been letting him away with shite all our lives. I'm not letting him away with this.'

Cal looks at the faces turned towards him. Out of nowhere he recalls the sudden fall of silence in incident rooms when he stood up to brief a team on the next phase of some investigation, or outline the operation that lay ahead of them. Those seem like places in another universe, like he could never have been real in those rooms and exist in this one too. These men, windburned and interwoven, in their battered work pants stained with grease and sheep shit, live by different rhythms and are made of different materials from the easy, smart-talking, forthright mix in his incident rooms. Even the light at the window seems to come from a different sun.

He has no right to lead these men anywhere, and no urge to do it. But it needs doing. All his life Cal has aimed to do the things that need doing, and now he's here.

'He's not getting away with it,' he says. 'I've got witnesses who saw Tommy heading for the old bridge, right around when Rachel went off it.'

No one moves.

'Jesus fuck,' Senan says, after a moment.

'I never knew,' Bobby says, stunned. 'If I'da known—'

'None of us knew, you gobshite,' Francie says, 'but we still didn't have our heads up Moynihan's hole.'

'All this time,' PJ says, with a kind of wonder. 'Everyone

going mental trying to work out what happened, saying this, that, and t'other. And all the time, there was people that saw him.'

'So you were right about getting loud,' Senan says. He's looking at Cal with a new alertness, now that Cal's way has turned out to get results. It didn't work exactly like that, but Cal doesn't correct him.

'Who was it?' Francie wants to know. 'And how come they said nothing before?'

'Teenagers out drinking,' Cal says. 'They didn't think much of it; they figured he had a side piece somewhere, went back to what they were doing.'

'He'll say they got it wrong, in the dark. Or they're talking shite.'

'Right,' Cal says. 'If that was all we had, Tommy could talk his way out, easy. But I've got witnesses for last night, too. Trey and her buddy saw Tommy heading for Mart's land, after two in the morning, carrying a spade.'

There's a surge of breath, close to a growl, around the table.

'What were they doing out?' Francie wants to know. 'Kids don't go drinking on a Monday.'

He means is this bullshit, and if so, will Trey and Kate be able to stand by it. 'They were there,' Cal says. 'I set them to watch the Moynihan place. I had a feeling.'

He doesn't go into the Eugene side of things. Eugene is the wild card who could win him the hand or come to nothing, and today the guys need solid things to grip; Eugene's precarious possibilities, rather than heartening them, would only wind them tighter. Cal feels, suddenly and sharply, the weight of being the one who has to make that call.

'He done it himself,' Senan says, low and dangerous. 'The fucker.'

'And I got photos of that hole in the ground,' Cal says. 'You could still see the spade cuts, in places. I got photos of the dirt that came out of the hole, too; he collected it in a garbage bag or something, and dumped it over by the wall. Tommy fucked up this time.'

PJ has his forehead furrowed, working to arrange all this; Senan has a grim one-sided smile. Their whole lives, Tommy has been all-powerful, untouchable, every move he makes has been a smooth checkmate. Tommy fucked up this time. Like everything else, Tommy is changing.

'So what you're saying is,' Francie says, 'we take all this to the Guards.'

The words fall heavily in the room. Cal feels the rejection, instant and instinctive.

'We can,' he says. 'I don't know how far that'd get. Tommy's got the local Guards in his pocket, and his buddy Whatshisname, Dickie O'Shea, he can probably pull some strings with the higher-ups. Everything we've got, if the Guards don't want to deal with it, they can just brush it off as local grudges, people getting jealous of the guy with the fancy house. If we had something solid, like if the kid had gotten video of Tommy digging that hole, no one would sweep that under the rug for some backcountry big shot. But we don't.'

'That's the fuckin' Guards for you,' Francie says, with centuries' worth of scorn. 'As much use as tits on a bull.'

'And regardless of what they do,' Cal says, 'there's still the business with the land.'

He gives the guys a second to find that in their minds. Today buried even that.

'I'll blow Tommy sky-high before I let him get his hands on that land,' Senan says. The words come slow and rough, from deep in his chest. 'After today.'

'We've got no way of knowing how far that's gone,' Cal says. 'Tommy's had it in the works for a while now. He's got investors in place, people on the council. If we get him locked up – or if we take him out – the whole damn thing could just keep on rolling along without him.'

They're Mart's words; Mart with a frying pan in his hand and a sidelong eye out for the squirrel. The full unreality of the day surges up on Cal. For a moment his breath jams in his chest.

'We need Tommy,' he says.

Senan is staring him down, arms folded. He says, 'So what's your fuckin' plan?'

'I figure we've got two choices,' Cal says. 'I can take what we've got to some detective up in Dublin. If we get lucky, I find someone who'll work it, and we end up with Tommy in jail and all his investors spooked enough that they take their megafarm somewhere else. If we get unlucky, the whole thing gets tossed straight in the garbage. Then we've blown our shot, and we've got nothing.'

Senan says, 'What's the other choice?'

'Or,' Cal says. 'We can take what we've got to Tommy. Like we were planning to do before. Tell him either he goes to his investors and his councillors and comes up with some reason why they need to pull the plug on their bullshit, or else we go to the Guards.'

There's a silence. It's still afternoon, but the light at the windows has a contracted, sparse quality; the men's faces are too dim for Cal to gauge. The kitchen is cold.

Bobby says, 'But then he'll get away with it. With Mart. And the young one.' His face has the raw disbelief of a kid slammed up against the impossible injustice of the world. PJ is unconsciously shaking his head.

'Yeah,' Cal says. Other people have killed and got away with it, around here, but he doesn't bring that up. To these guys, that was an entirely different thing. 'He'll walk away. But he won't walk away with anyone's land.'

No one says anything. PJ, troubled, glances around the table. Francie drinks. Bobby's eyes have welled up; he blots them, furtively, with his sleeve.

'You said we've no proof,' Senan says. He's looking down at his hands, clasped around his glass like he might crush it. 'No video of him digging the hole or nothing.'

'Right,' Cal says. 'Tommy doesn't know that.'

'What if he calls our bluff? Tells us fuck you, go to the Guards if you want?'

'Then we do it,' Cal says, 'and keep our fingers crossed. But Tommy's gonna know the Guards are a crapshoot, just like we do. If we put it to him right, I don't think he'll want to take the risk.'

'Tommy's a hard chaw,' Francie says. 'He never backed down that I know of.'

Cal says, 'I've taken down guys that could eat Tommy fucking Moynihan for breakfast.'

He watches them look at him and see, for the last time, a cop.

'If anyone can make Tommy back down,' Bobby says timidly, glancing around the table, 'it'd be a detective; someone that's had practice, like. And someone he hasn't known from a baba. A man that's never hadta do what Tommy tolt him, so Tommy won't be thinking he can scare him out of it.'

PJ is still gazing at Cal, but he's seeing something else now, something new. Francie is unreadable, scratching the day's stubble that darkens his bony face.

Senan's head is down again. He says, to Cal, 'I'm not leaving this to you. No harm to you; not saying you'd make a balls of it, or nothing. But this is our job.'

'All of our job,' Cal says. 'We go in together.'

Senan looks up. He says, 'And that's what you reckon we oughta do. Not the Guards. That.'

'What I want to do is beat that shitheel into mush and dump

what's left in a bog,' Cal says, 'but I gave Mart my word we'd use this. He didn't want it wasted.' He hears the quick hard breaths, all around the table. 'This is the only way I can think of that has a decent shot at not wasting it.'

There's another silence, this one full of things shifting. Bobby's eyes are welling up again.

'You can't go ignoring a man's last wish,' PJ says, suddenly and firmly. 'I'd say that's some kinda sin.'

'Fuckin' typical,' Francie says sourly. 'He was always an awkward aul' bollocks.'

'Right,' Senan says. He drains his bourbon and gets to his feet, the chair creaking under his weight as he pushes it back. 'Let's get a move on, so.'

21

This time, when they step between Tommy Moynihan's gateposts, the security lights don't snap on. The day is just starting to fade; behind the sprawl of the house, the sunset is a long band of gold and orange, flattened below the clouds. They go up the wide drive five abreast, their matched steps crunching the gravel.

With the light at its shoulder, the house is dark-faced and looks lower, masked. Cal can feel Tommy inside, watching as they come into focus on his little screen, deciding whether and how to meet the attack.

He calls it just in time. Cal is raising his hand to the discreet electronic bell when the door opens on Tommy, every silver hair in place, poised and easy in the suede-panelled taupe cardigan that Cal always knew he owned.

'Lads,' he says. His face is arranged in an expression of suitable gravity. 'I heard the news. 'Tis a terrible day for all Ardnakelty, but ye'll feel the loss worse than most.'

He's talking to Senan, presumably because Senan is both the biggest man and the biggest landholder there. Cal doesn't count; Tommy's eyes passed straight over him.

No one moves, but the anger rises. 'Mart's no loss to you,' Francie says.

'Francie,' Tommy says, reproachful but compassionate. 'Myself and Mart Lavin had our differences of opinion – haven't we all, sure? – but I'd be the first to say he was a fine man. And in a community like this, any tragedy touches us all.'

He sounds like he's practising for the eulogy. Cal says, 'We'd like a talk with you.'

Tommy turns to look at him with mild surprise. 'It'd be my pleasure,' he says. 'Will we say Thursday afternoon, around four o'clock? Or Friday?'

Cal says, 'We're here now.'

Tommy gives the other guys a remonstrating glance, nudging them to teach their pet Yank some manners if they want to take him out in public. He gets nothing back.

'Mr Hooper,' Tommy says, slowing down a notch so Cal can understand him. 'I know this has been a shock to you, and you're not yourself. But what you haveta remember is, myself and these lads, we knew Mart an awful lot longer than you did. So you'll forgive me if I'm not in form for a chat tonight.' He nods to Cal, dismissing him, and turns back to the rest. 'Have a talk amongst yourselves, decide whether Thursday or Friday suits ye better, and we'll put it in the diary.'

Senan says, 'Now suits us.'

Tommy measures them and gets it right: one more no, and they'll be on him. 'Right, so,' he says, almost concealing a sigh, noblesse oblige giving him patience with the unwashed masses. 'Come on in. We'll keep the voices down, if you don't mind; the missus and the young fella have enough on their plates as it is.'

The hall is high-ceilinged, with big gold-framed mirrors and a staircase that clearly calls itself a feature. Faintly, on a TV somewhere, a high monotonous voice quacks on and on. At the top of the stairs, in shadow, someone moves.

'In here,' Tommy says, opening a door. Cal could have described the Moynihans' living room without ever setting foot in it: enormous angular grey couches, enormous glass coffee table, ugly orange rug for a splash of colour, enormous art on the walls. Two grey armchairs are the only things built for comfort. The back wall is one enormous picture window, looking out over the long slope of the fields to the setting sun. Cal wonders how often Tommy has redrawn that view to fit his will: factory in one corner, the vast blank blocks of a megafarm stretching across the horizon, housing estates dotted around, and Tommy sitting here, lord of all he surveys.

'Have a seat,' Tommy says hospitably, closing the door behind them. He settles himself in one of the armchairs – the one in front of the window, so he gets a suitably impressive backdrop – and puts his fingertips together.

Cal takes the other chair, facing him across the coffee table, which raises Tommy's eyebrows a fraction. He doesn't want to deal with Cal. He's had all his life to take the measure of the other men, and they've had generations of training in doing the Moynihans' bidding. Cal is an unknown quantity, and has no such habit.

Senan and Francie take one couch, and Bobby and PJ take the other. Tommy waits for them to arrange themselves – the couches are constructed so that you can either perch on the edge or slump backwards at an awkward angle, putting you at a disadvantage either way. The room smells of some kind of air freshener named after plants that sound made up. Cal and the other men have come wearing the smells of the outdoors and Mart's death. He sees Tommy's nostrils twitch, and his glance at their muddy boots on the rug.

'Now,' Tommy says encouragingly, once they're all settled, with just the right note to remind them that he's a busy man. He's still talking to Senan. 'What can I do for you?'

When he came recruiting Cal, and at the funeral, Tommy showed up with the son and heir at his heel. Now he's shushing them so Eugene won't hear and join in the action. At Cal's shoulder, behind the living-room door, there's movement, faint as a stalking animal's.

'We got ourselves a situation, Tommy,' Cal says. He takes

care how he pitches his voice; he needs it to carry enough to reach the listener, but not enough that Tommy will notice. 'And we figured, what with you being kind of a big shot around these parts, you might help us decide how to deal with it.'

Tommy's eyebrows lift. 'I'm always delighted to give any man a hand,' he says, 'where I can. What's the situation ye've got yourselves into?'

'Mart's tractor didn't turn over by accident,' Cal says. 'Someone dug a hole in his field, right where the tractor tyre would pass.'

Tommy registers the right amount of shock. 'If that's true,' he says, ''tis a terrible thing. But – and no harm to any of ye – do ye not think ye're getting a wee bit carried away? There's nothing sinister about the ground sinking under a tractor tyre, specially not after all this rain. 'Tis natural to look for some rhyme or reason in a tragedy, but sometimes there's none to find.'

'That hole was dug,' Senan says. 'I seen a fuckin' hole dug in the ground before.'

'I'm sure you have,' Tommy agrees politely. 'But everyone's feeling a bit high-strung right now, and ye've had a hard day. When you're in that state, 'tis awful easy to work yourself up and start seeing boogeymen everywhere.'

A low mutter moves around the men. 'If you want to see for yourself,' Cal says, 'I got some photos.' He gets out his phone before Tommy can answer, pulls up a photo of the hole, and passes it across the coffee table.

Tommy takes reading glasses out of his cardigan pocket, unfolds them with a neat flick, and inspects the photo. 'Scroll left,' Cal says helpfully. 'There's a few that show the pile of dirt the guy dug up.'

'I'll take your word for it,' Tommy says. He hands the phone back to Cal.

'You're not gonna find anyone to argue that wasn't done by a spade,' Cal says. He puts his phone away.

Tommy purses up his lips and tilts his head, unconvinced. 'It mighta been, I suppose,' he says. 'It looks like a rabbit hole to me, but I'm no expert. Either way' – he takes off his glasses to point at Cal, for emphasis – 'I'd be careful how you say that, if I were you. That's an awful big accusation to be throwing around, and it could have big consequences.' It's fatherly admonition, out of concern for where their foolishness could land them. 'Ye're looking for someplace to take out all today's emotions, is what it is. But there's healthier ways of dealing with a loss, and ye'll see that once the shock wears off. Unless you've photos that show some man – or woman – digging that hole, my advice would be to forget all about your "spade marks".'

Senan moves on the couch. Cal hopes he can get them through this conversation without Senan punching Tommy's lights out. 'No photos of that part,' he acknowledges. 'But we got video.'

Tommy's head comes up from folding his glasses. His face is wiped blank, every muscle frozen. Behind him, the sun gilds the sweep of fields with the ghost of harvest radiance.

After a second he says, 'Of what?'

'You went out your back gate around two last night,' Cal says, 'carrying a spade.' Tommy's face doesn't change. 'You took the back lanes to Mart Lavin's bottom field, where you dug a hole on the path left by his regular tractor route.'

Tommy recovers himself. He leans back in his chair with his eyebrows high, staring at Cal like he just started stripping off. 'I'll say this much for you,' he says. The fatherly note has gone. 'You've balls the size of watermelons, walking into my sitting room and accusing me of murder.'

'You used a bag to collect the dirt,' Cal says. 'When you finished digging, you replaced the sod on top of the hole to conceal it, and dumped the dirt against the south-west wall of the field. Then you went back home.'

Tommy examines Cal for another long minute. Then he turns to the other guys. 'The fuck is this fella even doing here?' he asks, jerking a thumb at Cal. 'No offence, pardner,' he adds, to Cal.

'He's here,' Francie says. 'That's all you need to know.'

'And ye do what he says, is it?'

'And you oughta be grateful we do,' Senan says. 'I'll tell you now, boy, this isn't how I wanted to go about this conversation.'

'God almighty,' Tommy says, with a touch of wry amusement, 'I never thought I'd see Ardnakelty men taking orders from some Yank. Your daddies are turning in their fuckin' graves.'

'We don't take orders from any man,' PJ says. 'And we're done taking them from the likes of you.'

Tommy shrugs, still amused. 'I suppose sheep always find a sheepdog,' he says. 'But ye might wanta think twice, before this one herds the lot of ye into a bog. Have sense, for God's sake. All that rubbish' – he flicks a dismissive finger towards Cal's phone – 'what's it worth? Fuck-all. If those are spade cuts, and I don't think they are, then who's to say when they got there? Let's be honest, a few of ye have a grudge against me. I'm not saying ye'd go as far as framing me for murder – sure, I'd like to hope no Ardnakelty man would do that on another – but if push came to shove, it'd be awful hard to prove either way.'

'So what about the video?' Cal asks. 'We look like we've got the tech skills for deepfakes?'

'I'll tell you what I think about that video,' Tommy says. He tucks his glasses neatly back into his pocket and gives them a pat. 'I think *if* I'da done what you're accusing me of – which I'd call a grotesque allegation – and *if* someone had been videoing me, and *if* they'd been close enough to get my face on camera in the black dark, I woulda spotted them. There's no video. If there is, all it shows is dark.'

'You want to bet on that?' Cal asks. He could whip out a whole spiel about probable cause, how they've got enough that the Guards will track Tommy's phone and test the dirt on his spade and match his footprints to the scene, and he could throw in an account of video enhancement technology that would scare the bejesus out of anyone who's ever watched *CSI*. He has it all ready to go and he'd be using it, if it wasn't for that sliver of movement, almost too faint to hear, at the door. He wants this conversation to sound, to a listener, like Tommy is winning.

'Let's see this video,' Tommy says. He's smelled blood.

'You don't make demands here, Tommy,' Cal says. 'That's not how this works.'

He can feel the other guys around him, like there's a hard heat coming off each one of them. He doesn't look to check whether this is shaking them. All he can do is trust that their faith in him will hold.

Tommy is grinning. 'Listen to the big man. Are you hoping if you bluster hard enough, I'll panic and confess to something I never done? Maybe that worked on your suspects back in America, but I'm telling you now, boy, I'm not some halfwit teenager that robbed a petrol station for his fix. You're taking on the wrong man.'

He settles back in his chair, to finish this off at his leisure. 'I wouldn't know about America,' he says, 'but around here, we've got laws against slander. And I'm not the type to lie back and take this kinda vile attack on my reputation.'

'You want to air all this out in court,' Cal says, 'I'm in. I've got nothing better to do with my time. Your business buddies gonna like that?'

'Maybe you've nothing better to do, but I'd say these lads have. Amn't I right, lads?' Tommy looks the men over, giving them plenty of time to answer him. No one does. 'And it'll never see a courtroom. I'll have the lotta ye bankrupted long before that. One phone call to my solicitor, that's all it'd take. Will I get on to him right now?'

Out of the corner of his eye Cal can see Bobby and PJ glancing at him, worried. He says nothing.

'I'll tell you what,' Tommy says. Under the righteous outrage, he's swelling with victory. 'If ye're out that door by the time I count ten, we'll say no more about this. By rights I oughta demand apologies from the lotta ye, but I'll make allowances. One. Two.'

The room has the lush silence of rich people's houses, triple-glazed and thick-curtained. Francie is sunk into the couch, arms folded, like it'll take a crane to get him out. Senan is on the edge of his cushion, ready to rumble. Behind Tommy, the sun is a red coin balanced on the horizon.

'Three,' Tommy says. He reaches into his pants pocket and takes out his phone. 'Four.'

At Cal's shoulder, the living-room door opens.

Eugene's been caught without his finance-bro outfit; he's wearing a grey hoodie and black tracksuit bottoms, and he's in his sock feet. He looks younger, and tightened to snapping point. Cal has seen that look before, on guys who were past caring how many punches they took, as long as they landed some good ones.

'All this shit about Mart Lavin,' Eugene says. He's talking to Cal.

'Not now, Eugene,' Tommy says, like a six-year-old is up past his bedtime, but the glance he gives Eugene has a hard warning. 'I'm just finishing up a little chat with these lads. You go inside and watch the telly with your mammy, and I'll be with you in a minute.'

Eugene blinks, but he keeps his eyes on Cal. 'Fuck Mart Lavin,' he says. 'What about Rachel?'

'I told you what about Rachel,' Cal says. Out of the corner of his eye he sees the other guys' heads turn towards him, but all he can do is keep relying on them. 'We got witnesses putting your daddy at the bridge at the right time—'

'Ah, for fuck's sake,' Tommy says. 'This is getting beyond a joke. I'm a one-man crime wave, is it? Ye need a better hobby, lads.'

'But if we want to do anything about it,' Cal says to Eugene, 'we're gonna need what you've got.'

He feels the rest of the guys drawing breath, repositioning themselves, as they start to take in what he's been doing.

'Right,' Tommy says, loud and crisp. He shoves his phone back in his pocket and stands up. 'We're done here. I've cut ye some slack because of the day that's in it, but you've crossed the line. Eugene: upstairs, now. The rest of ye: outa my fucking house.'

Eugene snaps, '*Sit down.*'

His voice has a high, uncontrolled, dangerous note, and his hands are shaking. Something, Cal would love to know what, has cracked the dam open.

Tommy recognises it too. 'Eugene,' he says. His tone has changed; he's gone calm and firm, a headmaster expertly managing a tantruming child. 'This isn't the day for any more drama. Everyone needs to let the hare sit a while, and we'll come back to this when there's cooler heads all round.'

Eugene ignores him. 'You want the whole thing,' he says to Cal, 'you can have it. Just fucking *do something* with it.'

'You already got my word on that,' Cal says.

'Story time,' Senan says. 'I love a good aul' story.' He sprawls back on the couch, spreads his legs wide, and folds his arms, ready.

'If you've had enough of our company,' Cal says to Tommy, 'we'll all get outa your hair. Eugene can say what he's got to say somewhere else.'

After a second, Tommy heaves an exasperated sigh and sits down. 'All right,' he tells Eugene, adjusting the knees of his pants into place. 'Whatever nonsense this is, I might as well hear it. But make it quick. I've had enough nonsense for one night.'

'We're in no rush,' Cal tells Eugene. 'Start from the start, take your time.'

Eugene doesn't hear either one of them. He's already talking. 'So that morning, the morning before Rachel died. I told her the whole plan *he* had in mind.' He jerks his chin at Tommy. All his life, the two weightiest words have been *my father*. He's done with them. 'I was supposed to keep my mouth shut about it, but I was planning to propose to her that weekend, and I wanted to get this angle squared away first. I thought Rachel's initial reaction might need some managing, and I didn't want to end up dealing with that in the middle of wedding planning.'

His voice is cold and clipped, like he's giving a work presentation to people he despises. 'And yeah, no, she wasn't happy. At all. I'd expected this to be just one of those humps you have to get over, every couple has those, no big deal, right? But Rachel acted like this was *huge*. I explained to her: OK, some people would throw fits at first, but once they saw all the advantages in practice, they'd think this was the greatest thing since sliced bread. They always do.'

That gets a low growl from Francie. Eugene doesn't even notice. 'But Rachel . . . She didn't want anyone hating us, but it wasn't just that. She couldn't stand the idea of making people unhappy. That's—' Eugene catches his breath sharply. 'That's what she was like,' he says, after a moment. 'That's what she was like.'

'She was a good woman,' Senan says. 'You'll get no argument on that from anyone here.'

'You shoulda deserved her better,' PJ says.

'No shit,' Eugene says, with a bitterness heavy as stone.

'Ah, now,' Tommy says compassionately. 'You treated young Rachel like a princess – and she deserved it, I'm not saying she didn't. All I'm saying is, you've nothing to reproach yourself with.'

For a man of his experience, Tommy isn't showing the level of judgement Cal would have expected. Unsurprisingly, Eugene doesn't bother answering him. 'We spent the whole day on it,' he says. 'We went for a drive, we found somewhere for lunch, we drove around some more, and the whole time Rachel kept going back and forth – one minute she was all, "I trust you, if you think it's a good idea then it'll probably be fine in the end," and the next minute she'd be going, "No, everyone'll be devastated, you have to stop him . . ."'

He lets out something like a jagged laugh. 'Like it was that simple. "Just say it to him, tell him you won't run for the council, tell him you won't have anything to do with it—" I couldn't get it through to her that yeah, no, it wasn't actually that easy.'

Cal catches the quick, savage flicker of Tommy's grin. He spent Eugene's life making sure it wouldn't be that easy. 'And you were right, o' course,' he assures Eugene. 'Let's be serious: a man doesn't put years of work into something, and then throw the whole plan in the bin 'cause some young one doesn't like the look of it. Rachel was a grown woman, not a child; she shoulda known that herself.'

'She was working herself up worse and worse,' Eugene says. 'I never expected her to be so . . . Like, "Do I need to leave you, is that what I need to do, if I say it's this or me, then will you—" I didn't know what to do with that. I mean, I knew she wasn't going to actually break *up* with me, but just hearing her say it, she'd never talked like that before . . .'

The brittle professional veneer has cracked away; he sounds ragged and helpless, like he's begging Cal or Tommy or someone to tell him how to fix this. 'In the end she went, "I need to go home, I just need to be on my own and have a think." So I said yeah, OK, let's take a few hours, but I didn't want to leave it too long. Not with her that upset. And Rachel – I mean, I'd told her not to say anything to anyone, but she hated keeping secrets—'

'In fairness,' Tommy points out reasonably, 'you weren't after doing a great job of the aul' confidentiality yourself. You couldn't expect her to do better.' None of this is a surprise to Tommy. He's meditatively turning the gold signet ring on his little finger, watching them all under his eyebrows, waiting.

'I just wanted it sorted out,' Eugene said. 'I knew it would be, in the end, I just . . . I didn't like leaving it. So I told her to meet me at the bridge that evening.'

'In that weather?' Senan says. 'Fuck me. I thought this fella said you treated her like a princess.'

'It wasn't that bad. It wasn't raining. Where were we supposed to go? The pub? *Here?*' Eugene jerks his head at the house like it's a shithole. 'We needed privacy. And the bridge is where we go on, like, special occasions. It's her favourite place. I'd been planning to propose there. I thought maybe, maybe I could—' His face flinches away.

'You thought maybe a big diamond'd sweeten her,' Francie says. 'That's what you thought.'

That snaps Eugene back to them. 'Um, *no?* Rachel wasn't like that, and I'm not stupid. But yeah, *actually*, I thought if we got engaged and everything was great and she had that to focus on, it would give her some perspective, so she wouldn't be stressing out over the other thing.'

'Makes sense,' Cal says. 'So what happened?'

'*He* did. He'd run into me and Rachel, he knew something was up – like I said, she was never any good at hiding things. I told him everything was fine, I had the situation under control, but no, apparently that wasn't good enough. He spent the whole evening going at me, till he got it out of me.'

'Ya fuckin' dope,' Senan says. 'And here's you saying Rachel couldn't keep her mouth shut.'

'Bet your daddy wasn't a happy camper,' Cal says.

The memory makes Eugene blink. 'He went *ballistic*. Losing his fucking mind, kicking furniture, I thought he was going to, I don't know— "What the fuck were you thinking, are you fucking stupid, are you trying to wreck everything I've worked for—"'

Tommy is watching him in disbelief, eyebrows high, glancing around to invite the other guys to share the absurdity of this. Francie gives him a blank stare back.

'I told him Rachel just needed time to come round,' Eugene says. 'I told him. If he had *listened* to me, for once in his—'

'Ah, now,' Tommy says, 'I always listen to you. That doesn't mean I'll always agree with you.' The smoothness says these are words he's used plenty of times. He's trying to catch Eugene by the reflexes and bring him back into line, but Tommy's read it wrong again. Eugene is way past that.

'Then he asked me,' Eugene says, '"And what'll you do if she doesn't come round? Has she cut off your balls for you, boy, are you her bitch now, are you going to bend over and do whatever she wants?"' He's doing his dad's accent, with furious perfection. 'And I told him yes. I said yeah, actually, if Rachel didn't come round, then fuck the county council, fuck his whole bullshit *plan*, he could stick them up his hole, because I was out. And I said I was heading out to meet Rachel and tell her the same thing.'

Tommy is watching Eugene with the profound disappointment of a man whose wayward teenager, after all that good raising, just got caught shoplifting vapes.

Cal says, 'Only you didn't.'

'No,' Eugene says. 'I didn't.' Just for a second, his eyes close against the blinding flash of the ways things could have been different.

'Why not?' Cal asks.

'Why the fuck do you think? *He* told me to stay here, and he'd go talk to Rachel. He said . . .' Eugene's mouth twists. 'He said I'd made enough of a hames of this already, now I needed to get out of the way and let a grown man sort it.'

Bobby says, disgusted, 'And you done it?'

'Yes,' Eugene says, tight-jawed, 'I did. Exactly like you would have. Up until all this hit the fan, when was the last time any of you said no to him? Come on, go for it, I'd love to know. When?'

No one answers.

Cal says, 'How come you didn't text Rachel, let her know what was going on?'

Eugene's face goes fiery with shame. After a second he says, without looking at any of them, 'He took my phone.'

'I did,' Tommy agrees. 'For his own good. The lad was hysterical with worry over the mess he was after making. He was in no state to be talking to that poor girl; he'd only have put the both of them in a worse tizzy.'

'What time did he leave here?' Cal asks Eugene.

'Is this an interrogation?' Tommy enquires. His voice is leisurely and half-amused; he's humouring them, showing he's got nothing to worry about, letting this play out till he decides to stop it. 'Shouldn't you be reading us the aul' Miranda rights?'

Eugene doesn't look at him. 'Around nine,' he says. 'Rachel and I were going to meet at half-nine, and it's about twenty minutes from here to the bridge, on foot – he didn't take the car.'

'Well, that fits with what my witnesses saw,' Cal says, and hears Tommy's tolerant little snort at the word. 'When did he get back?'

'Like eleven.'

That leaves more than an hour unaccounted for. Cal wonders what Rachel thought, when she turned on the bridge to see Tommy coming out of the trees instead of Eugene; whether she was frightened. Tommy would have done a wonderful job of reassuring her. *Eugene said you were worrying your head, God almighty you have the poor fella in an awful state, he asked me to set your mind at rest. Sit down here and we'll have a chat, you must be frozen, I've brought a flask of lovely sweet tea to warm you up. Now, have a sup of that, and talk to me . . .* Probably he listened to all her arguments; maybe he let her talk him around, inch by inch, giving the antifreeze time to work. Once she had slipped too far to fight off either him or the river, he agreed with everything she'd said, helped her to her feet, and pushed. Cal thinks of the white moon blurred by cloud, and the white of Tommy's hair as he stood on the bridge watching the white of Rachel's jacket spin downstream, and all the miles of dark around them.

He says, 'And what'd he tell you, when he came in?'

'He said,' Eugene says, very clearly and with great anger, 'he said he'd changed his mind about talking to Rachel. He wasn't in the right frame of mind to do that, he said, after dealing with me throwing a tantrum like a child; he'd have to do it the next day. He said he'd just gone for a walk instead, to cool off. Up towards Kilhone. In the opposite direction from the river.'

'How'd he seem?' Cal asks. 'Still annoyed, calmed down, what?'

Eugene looks at Tommy. Tommy is leaning back in his chair, watching the scene with a weary disappointment in all of them. Behind him, the sun is sinking fast; the radiance has drained from the fields, and taken their solidity with it. They're made of mist, like you could walk into them and disappear.

'He hadn't *cooled off*,' Eugene says. 'He was in worse shape than when he left. Jumpy as fuck, obviously upset about something. At first I assumed things had gone wrong with Rachel, I was like, *Shit, what did he say to her, did he just make everything way worse?* But when I asked him, he roared at me not to be a fucking fool. Then he gave me that story about going for a walk.'

'Ah, now, Eugene,' Tommy says, waving an admonishing finger. 'If you really feel a need to go into all this, I won't stop you, but let's stick to the facts. I was in grand form. A wee bit ashamed of myself, is all, for trying to take matters outa Eugene's hands – sure, he's a grown man now, I shouldn't be poking my nose into his dealings with his lady friend, but isn't it awful hard sometimes to remember that the little ones are after getting big?' He throws a bittersweet smile to Senan, since Senan has kids. Senan stares back.

Eugene says, 'He was climbing the fucking walls.'

'Language,' Tommy reminds him.

'I didn't really clock it at the time,' Eugene says. 'I was focused on Rachel – like, what the fuck, he left her just waiting there, in the cold, thinking I'd ghosted her? Only when he gave me my phone back, she hadn't rung to ask where I was, so I thought maybe she was so upset that she hadn't even come out. So I phoned her, but she wasn't answering. I texted her and she didn't read it. In the end I rang her house – not that I was about to get into the whole thing with her parents, I just said I wanted to say good night. And they thought she was with me.'

He's talking faster, like if he can just speed hard enough, he'll reach her in time.

'I was like, "Jesus Christ, we need to call the Guards." But *he* was all, "Oh, she's just off having a sulk, crying on some other young one's shoulder about what a bastard you are, that's what women do, you'll have to get used to it if you're planning on marrying her, ha ha ha. She won't thank you for sending the Guards after her. Let her sleep on it, she'll be grand in the morning." Only I rang round her friends, and so did her mum, and nothing. I drove down to the bridge, in case she was still waiting for me or she'd had a fall or fainted or something, but she wasn't there. And I *still* couldn't convince him to call the Guards.'

'You coulda called them yourself,' Tommy points out. 'If you were that worried. Or the Holohans coulda.'

'The station was *closed*,' Eugene snaps at him, 'and I don't have a phone full of sergeants' numbers. Neither do Fintan and Claire. But they were worried too. They rang around and got people out looking.' He's spun back to Cal. 'And even then, right, *he* was taking over, *organising* people, handing out *assignments*, who should look where, and he told me not to say anything about Rachel being supposed to meet me at the bridge. He sent me off with Bernard McHugh in the opposite direction, up towards the mountains. We don't want people thinking you did something to her, he said.'

'And I'll stand by that,' Tommy says, lifting his head nobly. 'Ye all know what they're like around here for the vicious gossip. I was trying to protect my young lad. If I did wrong there, I don't regret it.'

Cal knows exactly what he was doing. Tommy was buying time. Every minute made it more likely that Rachel would be swept downriver, into the wide Shannon, out to sea and gone.

'So yeah,' Eugene says, to Cal. 'You were right. I thought something was dodgy from the start.'

'Fuckin' Einstein here,' Francie says. 'You swallowed that loada shite he fed you?'

'Man, that's his daddy,' Cal says. 'Would you jump straight to thinking your daddy killed your girl?'

'My daddy wasn't a prick,' Francie points out.

'Ah, he was,' Senan says.

'Sometimes, only. As a hobby. Not as a fuckin' *career*.'

Tommy is managing a set, patient half-smile, but he's having a harder and harder time rising above the peasants using his living room like it's their pub alcove. 'So you're saying you wouldn't,' Cal says to Francie. ''Cause nobody would. If the idea came into your head, you'd just tell yourself to quit thinking crazy.'

'Exactly,' Eugene says, pointing a finger at him. His voice is rising. 'Exactly. That's what I kept telling myself, that the whole idea was insane, I was just letting my imagination run away with me because of all the stress—'

'And that's entirely understandable,' Tommy says magnanimously. 'Sure, anyone'd be losing the plot a wee bit, after what you've been through. We'll come back to this in a few months, when you've had a chance to—'

'Only then,' Eugene says to Cal, 'you told me he went to the bridge that night. And I couldn't work out, I kept thinking, why would he lie about that? To other people, yeah, sure, so they wouldn't talk shit. But why me? I wasn't about to go spreading rumours. Why would he be arsed, why wouldn't he just tell me, unless—'

'Right,' Tommy says, slapping his hands on the arms of the chair. 'I'll take it from here, lads. My young fella's had a tough time, like he told you, and he's having a bit of a meltdown here. I'll apologise on his behalf later, but first let's get things straight.'

'I'm *getting* things straight,' Eugene says, through his teeth.

'You've said your piece,' Tommy tells him. His voice hasn't risen, but it has a weight that flattens Eugene's. 'Now you're going to behave yourself while I do the same.'

'Let your daddy talk a while, Eugene,' Cal says, and sees Tommy's jaw tighten at someone else giving orders in his house. 'I'm interested to hear what he's got to say.'

After a second Eugene bites down on his lips, leans back against the wall, and folds his arms hard.

Tommy takes his time, to make it clear again who's running this show. He breathes his temper down. Then he leans forward in his chair, clasps his hands between his knees, and considers them. The sunset behind him has paled to a cold streak of yellow; the sun is gone.

'You've small bits right,' he says to Cal, 'here and there. I made the decision to keep some things to myself, and fair play to you for spotting that. But you've got the big picture wrong.'

He waits for someone to ask how. No one does.

'Rachel was a lovely girl, God rest her,' Tommy says, 'and here's the thing: she was no fool. If someone hadda sat her down and explained properly what was on the cards, she'da been well able to understand that this factory's a windfall for the place, not a tragedy. But as it was, all she heard was, "That factory's going to take over the whole townland till there's nothing left." And you couldn't hold that against her. Sure, there's plenty of older and wiser people that fell into the same trap.' He runs a wry, weary eye over the men watching him. 'Eugene's only young; he's had no practice putting ideas across to people in a way they'll understand. You can't blame him either.'

Eugene moves, against the wall. He's not looking at Tommy.

'So,' Tommy says, 'I went out to put Rachel's mind at ease. She deserved that. Maybe she was a wee bit on the dramatic side, we'll put it that way, a wee bit inclined to go straight to Defcon One, but she was a good girl; she only wanted the best for her home place. But I never saw her. All I found was a note on the bridge, with a rock weighing it down.'

'A note,' Cal says. 'Saying what?'

Tommy sighs. He gazes down into his locked fingers, his head bent under the weight of this.

'That note would break your heart,' he says. 'I blame myself. If I'da just got to her quicker, or if I'da talked to her when I saw her earlier in the day, I coulda had everything straightened out, but . . .' He runs a hand over his face. 'Rachel still had herself convinced the factory was some kinda disaster, and she thought Eugene would leave her if she didn't come round to our way of thinking. I can tell you now, she was wrong there; we're big believers in loyalty, in this family. But apparently he'd got awful frustrated with her earlier, and that's what she took away from it. And she couldn't do without him.'

Eugene's face is curled tight with fury and disgust, but there's no surprise in there. Somewhere along the way, probably after Cal cornered him in the lane the other day, Eugene has heard this story. Tommy put plenty of skill into crafting it; it's loaded with enough guilt-trip to turn all Eugene's blame away from Tommy, right back onto himself. Maybe he believed it the first time he heard it, at least halfway, but he doesn't believe it now.

''Twas clear enough what the poor girl had done,' Tommy says, 'God forgive her. I went down the riverbank as far as I could, but I mustn'ta gone far enough, because I never saw hide nor hair of her. Not that it woulda done any good if I had – not a chance I coulda pulled her out in time – but I hadta try.'

'So,' Cal says, 'instead of telling Eugene all this and calling in rescue teams, you gave him some bullshit about going for a walk.'

'For God's sake, man,' Tommy says, with a sudden surge of anger. 'D'you think I wanted to destroy my own son altogether? He was after losing the woman he loved. Rescue teams wouldn'ta changed that. If I'da told him she did it on purpose because of what he said to her, it woulda broken him. So I did, yeah: I ripped that note to bits and I gave him a story. There you go, I'm holding my hand up to it. I took that onto my conscience for my son's sake, and I'd do it again. And if you hadn't come along sticking your nose in, he'd never have had to know any different.'

His face has gone red, and he's thrusting towards Cal like he wants to take him. The little speech is garbage, but the rage is real, and too close to the surface. If Tommy recognises that, what he should do is end this conversation right here.

'Well that's mighty noble of you,' Cal says, grinning straight in his face. 'What a hero.'

'*Bullshit*,' Eugene says. He's not leaning against the wall any more. 'My *feelings*, what the actual fuck, he never gave a *shit* about my feelings. The only reason he ever did anything in his *life* is to get what he wants. He fucking killed her.'

'That'll do, boy,' Tommy says sharply. He's on his feet and moving. 'You're losing the run of yourself.'

'He admitted it,' Eugene says, to Cal and all of them. His voice is rising again. 'I asked him, after you told me he was at the bridge, I asked him why. He said Rachel was going to talk, and he shut her mouth. He said someone had to.'

'Loada shite,' Tommy says. He gets a grip on Eugene's arm, hard enough that Eugene makes an involuntary sound.

'Let him talk,' Cal says. He's out of his chair.

'You,' Tommy says, 'you stay outa this.' His voice has thickened. He aims Eugene at the door and shoulders him along like a bull. 'My fuckin' son in my fuckin' house. He'll talk when I say he talks.'

'And,' Eugene says, louder and faster, trying to wrench free, 'and he said someone needed to put a stop to Mart Lavin. This shit was getting out of hand, he said, that little scut was getting above himself, playing at leader of the resistance for a bunch of morons who couldn't organize a piss-up in a brewery—'

'Shut your mouth, you little—'

'—he said if Lavin was gone they'd fall into line like sheep, he'd send me to handle it if I wasn't a useless little prick, now he'd have to handle it himself—'

Tommy spins Eugene around and backhands him right across the face. Eugene staggers, but Tommy's grip keeps him on his feet.

'Who do you think you're dealing with?' Tommy says, into Eugene's face. His breath comes in growls. 'Answer me. That's what Lavin done, he forgot who he was dealing with. *I'm the master here.*'

Cal shoves between them. 'Hey,' he says, loud and sharp, full cop voice. 'Break it up. You're done.' He twists Tommy's hand off Eugene's arm. The other men are on their feet, ready.

Tommy almost goes for him, his fist is pulling back, but he has just enough left to stop himself. He says, deep and lethal, his face close to Cal's, '*Don't fucking cross me, boy.*'

'Or what?' Cal asks. He has a hand lifted, warning the other guys to stay where they are. 'What are you gonna do?'

Tommy keeps staring at him, but his face has gone blank, just the thoughts running hard behind his eyes.

Cal leaves him time to scan through every option, and discard it. No going to the police with some story about harassment. No more siccing his dog-pack on anyone, and no more calling in favours from his big-shot buddies. No more screwing around with tractors, or hunting accidents, or whatever else he might have considered. All the artillery Tommy's accumulated so methodically, over a lifetime, is useless now. With what Eugene just said, Cal and the guys have enough to take to the Guards, and too much for even Tommy to bury. Unless he can crash a helicopter on top of all five of them and Eugene too, he's run out of road.

'You heard him,' Eugene says. His voice is shaking, but he's on his feet and standing straight. 'You heard that. And he went out last night, late. He took the garden spade. He was gone ages.'

His cheek is starting to swell, and there's a trickle of blood where Tommy's signet ring caught him. 'I'll testify to that anywhere you want,' he says. 'The Guards, or court. Wherever.'

'Don't talk like a fuckin' fool,' Tommy says. The red has faded out of his face, but his eyes haven't moved from Cal's. 'No one's testifying to anything. If these shams were going to the Guards, they'd be there, not here.'

He steps back and spreads his hands to the other men, beckoning like he's calling for a fight. 'Come on, ye've wasted enough of my time. Let's be having you: how much do ye want?'

Francie clears his throat and spits on the rug.

'That factory's got all the land it's getting,' Cal says. 'If I get wind of one compulsory purchase order, that's when we go to the cops.'

Tommy wasn't expecting this. He stares for another second; then he laughs. 'Are you laying down the law to me, boy?'

Cal says, 'I'm telling you how this is gonna work.'

'What's it to you? Your land's safe enough.'

'Yeah,' Cal says. 'So's everyone else's.'

Tommy laughs again. It's a rough, raw sound, with too little control. 'You haven't a clue how any of this works. Not a bull's notion. Off you go, boy, back to your carpentry. Back to America. Off you fuck, and don't be annoying me.'

'No compulsory purchase orders,' Cal says. 'No more hassling people. No more bullshit. You're done.'

'What are you talking to me for? I don't own the fuckin' factory. I don't run the fuckin' council.'

'That's right,' Cal says. 'So you're gonna have to talk to the people who do.'

Tommy aims a finger at him like he's scored a point. 'See that, that shows you know nothing. You're years too late, boy. Have you any idea how big this is? Once a project this size is up and moving, you can't just slap the brakes on.'

'You'll think of something,' Cal says. 'Make it good.'

Bobby says, 'You said you were master here.'

Tommy's eyes move to Bobby. 'You ungrateful little scut,' he says heavily. 'You were only delighted to hand over your land. Nearly bit my hand off.'

'If I'da known what you were at,' Bobby says, 'I'da told you to shove your money up your hole. You made me into a fuckin' traitor. You won't do that on anyone else.'

The room is silent. In its warmth, the smell of earth and tractor grease has risen. Beyond the window, the fields are dark.

Tommy says, 'How do I know ye won't fuck me over? Wait till my deal's gone down the tubes, then off ye go to the Guards.'

'We're not fuckin' scumbags,' PJ says.

'He's a cop. Ye brought a cop into this.'

Francie snorts. 'You've brought in enough Guards when it suits you,' he says. 'The difference is, we didn't buy ours.'

'You're gonna have to take our word for it, Tommy,' Cal says. 'I know you're not happy about that, but sometimes life's a bitch.'

'And you can take my word on this as well, boy,' Senan says. 'One foot outa line, and we'll have you. And mind your step, 'cause I'm only dying for the fuckin' chance.'

Tommy looks them over, one by one. His lip is lifted with disgust.

'You give me the sick,' he says. 'The lot of ye.'

'Your own kid, man,' Cal says. 'Who the hell pulls that shit on his own kid?'

Tommy is straightening his cardigan, rumpled from the tussle with Eugene, but he glances up at that. 'You've a small mind,' he says. 'Like the resta these. Small thoughts; small goals. You think you're great now, boyo, 'cause ye all get to keep your small things a while longer, but that's just luck. Let me tell you something: the next man that comes along thinking big, he'll splatter ye like ants.'

'That's what you thought a month ago,' Cal reminds him.

'Get them outa here,' Tommy says to Eugene. 'Make sure they're gone. Then clean that rug before your mammy sees it.'

'You fucking clean it,' Eugene says. His cheek is still bleeding. To Cal: 'Come on.'

No one looks back at Tommy as they leave the room. Off in the depths of the house, the TV quacks on, where Clodagh Moynihan sits oblivious from habit or from sheer force of will.

Eugene opens the front door for them. The security lights

blaze on as they cross the threshold; darkness has come down while they were inside. After the heavy warmth of the house, the air is icy and sweet.

On the doorstep, Cal turns back. 'You gonna be safe here?' he asks Eugene.

Eugene looks at him with a mixture of exhaustion and distaste. 'What would *you* do about it if I wasn't?'

Cal supposes Rachel must have seen some value in Eugene, although then again she did seem to favour hopeless causes. 'I'd figure something out, son,' he says. 'I'm good at that.'

'Yeah, thanks but no thanks. The last thing I need is you figuring things out for me.' Eugene blots his cheek with his sleeve, and stares at the bloodstain like he doesn't understand it. 'I'll stay over at someone's tonight. And I'm heading up to Dublin tomorrow, anyway. I never wanted to move back to this shithole to begin with.'

'Good call,' Cal says. 'If we need you, I'll find you.'

He's turning to leave, but Eugene doesn't shut the door. 'You want to know the part,' he says, 'like, the part that really blows my mind? When he came in that night, I told you he was climbing the walls. He wasn't. The whole time, he was *totally fucking normal*. She was out there in the river, and he was cool as a cucumber. Like nothing important was happening. Isn't that the best part?'

His hand on the doorframe is shaking. In the cold white light of the yard the other four men wait for Cal, watching, their breath smoking on the air. 'Good luck out there,' Cal says.

Senan says, outside the gates, 'I need a fuckin' drink.'

The pub is quiet. Small groups of men are sitting in corners, silent, spaced well apart; the TV is turned down low. Apparently Cal and the guys have been un-barred: when Barty turns from wiping the counter and sees them coming in, all he does is put down his cloth and start setting up their pints.

Men glance across and nod to them, as they settle in the alcove, but no one comes over. Cal knows what to say to the loved ones of the dead – *Sorry for your trouble* – but there's no one who was close enough to Mart to warrant those words.

Barty brings the pints and a round of whiskeys on the side, as a gesture of condolence or reconciliation or something along those lines. The whiskey hits Cal hard, loosening his muscles with an abruptness that almost leaves him limp. He realizes he hasn't eaten since breakfast, which feels like days ago.

'I'll get onto his cousin,' Senan says. 'Myles, over to Gorteen. He'll be the one to make the arrangements. For the funeral and all.'

'And I'll make the arrangements for throwing Dickie O'Shea out on his arse,' Francie says, 'if he has the brass neck to turn up.'

Senan is watching Bobby, who's tucked into the corner of the alcove with his head down over his pint. 'Bring your Róisín along,' he says. And when Bobby looks up, startled: 'It's not what I'd call a romantic day out, but she might as well have a look at what she's getting herself into.'

'Ah, no,' Bobby says hastily. 'Sure, I wouldn't do that to her.'

'It'll have to be done sooner or later. And with everyone's mind on other things, no one'll go giving her the third degree. I'll have Angela keep them off her.'

'I might,' Bobby says dubiously. And with more conviction, as the idea takes hold: 'I might do that, all right. Herself and Angela'd get on.'

They drink. Cal finds himself checking the details of the pub, methodically, like they might have shifted in ways that hold importance. One of the faded newspaper clippings framed on the walls has a new crack in its glass, probably from the other night's ruckus; a trickle of damp from all the rain has bubbled the painted-over wallpaper in a high corner. Senan's holy-water Mary is still stuck at a rakish angle in the fishing net.

'You'll give me a hand keeping his farm going,' PJ says to Cal.

'Yeah,' Cal says. 'Some of the ewes have scald; we're gonna need the footbath.'

'I'll send over a couple of my lads,' Senan says.

'He told me he left the farm to Ruairi,' Cal says. He'd forgotten all about that. Just a few weeks ago Mart was considering, with no particular urgency, where to leave his land. Cal wonders whether Ruairi was a placeholder set up long ago, or whether somewhere in those few weeks, Mart understood that he couldn't afford to wait.

'Right,' Senan says, after a moment. 'Fair play to him. I'll send Ruairi over, so. He might as well get the feel of the place.' He clears his throat and takes a swig of his pint.

'And he wanted you to take Kojak,' Cal says to PJ. 'So's he'll have sheep to work.'

PJ nods. 'That's a fine dog,' he says. 'You wouldn't get better anywhere.'

'We oughta have the wake here,' Bobby says, struck by an idea.

'The fuck are you on about?' Senan demands, staring at him in disbelief.

'I'm only saying. His favourite place, like. What's wrong with that?'

'And have the coffin on the bar, is it?'

'I've seen worse on that bar,' Francie says darkly. 'D'you remember the time—'

'You'll give the tourists a fuckin' heart attack. They walk in here looking for Aran jumpers and leprechauns, and there's a fuckin' corpse staring them out of it—'

'How many tourists do we get in November?' Cal points out. He has no opinion on the wake, but this argument – vehement, elaborate, low-stakes, the kind of bickering that's been currency in Seán Óg's ever since he got here – feels like a good thing.

'All it takes is one, and it'll be all over Instagram. Making a holy show of us.'

PJ has stopped drinking so he can think better. 'Father Eamonn wouldn't say the rosary in here,' he says firmly, having considered the issue long enough to reach a conclusion.

'That's an upside, not a downside,' Senan tells him. 'All the same—'

The argument lasts them through the rest of their pints. No one says a word about Tommy. When their glasses are empty, they head for home, in the windless dark that smells like coming frost.

22

Cal gets in his car and heads for Lena's early the next morning, as soon as the sun is up. He and PJ need to see to Mart's sheep, but PJ has his own work to get through first. Cal has a while. If it turns out not to be long enough, he can try again later.

He was right about the change in the weather. The air has a new hard bite, and frost lies white over the fields, patterned with long meandering lines of black dots where farmers, dogs, rabbits, birds have gone about their accustomed business. The cloud is paler; small sounds, the burr of an engine or the ring of metal on metal, come clear-edged from far away on the cold air. Old songs in the pub start like this, with a man rising early and setting out to see his sweetheart, appreciating the beauties of nature along the way. This doesn't feel like a song.

No one else is out on the roads except Con McHugh, pushing a wheelbarrow of sheep lick buckets along the back lane that winds between his land and Flapper Deery's. When he sees Cal coming, his head snaps up and he steps out into the road, arm raised, to block the car.

Con is the youngest of the McHugh brothers, a big, rumpled, sweet-natured guy who seldom gets a word in edgeways. Cal has always liked him, but then, he always liked Bernard. He stops the car and rolls down his window, but he keeps the engine running and his eye on the hedges around.

'Sorry for your trouble,' Con says, at the window.

Cal is taken aback. He would suspect sarcasm, except Con

isn't the type. Instead he's startled to find his throat swelling. 'Thanks,' he says.

'He was a great worker,' Con says. 'Kept that farm going all on his own for years. You wouldn't find finer sheep anywhere.'

'He was good to me,' Cal says. 'I would've had a hard time settling in around here, if it wasn't for him.' Which, while it barely scratches the surface, is the truth.

Con nods. He takes off his woolly hat and examines it. 'I was meaning to say to you,' he says. 'About the, that chair. Just if—' He shifts, glancing at Cal like he's expecting a rebuff. 'If ye'd got around to it, yourself and the young one. 'Cause I know ye're busy.'

'It's coming along pretty good,' Cal says. 'It'll be ready in plenty of time for Christmas.' Senan has talked to Angela, Angela has talked to Noreen, and Noreen is talking to everyone and their mama. All across the townland, under this pale sky, things are rearranging themselves. Cal catches himself making a mental note to ask Mart how this is going to unfold, and what he should do in order to avoid fucking up.

He turns off his engine. 'How's Aileen doing?' he asks.

Con's face relaxes into a smile. 'Ah, she's great. The midwife says they're both doing great, thank God. She's getting big now; she says by Christmas I'll have to roll her along.'

'Give her my best,' Cal says. 'Any time you want to take a look at how the chair's going, see if you want to make any changes, come on over. If you don't get a chance, I'll phone you when it's ready.'

A movement beyond the wall makes them both turn quickly, but it's only Flapper Deery's pony trotting up in hope of treats. Cal understands who Con doesn't want walking in on this conversation: his own brothers, or at least some of them. The McHughs are known for sticking together to the point of lunacy, but even that has been frayed at the seams.

'I was talking to Malachy Dwyer,' Con says. 'He says tomorrow night he'll bring a few bottles down to Mart's place. If that suits, like.'

He means the wake. Malachy is the local moonshiner; Cal has experience of his poteen, which has a reputation for being the purest in several counties and which kicks like a mule. Mart would rise up out of his coffin if they tried to bury him without getting hammered on Malachy's finest. 'Sounds good to me,' Cal says. 'I'll check with Senan and the guys, let you know if tomorrow night works.'

He has a question. He's not sure of the right way to ask it, but he's going to have to navigate these things for himself now. He asks, 'There gonna be trouble at the wake?'

'No,' Con says, instantly and with force. 'God, no. It's not . . .' He trails off. 'Mouth won't come,' he says in the end. 'Tadhg mightn't either, I don't know. But the rest of us'll be there. Bernard and all, like.'

Cal understands what Con is telling him. For the people who have weight around here, this is finished. There'll be holdouts, on both sides – probably Cal should avoid Mouth for a while – but the townland as a whole is beginning the slow process of laying the sod and leaving the grass to grow over this last month. Ardnakelty is skilled in this, having done it a thousand times; it can do it again.

'Bernard's a good guy,' he says. 'See you there.'

He starts the ignition, but Con stays put. 'Say hiya to Lena from me and Aileen,' he says.

'Will do,' Cal says. 'Thanks.'

He puts the car into gear and lifts a hand to Con as he moves off. In the rear-view mirror, Con hefts his wheelbarrow and heads on down the lane, his boots leaving black marks in the frost.

Lena's Skoda is in her front yard. Cal parks next to it, where she'll see his car from her kitchen window. Then he sits down on her front step and waits.

He thinks, mainly, about Mart. Up until now he's had no time to do that; when he got home last night, the friendly woman Guard was waiting on his doorstep to take down his account, and once she left he was asleep almost before he could get under the bedcovers. His mind hasn't had a chance to start absorbing things – he catches himself thinking that Mart isn't going to take well to being murdered, and wondering what he'll do about it. Cal wishes he were a religious man, not so he could believe that Mart is in heaven – an image he has difficulty picturing – but so he could believe that Mart had a bird's-eye view of what went down in the Moynihan house yesterday evening. He would have got a kick out of it.

The frost glitters in the strengthening light. It'll be good for the ploughing, if the rain holds off to let the land dry out. The cold strikes up from the stone into Cal's ass, but his jacket is solid enough that the rest of him stays warm. The jacket still smells of Mart's tobacco smoke, but he has no other that's fit for this weather.

After a while Lena comes out of the house, closing the door behind her to keep the dogs in.

'Are you here long?' she asks.

'Little while,' Cal says. 'Half an hour, maybe.'

'I was hoovering,' Lena says. 'I didn't hear you come.' She sits down on the step, a couple of feet from Cal, and pulls her sweatshirt sleeves over her hands against the cold.

'I was going to call over to you yesterday,' she says. 'Only then I heard about Mart. Noreen said you found him.'

'Yeah,' Cal says.

'How're you doing?' Lena asks. She's turned to look at Cal full on.

'Not sure yet,' Cal says.

Lena nods. It feels like a long time since Cal last saw her face. She's thinner and pale, and the lines from her nose to her mouth have deepened, but the way she's looking at him, like she's actually there on the step and seeing him, gives him a flicker of hope. He was afraid she'd be the way she was that day at her kitchen table, right next to him and gone far beyond reach. Her voice doesn't sound like an echo any more. He wants to know what she was coming to say to him, yesterday.

'Few of us went over to Moynihans' yesterday evening,' he says. 'Tommy's done here.'

Lena is unsure whether he's telling her this as reassurance, or out of pride in his achievement, or as justification for using her as a tool. 'How?' she says.

Cal tells her. When he's done, Lena sits looking at her front yard. A wren is flipping in and out of the hedge, scrounging in the frosty grass. She needs to fill her bird-feeders; winter is here.

'What does Tommy say was in that note?' she asks.

This clearly isn't what Cal was expecting. 'There wasn't any note,' he says. 'He was just trying to guilt-trip Eugene.'

'Let me guess,' Lena says. 'The note said she was doing it 'cause of Tommy. She couldn't stop him, and Eugene wouldn't be able to even if he tried, not unless he had something massive to use. This was for Eugene to use.'

Cal has turned sharply to look at her. 'Tommy said it was mostly her worrying that Eugene was gonna dump her.'

'I suppose he would say that, yeah,' Lena says. 'There was a note. And Tommy didn't kill Rachel.'

Cal says, '*What.*'

'When me and Sheila were no help to her,' Lena says, 'Rachel went to Dymphna Duggan. Mrs Duggan told her there was only one way to stop Tommy.'

Cal says, after a second, 'Jesus Christ.'

'She told her where Noreen and Dessie kept the antifreeze,'

Lena says. 'That shouldn't have me raging, not with everything else. But there was Noreen, in bits over this. Her own antifreeze.'

Sometime soon she'll have to buy a bottle of antifreeze and put it in Noreen's shed, so nobody will miss the one discarded somewhere along the road to the bridge, or spinning away downstream. The antifreeze to ease the leap into the river, the river because the antifreeze would take too long, and each to make sure the other one didn't fail. Lena thinks of Rachel on the bridge, the night around her starting to blur, the river's roar and the utter loneliness filling her ears and her mouth like dark water.

Cal says, 'You sure about this?'

'I'm sure,' Lena says. 'Mrs Duggan told me herself.'

'Doesn't mean it's true. From what I hear, she likes getting people worked up.'

Lena shakes her head. 'She doesn't tell lies. If she did, people'd stop believing her; she couldn't be having that. And anyhow Yvonne McCabe saw Rachel going into Duggans', that night.'

'Rachel would've texted someone. Not left a note.'

'If she'd texted anyone,' Lena says, 'they'd have gone looking for her straight away, and they mighta found her in time. And then she'da been bundled away somewhere on a psych hold, nice and safe, and anyhow she'da been just some young one with mental health issues. Unstable, like. Crying out for attention. You wouldn't want to listen to anything she said.'

She hears the tightening in her voice. Tommy would have done it perfectly, grieved by the bizarre accusations, but compassionate towards human frailty. Rachel knew Tommy, better than Lena does. She knew what to fear.

'She thought Eugene would find the note,' she says, 'when he came to meet her. If anything could give him the guts to go against Tommy, it'd be that. He'd tell the world, and everyone'd be up in arms, and that'd be the end of Tommy.'

Cal arranges all this in his mind, drawing patterns with a finger on the step between them. Lena leaves him to it. The two of them may be here only to recognise that what they made has been damaged beyond repair, and to do this one last thing together, lay it to rest. But whatever they're doing, they need to start from the same ground.

'It could've worked,' Cal says. 'Eugene's a little shit, but he seems like he actually cared about Rachel.'

'It woulda worked,' Lena says. 'I shoulda seen it ages ago.' She thinks of Sheila telling her *A grown woman knows sometimes there's nothing to be done, so you do nothing.* When there was nothing to be done, Rachel made something.

'Sheila says Rachel was soft,' she says. 'Soft as butter. I'm not so sure.'

Cal is thinking about Eugene, so convinced his father killed Rachel that he's ready to get up in court and swear Tommy confessed. He says, 'Are you gonna tell people?'

Lena watches him. She says, 'How about you?'

It takes Cal a while to answer. 'It's been a bad time,' he says. 'This place pretty near ripped itself apart. Now it seems like maybe people can quit going at each other's throats and start fixing up the damage, getting back to normal, even if it takes a while. I don't see much use in stirring things up again.'

Lena nods. 'That's very sensible altogether,' she says. 'Whatever you say, say nothing; sure, talk only ever led to trouble. If it wasn't for the accent, anyone'd take you for a local.'

Cal can't read the edge in her voice. He doesn't answer.

'And o' course,' Lena points out, 'you need to stay quiet, to keep Tommy in line. If he gets proof he didn't kill Rachel, that's half your leverage gone, and you wouldn't want that.'

'Well, it's not proof,' Cal says. 'Mrs Duggan's word against Eugene's. That's not gonna get Tommy off the hook.' He knows that's not the point.

Lena says, 'I told Eugene.'

Cal turns to stare at her. Her face is lifted to look out over the frost-bleached fields; her profile shows nothing. He doesn't understand any of this, what she was aiming to do, why she never told him any of it, why she's telling him now. He says, 'When?'

'Julie Quinn had his number,' Lena says. 'He usedta hang around with her Niall. I rang him to meet me, after I left Mrs Duggan, and I told him. He's in rag order, isn't he?'

Cal remembers how he wondered, yesterday evening, what had pushed Eugene over the line. He asks, 'What'd he say?'

'At first he was bulling to go after Mrs Duggan,' Lena says, 'although I'm not sure what he had in mind; loads of noise about the Guards and suing, I don't think he knew himself. I said to him, you can do what you want to do, or you can do what Rachel wanted done. Take your pick. Then I left him to it.'

Cal says, 'Why tell him?'

Lena rearranges her hands, tucking them into the opposite sleeves of her sweatshirt for warmth. 'Like you said,' she says, 'he cared about Rachel. In the end, he let her do what she wanted with her own death. No one else would. I thought she oughta have that.'

Cal draws more patterns on the step and goes through yesterday's conversation. As far as he can see, Tommy told the truth on pretty close to everything. Presumably Cal should feel a twinge of conscience somewhere around this, but he doesn't.

'I'll keep quiet,' Lena says, 'but not to suit anyone around here; to suit Rachel. She went into that river to get a job done. It's done.'

The finality in her voice comes to Cal like grief. All around, things are ending, without fanfare, falling as simply as leaves.

'I'm going to tell Claire and Fintan, just,' Lena says. 'I wouldn't say they'll do anything with it, but I could be wrong.

Either way, that's up to them. It might break their hearts all over again, I don't know, but they oughta know Rachel had her reasons.'

Her eyes move to Cal, measuring him. 'Are you going to say I oughta keep my mouth shut, leave well enough alone?'

'No,' Cal says. 'I think you're right.'

'Well, that's a relief,' Lena says, and this time the edge in her voice is clear and sharp. 'I was worried you'd gone native altogether. At least you're not that far gone.'

Cal feels a sudden burst of anger. He says, 'You never told me any of this.'

'You would've handed it over to Mart,' Lena says, 'for him to use. That wasn't what I was doing it for.'

'Not if you didn't want me to. All you had to do was ask.'

'I never aimed to make your decisions for you,' Lena says. 'The only decisions I make are my own.'

'What the hell,' Cal says. His voice is rising. 'That's not how it works. We're supposed to be in this together.'

'We weren't,' Lena says flatly. 'When I found out what Tommy was up to, you brought it straight to Mart. When you heard what people were saying about us, you did the same again. You were in this with Mart Lavin and his boyos.'

'I was trying to *fix* things. That's all I ever aimed to do. Maybe I could've found some other way if you'd told me what was going on, but you weren't talking to me. I didn't even *see* you. You made those damn decisions for me just fine. What the hell was I supposed to do? Sit on my ass while that shitbird Moynihan trashed everything?'

He wants to get up off the step, move somewhere, hit something. His hands are shaking. He clasps them together to still them.

'I was trying,' he says. 'Maybe I did it wrong. You didn't even try.'

His anger doesn't bother Lena; it's another thing that puts them on the same ground. He has a point, and she welcomes that. She takes her time getting her answer clear.

'When I first found out what Tommy was at,' she says, 'I was going to tell the whole place. I couldn't wait. Wild rebel, me, all ready to watch the world burn.'

Probably some of it was for Trey. Maybe some, whether she liked it or not, was for Rachel. Some was for herself, and for Cal, to show him that he didn't have to end up what he is now: Ardnakelty's man, subject to all its pulls and its requirements.

'And then,' she says, 'Tommy showed up here and explained if I didn't behave myself, he'd land me in jail or in a mental ward. And as soon as the pressure was on him, he sent over a Guard to get the ball rolling.'

'And if you'd told me any of that,' Cal says, 'we could have figured out what to do about it. Together.'

'Probably I should have,' Lena says. 'But it was never that I wasn't talking to you. After Tommy got to work on me, I had no talk left in me for anyone that was part of this place.' Her voice is level, but she doesn't try to keep out the traces of these last weeks. 'All I wanted was to get it off me, before it ate me alive. I would've got in that car and left, only I had nowhere to go.'

She watches Cal hear the parts she isn't saying; his eyes close against them for a second. This is a space she never intended to let anyone enter. But wherever they go next, he needs to know how they got here.

'Tell me something,' she says, after a while. 'When ye went over to Tommy yesterday. Which one of ye did the talking?'

'I did,' Cal says. The anger has gone out of him.

Lena nods. 'It sounds like you did a good job,' she says.

Cal understands what she means. Most things he's offered this townland, pretty much anyone could have offered the same, but not this time. He's stepped into a place. Who he is may be no different from the man Lena took up with, but what he is, and what he brings to her, has changed.

'I live here,' he says. 'I'm just trying to do that right.'

'I know,' Lena says. 'It's not as easy as it looks, is it?'

'I didn't plan on this,' Cal says. 'Things seemed like they'd finally settled. You and me, and Trey was on a good track, and people had quit treating me like a tourist and trying to get me to wear a leprechaun suit to the pub. Things were working great, far as I could tell. I guess I figured they would just keep on going the same way.'

'I wanted to think that,' Lena says. 'I almost had myself convinced, for a while there.'

The anger has gone out of her, too. Back when she wanted Cal partly because he had nothing of this place built into him, she was an eejit to think that would stay unchanged. He's growing in this soil now.

If his outsiderhood was ever what she prized most in him, it isn't any more. She's changed as well. When Cal felt it happening, he held on to her as best he could, steadfast, hoping if he held on long enough they'd know each other again. It's not that she feels she owes him the same in return; it just seems like, of all the things people have done over the last weeks and hoped they were doing right, that was the only one that didn't have a payload of darkness enclosed somewhere inside it. Lena values that, more than she ever noticed before.

'Sheila and a couple of others called round here a few days ago,' she says, 'to say they'd tell the world they were with me when Rachel died. That was the last thing I expected. I hadn't seen Yvonne and Julie since school, not properly, but there they were.'

She lets out a long breath and watches the smoke of it spread and dissolve in the cold air. 'Looks like I live here as well,' she says. 'I'll have to work out how to do that.'

Cal nods. They sit in silence for a while, listening for each other, trying to find each other in this unfamiliar place. The wren is still at work, indefatigably combing the grass.

'I'da given a lot to see Tommy Moynihan's face,' Lena says, 'when some blow-in put him back in his box.'

'He said I had a small mind,' Cal says. 'You figure my feelings should be hurt?'

Lena laughs. 'God,' she says. 'He's some dose, isn't he?'

'I guess Rachel thought big,' Cal says. 'For better or for worse.'

Lena stands up and dusts off the seat of her jeans. Cal watches her. The frost has purified the light so that the pale landscape stretches out for miles, to a faint horizon of hills in some other townland.

'I'm freezing my arse off out here,' she says, and holds out a hand to him. 'Come inside.'

After lunch Cal and PJ get started on Mart's farm. The work goes clumsily. Mart's sheep are accustomed to Kojak, but Kojak is curled in a corner of Cal's living room, motionless except for the flicker of his eyes and the lip that lifts when anyone gets too close. PJ brings up his tractor – even once the oil drains back into place, Mart's won't be an easy thing to touch. PJ, who yesterday was solid as rock right through everything, flinches like a spooked horse whenever he looks at it. The earth in the bottom field, with no rain to blur it and the frost to preserve it, still shows the dents of the tractor's weight and the lighter imprint of Mart's body. When the inspectors come with their notebooks and questions, it'll tell the chosen story.

Senan brings Ruairi over. Ruairi is twenty, a big, open-faced kid with a broccoli haircut, his usual cheerfulness muted by the circumstances. What with Mart not even in the ground, no one makes any mention of the land going to him; but Senan, with a delicacy Cal never expected, strolls casually through all that'll need deciding over the next while – we could turn the sheep back out after the footbath or we could house them till the scald's gone, when d'you reckon the ewes'll need scanning, that one's lost both ear-tags, some of those lambs oughta go to the mart. Ruairi answers readily and solidly. A couple of times he glances at Senan like he's expecting disagreement, but all he ever gets is a nod.

Eventually the four of them manoeuvre the whole flock through the footbath and let them mill around for a while till their hooves dry off. Ruairi finds the ear-tagger and the pack of tags in Mart's shed and puts new ones on the ewe who's lost hers, making a careful note of the number. The squirrel watches them from the roof of the house, before whisking around and vanishing into some new hole in the eaves with an impertinent flick of its tail.

By that time Angela Maguire has arrived, chivvying a small flock of teenagers she's collected to help get Mart's house ready for the wake. The sound of vigorous hoovering pours through the opened windows, and occasionally someone comes out to the yard to shake curtains or beat puffs of dust from cushions. When Cal sticks his head inside for a drink of water, Angela shoos him and his mucky boots away and brings him a glass on the doorstep.

'Thanks,' he says. 'I ran into Con McHugh, we were saying probably the wake could be tomorrow night. That sound about right?'

'Ah, yeah; that's when I was thinking, all right. Leave us time to get everything sorted.' Angela, pushing hair off her forehead with the back of her wrist, shoots Cal a quick look. 'D'you reckon Lena would give us a hand making the sandwiches?'

'Probably,' Cal says. Lena may kill him, but he gets what Angela is doing, and so will she. 'Sure.'

'Great,' Angela says, taking the glass back. 'I'll give her a ring.' Behind her, the floors are wet and shining, and her Finbarr and Noreen's Cliona have cleared the breakfast things off the kitchen table and are giving it an energetic scrub. In the living room, someone has turned the old mirror over the mantelpiece to face the wall.

Cal leaves Senan and Ruairi going through Mart's books, looking for the date he put the rams in with the ewes, whether he's dosed for fluke yet, what lick buckets he's ordered. Presumably Cousin Myles and a solicitor and various other people will show up at some point to put in their two cents' worth, and the whole thing will take a while to shake out, but the land and the sheep are oblivious to all this; their requirements move on, unaffected, along their accustomed rounds.

When he gets home, the workshop radio is playing some cheesy pop song. Trey has her wood burl out on the worktable, along with a big piece of paper covered in neat, indecipherable diagrams and notations, and is carefully drawing in guidelines for the hollows that will make cubbyholes. Rip and Banjo are getting under her feet.

'Tommy kill Mart Lavin?' she asks, by way of greeting.

'Yeah,' Cal says. The dogs have bounced over to investigate his smell of sheep and sweat; he bends to rub their heads. 'Not Rachel, though.'

Trey stares, her pencil in mid-air. 'You serious?' she says. 'For definite?'

'Yeah. She did that herself. Aiming to turn people against Tommy, sink his big plan.'

'Huh,' Trey says, after a moment, the same way Cal says it. She snaps her fingers for Banjo and lifts his hock to disentangle a wood shaving from his fur. Cal can't tell what she's making of this, whether she thinks Rachel was an idiot or whether she sees logic in her choice.

'You'd've thought of something better'n that,' he says. 'To stop him. Right?'

'I did,' Trey points out. 'We did.'

A couple of years back she would have stated it as plain fact, no different from *I sanded that table*. Now Cal can tell, from her straight glance at him, that this is reassurance.

'Right,' he says. Trey frees the wood shaving and gives Banjo a pat, dismissing him to go back to sniffing Cal's socks.

'Keep that about Rachel to yourself,' Cal says. 'Miss Lena knows. No one else needs to.'

''S Tommy's fault anyhow,' Trey says. 'You gonna get him now?'

'That's done,' Cal says. 'Tommy won't be giving us any more trouble.'

'He going to jail?'

'No,' Cal says. 'Not unless he gets feisty. We need him, to pull the plug on his buddies' plans. He so much as looks sideways at anyone, then yeah, we're going to the Guards. But he won't.'

'So he's not gonna pay for any of it,' Trey says flatly. 'What he done on you, or Lena. Or Mart.'

'Kid,' Cal says. 'You remember what I said to you a few days ago? What I wanted was Tommy Moynihan tarred and feathered and run out of town.'

'He hasn't been.'

'Closer than you think. Tommy's not gonna be giving orders and getting his ass kissed around here any more. He's not even gonna be able to walk into Noreen's or Seán's. He shows his face in the village, someone's gonna spit on his shoe. He tries to drive down the street, people are gonna block his way.' Cal knows enough, now, to feel the immensity of that shift. 'Tommy's nothing,' he says.

Trey winds the wood shaving around her finger. In the end

she gives that a reluctant nod. 'He might haveta leave town,' she says.

'He might,' Cal says. That would probably be a good call. Once Tommy's fulfilled his function, there are people who might feel he's surplus to requirements. In any case, the landscape Tommy sees out his window is redrawing itself, not in the ways he envisioned, and Cal can't picture him reshaping himself to fit its new form. 'Either way,' he says, 'he's gone.'

After a moment Trey says gruffly, 'Sorry 'bout your man Mart.' She's gone back to her pencil and ruler; Trey abhors being on the receiving end of sympathy, so she's unskilled at offering it. 'Ye were mates.'

'Sort of,' Cal says. 'I guess. Thanks.' His feelings about Mart were complicated, and are getting more so. He can't tell how much is personal grief, and how much is the broader loss that comes from an old oak wantonly chopped down or a standing stone vandalised. The distinction hasn't seemed important, since the work that needs doing is the same either way.

'Miss Lena's coming for dinner,' he says, and enjoys Trey's fast spin towards him. 'I want to make her something good. What do you figure?'

The kid stares at him like she suspects some trick. 'You talked to her?'

'Yeah,' Cal says. 'Everything's fine.' Which, while it may not be exactly true, feels close enough to hold up.

Trey keeps up the stare for another minute, but whatever she sees satisfies her. 'Fuck's sake,' she says in the end. 'About fuckin' time.'

'You know what?' Cal says. He feels like he's going to crack open on something, maybe tears or laughter, he can't tell which. 'Your language sucks. That's no way for a proper young lady to talk. I'm gonna send you to charm school.'

Trey, turning back to her burl, snorts derisively. 'Charm schools'd run a mile if they saw this place.'

'I'm gonna start one. Noreen can help me out. We'll have you lifting up your little finger and curtseying in no time.'

The kid gives him a look like he's lost his mind, which Cal agrees is a possibility. 'Make tacos,' she says. 'Lena likes them. We've got the shell yokes, and mince.'

'OK,' Cal says. 'We'll do that.' He wants to give both her and Lena something extravagant and elaborate, something magnificent enough to blow away every particle of the last few weeks, but tacos will have to do. Probably Tommy was right and he has a mind for small things, but he's OK with it.

Trey is bent close over her burl, taking complicated measurements. She says, 'C'n Kate come for dinner as well?'

Cal is hit by a sudden sense of wonder. 'Sure,' he says. 'She like tacos?'

'Dunno. Probably. She likes most things.' Trey glances back and forth between the wood and her diagram, and pencils in another careful line. 'We're kinda going out,' she says.

Cal can feel every cell of her alert for his reaction. He wants to put his hands on her shoulders and turn her to face him so she can see his great big grin. 'Well, congratulations,' he says. 'You guys arrange the whole thing through ambassadors, like Aidan and Ciara? Schedule a reminder on your calendars?'

'Nah. Just sorta happened.'

So all those hours surveilling the Moynihan house, whatever else they accomplished, did at least one purely good thing. 'I dunno,' Cal says. 'Maybe I should interview her first. Make sure she's not a bad influence.'

'Fuck off,' Trey says. He can hear her grinning too.

'Charm school.'

'Fuck off.'

Cal feels like he should be giving her an educational speech here, but he's unequipped for it, not yet having been able to bring himself to add 'do lesbians need to use some kind of condom or what' to his search history, and anyway the kid appears to be doing just fine without his input. 'You guys be good to each other,' he says.

'Duh. We are.'

Maybe not entirely without his input. He looks at Trey's messy bent head and remembers her three years ago, all claws and prickle, no more willing or able to forge human ties than a wild animal. If she's moving away from him, building her own world where she and Kate are good to each other and sing songs he doesn't know and goof around with hat emojis, he had a hand in getting her there.

His phone beeps. Lena: *Will I bring anything?* He texts back, *Nah we're good. See you soon.*

'I gotta take a shower,' he says. 'You run down to Noreen's, pick us up some sour cream and a lettuce.'

'C'n I take the car?'

'No.'

'I drove my mam's before.'

'So don't. This weekend I'll start teaching you. Today you take your bike.' Her hands on the wood have lost the soft formlessness of a little kid's; they're calloused and wiry from work, scarred here and there by tool-slips and splinters. They still catch at Cal's heart. 'And if Kate's coming over,' he says, 'you better hide that thing.'

This seems like the kind of evening where everyone might feel a little clumsy, what with one thing and another, so Cal heads that off by giving people stuff to do. As soon as Kate arrives, he sets her and Trey to cutting vegetables for taco toppings. Trey has apparently texted Kate whatever updates she needs, because she doesn't ask questions, just starts in slicing bell peppers and giving the lowdown on the musical differences in the band where she plays bass.

Cal, mixing spices, stays quiet and watches the two of them sideways. He has the radio on, some Irish music station, to give Trey something to rib him about. Trey has lit the fire and it's burning steadily, no spitting, sending out a tang of spruce; the wood Cal chopped, stacked high in the corner by the fireplace, is well seasoned after all.

Trey and Kate seem the same together as they always have: at ease, working deftly side by side at the tiny counter, expert in each other's movements from the football pitch. Kate brought a box of brownies for dessert, which Cal approves of as a sign of good raising. She hasn't exactly dressed up, but unlike Trey, she appears to have actually picked out her clothes – she has on cargo pants and a Foo Fighters sweatshirt, both clean. Trey is wearing much the same outfit she had on the first time Cal ever saw her, jeans and a red hoodie, except now the jeans fit and the hoodie looks like it was bought for her rather than inherited from a random sibling.

That first day, she wouldn't come within grabbing distance of him. He doesn't think she spoke more than a dozen words. Before that, before he even got a good look at her, she bit him. She's shredding lettuce in time to 'Chasing Rainbows', head-bopping along, pausing to snitch a slice of pepper from Kate's chopping board. He has to look away, before she turns and catches him staring at her like a big dumb goofball, or before he puts a hand on her head and embarrasses her in front of her brand-new girlfriend.

Lena comes in the door red-nosed with cold; when Cal kisses her, she smells icy. 'Kojak's not doing too good,' he says, as he takes her coat. 'He's going to PJ tomorrow, but I said I'd keep him one more night, in case being around Rip might help.' It's not working. Kojak is still motionless in his corner; Rip and

Banjo are sprawled by the fire, giving him the wide berth that combat-eyed guys get on buses. 'He won't eat. I thought maybe you could do something with him.'

'I'll give it a shot,' Lena says. 'Is he drinking?'

'Yeah. Some.'

'That's a good sign, anyhow,' Lena says. She moves towards the corner, taking her time. When Kojak lifts his lip a fraction, she stops and sits down on the floor, sideways on, not looking at him. 'What's for dinner?'

'Tacos,' Trey says.

'Beef ones,' Kate says. Cal sets the frying pan heating, and tilts it to spread the oil around.

'Lovely,' Lena says. She settles herself comfortably against the wall and snaps her fingers for Rip and Banjo. They come over, glancing warily at Kojak, and she strokes their heads. 'Pass me over a bitta mince for these lads,' she says, 'before you put the spices in.'

The radio is playing 'The Irish Rover', fast and scrappy. PJ taught Cal the words to this one, back when they were cutting brambles; he sings along, in an undertone, while he scoops a chunk of ground beef onto a plate for the dogs. Kate does a half-mocking dance step.

Cal expects Trey to bitch about this level of folksiness, but she's keeping an eye on Lena, sideways, checking her over. 'When's your rematch against Lisnacarragh?' Lena asks her.

'Next weekend,' Trey says. She's moved on to grating cheese; she cuts off a chunk to eat while she works, and gives Kate half. 'Unless the pitch is rained out again.'

'I'll bring ye,' Lena says. 'As long as Aidan goes in the boot.'

'Aidan's sound,' Trey objects.

'He is, yeah. And he's like having a chimpanzee in the car.'

'He nearly got himself killed last month,' Cal says, 'hanging out my car window to throw a sandwich at some other kid.'

'He wasn't trying to *hurt* him,' Trey explained. 'They're mates.'

'We could be bringing Zoe Greaney,' Kate says. 'Mr O'Donnell only lets her ask three questions a class, 'cause he says otherwise his brain'll shrivel up and die.'

'When he told us stratus clouds can cover the whole sky,' Trey says, 'she asked if that's why it gets dark at night.'

Lena is laughing, keeping it quiet so as not to startle Kojak. Cal brings her the plate of ground beef and a spoon, and she smiles up at him and touches his wrist before she takes it. His ring is on her finger.

'Or Jayden Crilly,' Trey says. 'He licked sheep shite off the back of a school bus seat.'

'Aw, jeez,' Cal says. 'He have a good reason, or was he just hungry?' He tips the rest of the ground beef into his frying pan. It sends up a sizzle. Condensation is misting the windows against the cold outside.

'He was dared. And he's weird.'

'If that's John Paul Crilly's young fella,' Lena says, 'I'm not surprised. John Paul put a dead bee in his ear on a dare, one time. He hadta go to Emergency.' She's feeding Rip a bite of mince off the spoon, while Banjo writhes with anticipation. Kojak, watching, twitches an eyebrow.

'Well, I can see why you want to stick around here,' Cal tells Trey. 'You wouldn't get that kinda action up in the big city.'

He catches Trey's glance at Lena, watching for her response.

'I suppose you could do worse,' Lena says. 'You haveta live somewhere, sure.' She gives Banjo his bite of ground beef. Kojak's nose is stretching forward. She ignores him.

'Kate's staying here as well,' Trey says. 'Once we leave school.'

''M going to train for a paramedic,' Kate says. 'I can live at home for that; it's only over in Ballinasloe.'

Cal finds himself blown away by them, all their plans. When

he was that age, his only plan was to save up a few bucks so he could hit the highway the day he turned eighteen, and maybe take Darla Myers on a date or two first. 'Sounds good,' he says. 'And Aidan's gonna be an electrician, right? All you guys need to do is get Ciara into plumbing and make Ross into a mechanic, and you'll be ready for anything.'

'Did Aidan break the bad news to his dad yet?' Lena asks.

'Last week,' Trey says. 'His dad didn't even freak out, just said the farm'll be there if he changes his mind. Aidan reckons he must be on chill pills.'

'Nah,' Kate says, putting the vegetable dishes on the table. 'It's 'cause of everything that's been going on. He doesn't care if Aidan turns out to be an electrician, or a binman, or a YouTuber, as long as he's OK.'

'Makes sense,' Cal says. He remembers Kate heading home to her mama, the other day, to prove she wasn't dead after the party. A kid who has an inkling that adults have viewpoints of their own, rather than just being gratuitous pains in the ass, might be able to see Trey's complicated parts and take them as they are, maybe even with gentleness. He would like Trey to have some gentleness around her, in whatever world she's building for herself.

'Then c'n I start my apprenticeship next year?' Trey says, to Cal. 'As long as I'm OK?'

'I'm not the boss of you,' Cal says. He sprinkles his seasoning mix into the pan.

'You know what I mean. You gonna keep giving me hassle about finishing school?'

'Nah,' Cal says. 'You're no dummy. If you figure next year's the right time, it probably is.'

Trey's double take makes him grin. She gives him a stare that's somewhere between baffled and suspicious. He wiggles his eyebrows at her.

'Now,' Lena says softly. 'There we go.' Kojak is snuffling at the outstretched spoon. When he snaps the ground beef off it, Lena moves the plate under his nose, ignoring the other dogs' reproachful gazes, and he eats.

Cal adds tomato paste and water to the pan and watches Trey and Kate trying to work out how much lime juice to put in the salsa. For a second he sees them vividly, sturdier and better brushed, telling work stories in this kitchen with grown women's voices while he and Lena, greyer, laugh along. He and Lena won't be exactly what he used to picture. The boundary walls they set in place haven't held up, on this shifting terrain; what they share from now on won't have the simplicity and the clarity that both of them loved. But they'll be something; they'll be here.

He wishes Mart could see this too. Maybe he was right, and it's only a matter of time before some other Tommy comes along to raze the stone walls and the hedgerows, cram the animals into hangars, strip the names from the fields. Ardnakelty will carve itself new channels, the way it always has, and keep on going.

Kojak has scoured the plate clean. He gets up, with some difficulty, and stalks stiffly to the front door.

'Let him out,' Lena says. She unfolds herself from the floor and brings the plate to the sink. 'He must be bursting for a pee.'

'He might not come back,' Trey says. Cal was thinking the same thing. The food could have given Kojak enough strength to find somewhere he'll be allowed to die.

'He mightn't,' Lena says. 'That's his choice.'

Trey opens the door, and Kojak vanishes into the sweep of cold dark air. 'Hey!' Trey says. 'It's snowing.'

They all go out to the step to look. Cal has never seen snow here before. It's falling thickly; all across the garden, in the wide

V of light spilling from the door, the air is filled up with big, soft, unhurried flakes and silence. It smells changed, scoured to utter purity, like it's preparing for something to happen.

Snowflakes brush against Cal's cheeks and get caught in his beard. Lena turns up her face to meet their fall. Trey puts out her arm to catch some on her hoodie sleeve and shows them to Kate, the two of them leaning shoulder to shoulder. In the oak, the rooks complain about the inconvenience and tell each other to shut up and go back to sleep.

'I can't remember the last time it snowed,' Lena says. 'Snowed properly, like, and stuck.'

'This'll stick,' Cal says. In the morning the fields will lie smooth under snow; high on the mountains, where Trey used to live, the spruce trees will be dark scrawls against white.

'Cumulonimbus,' Kate tells Trey, pointing upwards.

'That's why it's dark,' Trey tells her, and they both snort with laughter.

The stillness is immense. The light shows a slice of garden, the gate hanging open, the patch of road outside, all whitening fast. Everything beyond that is invisible in the night. Cal can feel the miles of it around him on every side: snow falling on Ardnakelty, on the fields and the scattered rooftops, into the crevices of the drystone walls, on the backs of the patient cattle, over the curled small creatures and the seeds that wait deep underground for spring.

A low dark shape shambles into the light. 'Hey, boy,' Lena says softly. Kojak, head down against the snowflakes, plods towards the door.

'Good boy,' Trey says, as he nudges his way between her and Kate. He shakes himself and heads for the fire to warm up, leaving a trail of wet paw prints across the floor.

'That beef's gonna be ready,' Cal says.

After the outdoors, the house surges with warmth and rich

smells: woodsmoke, dogs, meat and spices. On the radio, Jessie Buckley is singing 'When I Reach the Place I'm Going'.

Kate puts more wood on the fire with one hand and phones her mam with the other, to reassure her that she won't bike home in this, she'll get a lift off Cal or Lena. Cal gives the ground beef a last stir, Trey deals out taco shells onto plates, and Lena sets the table, while outside the windows the snow falls on.

Acknowledgements

I owe huge thanks to Darley Anderson, the finest agent I can imagine, and to everyone at the agency, especially Mary, Georgia, Rosanna, Rebeka, Ilaria, Francesca and Kristina; everyone at Viking US, especially Rebecca Marsh, Becca Stevenson, Kristina Fazzalaro, Molly Fessenden and Elizabeth Pham Janowski; my lovely editor Harriet Bourton and everyone at Viking UK, especially Olivia Mead, Rosey Battle and Georgia Taylor; Cliona Lewis and everyone at Penguin Ireland; Susanne Halbleib and everyone at Fischer Verlage; Steve Fisher of APA; Ciara Considine, Clare Ferraro and Sue Fletcher, who set all this in motion; Roger Clark, for giving Cal and all of Ardnakelty a voice with such skill and richness; Aja Pollock, for another expert copy-edit; Darren Haggar, for another stunning cover; Fearghas Ó Cochláin, for answering more questions that probably have both of us on a list; Lucian Pieterse and Ava Sturdy, for trying out horrifying chat-up lines on their AIs; Linnet Walsh, for intel on music, Pritt stick and stratus clouds; Jessica Ryan, for being my North Carolina dictionary again (any mistakes are mine and not hers); Graham Murphy, for always knowing what's on the telly in the pub; David Ryan, this end up, may contain nuts, do not inhale, fold along dotted lines, may cause drowsiness, banana for scale; Kristina Johansen, Alex French, Susan Collins, Ann-Marie Hardiman, Jenny and Liam Duffy, Oonagh Montague, Paul and Anna Nugent and all the Orson gang, Kathy and Chad Williams, Noni Stapleton, and Karen Gillece, for laughs, long talks, coffee, pints, creativity, support, and all the other essentials; my mother, Elena Lombardi; my father, David French; and, as always and in so many ways, my husband, Anthony Breatnach.